I0740142

Also by Doug Richardson

Lucky Dey Thrillers
Blood Money
99 Percent Kill
American Bang
The Night is Never Black
Hip Slick and Dead

Other Fiction
The Safety Expert
Dark Horse
True Believers

Nonfiction
*The Smoking Gun: True Stories from Hollywood's
Screenwriting Trenches*

A LUCKY DEY THRILLER

DOUG RICHARDSON

REAPER

los angeles

Velvet Elvis Entertainment
6038 Tampa Avenue
Suite 366
Tarzana, California 91356

More information at www.dougrichardson.com
ISBN: 978-0-9964563-3-3

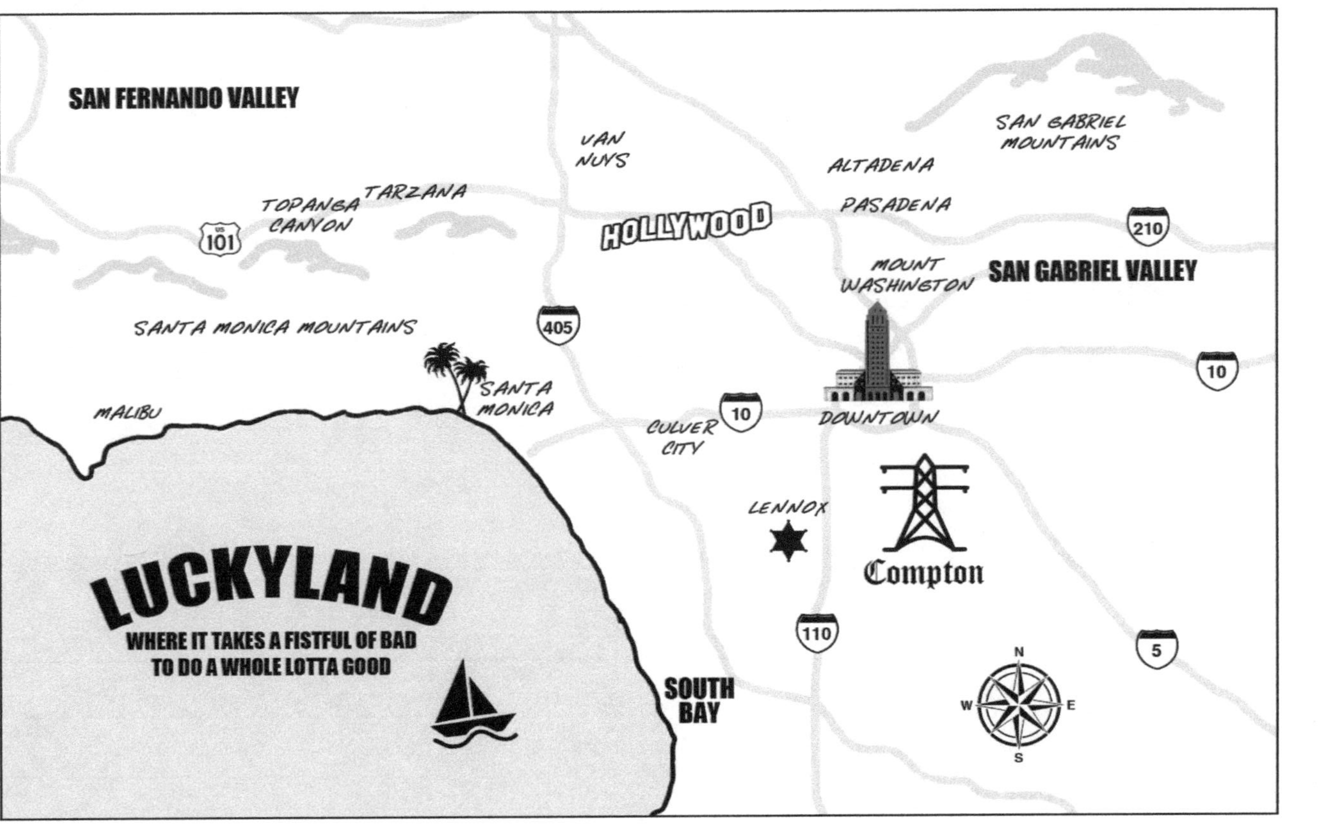

SAN FERNANDO VALLEY
TOPANGA CANYON
TARZANA
VAN NUYS
101
HOLLYWOOD
ALTADENA
PASADENA
SAN GABRIEL MOUNTAINS
210
SAN GABRIEL VALLEY
MOUNT WASHINGTON
SANTA MONICA MOUNTAINS
405
10
SANTA MONICA
MALIBU
CULVER CITY
DOWNTOWN
10
LENNOX
Compton
110
LUCKYLAND
WHERE IT TAKES A FISTFUL OF BAD
TO DO A WHOLE LOTTA GOOD
SOUTH BAY
N E W S
5

For my sister
Laurie Adele Paredes

Monday

1

Frosty checked his phone screen. It was an unconscious act and only three slow-motion minutes since his last glance. Every passing second felt as if it were creeping like a caterpillar on a tenuous twig. It wasn't the waiting that chapped the twenty-two-year-old. Waiting was what he did. Waiting for Julius to hand out his next instruction. Waiting at the bodega to cash his Gran'nana's social security check. Waiting was process. After all, what was life? As his Gran'nana always say, all to livin' was about waiting to die 'n' meeting her lord and savior, Jesus Christ.

No. What bothered Frosty was the San Fernando Valley zip code. He would generally call his comfort zone anywhere south of Interstate 10 and east of the 405. Crossing north of South Central Los Angeles might as well have been a snowy slog across the Canadian border. Only Canada would at least be predictably opaque with white people. Frosty could handle white people. They'd take one look at his skinny black ass and his yellowed, alien-like wide-set eyes and be afraid. Either that or they'd overcompensate with their polite white guilt. White folk were so goddamn easy that way.

It was the mixed bag outside South Central that caused Frosty's anxiety. The ever-growing polyglot of ethnic minorities and the assimilation from the old known demarcations of black, white, and brown—it was all too confusing to keep current.

Frosty's Gran'nana said it best:

"Used to be able to tell who was who. Now all the mixin' makes you wanna start ev'ry conversation with, 'What the heck kinda race is you?'"

Up until that Monday, the summer had been cooler than the usual swelter. If only it had stayed cool for one more twenty-four-hour sweep and the Santa Ana winds had held at bay. Then Frosty might not have had to worry about his perfectly functioning sweat glands. Perspiration contained DNA. And everybody knew DNA was what got even the best bad guys caught. In his Jordans, black Wrangler jeans, and a thin, navy blue hoodie, Frosty needed to fit into character, otherwise known to law enforcement as a "black male usual"—an African-American man in his late teens to twenties—a descriptor that, in America, fit tens of millions.

That's right. Try and pick me out of a lineup, motherfuckers.

It was the second day of July. And Frosty had made sure to ride the most obvious transit routes. The Blue Line to downtown. The Red Line to North Hollywood. The Orange Metro bus to some Valley neighborhood called Tarzana. On that route he'd be certain to pass plenty of security cameras and, depending on their operational status, each was guaranteed to capture his image. But the average lens would record little more than a five-foot-ten-inch black man's silhouette in a ubiquitous dark hoodie. Daylight would soon be waning into a dusty twilight. If any enterprising LAPD cop had figured Frosty would be worth a stop 'n' frisk, they'd have come up with little more than a few crumpled dollar bills, a nearly empty container of orange-flavored Tic Tacs, and a stick of CVS-brand lip balm. But the gig itself would be flushed. A new plan would have to be formed.

Near the corner of Reseda and Ventura, Frosty slipped into a supermarket parking lot. Keeping his gaze just south of level, he easily marked the four security cameras, each boxed in what looked like a tin-covered birdhouse and mounted high on a light post.

Sweet. I like me lots of cameras.

Knowing that every captured move would be recorded and eventually catalogued by detectives, he slid up and down the aisles of cars, pretending to test for unlocked doors, only showing interest in the more expensive luxury brands—Lexus, Cadillac, Mercedes-Benz. The exercise lasted less than two minutes. But it was guaranteed to super-glue an easily digestible motive to the crime Frosty was designed on committing.

Frosty crossed Ventura Boulevard near the old Taco Bell and soon melted into the dark and forested residential streets of the Tarzana hills. His path was circuitous. Yet all the while he was precise about his destination. The address was locked in his head. That, and he'd already visited the house on three previous occasions—the last time to conceal his murder weapon of the moment, a .22-caliber Taurus pistol, which was nearly as small as the palm of his hand. Frosty had double-Ziplocked the pistol with a pair of blue surgical gloves before burying the bag four inches deep in the freshly mulched flowerbed that fronted a Tudor-style house two driveways to the west.

It had been some twenty or so minutes since the sun had dropped below the crest of what locals called the Santa Monicas— a low-lying mountain range that bordered the Pacific Ocean, stretching east to west from Bel-Air to Point Mugu. In the gray before night—and more importantly, before the streetlamps had fully sparked—Frosty recovered the weapon, made sure to stuff the baggies in a front pocket, and did his best to make himself comfortable in a concealed corner of the empty home renovation site across the street from the target driveway. The clock on his phone read 8:43 p.m.

There was nothing left to do but wait.

At half past ten, perched on a short, sawed-off chunk of two-by-six, Frosty's bony butt began to ache as he kept shifting from one weak cheek to the other. What he'd have given for the "high motor" his track coach had so valued. So many of his school homies were built with popping gluteus muscles that not only made for fast legs, but also made baggy jeans a cinch to hang low. Somehow Frosty had been born with an ass as slight as the rest of him. For a while in middle school, he was even nicknamed Plank until Frosty shut up the instigator with an after-the-bell beatdown. Though the nicknaming perp ended up in the hospital with three broken ribs and a concussion, he never ratted on Frosty for the simple fear of getting capped by any one of Frosty's compadres—the Palmer Blocc Compton Crips.

Superiority through extreme violence, one of his O.G.s used to say.

That's right, Frostman. Superior violence always comes out on top. Like that Hiroshima and Nagasaki shit. Boom-boom and it's goodnight war in the Pacific.

A pair of headlights swept up the hilly curve. From just under an eighth of a mile away, the lights flashed across the neighborhood trees—a mix of eucalyptus, ancient oaks, and reaching cypress, with not a leaf wiggling in a non-existent breeze.

"Fuck all, it's hot," moaned Frosty to himself, slightly surprised to hear his own voice before he whispered back to himself, "Shoulda brought you some bottles of water, dumbass."

The car attached to the headlights—a freshly waxed white Range Rover—accelerated past the address.

Thirst was becoming an issue. Somehow, Frosty had journeyed to the Valley already dehydrated, then marched from mass transit to mass transit before trudging into the Tarzana hills. His throat was dry and when he swallowed, his tongue stuck to the top of his mouth as if it were coated in Jif. He thought to leave his perch, search for a garden hose or a waterspout or even a half-supped bottle of Arrowhead, and quench his thirst. Only the thought itself was overruled by his wiser, quieting brain centers. He'd made personal admonitions to touch absolutely nothing on which he could leave a trace—a single solitary skin cell. Despite his thirst, leaving no trace was Frosty's governing thought. Patience would be rewarded. Just wait it out, do the thing Julius asked, and get back to life south of the 105.

Then came another flash of headlights, only these were the whiter, more ethereal shade of halogen. Yet despite the oncoming presence of a moving vehicle, there was zero sound of a surging gasoline engine propelling the car up the hill. If Frosty's ears were keener, he'd be able to hear the slight hum of an electric motor and the rubber-on-asphalt friction of four performance Pirellis.

But will it be my *Tesla?*

The battery-powered car—four doors and sleek as a Maserati sedan—softly wound down to almost perfect silence as it neared the address. The corner streetlamp threw a blue-gray cast, making the car's skin appear like a fish darting into the shallows.

Yes, sir. That's my *guy driving* my *car.*

From that moment until the ugly deed was done, Frosty's movements could almost be described as robotic. Each step had been thought through days in advance. All Frosty need do was execute his most simple plan. The Palmer Blocc Crip quickly rose and skipped in the direction of the street with speedy deliberation. As the Tesla slowed and pulled up to a residential gate, the driver's window rolled down so the gray-haired man behind the wheel could punch in a code he knew as well as his own name. When his brake lights flared, he wouldn't think to peek cautiously in either his rear- or side-view mirrors. It was getting late on a Monday night. The driver was probably buzzed or even drunk and, only yards from his bed, barely aware of little more than his next task—pressing the four numbers to engage the motor that would swing the gate open.

Frosty noted the seersucker sleeve stretching for the keypad and a pricey timepiece glinting in the glow of the nearby streetlamp. His Jordans made little sound as he covered the short distance across the asphalt. So far, Frosty had touched nothing besides the pistol, an item he'd be certain to take with him. He passed it to his left hand, confident he'd switched the safety into the off position. Next, he automatically quickened himself as he counted out the telephone tones chirping from the tiny speaker box below the keypad.

At the open window, Frosty hooked his left arm inside the doorframe, bending sideways at the waist to make certain the muzzle of the .22 touched the Tesla driver's bristled temple. He pulled the trigger twice, releasing a pair of high-pitched pops. The skin contact and the acoustics of the car behaved as baffles, disguising the sounds to little more than finger snaps.

The driver jerked and lolled. His body barely had time to slump when Frosty cracked open the car door. It was when he reached across the seat to unhitch the man's seat belt that he was assaulted by the scream.

The unholy howl came first as a blast of unwelcome air from the maw of the woman passenger. A hooker or a secretary, Frosty would later surmise. She'd been both unexpected and had already thrown the lock on her own door. She was in the process of hurling herself toward the driveway when she had realized that she was still restrained by her own seat belt. Nearly forty years old, redheaded, and her blouse unbuttoned enough to show off her new pair of surgically minted double-D breasts, she was sucking in her first breath to unleash a second howl when she discovered herself facing the small-caliber muzzle.

Again Frosty squeezed on the trigger. The microsecond flash of gunpowder afterburn camouflaged the actual bullet penetrating the colored contact lens in the passenger's left eye. The woman slumped four inches, threw a quick spasm, then fell away with her legs kicking. Without the safety belt, she'd have spilled completely out of the car.

With the driver's seat belt unhitched, Frosty tugged the male victim from the car. Next, he climbed in behind the wheel and popped the lock on the dead woman's seat belt, allowing her to crumple into a polyester pile outside her open door.

Frosty pressed down on the brake, geared the Tesla into reverse, and carefully backed onto the street. The passenger door shut itself once Frosty had shifted into drive and tested the electric car's well-advertised acceleration. In less than two minutes, Frosty was on the freeway, pointed out of the Valley, and finding himself cooled by the comfortable breeze provided by the Tesla's electric-powered air conditioning.

"Thank Jesus for motherfuckin' air conditioning," shouted Frosty to nobody other than himself.

2

Compton Station, L.A. County Sheriff's. 11:03 p.m.

The pain wasn't quite excruciating. Yet the muscle memory of how debilitating it had once been wanted to convince Lucky that popping a pain pill would be more efficient than the twice—sometimes three times—daily sessions of self-induced traction. The prescribed series of stretches, contortions, and exercises were designed to build core strength and relieve the stress on his surgically repaired back. Lucky could only suppose they did as advertised, but simply recalling the old pain would trigger Percocet cravings every time he unrolled the foam rubber yoga mat he kept in his locker. He'd lie in the most remote corner of the Compton station's locker room, its permanent mildew smell filling his nostrils. He'd set a thirty-second timer on his phone and once again begin breaking through the adhesions that always seemed to have reformed since his last horizontal bout with himself. Lucky would generally top off the session with eight hundred milligrams of ibuprofen chased by a can of Red Bull.

It was week two of Lucky's reassignment as a Los Angeles County sheriff's deputy. And the next check mark to address on his return-to-duty list was a name on a slip of thin, hand-cut paper. As if to save the environment, all four of the trainee assignments had been printed on one sheet of cheap white copy stock, then quickly quartered with a guillotine cutter. Pretty archaic, thought Lucky, for a modern, urban police department. But this was both County Sheriff's *and* Compton, where they hadn't changed the bolted seating in the lobby since it had been Compton City PD in the 1970s.

Deputy Lucky Dey flicked the slip of paper, folded it into his shirt's buttoned pocket, and performed one last check in the locker room mirror. As usual, his own handsomeness evaded him. Aside from his mother's blue eyes, he saw only wreckage. Scars. A nose permanently misshapen from collisions with both cars and fists. He checked his equipment to make certain he hadn't forgotten something important, like spare magazines for his SIG Sauer. Carrying either a nine or a forty was standard for uniformed deputies. Not quite what Lucky had been used to packing back in the days he'd worked as a detective for both L.A. County and then up north in Kern. A Model 1911 .45 was his preference. It was heavy as hell, which absorbed the recoil. It was also louder and generally smacked a target harder both wherever and whenever Lucky aimed. In other words, a bad guy spanked with a .45 slug generally went down and stayed down.

"Uniform looks good," said Watch Commander Lieutenant Eugene Torres. The stout ex-Marine with a throwback mustache slapped Lucky's shoulder as they squeezed past each other in the tight corridor that shortcut through the dispatch room. "Betcha you were surprised it still fit ya."

"Desk jobs are ass-spreaders," replied Lucky.

"Same with a seat on patrol," warned Torres. "Had this one TO who told his rooks that traffic stops were the best way to supplement the cardio. That, and watching the greasy lunch breaks."

Patrol.

How many years had it been since Lucky had manned the wheel of a black-and-white? No matter. That was the deal he'd agreed to for the sheriff's department to take him back. As well as the responsibility of working as a training officer saddled with two trainees a year. It wasn't quite detective grade. Yet it would have to do.

Lucky stuffed Torres's unsolicited advice with a sideways wink and stepped out into the night. The motor yard was rectangular, a hundred yards deep, and cast in a yellowish blaze of sodium street lamps. Sheriff's patrol units were parked like soldiers waiting for orders. Ford Interceptors, Suburbans, and the old standbys, Ford Crown Victorias. The rumors were that all the sedans would eventually be replaced by roomier, all-wheel-drive SUVs. Swell, thought Lucky. The modern-day cops' black-and-whites were simply a bunch of supercharged mom-mobiles.

His assigned black-and-white was already backed up, wheels touching the curb, gassed and ready to roll. The exhaust was smoothly belching downward in the direction of Lucky's squeaky new tactical boots. The passenger door swung wide and out stepped Lucky's trainee. Despite her own new boots and a lousy-fitting uniform cut to erase any essence of what might be considered feminine, Lucky guessed the young deputy couldn't have weighed more than 110 pounds naked and blown dry.

"Deputy Dey," the trainee spoke up, assuming a strong-spined stance. "I'm—"

"No, no," interrupted Lucky, holding up a single index finger, then using it to fish that slip of paper from his shirt pocket. "Lemme see if I can get this on the first go."

Lucky cleared his throat and again snapped the piece of paper. He remained on the curb, using the extra five inches to accentuate his own six-foot frame over the trainee's five-foot-four.

"Deputy Mequashia Saint George," read Lucky. "I get that right?"

"Shia," corrected the trainee. "That's what I go by. Been that way since kindergarten."

"Mequashia, though," grinned Lucky. "That's pretty fuckin' exotic."

"Grew up in the West Valley," said Shia, unblanched by Lucky's f-bomb describer. "Nothing exotic about that."

"'Less you live in Pacoima."

Shia offered her open palm. Her fingers were delicate, like a hand model's, with a tinge of peachy-pink on her palms to contrast her flawless ebony skin. Shia's nails were short but manicured; her teeth, perfect rows of enamel, the probable work of a gifted orthodontist.

A real beauty, thought Lucky. Slight as she might have been beneath her Kevlar vest, even with the lowered physical bar for women recruits, she'd most likely be able to surprise most males with power well beyond her stellar looks.

As for what Shia saw in Lucky? The training officer didn't much give a rip how she viewed him. At first glance she could have seen him as a muscle-head whitey with a buzzed scalp. Or at almost forty years of age, too old for the uniform. Was he a closet racist after too many ghetto-serving years as a sheriff's deputy? Or an overreaching apologist?

Whatever I am, she'll have to figure it out for herself.

All that mattered to Lucky was that she saw him for who he was: her TO—or training officer. For the next five months, he would be her boss, sensei, guru, and closest ally on earth were she to get herself into a shit storm. And working out of the Compton station, there was guaranteed to be plenty of opportunity for that.

"What do I call you?" asked Shia, her head slightly cocked into a question mark. It was as if she were really asking, *Did you really forget to introduce yourself?* "TO Dey?"

"Lucky," he answered in a simple monotone. "Luck if you want to save on the syllables."

"Lucky works," said Shia, taking her cue as he circled around to the driver's side door.

"You up to speed on the Box?" asked Lucky upon his slide behind the wheel. The Box he referred to was the touchscreen laptop that was standard in every patrol car and mounted on a swivel for both the driver and passenger to operate.

"Top of my class, sir," answered Shia.

"That's good," said Lucky. "Because I'm a moron with machines."

The comment earned him a sideways look from his trainee.

"Been fourteen years since I was in a patrol unit," volunteered Lucky. "So in a way we're both rookies."

Shia, her whip-smart brain beneath efficient cornrows pulled neatly into a decorative knot at the back of her skull, appeared wisely skeptical at Lucky's rookie remark. She'd likely heard tales of training officer shenanigans, hazing, and the general head wrecking of trainees. And this Monday night would be day one of a nearly half-year journey to full street-cop status.

"No reply," grinned Lucky. "Smart girl . . . But I wasn't lyin' about how long since I'd been in a black-and-white. Wouldn't worry, though. Seat belt?"

"Oh, yeah. Right," said Shia, slinging the belt across her torso until the tongue clicked into the receptacle. However, as Lucky gassed the unit forward toward the steel-reinforced gate leading out of the motor yard, she noticed her TO hadn't made a move to secure his own restraint. Nor would he as he eased the Interceptor onto South Willowbrook. Shia's eyes briefly landed on the yellow and black warning decaled on the dashboard of each and every sheriff's patrol car:

ALL VEHICLE PASSENGERS
MUST WEAR SEAT BELTS!

"Something wrong?" asked Lucky without even glancing at her. With his right hand he double-clicked the power button on his tactical flashlight, testing the penetrating beam before resting it between his legs. The phallic appearance of the gesture wasn't lost on Shia.

"No, sir," braved Shia. "I'm good to go."

3

Compton.

"Whoa, whoa, whoa!" harped Andre, better known in the neighborhood as Mush Man—or simply Mush. His customized shopping cart, outfitted with polyurethane skateboard wheels and a two-by-four plank for a riding step, had nearly tipped sideways on the tight street corner.

"That was almost a double bad-bad," announced Mush Man aloud to nobody but his dogs, four big mutts he'd harnessed to the front of the cart with an organized tangle of found rope and plastic crate strapping. Each of the quartet of street mongrels was named for one of his favorite African-American heroes.

"Oprah, baby? We lose us anything?"

The black lab mix with the white whiskers at the front of the pack perked at her name, panting, then licked her lips.

"No snacks till we cash our cargo," reminded Mush Man. He

circled the stuffed cart, examining his haul of aluminum cans and bottles, mostly gathered from a warm weekend of Compton-wide partying. "Shit-fuck-shit-fuck," he involuntarily ticked. "Gotta slow us down some before we make them turns. You hearin' me, Rosa? Hank? Yeah, I'm talkin' at you, mutt-bags. Oprah, she the lead dog. That mean you gotta follow how she does it. Crap, crap, crap."

The fourth dog, a shoulder-strong pup Mush Man named Thurgood, after the late, great Supreme Court justice, sat obediently and wiggled his body for attention.

"Lookit Thurgood there. He not makin' a fuss of nothin' and he's way newer than the two of y'all."

Mush Man checked his harnesses. "Now we got four blocks up Poinsettia—ass-cracker shit-shit!" he ticked again, chin jerking left with each nervy syllable. "Then right turn on Rosecrans. Cross the boulevard and we back north on Bullis Road. Everybody got that?"

The dogs didn't need to answer. Their faces spoke up with every adoring tone from their savior and master. They lived for the little Mush Man, a skin-and-bones character who barely topped a defiant five-foot-five. His dirty curls were screwed under a black USC cotton beanie he'd long ago swiped off a chain-link fence.

"Ready, Oprah? Let's—suck me, suck me, suck me—damn it all. Mush it, girl!"

Mush Man wished like hell that it wasn't so damned hot. Just a degree or two cooler and he might have been able to feel a breeze on his flushed cheeks, a perk of the self-made sport he'd coined as Urban Dogsledding. Of which, Mush Man would inform any inquirer, he was a five-time world champion.

Tough sledding tonight, said Mush Man to himself. Simply and succinct. It was weird to him that the words between his ears were always clean and curse-free. Inside his own brain, there were no awkward verbal ticks like the ones he suffered when speaking aloud. No bursts of slurs or ugly invectives. But for the mental disorder the local VA had diagnosed as Tourette syndrome, Mush Man imagined himself cleaner than Bill Cosby.

Well, the old *Bill Cosby.*

"Dr. Motherfucker-shit-crack-Huxtable," Mush Man said aloud.

The Compton sidewalks Mush called sled trails were cracked from age, decades of disrepair, and tree roots inching shallower in search of available water. It wasn't much of an issue for the dogs. But for Mush Man, the wrong bump could spill him and his valuable payload into a splash of Tecate cans and Magnum 40 bottles. On top of the challenges posed by the irregular surface, it was nearly too dark to see. Poinsettia, like most residential streets in the zip code, was poorly lit due to a lack of working streetlamps and unpaid electric bills.

Stucco-faced homes flanked the street. Domicile boxes, mostly. The houses averaged barely a thousand square feet and most were fit with burglar-proofing over the windows—otherwise known as ghetto bars.

"Whoaaaaaaaaa," Mush commanded and braked before taking two long looks up and down the tree-lined street. There were no cars in sight. Safe for humans to cross. It was the dogs, though, who made Mush Man so careful. His mutts were trained as well as a vagrant could instruct. It was his own marginal schizophrenia that Mush couldn't trust. Unmedicated and untreated for eight years, mental illness was Mush Man's cross to bear. But it was *his* cross and damn anyone else who wanted to change him.

A backyard dog barked. A big bully of a beast who'd gotten a whiff of the dog team. All the mutts' ears swerved in unison. Thurgood barked back. Rosa joined in with a lunar howl.

"Eaaaaaasssy now," warned Mush Man as he coaxed his team onto the street. The defined and familiar sound of sixteen padded dog feet slapping the pavement was replaced by a cacophony of shallow splashes. A wetness spritzed Mush Man's face. In what scant light there was, he could make out a low wake left behind his rickety shopping cart.

The cart began to drag.

"Shitter-shitter-shit!" Mush Man complained, before adding a new command. "Drive hard, Oprah! Drive HARD!"

The blacktop underneath him was covered by a four-inch-deep

river of water, silently coating the surface before getting sucked back into the storm drains. But as far as Mush was concerned, he might as well have been fording roaring rapids in a hydroplane pulled by a team of thoroughbreds.

Then he missed the opposite driveway.

Though the four mutts cleared the curb easily, the shopping cart's front wheels stopped dead. The rear of the cart pitched forward, rotating over the fulcrum and twisting. Mush Man smartly bailed right while the cart spun left and emptied in a spray of recyclables. The clatter of cans and bouncing and shattering bottles shocked the neighborhood's silence and alerted nearly every chained or fenced dog for a square block.

Mush Man crawled onto the sidewalk. If he was bleeding he couldn't tell. Most of him was soaked to the skin. Feeling little more than bruised—and disappointed for having tossed his haul—he allowed his pups to gather around to lick him back into reality.

"Musta lost half our shit," Mush Man confessed to his team.

Indeed, it appeared a good portion of his load had tumbled into the street and was rushing away, carried by the blackened river lit by the low-hanging moon, nearly full and magnified in a sky atmospherically tinged with summer hues of amber and yellow. A magical river where there had been none, appearing out of the darkness and flowing like a moving belt of black gelatin.

"Beautiful," grinned Mush Man.

4

Lucky hadn't a set plan for his trainee's first loop in a black-and-white. Other training officers surely had a formula or technique for breaking in their charges. To hell with that, he decided. Working patrol is about dealing with what came. The streets would provide their own baptismal rite. Lucky's job was to make sure she survived the monsters that were certain to crawl from the night.

Or whatever shit I might get her into.

Despite the time away from commanding a black-and-white, Lucky's muscle memory was intact. And though Torres had advised they spend their initial shift assisting other units, the moment Lucky had put rubber to the road he was back in what he'd always referred to as street sweeping. His cop job, no matter the stripe or assignment, was to solve a simple axiom: identify and bag anybody within his authority who posed a risk to the public safety.

His trainee would have a different perspective.

Prepared as Shia was to take on whatever came her way, she'd already catalogued a potential red flag with her training officer. It was that phallus of a flashlight Lucky kept propped between his legs. She wondered if it was some kind of sexual test. Would the trainee take offense? Or dish out some kind of probative comment, joking or otherwise? Or maybe her TO was just trying to remind her that he was *the man* in all matter of reference, gender or otherwise—and she was the weaker sex in all and equal measure.

Within a matter of minutes, though, Shia was corrected. She quickly observed that when Lucky spotted a suspicious oncoming vehicle—a potential stolen car or a ride preferred by gang bangers—he'd snatch that flashlight between his legs and use the concentrated beam to cut through the headlight glare and ignite the face of the driver as the unit rolled past. In that one second of clarity, he could read the occupant's sex, age, or even attitude. The flashlight would then be returned, ready for the next drive-by. Sex or power had nothing to do with it.

Shia wondered if the passing driver being "flashlighted" felt harassed. Yet she marveled at the simplicity and succinctness of Lucky's trick. Especially when, minutes into their shift, he'd initiated a traffic stop on a beat-up Honda with a broken taillight, and illuminated a pair of male Hispanics with shaved heads. With the black-and-white's overhead lights on full spin, the Honda pulled to the curb. Lucky was out of the unit in a heartbeat, pistol unskinned from his holster and tucked against his ribcage.

He gave no order for Shia to either stay in the car or assist.

"Shit!" Shia mouthed to herself, unhitching her seat belt and nearly face-planting upon stumbling out of the car. By the time she'd found her wits and balance, Lucky had already holstered and locked his pistol and was asking both men for their IDs. He ordered his trainee back to the car to work the Box and run the head-shaved duo for wants and warrants. Lucky then cut them loose with only a warning.

The traffic stops continued at a feverish pace until Shia became accustomed to the timing. It didn't take long for her to lose her zeal for the seat belt. In their first two hours Lucky and Shia stopped and walked on eight cars without citing a single one.

"Having fun yet?" Those were Lucky's first non-instructive words since they'd departed the station parking lot. He wheeled the Interceptor up a residential street overgrown on both sides with over-arching shade trees.

"Better 'n Disneyland," replied Shia.

"Mmmm hmmm," Lucky nodded, switching on his post-mounted floodlight and sweeping it across the tree trunks on both sides of the street.

"May I?" she began to ask.

"Ask."

"Your approach on a stopped vehicle," she continued.

"What about it?"

"Your weapon is out of the holster before you exit the unit."

"And yours isn't?" asked Lucky, though clearly he already knew the answer to the question.

"Not long outta the academy, sir, so forgive the question."

"I said ask."

"Isn't it out of policy?"

"To unskin my gun?"

"Unless you perceive a reasonable threat."

"Exactly."

"Yes, sir. I understand—"

"Call me anything but *sir*."

"Lucky. Okay," stammered Shia. And she wasn't at all used to stumbling over words. "I've counted eight traffic stops."

"And my gun came out every time," Lucky confirmed.

"Yes. My question concerns practice versus policy. If eight out of eight would be considered perceived threats? I ask this understanding that traffic stops are, by their nature, a potentially dangerous situation. But does, say, a broken taillight warrant—"

"Each stop is its own situation."

"Exactly."

"And what is the situation?" Lucky asked.

"'Kay. First stop. Broken taillight. You light 'em up. I run the tags. No wants or warrants."

"So in your opinion, there's no perceived threat?" Lucky pressed.

"Enough to unskin my weapon?" asked Shia.

"Your situation is incomplete."

"Two young men—teens to twenties—in a Honda?" she guessed. And Shia hated herself for guessing. "Two Hispanic males? But that would be profiling."

"And we wouldn't want to do that," said Lucky, his voice so flat she couldn't gather if it was sarcasm or something else. "Situation?"

"I'm blank, sir," said Shia, her voice giving away in a hint of frustration.

"Eight out of eight cars."

"I don't see the common thread, sir."

"Is that an opinion or a surrender to the question?"

"Neither? Both?" Shia crossed her arms.

"Situation?"

"Training officer and trainee on first night patrol in a black-and-white."

"Are we in West Hollywood?"

"No, sir."

"Santa Clarita? Calabasas?"

"No, sir."

"Stop with the sirs."

"No, Lucky."

"We're in fucking Compton?"

"Yes."

"And that is our situation. Every minute of every day we're in this radio car in the city of Compton. And based on crime stats alone, could I argue that *any* approach on *any* car at *any* time in Compton is a reasonable threat?"

"I see your point."

Lucky ended the discussion. Abruptly. It left Shia to stew on her own assumptions, actions, and arguments. If Lucky's design was to leave his trainee off balance, it had been a successful exercise.

The following two hours were dedicated to assisting other sheriff's units on what Lucky dubbed garden variety calls. The conversation between training officer and his charge remained sparse yet polite. Lucky learned Shia had spent barely a year working duty at the county jail, a requirement for every deputy after graduating from the academy. Depending on new hires and retirement rates, it could take up to eight years for a rookie cop to matriculate out of any one of the L.A. Sheriff's jails. Yet Shia had escaped the downtown dungeon in less than a year. Lucky's affirmative action calculator ticked the probabilities. Shia was clearly beautiful, articulate, and intellectually adept. Rising stars tended to shoot upward at an exponential rate. Ambition was rewarded, especially for minority women who could solve the political Rubik's Cube.

"Finished high school at sixteen. Undergrad at Cal Poly," she'd answered when he asked about her schooling. "After growing up in the Valley, had to have me some beach years. Then grad school at UCLA and another pair at CSUN."

"Just because," said Lucky.

"Had this notion I wanted to be a shrink. So, I took the GRE, scored high enough for a two-year ride," finished Shia, not so much wearing her education on her sleeve, but more so as if she were accustomed to reciting her university curriculum vitae to superior officers.

"Bright girl," teased Lucky, curious to see if her pupils would swivel left or even roll from the feminine slight. Instead, Shia's eyes remained fixed and forward, which in Lucky's opinion was equally demerit-worthy.

During her recitation, Shia hadn't noticed Lucky buckling his seat belt. He crawled the black-and-white onto Lime Street, a sleepy nondescript strip.

"When did you psych yourself out of the psych biz?" Lucky semi-joked.

"Funny and apt," she replied. "I think it might've been—"

Lucky stomped on the brakes, turning Shia into a low-speed projectile. Lucky's right hand reached across to retard her momentum. Then with his left, he twisted and hooked the back of Shia's neck, pulling her down, practically folding her at the waist.

"SHOTS FIRED!" Lucky barked. "I'M HIT AND NEED MEDICAL. RADIO YOUR LOCATION!"

Shia's instinct was to wrench herself from Lucky's grip. She strained upward.

"You wanna get shot?" pretended Lucky. "They're still shootin'! Radio our twenty!"

"So lemme look," she leveled.

"Look up and you're shot," said Lucky. "Radio! Your! Twenty!"

"The Box," she argued. "I can see on the Box."

"You're betting my life on a machine?"

With that, Shia stopped struggling. She breathed. Tried to summon an answer.

"I . . . I don't know where we are," she finally admitted.

"Then I'm dead," said Lucky, releasing her and returning to his seat. "I bleed out waiting for EMS. You're dead too. All mommy and daddy have left of you are your two master's degrees over the mantle."

"They're divorced," she sighed.

"Sweet. So, they fight over diploma custody. At least they have proof their baby girl was book smart. But still not smart enough to stay alive on her first night on the job."

"Shit."

Lucky swiveled the Box over to Shia.

"Code Six us so you can investigate our location," ordered Lucky.

"I can see it right here," she pointed at the monitor. "Lime. Fifty yards south of Rosecrans."

"Bullet grazed the antenna. GPS compromised."

That's when she looked at him. Hazel-brown eyes and narrowed eyebrows as if to say, *So this is how the next five months are gonna go?* Lucky gave back nothing. He snapped the plastic lock off an Arrowhead water sports bottle, sucked back five quick ounces, and waited.

Shia swung her door open and climbed out into the dark. Lime Street was pretty much black but for the moon and distant spill of streetlamps coming from Rosecrans. Shia took in a quick three-sixty sweep of the landscape, adjusted her tactical belt an inch lower onto her hips, and strode toward the boulevard. Lucky followed in the black-and-white.

When Shia arrived at the intersection, she stuffed the impulse to gesture like a *Price is Right* model, mocking the assignment while revealing a task completed. Code Six was defined in the call book as "out of the vehicle for investigation."

So, I'll investigate, she reasoned. Because investigations required evidence, it was incumbent for the first uniformed officer on the scene to ascertain and gather. Out came Shia's smartphone. She snapped digital images of both street signs. It was when she was considering a third angle of the intersection that a strange sound caught her attention. It was a rattling. Loud and closing fast. Wheels on rough asphalt and the vibrato of clattering metal and glass.

Shia touched her gun and spun toward the noise. From under a streetlamp appeared a swerving shopping cart hauled by four panting mongrels. At the helm of the odd contraption was a small black man in a beanie and a pair of plastic carpentry goggles.

The trainee cop threw up a hand, signaling for Mush Man to stop.

"Whoa, whoa—pussy-crack-whore-pussy," called out Mush Man.

"Sir, may I please talk to you?" asked Shia, angling across.

"You wanna talk to me?" stalled Mush Man. "I wanna talks to you all about the damn river I found—nigga cop, nigga cop."

"You don't need to use foul language, sir," calmed Shia, trained to handle aggressive words after working the jail. "Lemme ask you a quick question. Can you please tell me where we are?"

"You askin' what?" snapped Mush Man. "If you's in Compton? You lost or somethin'?"

"No. And yes, we're in Compton," confirmed Shia, switching her phone to video mode. "I was just wondering if you could confirm for me that we're at the intersection of Rosecrans and Lime."

"Some kinda candid camera thing?" he asked, before his chin jerked left. "Cock-suck, cock-suck."

"Sir. Please."

"So how about this—shitferbrains?" offered Mush Man. "I tell you which intersection you at, then you lemme show you where I found—bitch, bitch, bitch—a river going right through the middle of the hood."

"Like the L.A. River?" Shia was referring to one of the many massive drainage arteries that run through all parts of Los Angeles, funneling rainwater and just about everything else that flows to a final destination in the Pacific Ocean. Every channel, no matter where, bears the same name: the L.A. River.

"I know me the L.A. River," replied Mush Man. "And this ain't that—fucker, fuck-fuck-fuck-ASS." Mush Man cleared his throat as if that would cleanse his verbal palate. "Place I'm talkin' 'bout used to be jus' this plain ol' regular street—"

"As I live and breathe," sounded Lucky. "Is that the Mush Man?"

"Hey, now!" grinned Mush Man. "Lucky-fuckin'-fuck-fuck-Dey! And wearin' him his park ranger duds at dat!"

Lucky released an easy laugh, acknowledging one of the biggest knocks on the L.A. Sheriff's—that their uniforms of forest green pants and khaki shirts appear more like those of US Forestry Service Rangers than actual street cops. A stark contrast to the LAPD's sleek, blue-black togs.

Shia found herself startled by Lucky's clean rows of white teeth. Only then did she recognize that in their hours together, Lucky hadn't revealed more than a smirk. She now witnessed Lucky's hardened eyes light up with warm recognition at the vagabond and his sled team of matted mongrels.

"What you doin' all the way down here?" asked Lucky.

"Ran outta sidewalk up Lennox way," said Mush Man. "Me 'n' my dogs needed new streets to beat—sweet-bitch-bitches."

"That Miss Oprah as lead dog?" Lucky dropped to his

Neoprene kneepads much to the dog's excitement. Oprah nuzzled up like she knew him.

"Was her time to step up," said Mush Man. "Had to put ol' Freddy Douglas to sleep, you know. Buried him right next to Jesse."

"And I remember Rosa," said Lucky, greeting the number-two dog with a cheek rub.

"That there's Hank," introduced Mush Man. "After Hammerin' Hank, of course—big dick nigga man. And the newest fella here is Thurgood."

"They look healthier than you, Mush."

"We all shares equal. And jus' like me, they don't get no brain poison."

"Head clear?" asked Lucky despite knowing otherwise. An unmedicated schizophrenic was often a danger to himself and others. But he knew Mush Man had enough of a hold on his disease to shelter in place when he lost all sense of control.

"Clear as nightingales singin' in church," declared Mush Man. He self-mockingly rapped the heel of his palm against his skull. "'Cept for the—you know—the bad words."

"Just makes you colorful," admired Lucky.

"So where you been? You get lost, then come back as a street sweeper?"

"Tried doin' the deputy dance up in the boonies," admitted Lucky. "Didn't stick. I'm back as a training officer."

"*Her* training officer?" Mush Man was pointing at Shia like she was fifty feet away instead of only five. "Cunty-cunty-cunt-cunt."

"He *is* colorful," smiled Shia, uncomfortable, but zeroing in on the hitch in Mush Man's mental bent.

"Then you listen and learn from Deputy Lucky," implored Mush Man. "Nobody knows better at bein' the po-po than Lucky Dey. And he badder than all the bad boys I ever seen—here 'n' over in towel-head country."

"That so?" teased Shia.

"Got him the tat that proves it." Mush Man kicked at Lucky's left calf before his voice lifted into a shuddering falsetto, "Eat-me-now-brown-cow."

Shia turned away, working every ounce of herself not to burst out in laughter at poor Mush Man's expense.

"First night back in the black-and-white," revealed Lucky. "Don't go scarin' my rook."

"I know, I know. Mush Man's mouth's got a mind of his owns," confessed the dogsledder. "But you gonna check out my river, right?"

"River?"

Mush Man nodded along while Shia explained what he'd reported.

"We'll check it," assured Lucky. "You got a roof down this way?"

"You know me. Say I'm shelter-resistant. But we gets by," winked Mush Man. "Now you get on protectin' and servin'."

"That's LAPD," reminded Lucky. "We say, 'A Tradition of Service.'" He pointed out the door of the Interceptor where, just underneath the county sheriff's logo, there was a decaled word strip in black cursive.

"Tradition, yeah?" laughed Mush Man. "I can think of a tradition of somethin' else. And I'm gonna leaves you with dat—nigga bitch bitch bitch."

Mush Man whistled softly, bringing his dog team to attention before urging them forward. Oprah, the lead dog, pulled, and the rest followed, snapping Mush Man and his urban shopping sled onto two wheels. The slight vagrant balanced on his running board with expert grace, much like a teen skater flexing his skills. Mush Man then righted the cart and angled the clattering throng across Rosecrans and up the wheelchair ramp onto the opposite curb.

"Like dogs, sir?" asked Shia before correcting herself. "I mean, Lucky?"

"Like 'em just fine. Too bad they don't like me. Allergic. Quick stop, Planet Benadryl. Then we find this river."

Tuesday

5

Topanga Canyon. 2:49 a.m.

"Holy God," breathed in the boy wonder, eyes wide orbits and desperate to savor the moment. It was, quite possibly, the greatest moment of his life. Or, at least, he couldn't imagine anything that came close until one particular memory flashed. And that might have been the look on the faces of those privileged doubters at the Buckley School who'd laughed when fifteen-year-old Atom—then named Adam Blumquist—had announced he was not only going to be a famous movie director, but the most successful movie director in Hollywood history.

After Atom gifted Buckley's development and scholarship funds with a mid-six-figure donation, the headmaster had asked the boy wonder to deliver the commencement address at their most recent graduation ceremony. From the dais, Atom had not only made a point to stare down each of those teachers who had lacked faith in his talent, but had the balls to call them out by name.

Yeah, man. That moment and this *moment.*

The present moment was both a collection of images as well as a flood of feelings. Though feelings weren't entirely important to the boy wonder compared to his beloved moving pictures. The picture frame was everything to him. And, from Atom's perspective, his life deserved to be experienced in theatrical wide-screen glory. Thus, the backdrop he'd chosen for the present moment—the view from atop a Topanga turnout overlooking the West San Fernando Valley. Below, a blanket of lights curtained by distant mountains glowing in the spill of their candlepower.

"Don't stop," begged the naked swimsuit model splayed face-down on the hood of his blood orange Lamborghini. Her sweaty hands smeared disappearing palm prints on the finish, aptly named by the automaker as Arancio Borealis.

The boy wonder dug in with his python-skin cowboy boots, gifted to him by the cast of young stars who'd populated his most recent action opus, *Roadkill 3: TransAmerica.* As the worldwide gross crossed the billion-dollar threshold, Atom celebrated the night with a bottle of rare tequila and a panoramic round of unprotected outdoor carnality. Still, his thrusts were less about below-the-waist pleasure than his rocks-off-between-the-ears fantasy.

I'm king of the world! he wanted to shout to the heavens and anybody else within earshot.

"Harder," urged the girl, barely eighteen—he hoped—blonde and demonstrably experienced.

The boy wonder briefly wondered if she'd really meant it. If she was indeed experiencing her own fantasy of being rear-mounted by a famous movie director while across the hood of an exotic Italian car. Or was she just selling? Why not and who cares? he figured. In Hollywood, everyone's selling. And this was Atom's unholy fairy tale.

He bent his knees and briefly lay across her, tasting her sweat with a tongue he'd sometimes wished was as abrasive as a cat's. A breeze kicked up and rustled the leaves of an overhanging oak. He felt the rush of air cool against his bared ass. If this were a scene in a movie, he wondered how he would cover it. With multiple cameras, making certain not to miss an angle of ecstasy? Or with a single camera, allowing himself to record the moment over a period of hours instead of minutes, savoring every drop of her perspiration onto film and keeping her goose-pimpled and naked until the sun breached the horizon.

Thank God I popped that Viagra.

Thank God, indeed. Otherwise the moment might have ended that much earlier, putting a cap on the fantasy and leaving the experienced model sexually unsatisfied.

"Tequila," she demanded, twisting her body, neck, and face enough for him to spill a shot from the open bottle into her mouth.

Atom followed by guzzling back a swig for himself. That's when he got the idea that he might pour a bit of the expensive juice onto her creamy back for him to lick. With that, he turned the bottle and splashed some on her. She wriggled with excitement and made an *ooohhh* sound. It set off a surge in him. Adrenaline. As if he'd just been fuel-injected with an extra hundred cc's of lust. The boy wonder lifted his heels and dug at the dirt from the balls of his feet for more leverage. The girl beneath wanted a pounding and damned if he wasn't going to give it to her up to the hilt.

"I'm king of the fucking world!" Atom finally shouted, arms spread wide like James Cameron at the Academy Awards. Only instead of holding an Oscar in one hand, he gripped that bottle of expensive Don Julio Real.

Then reality happened.

Cowboy boots, python-skin or otherwise, aren't known for their traction. The leather soles, relatively slick from a lack of true wear, slipped against a surface of sand and decomposed granite. Once the g-forces of Sir Isaac Newton took over, any hope of Atom regaining his dignity was lost.

In order to maximize the moment for his demanding eyeballs, Atom Blum had parked the Lambo up against a ravine. He had been so keen on getting the busty eighteen-year-old out of every stitch of her clothes, he hadn't noticed he'd left barely two feet of a sandy ledge for himself to orchestrate his sex scenario.

Then there was the tequila effect. The boy wonder later recalled the feeling of his feet giving way, yet the next part of the fall was barely a blur. Consciousness quickly returned as Atom felt himself tumbling backward, crashing through thorny brush and pointy dead oak leaves for some fifty feet until he hit the rock-covered bottom. All the way, his boots remained on, as did his designer dungarees, tangled and torn around his ankles.

There were cuts and scrapes and his skin stung. The only part of Atom that didn't seem to hurt instantly was his chemically enhanced member, which, he couldn't help but notice, was still unsheathed and pointing awkwardly to the sky.

The swimsuit model screamed like she'd discovered her own nakedness, grabbing at her clothes until she heard Atom shouting from down in the ravine. At first, his was a stream of foul and angry invectives. Each loaded with blame for anyone but himself. Eventually came a pause and a plaintive whimper of a request.

"Call 911!" squealed the movie director.

If he'd thought to check his watch, Atom would've known the exact time he lay there drunk, half-naked and exposed at the bottom of the ravine before he'd begun to form anything resembling cogent thought. The girl, whatever her name was, had only once dared a look into the dark chasm. Since his demand that she dial 911, he'd heard nothing from her. He'd first imagined her leaving the gravel cutout for the blacktop of Mulholland, dutifully waiting to flag down the responding paramedics. As his mind played out how he imagined his rescue occurring, clearer thinking prevailed. Most likely, both police and fire departments would be scrambled. There would be a public record of that, all the way down to the 911 call. Had the girl used her name? Or even more terrifying, had she dropped *his* name?

Fuck!

The boy wonder knew how the online tabloids monitored emergency alerts that might involve a celebrity. And they weren't beyond paying for and publishing the slightest hint of scandalous innuendo. Had the girl already sold him out? How many hours before the dirty details of his sex fumble were bannered across the front page of TMZ?

Fuck! Fuck!

As was his narcissistic habit, Atom began to shoot the scene in his head. With a crane to start. A booming camera shot that would capture the flashing lights of police and fire crews surging to the rescue. As the trucks and cruisers pulled into the cutout, the crane would track and lower into a tight close-up of a gritty first responder. Next, Atom would continue the scene with a chasing point-of-view shot as the paramedics raced toward the edge of the ravine. Lastly, he imagined the visual payoff as he'd direct the camera to tilt and zoom into the rocky chasm. Flashlights would search and suddenly focus on a skinny and scared thirty-five-year-old man with a Beverly Hills haircut and barely the strength to shade his eyes from the glare. Still stunned from the fall, the poor accident victim hadn't the awareness to pull his pants back up to cover his awkward nakedness—his glistening and chemically charged prick.

Firemen and police would be certain to chuckle to themselves before roping in for the final rescue.

Fuck that shit.

With that, the boy wonder rediscovered his mojo. He straightened his legs and only half-hitched up his ripped pants before beginning his climb out. To avoid slipping any further, he abandoned his pricey cowboy boots, leaving the python-skinned pair where his bony tailbone had come to rest.

"Fuck those boots," slurred Atom aloud to nobody but the snakes and lizards.

The calf-high silk socks tore almost instantly, leaving his soft and manicured bare feet seeking a grip against the rocks and decomposed granite. Atom was far more inebriated than he realized. The climb forced his heart to race. The crevasse spun. And almost as if he'd imagined rerunning his own bad movie, he skipped and bumped his way back down to the bottom. Back where he had started and seeking some calm behind his closed eyelids. Perhaps when he reopened them he'd discover it was only a nightmare.

The sky above him lit up, penetrating his thin-skinned shutters in a flare of veiny red—the thumping Atom imagined betrayed by his own damned ears. He found his hands instinctively protecting his face from the super-kilowatt lamp that turned the crevasse from black to white hot.

"THIS IS THE LOS ANGELES SHERIFF'S," boomed a voice from a speaker mounted to the undercarriage of the helicopter. "ARE YOU IN NEED OF ASSISTANCE?"

Shitballs, bitched Atom at himself. *Please, God, tell me my pants aren't still around my knees.*

A quick glance across his body returned the correct answer. His denims had only made it up to his thighs. His Viagra-powered member was, despite both tumbles, still at attention, overblown and overexposed in that wash of bright light.

6

Compton.

"When you woke up this morning," said Lucky, "betcha didn't imagine you'd meet the likes of Mush Man." Lucky had the black-and-white's trunk lid up and was rummaging for the first-aid kit.

"Tourette's?" asked Shia, though it was more of a known than a question.

"Chapter in one of your schoolbooks?"

She nodded that indeed it was. The DSM—or the Diagnostic and Statistical Manual of Mental Disorders—referred to Mush Man's bizarre, rat-a-tat of dirty invectives as Tourette syndrome or Tourette disorder or GTS, the classic neuropsychiatric diagnosis where the afflicted often has little to no control over physical tics such as eyeblinking or twitches. For some, though, the tics manifest as shocking vocal bursts of antisocial cursing.

"Awful illness," replied Shia. "And schiz too?"

"His mutts don't seem to mind," answered Lucky, finding the kit and unzipping it until it flopped open like a clamshell. He dug for a tube of antiseptic gel, squeezed out a golf ball–sized dose, and began working it into his palms, up his forearms, neck, and face.

"Interesting taste in dog names."

"For a minute, SPCA was on his case," said Lucky as he returned to the driver's seat. "Somebody in Venice complained. Cruelty to animals bullshit. Hell. He's a schiz. Rescues dogs. Keeps 'em fed better than himself. Names them after black people he admires. What's not to love?"

"What happened with the complaint?"

Lucky smirked without meeting her eyes.

"'A Tradition of Service'," he said in a mocking monotone.

"Okay," bit Shia. "I'm the rook. But is that some kinda code I'm supposed to figure out?"

"No code," answered Lucky. "Mush Man is good peeps. Two-tour combat vet with a bad case of postwar heebie-jeebies. And some of us in Sheriff's have our own ways to serve and protect."

"So the complaint went away."

"I can be convincing."

Lucky assigned Shia to record the stop on the black-and-white's computer, including Mush Man's statement concerning "the river." Suspecting a car or truck accident involving a fire hydrant, the duo proceeded on the short half mile over to Poinsettia Drive and slow-rolled with their spotlight on full blast. Halfway up the block, the front tires touched wet asphalt.

Shia keyed the Box, recording that both officers had stepped from the vehicle, then followed Lucky onto the street. The pair walked into the car's flood lamps. There they discovered a gush of water spilling over the crown in the road before splitting into uneven streams in search of street drains.

"Compton fire hydrants are yellow," said Lucky. "Probably some local drunk. Check the driveways for dented bumpers and paint transfer."

"Call the FD?"

"Could be from a house," replied Lucky. "Busted pool or hot tub or main. Find the source first."

Shia was already making an about-face back to the car when Lucky clucked.

"Where you going?" he asked. "You take point. I'll follow and sweep with the spot."

"Right," said Shia, trying to *sound* agreeable. Though something about the point-of-the-spear part of the assignment smelled. As if it bordered on hazing. Still, she reminded herself that she was the Princess of Suck-Up. She'd clarify to others that her personal nickname wasn't about the act of sucking up. No, ma'am. Her version was about sucking it in, gritting her teeth, and pushing on.

Once she heard Lucky drop the Ford into gear, she began to walk the make-believe center stripe. The road in front of her was blanketed in a blast of white light. The radio unit's headlamps were clicked to bright and Lucky continued to angle the post-mounted spotlight.

The water climbed to her ankles.

When Shia's ultra-light boots flooded, she cursed herself for not choosing the heavier, waterproof pair she'd left in her locker. The choice of the micro-weight pair had everything to do with optimism and a simple calculation: if she were to get into a foot-chase during her virgin night, she'd hoped to out-sprint both cops and criminals.

The water moved with greater volume, climbing to her lower calves with a chill.

"Can you hear a source?" chirped Lucky though the black-and-white's loudspeaker. The sound came as a shock, causing her to jolt. "If it's a hydrant, it sounds like you're near a waterfall."

Shia shook her head and trudged forward, remembering to shoot her tactical light up each driveway in search of dented bumpers and yellow paint transfer. But for the low hum of the Interceptor's engine and the splashing of her own deepening foot-falls, the neighborhood appeared abandoned.

Behind the wheel, Lucky kept his left grip guiding the spot-light, his other skipped from the steering wheel to the Box, where he keyed though screens looking for any alerts that might explain the source of the flooding.

Then Lucky felt it.

Like most native Angelenos, his nerve endings had a particular sensitivity to tremors. The earth shook so often that locals would usually register the shaking, coolly measuring for a sign that the shaker was either significant or not worth the worry. The fact that Lucky could sense the ground moving while seated in the shock-absorbing Ford Interceptor was telling.

But there was a visual cue.

The picture in front of him—that panoramic windshield frame of Shia and her flashlight slowly stalking the source of the flooding—shifted and tilted slightly downward. In unison, the asphalt underneath the trainee and the radio unit gave way like a gallows trap door releasing underneath a condemned man. As the black-and-white pitched forward, the headlights tracked with Shia as the ground beneath opened and swallowed her in a forty-foot spray of frothy saliva.

And all Lucky could do was hang on.

7

Before his job at the Department of Water and Power, Tim Gilligan had managed fast-food restaurants. If he were ever to apply for another job, he'd have to worry that his resume would reveal a strange trajectory. The Southern California native had begun his work career in the most menial position at a Carl's Jr. in Hawthorne, climbing his way up to assistant manager by the time he was eighteen. From there he'd hopscotched to managing a nearby Wendy's franchise, a Del Taco in Tustin, and a collection of Subways in Anaheim, a stone's throw from Disneyland. Without a college education, Tim's next logical step was to raise money from family and friends to buy his own franchise. Instead, a customer introduced Tim to a career with the largest municipal utility in the United States. In a matter of months he'd gone from managing pimpled teenagers and English-challenged Vietnamese and His-panics to organizing DWP work crews.

As the department's manager for maintenance and repairs, Tim was all too accustomed to being awoken at odd hours by a favorite Travis Tritt tune he'd purchased as a ringtone. Not that he was the first call. He had minions who handled the hourly reports and service breakdowns. Assistant managers and field responders were more than capable of jumping into the fray of water main failures and arcing transformers.

Tim Gilligan was upper management, albeit the lower tier of upper management. His $175,000-a-year salary placed him in the higher pay-grade echelon of municipality management. Not bad for a city employee and college dropout.

The odd-hours calls had become more frequent of late as the mighty LADWP had been suffering almost weekly water main failures. The overworked pipes, many of which were up to one hundred years old, had been bursting citywide at an alarming rate.

Simple math, Tim had explained in a series of memos. The original riveted pipes, a full third of which had been sunk below city streets prior to the year 1930, were simultaneously breaching from decades of stress and corrosion. The reason these blowouts—as they were called within the public utility—were occurring in the wee hours of the night was due to low water usage. Pressure in the pipes would build during the hours of minimal utilization. Then *ka-boom!* The rivets would fail and a gaping chasm would suddenly appear in the middle of a city thoroughfare.

Tim picked up his phone, clicked receive, but before he put it to his ear, he allowed a moment for his eyes to adjust.

Damn.

Instead of the bedroom he'd become used to—a cozy country nest of pine and lacy frills his wife, Stacy, had cultured—he was slapped back into a dull depression by the plain, Navajo White walls of the Oakwood Apartments.

Damn it all to hell.

The waking reminder of his imminent divorce—number two

for Tim Gilligan—and the bad news of what was in all likelihood another blowout waiting for him at the other end of the phone call gave him every reason to bury his head back in his sweaty pillow. Any random nightmare would be more welcome than the life he was living separated from his kids by another vicious cur of a future ex-wife interested in both blood and money.

Because I'm a dirty, whore-loving SOB.

"Yeah," said Tim into his phone. "What time is it, anyway?"

"Half-three," said the Irish-accented managing engineer.

"Oh. Hey, Liam," said Tim. "Blowout?"

"And the hits just keep on comin'," quipped Liam.

"Where this time?"

"Compton."

With the news, Gilligan let out a sigh of relief. At least the blowout wasn't located in a high-profile zip code. The worst case benchmark being the 2014 collapse of a section of Sunset Boulevard, right in the heart of Bel-Air. Millions of drinkable gallons gushed onto the UCLA campus, flooding Pauley Pavilion, home of the storied Bruins basketball program. That same year, there'd been a blowout in tony Encino and one next door in equally posh Sherman Oaks the year before. Each came with monumental headaches for the utility both in man-hours, money, hassle from the community, and all-important public relations.

But Compton? A blowout there was likely to remain under the radar.

"You at the hole yet?" asked Tim.

"'Bout ten out. How long for you to get down here?"

"Gimme forty minutes."

Tim reached for the TV's remote control. Not to check the news. For the noise. He hated being alone. A flaw, a marriage counselor had surmised, that would continue to get him into another marriage quicker than was advised or into marital hot water when a relationship got sticky.

Then Tim saw what was on the TV.

"Aw, fuck me with a fork," Tim exclaimed.

"Rather you buy me dinner first," joked Liam.

"Goddamn Channel 5's already got a helicopter on it."

"Big hole with a sheriff's cruiser in it?"

"Don't tell me we got hurt cops."

"I won't tell you," said Liam flatly, "but I reckon your imagination can put it together."

It was agreed. Tim Gilligan should throw water on his face, find the nearest quadruple espresso to suck down his gullet, and hustle his ever-widening rear down to Compton.

Compton, Tim. You know the place.

Tim sure as hell did. He had a dirty secret down that way. And he hoped to Satan's hell to keep that secret buried and forever off of Stacy's divorce lawyer's forensic radar.

A secret and now a big-ass hole in the ground.

Tim Gilligan hadn't the faintest that his dirty secret and the latest DWP blowout would soon be one and the same—that when the pipes blew and the earth opened, the hole would swallow a hell of a lot more than just a sheriff's black-and-white.

It would soon swallow just about everything and everyone else with chips in the game.

8

Compton.

From street surface to underbelly, the sinkhole was two inches shy of eleven feet deep. When the asphalt gave way under Shia's lightweight boots, it felt exactly like that horrid Disneyland attraction she loathed to her bones—the Hollywood Tower of Terror. Modeled loosely after the historic Hollywood Tower apartments on Franklin Avenue, the ride is a hairy, out-of-control elevator violently propelled up and down in random fits. In Shia's opinion, the drops were the worst part, forcing her stomach up into her throat. After each group trip, she swore to Jesus she'd never partake again.

A foamy explosion of water, crumpling asphalt, and mud had buffered her fall. Instinct had kicked in, as did her feet, as she struggled to find buoyancy amidst the churn. But her duty belt—including her pistol and extra ammo mags—acted like diver's weights, repeatedly tugging her back down. When she reached for her buckle, it wasn't at her navel as the belt had twisted. But which way? Left or right? Without her arms to help propel her upwards, she sunk deeper with every search for the clasp. Her chest screamed for air, her calm all but submerged with the rest of her.

Shia felt her feet hit bottom. How far down? Jesus, was she going to drown on her first shift? She pushed off and, using her arms for lift, she aimed for the surface, ignited from above by the Interceptor's angled headlamps. So close, she thought. Home. Closing fast. All she had to do was reach up and grab the bumper guard. The lights, though, weren't waiting for her. They were upon her, charging downward as the black-and-white plunged into the hole. Four thousand pounds of metal and gravity. Shia snap-twisted her torso. A reflex. Her back to the behemoth, she fully expected the grille to pin her to the bottom of the hole. Her lungs would give in and her last breath would be spent inhaling liquid instead of air, a deathly return to the womb.

God, please make it quick.

The bumper missed and stopped halfway to the bottom. The turbulence and churn spun Shia, and she found herself breaching towards the surface. She flailed, unable to turn her face to the sky, only to find the Interceptor pushing her under yet again.

Jesus, no!

Then she felt the hook.

Like that terrible amusement park ride, the elevator was again propelling her body upward. Suddenly clear of the water, she found herself thumped upon the angled roof of the black-and-white with her legs tangled in the fixed light array.

"You breathin'?" she heard Lucky ask. Yet somehow the shock of the moment had left her too breathless to form a word. So, Lucky reminded her, "You're okay! Now, you gotta move with me!"

With his hand still hooking the back of her Kevlar vest, Lucky dragged her across the rear windshield, up the canted trunk, then at last onto the jagged asphalt.

"Stand or crawl!" demanded Lucky. "Just get the hell away 'cause I don't know if this hole gets any bigger."

Shia found her feet and stumbled after her TO to the sidewalk and a scrubby lawn. Lucky pounded on the ghetto bars at the front door until the porch light ignited and the robed occupant answered. He borrowed a cell phone, called 911 for assistance, then asked for a couple of towels and a plastic bag packed with ice. Ever grateful, Lucky slipped the ice bag between his waistband and the small of his back in defense of certain and painful inflammation.

In minutes, the scene was secured with sheriff's units shutting off access to the street. Fire engines were scrambled and, as a crowd of neighbors rimmed behind yellow police tape, paramedics checked out both Lucky and Shia for signs of injury.

"Only thing broke is her first night cherry," Shia overheard one distant deputy guffaw.

"Stuff the ten-cent commentary," barked the Mustache, a.k.a. Lieutenant Torres, who'd arrived at the scene to supervise. "Don't make me assign gender sensitivity training!"

While the sheriff's deputies and first responders kept the sinkhole safe and surrounded until officials from the Department of Water and Power arrived, Lucky and Shia were shuttled back to the station house. Once they were showered and back in their civilian garb, Lucky remanded Shia to the drudgery of writing reports. In addition to the chores generally reserved for trainees—writing the incident and end-of-watch summaries—Shia also had to complete the accident and damaged vehicle reports plus requests for all replacement equipment ruined in the water. As Shia toiled, Lucky commandeered an empty desk chair in the dispatch room, propped his sneakered feet on a table, sipped orange Gatorade, and watched the blowout story unfold on the KTLA Channel 5 News. When his new deputy interrupted with printed pages for his approval, he'd suggest corrections and return to the TV, contemplating everything from what it might take for the DWP to repair the massive mainline, to whether he should capitulate on Gonzo's desire to make an offer on the Altadena house they'd been co-renting, to the always fleeting memories of his deceased younger brother—a still-festering wound that was never far from emotional reach.

Lucky was finally satisfied with Shia's written reportage as the clock ticked minutes from their shift's 7:00 a.m. conclusion.

"Leave your service weapon in the dehumidifier and go get some rest," was Lucky's final remark to Shia. "I'll see you back in a new car at nine."

If the new deputy was uncomfortable with the arm's-length affect employed by Lucky, she would need to swallow and get used to it. There wasn't much warm or cozy about Lucky. The veteran cop wasn't wired that way and, from his own prismatic perspective, doing things his way had served him well enough.

The early morning trek back home to Altadena was full of yawns and a couple of strong air conditioner blasts just so Lucky could stay awake. He was half hoping the suburban rental house he shared with LAPD pilot Lydia "Gonzo" Gonzales would be empty. If he'd driven any slower—or stopped to shop for shaving cream or some other distractible item—he would've been assured of a family-free path from the driveway to a bedroom blacked out with opaque motel curtains.

Family-free?

Not a one of Lucky's made-up "family" was an actual blood relative. There was Gonzo and her fourteen-year-old son, Travis. Newest to the made-up clan was sixteen-year-old Karrie Kaarlsen. The pretty teen, originally from Wisconsin, was a runaway who'd tried to exchange a dark past in the freezing Midwest for the sunny skies of Southern California. To describe her adventure as a bump-filled hell ride would have been kind. Yet she'd found healthy parental attachments in the unmarried duo of Lucky and Gonzo, plus a strength of purpose in serving as a surrogate big sister to socially challenged Travis and in her ongoing obsession with Muay Thai.

"You look like shit," deadpanned Karrie before Lucky could roll up the window of his '99 primer gray Crown Victoria.

Lucky squinted into the glare, barely able to make out the outline of the strawberry-blonde teenager. He could picture her, though. Her image had been branded onto his brain ever since he'd first seen her picture. Freckles. Green eyes. Gone were the heavy makeup and pretense of being an adult. The girl was apple pie

Americana in a five-foot-three-inch package. Sixteen and, Lucky could only guess, happy.

He'd pulled into the driveway at the same moment Karrie was about to roll out in her nearly new Toyota Prius, a sweet-sixteen gift from Conrad Ellis, an old family friend turned patron and rich Dutch Uncle. The metallic lime green paint job just added to the burn in Lucky's retinas.

"If I could see what you're wearing, I'd probably tell you it's inappropriate," swung Lucky.

"Called summer school," gibed Karrie. "No stupid uniforms."

Kushunk-thunk. Lucky heard the Prius's passenger door open and shut in a simple one-two cadence. Travis, he easily figured, climbing into the Toyota. The boy hadn't summoned so much as a "Hi, Lucky," let alone a "Good morning" or "How are you?" He was, after all, fourteen and cursed with the weird kid gene. And though Travis worried his mother into sleeplessness, Lucky reckoned the boy was just fine. Travis was odd and Lucky was the odder surrogate dad. Perhaps that was why they got along so well.

As Lucky stepped gingerly from the car, he knew he was something shy of thirty-nine aching paces to a bed and a fast slip into unconsciousness. Between the driveway and the mattress, he'd surely encounter Gonzo, the matriarch of his *faux familia.* He knew she loved him with little condition—having nursed him back to living twice—the first after a head-on collision with a speeding Volvo—the second and more recent rescue was from his addiction to opioids, namely Percocet and Vicodin.

Hello. My name is Lucky and I'm a drug addict.

Lucky, in turn, loved Gonzo. He just loathed the ambivalence of his own affection. While he appreciated the onset of sudden stability in his life, he felt he neither deserved nor trusted it—that where he was truly meant to live and breathe was amongst the miscreants and the deadbeats of the streets.

Let's be frank, Lucky. It's a miracle you're not in jail.

"Honey, I'm home," Lucky called out.

The Craftsman bungalow was sturdy. Most of the exterior

shingles were still in place. Not to mention it was full of tax incentives for anyone who restored it (another reason why Gonzo wanted to buy instead of rent).

"Bedroom," called out Gonzo.

Lucky lumbered down a tight corridor that was two shoulder widths wide. Karrie and Travis, both on the slight side, could slip past each other without having to turn sideways, but Lucky and the swimmer-built Gonzo could barely maneuver without bumping uglies.

Gonzo called it architectural foreplay.

The master bedroom was two steps up—small, but neat and warm and decorated in a collage of fabrics and soft textures in contrast to the floor-to-ceiling hardwood. The room was rather dark on the most blue-skied of days, yet Lucky couldn't wait to pull the blackout drapes and erase all evidence of sunlight.

"You around for that water main thing?" asked Gonzo almost absently.

Lucky's eyes flicked to the TV angled atop the dresser. From first glance he could see the news helicopters were still in the air, telephoto lenses focused on the sinkhole with the sheriff's black-and-white stuck nose-down in the water.

"It's all hands on deck down there," deflected Lucky. It wasn't that he didn't want to debrief Gonzo on his first night's adventure with his trainee. He just wanted sleep so badly. If he'd copped to his involvement, Gonzo would've demanded he describe every last detail.

"I'm late," offered Gonzo as she finished folding laundry. She moved the neat pile from the mattress top to a nearby chair, clearing the way for Lucky to flop. "When you wake up, could you move what's in the washer to the dryer?"

"Sure, sure." Lucky kicked off his sneakers and fell facedown onto the bed. His arms scrunched a pillow up underneath his head.

"Not even a kiss hello or goodbye?"

"How about goodnight?" he asked, his words half muffled by his bicep. "Does that count?"

Gonzo crawled onto the bed, straddling Lucky with her

gazelle-like legs, hugged her man from behind, then lightly bit his ear.

"I'd say ow, but I'm toast," said Lucky.

"That didn't hurt."

"The back," he nearly complained.

"Noob put you through your paces?"

"Just sore, that's all."

"Trainees wear old men out," said Gonzo. "Except me, of course. I was a perfect and efficient trainee in every imaginable way."

"Bet you were a nightmare."

"I'll be one if you forget the laundry."

"G'night," said Lucky, eyes closed and hoping to drift off.

"You got AA before shift tonight?" she asked, before realizing he was already comatose. She left him, dressed, asleep, but not yet snoring. She made sure to lock the front door behind her.

9

Downtown Los Angeles. 9:11 a.m.

Face it, Timbo. You're fat.

At least once a day, Tim Gilligan chastised himself for letting his weight climb out of control. He would sometimes blame the divorces and subsequent calorie-boosting drinking binges. But just getting in and out of his DWP-issued Hyundai was becoming a strain. His knees hurt. His lung capacity felt shallow. He was a heart attack on a stick waiting for life's last lick.

Short of sleep and not receiving a scintilla of satisfaction from his behemoth McDonald's McCafé, he'd rolled down to Compton and witnessed firsthand the damage done by the DWP's most recent blowout. But for the sheriff's radio unit partially consumed by the sinkhole, it was pretty much like most of the other incidents—a water-spewing crater roughly the depth of the mainline with a circumference matching three-quarters the width of street.

In essence, a pothole big enough to swallow a blind elephant.

After putting a cork in his nerves, Tim made sure to check in with each department—fire, police, street services bureau, and even the Compton assistant mayor, who lived just three blocks to the west. He'd made sure to thank them for any and all early morning efforts of support before promising that the DWP would contain and repair the damage as quickly as humanly possible.

Or bureaucratically possible.

The Water and Power manager kept up his political presence, if only inside the safety tape. With the media throng that had begun assembling just shy of 6:00 a.m., Tim thought it wise to leave both video and live camera interfacing to the perky Ann Marie Callahan, the department's Ivy League–groomed public affairs officer.

As for his personal inspection of the blowout hole, with the presence of so much mud, foaming water, and crumbling asphalt, Tim couldn't tell if anything incriminating had been unearthed. The odds, he knew, were against it. But the street name—Poinsettia—it struck him as familiar. Worrisome. Not until he'd returned to the office and checked the schematics would he know for sure if there was any more to the Compton water main break than what it hopefully was—just another lousy blowout.

At ten past nine, Tim parked in his assigned DWP parking spot. As he waddled the short distance to the garage elevators, he could have sworn his knees were popping so loudly that the noise could be heard reverberating throughout the entire underground car park.

You're not only fat, Timbo. You're also a corrupt SOB.

Stuffing his self-flogging long enough for an elevator ride, Tim stepped onto the twelfth floor of the downtown John Ferraro Building to discover fifteen thousand square feet of unmanned desks, empty cubicles, and unanswered ringing telephones—reminiscent of scenes from the post-apocalyptic sci-fi films he'd loved as a preteen. The government-gray-on-gray space had the look of a fluorescent-lit sea of inefficiency, devoid of the slow-moving human slugs often attracted to civil service. The seemingly lifeless space curried a chill of mausoleum coldness.

Then came the low hum of human grumbling—muffled from somewhere within the office space. Tim swung left, expecting to find a crowd assembled in the windowless break room, which was barely large enough to contain a couple of adult carloads. Instead, his eyes were drawn to the newly redecorated conference space, a generous glass-encased room with a view of the intersection of the Hollywood and Pasadena freeways—famously known as the Four Level—and beyond, Dodger Stadium cast in a soft low-soaring cloud-fill affectionately known as June gloom.

Gloom indeed, thought Tim. Only it was already July.

Crammed into the conference space was what Tim perceived to be the entire engineering department staff. Heads were lowered, but Tim could pick out his favorite receptionist—a pleasing-to-the-loins twenty-something redhead he'd privately named Front Office Peggy—who was passing around pink tissues from a floral-printed Kleenex box. When she spied Tim, she handed off the tissue box and moved to the door to greet the latecomer.

"It's Hal Solomon," said Peggy.

"He's here?" wondered Tim.

"God, no," she said. "He was killed last night. He and his ex-wife. Right in front of his house."

"Hal Solomon?" duplicated Tim, oddly uncertain that he'd heard correctly, even though Peggy's diction was pretty clean and without the vocal up-lilt of a typical Valley girl.

"As in *our* Hal Solomon," replied Peggy. "He was just visiting last Thursday."

No doubt Tim knew Hal Solomon. The sixty-year-old was a former engineer and DWP lifer who'd been elevated to a career peak as Water and Power board member.

"Jesus," said Tim. "And sudden, yeah? Heart attack?"

"You haven't seen the news?" asked Peggy.

"Blowout down in Compton. Where do you think I've been?"

"Not that. In the West Valley, you know? The 'deadly carjacking'!" she stressed, already utilizing the banner adopted by the local TV news outlets.

Tim could only shake his head, still putting the pieces together. "Hal was carjacked?"

"He and the ex-Missus Solomon were found dead in their driveway," whispered Peggy, as if it were some kind of inside DWP secret. "Shot in the head."

Tim's fingertips touched his cranium, massaging his own thinning follicles. As if the idea of Hal Solomon's murder needed assistance penetrating his own thick melon.

"Chandra invited everyone into the conference room for prayers," said Peggy. "Not that it's mandatory or anything. I mean, I'm not even Catholic anymore. And I think Kevin's an atheist. But he's in there. I'm sure everyone would appreciate if you came too."

There came a tingling beneath Tim's skin—an uncomfortable agitation that arrived without warning. His pores were opening and his sudden flop sweat was instantly chilled by the wafting air conditioning.

"I feel sick," said Tim, not even meaning to excuse himself. He pivoted and made a dead reckoning for his office.

The notoriously windowless tomb—which was well beneath Tim Gilligan's managerial station—was in a cramped L-shaped space that hugged the floor's main electrical box. The thermostat was also in there to make certain the temperature was correctly adjusted for the equipment. Tim's seniority could have easily afforded him a corner suite with a view, but he found the constant hum of electricity regulated by the industrial breakers to be soothing and privacy-enhancing. He'd configured his desk and computer screen in such a way that if he saw someone coming, whatever private correspondence or conversations in which he might be engaged could be terminated without a hint of suspicion. That and the waves of electrical interference would make it almost impossible for anyone with an agenda to plant a listening device.

Turning to his desktop PC, Tim performed a quick news search for Hal Solomon. Within an eyeblink, media sources unfurled across his screen with clickable links. Each station had produced familiar video packages—a ridiculously telegenic stand-up reporter under a blaze of white camera lights, replete with B-roll footage of pools of coagulating blood and a driveway roped off with yellow crime scene tape dramatically fluttering in the early morning breeze.

"Sheezus hell," mouthed Tim.

The details of the murders were currently just guesswork and possible scenarios. Police sources called it a "carjacking gone horribly wrong." There were rumors of an African-American suspect in black jeans and a dark hoodie captured on a nearby supermarket's security cam. The suspect could be seen in the parking lot, testing the doors of luxury cars. More tangible details were being kept under lock and key by the LAPD while unnamed sources were already floating theories that after the hooded felon failed to shoplift a parked luxury ride, he'd shifted his focus to the sleepy driveways south of Ventura Boulevard.

Carjacking gone wrong?

Early reports claimed the spindly, sixty-year-old Hal Solomon had put up a fight. Tim couldn't even imagine the older man struggling with man or woman over a dinner check, let alone a fully insured car. Then there was the black suspect in the West Valley. Tarzana was hardly lily white. In fact, there was little of Los Angeles that hadn't been integrated by nearly every stripe of ethnicity, except possibly the eight-mile-deep black and brown swath that cut from South Central Los Angeles southwest to Compton, where very few Caucasians chose to live.

Still, wondered Tim—an armed black man jacking cars on the slopes of Tarzana? What was the likelihood of such a scenario versus something . . .

. . . more malevolent?

Tim rolled his desk chair deep into the corner of his odd-shaped office. He pressed his seat back against a wall of steel shelves, which held stacked schematics of every Water and Power pipe that had been sunk into Southland earth since William Mulholland had overseen the installation of the Los Angeles Aqueduct, forever changing the city's destiny. He thumbed his mobile phone to a number on speed dial. There was barely a single ring before his call was kicked to voicemail.

"This is Catalina Rincon. I'm not available, so leave a message."

A finger swipe and Tim had hung up. Cat would surely know. For a moment, he considered leaving word for her at her office. What could be suspicious about an executive on the engineering floor phoning a Water and Power board member? He might be calling to offer his condolences over the tragic circumstance of losing an esteemed colleague.

Tim's phone vibrated in a pair of quick bursts. He glanced at the incoming text contained in a white-on-green bubble.

in a meeting. usual spot? 1245?

He exhaled, then replied in a three-letter affirmative. His unanswered questions swilled like spoiled milk. Tim rationalized it would be better if he waited. Cat—or Catalina—was guaranteed to come with her own queries concerning the blowout in Compton: how it compared to some of the more recent failures; plans for cleanup and repair; and if, by ugly chance, it could endanger the dirty secret the two of them had shared with Hal Solomon. The very dead Hal Solomon. Murdered by a hooded assailant in his West Valley driveway. A black assailant, at that. Coincidence? Or an early sign of oncoming calamity?

The odds of a connection between the blowout and the murder appeared astronomical. Yet if Tim were a betting man instead of a man afflicted by constant cravings for food, drink, and prostitutes, he'd have wagered most of his money roll on the calamity.

10

Pasadena. 1:00 p.m.

"Hi. My name is Lucky. And I'm an addict."

He'd said the words many times over, but he wondered if he'd ever truly believed them. Even as an afterthought the moment they'd crossed from his tongue to his lips. The personal and public admission was the assumed and de facto requirement for attending AA meetings. Addicts need only apply. All attendees were there to surrender to the God of Almighty Dependency. Through the help of a sponsor and consistent meetings, Lucky had kicked his habit of greater mobility through over-prescribed pain medications. Yet when he cocked his ears and listened to the other addicts and the life stories they shared, he couldn't quite personally relate to the depths of their former depravities.

Not that he didn't pretend. Lucky was adept at pretending—mostly, in his odd prismatic opinion, at pretending to be human, or at least a regular guy. In part, that's what Gonzo loved about him. He was middle-class, blue-collar, and suffered little of life's bullshit. Keeping things simple was both credo and calling. Like sorting out the good guys from the bad guys. His tool-like purpose was as a valid societal need. There was no demand to complicate things any further, let alone dig deep for unscrubbed emotions. There was too much darkness down there. Lucky thought it best to keep those trap doors barred, bolted, and secured to a fault.

Yet there Lucky sat in a circle of folding chairs in an old church basement. Transom-styled windows flooded the all-purpose space with fuzzy daylight, igniting the microns of dust into shafts of gold. Eleven adult men and two women—one who was so emaciated it was hard to believe she was more than three weeks sober—took turns putting words to their own intestinal wrestlings.

Then there was the familiar-looking fellow with the over-sized forehead. At least that's how Lucky clocked the man. A peer. Maybe a year or two younger than Lucky, inches taller, with the hair of a man in his late fifties, gray and neatly trimmed, harshly receding around a perfect dome of skin. Lucky guessed the man in the buttoned-down business shirt and conservative tie either drove a convertible or was a hardcore tennis addict. That would explain the man's over-tanned complexion.

Feeling like he was staring, Lucky tuned back in. The subject at hand was reliving their rock bottoms—those seminal moments when addicts realize that it's either accept their own deaths or seek help.

Do I even have a rock bottom?

This was Lucky's true struggle. He'd hit some lows in his life— awful and debilitating turns. But a bona fide floor in his subterranean self? His commitment to treatment and sobriety had begun with little more than a conversation. Gonzo had expressed her uncon-ditional affection for him. Yet she wouldn't commit to rekindling their relationship or be teenaged Karrie's surrogate mother without Lucky agreeing to a sobriety program. She'd also suggested that, should Lucky decline her request, she might anonymously inform the L.A. Sheriff's Department of his untreated condition. Lucky weighed the choices—kick the pain meds or suffer the obvious consequences—and picked the former with little more than a shrug. Not what most in recovery would call an undeniable rock bottom.

Conclusion?

I haven't yet touched my bottom. It's down there. If I survive another day as a cop, I might get that much closer.

Lucky's turn to share came around. He summoned what truth he hoped would sound tragic enough—the fiery death of his little brother—the faces of crime victims he couldn't save—the general plethora of cops 'n' robbers crap that reeked of verisimilitude. All the while, as he spoke, he was desperate to be the kind of man who could connect with his own words. But that would require Lucky to believe in words with the same conviction he had in verified human behavior.

In Luckyland, actions spoke.

The hour-long AA meeting wrapped up at 2:00 p.m. straight up, with more than half the attendees making beelines for their next destinations while the remainder lingered at a buffet table stained from coffee and the crumbs of leaky jelly-filled donuts. Lucky's intent was to grab a free cup of tar-to-go and a mouthful of something doughy and glazed if there was anything left in the flimsy pink box.

"Hey, man. Your share really hit me."

The voice came from Lucky's right. Somehow Lucky instantly knew who it was—as if he'd been able to picture the vocal tone of the smart-shirted guy with the obvious forehead. That pronounced space above his eyebrows—the obvious permanent hitch in his gait.

Something.

"Steve Wimminger," the man introduced himself with a strong, confident hand.

The name didn't make an impression on the sheriff's deputy, who accepted the handshake.

"Lucky. And thanks, I guess. Sorry. It was Steve?"

"Friends just call me Wim—or Wimmer," he admitted with a nervy bounce. "Anyway, kinda new to the AA thing, if you couldn't tell."

"How many days you got?" asked Lucky.

"Three weeks sober," said Wimmer. "Hard shit."

"Musta thought you were somebody else 'cause I coulda swore I'd seen you in the rooms before."

"Might have," agreed Wimmer. "Not my first pony ride. You know. Stops 'n' starts. I'd hit a meeting. Like I thought it was some kinda magic, you know? Two hours later I'm in the office men's room with a straw up my nose."

"Sounds glamorous."

"Lawyer. Long hours. Late nights."

"Well, three weeks is better than no weeks," assured Lucky, preparing to wrap up the brief conversation. "One day at a time, man."

"Hey. Got this uncle in Philly," Wimmer segued, revealing a slight limp as he half-stepped closer. "Thirty years in the sobriety bank. So, he suggests that, for a sponsor, I hit a meeting every day until I find someone who really hits my button. Got me in here." Wimmer gently performed a three-fingered tap to his chest. "You did that for me today."

"Thanks," replied Lucky. "But I'm not sponsor material. Not even a year in."

"But you got your shit down."

"Two minutes of me doing the circle-time rap doesn't give that much away."

"So don't sponsor me," said Wimmer, pulling on his own reins. "But maybe help me find somebody. Because this time I really need to make it stick."

"Really," explained Lucky. "I'm not your guy—"

"Who's your sponsor, then?"

"Guy I know a long time. Dwayne Conroy. This isn't his side of the city. Not his meeting."

"Think he might know somebody? Like, if you asked him for me? 'Cause like I said, your share gave me goose bumps. Dunno why, but I think somebody like you—but with some more road underneath his wheels, someone who could prick up my ears— might be just what I need to stay on the path."

Lucky's chitchat meter had run out of quarters. So, before Wimmer had let go his last syllable, the cop produced a vellum business card with an embossed Los Angeles Sheriff's Department logo.

"Deputy Lucas Dey," read Wimmer. "Figured you were a cop from, well, the share."

"Just keep it anonymous," said Lucky.

"Yeah, yeah. That's your number?"

"My cell. Call me in a coupla days. I probably won't pick up but leave a message. Maybe I'll have caught up with Dwayne. Fair 'nuff?"

"Thanks. Really."

"Hit more meetings," advised Lucky, instantly regretting how he was already sounding sponsor-like. "Twice a day if you have to. Whatever it takes."

"I'm callin' you," pointed Wimmer. He was backing away, flapping Lucky's business card in front of a grin so wide it stretched his face in all directions but up.

Lucky was briefly amused. If he ever ran into Wimmer again, he might remember him as the fellow who could sell his forehead as a human billboard, renting the space over his eyebrows to the top-bidding advertiser.

The basement door was atop a short flight of linoleum-tiled steps. On another day Lucky might have climbed them two at a time, arriving at the top landing in half the strides. But the tightness he felt at the base of his spine advised him otherwise.

Meanwhile, Wimmer remained until Lucky had cleared the basement stairs. He dropped that winning grin, spun left, and sought a quiet corner with his mobile phone. He dialed, checked once to make sure he'd put enough space between himself and the remaining addicts gathered around the coffee urns, and waited five rings for an answer.

"You wouldn't believe it," said Wimmer right off the top with relish. "Woulda placed fifty-fifty odds the asshole would've made me. But nothin'. Sure of it. Not a spit of recognition. I even talked him up about a sponsor . . . Seriously . . . Yeah, yeah. Take it from me, Lucky fucking Dey doesn't have a clue the size of the bat I'm gonna take to his little world."

11

Downtown Los Angeles. 2:32 p.m.

Tim bitched at himself. It was sticky hot and he could feel the moisture from his butt crack sucking at the fabric of his fat-man khakis. He seemed to be suffering a walking wedgie at the end of every city block. More concerned about how it might look than the discomfort, he'd pulled out his shirttail, hoping to conceal the embarrassment.

A city bus trucked past. He cursed himself for knowing nary a lick about the metro transit system. Yet why the hell should he? In his universe, subways and buses were for immigrants. Conversely, Tim Gilligan was a lily-white Anglo and a Southern Cal native. Those of his extraction either drove cars, biked, or hoofed it. And that was tragically that.

At least he'd made something out of his ninety-minute lunch with Catalina Rincon, hydrating himself with every glass of water the buxom, Turkish-blooded twenty-something server poured. He kept stealing looks at the cleavage peeking out from her black yoga top and she kept pouring as long as his eyeballs promised a tip befitting her service. Despite her available looks, the waitress couldn't hold a candle to Tim's lunch date. Catalina Rincon. The petite thirty-five-year-old must have been turning heads since she was twelve. Though she was fully Hispanic by birth—equal parts Salvadoran and Colombian—Cat shaded closer to African-American, complete with a shock of tantalizingly frizzy brown hair, freckled cheeks, striking jaw, and lips that could only have been formed by a design committee of heterosexual men. Then there were her eyes, hazel and so penetrating that men in her life complained she could read their most sacred thoughts.

The rest of Cat was chiseled from a workout regime that began weekday mornings at 5:30 a.m. Or so she'd proudly brag as she and Tim split their usual order of a rib-eye steak with mashed potatoes, falafel, hummus, and a tart green salad. Tim was self-conscious with every delectable bite that his girth was filling the entirety of his mesh-wire chair while Cat could have shared her identical seat with a pair of pet Corgis.

Tim pressed Cat about her fellow board member Hal Solomon, shockingly gunned down in his Tarzana driveway. Cat was quick to push past what she termed the "sad shit" and maneuver the conversation to updates on Tim's two families, the Damocles's sword that was his pending divorce number two, and what it was like for a man in his forties to be single again. Was he seeing anybody? Trolling for honeys on social media or dating sites? Or was he fisting his way through Asian porn sites again? Cat was all about sex talk as it related to Tim, but not at all herself. It was a constant tease and tactic as she was going out of her head-turning way *not* to discuss Hal Solomon.

"What do you know about the murder?" Tim pressed again, "Beyond what's on the news?"

"It hasn't even been twenty-four hours," defended Cat. "What more could anybody know?"

"How about that Hal wasn't on board?" Tim was leaning in

so he wouldn't have to raise his voice over the rumble of a nearby diesel engine on idle.

"Don't have a clue what you're talking about," answered Cat.

"Shit if you don't," Tim countered. "You act like I'm wearing a wire."

"Are you?"

"Like that's where we're at? After all this time?"

"Hal was on the fence but coming around," insisted Cat. "More important, if he didn't want in, then he was happy just to get out of the way."

"Well, he's out of the way now, yeah?"

"It was a carjacking. That's all."

"In Tarzana? Brother from the hood just hanging out, waiting to steal the old man's Tesla?"

"We don't know who he was or if he was from Bakersfield, for all any of us know. Let alone *the hood*? You're reaching, Timbo."

"Think I've earned the right to some paranoid thoughts," defended Tim. "And so should you."

"I don't operate that way." Cat tried a come-on smile. Confident. Calculated. Like she knew some kind of secret password to a safe room.

"Just trying to stay a step or two ahead," Tim tried to explain. "No surprises."

"Three hundred million dollars, Timbo," said Cat. "That's what the DWP injects into the city coffers per year. You don't think I've got my bases covered?"

"*Your* bases. As in Cat Rincon's sweet ass."

"Don't forget we both have stock in this," she said. "Five million by year's end . . . And thanks. Not sure you ever noticed my ass. God knows I work hard enough to keep it worth looking at."

Tim hardly looked sated by her answer.

"You want dessert?" asked Cat.

"I wanna sleep tonight without wondering if I'm next."

"Why would you be next? Big Tim brings the juice. This doesn't happen without you."

The juice!

In all Tim's fear and paranoia over Hal Solomon's murder, he'd forgotten to cross-check his private schematics against the master DWP map detailing the Compton blowout. If there was no conflict, he sure as shit didn't need to tell Cat.

"Did you hear me?" queried Cat. "We're partners. You 'n' me. Thick and thin all the way to the payoff."

"Yeah, yeah," groaned Tim. "But does Cat's Compton partner know that? Huh? Does he even know who I am?"

"He knows what he needs to know," calmed Cat. "Just like you only know what you know. And as long as you both trust me . . ."

The end of lunch came with a cash split of the check. Cat kissed Tim on his scruffy cheek and he was soon hoofing it back to his office in hopes the walk and perspiration would melt off the calories from having nervously polished off the last of the garlic mashed potatoes.

"Fuck her," groaned Tim to nobody but the corner panhandlers.

Fuck her? Unlikely.

He couldn't imagine someone with Cat's appeal getting cozy with a man whose ass crease could sweat like a lumberjack's armpit.

Yet besides me, who hasn't fucked her?

The label "climber" wasn't fit to describe a woman as ambitious and willing as Cat Rincon. Her rise from city council volunteer to mayor's chief of staff to running her own real estate management firm to Department of Water and Power Board of Directors was nothing less than meteoric. Which made Tim wonder: What else could Cat Rincon do or with whom was she willing to make a bargain to achieve her next bloody goal?

Bloody goal?

Tim caught himself, stopping mid-trudge. Had his brain pulled a Freudian slip on him? Or was the heat playing tricks between his subconscious and his affection for Cat?

Cat Rincon. So ambitious she'd kill?

Tim stuffed the thought, wiped his brow, and resumed his walk.

12

Trees. They were the last image Frosty hoped to recall before falling asleep and the first when he woke. Even if the time was as late as three in the afternoon. Frosty's eyes fluttered open and focused on a mature *Podocarpus* or *Afrocarpus*, also known as a fern pine. The one pictured on the magazine cut-out scotch-taped to his wall was forty feet tall, alone, and throwing shade over a small Cape Cod–styled home.

"Laaaaaammmmaaaaaarrrrrrrr!" his mother's voice called out from the kitchen. "How late you gonna lay up?"

Frosty allowed his eyes to slide to the next magazine photo. *Schinus terebinthifolius.* Or better known as a Brazilian pepper. He liked to quiz himself on the Latin. Knowing the scientific genus of every species wouldn't be required once he finally acquired his dream nursery. But being able to rattle off the Latin in rapping licks would be sure to sound badass. Educated. Hardly like the ghetto trash he felt deep in his bones.

"Lamaaaaaaaaarrrr!"

Frosty hated his birth name. Nobody but his mother and Gran'nana were allowed to call him that.

Lamar Otis Clayton III.

His grandfather, the original Lamar, was a man of respect. He was both preacher and proud Compton tobacconist. His corner shop was a famous gathering post where Lamar, the senior, would sell good smokes and God's mercy to whoever walked through his door. Frosty's own dad, otherwise known as Deuce amongst his Crip brethren, was long since dead, killed in a drive-by only two blocks from the converted garage where Lamar number three laid his head to rest.

Frosty sat on his single cot. Stark naked. Seeing his skinny legs beneath him ushered in a flood of memories from the night before. After ditching the stolen Tesla behind the razor-wire fences of a Lynwood chop shop, he'd bummed a ride back to the eight-hundred-square-foot duplex he shared with his mother and his Gran'nana. In the dark of his backyard, he'd stripped out of his bloody clothes and stuffed them into a large trash bag along with the .22 pistol. He had hidden the evidence in the empty wheel well of his black-on-black Cadillac Escalade's trunk with a plan to discard all fouling evidence the next afternoon. Frosty had quietly showered, smoked a leftover joint while sitting on his toilet with the window open, and eventually passed out amongst his beloved trees.

"Laamaaaaaaaaarrrrr!" This time his mother double-thumped a heavy fist against the wall.

"I hear ya!" bit back Frosty.

"Need a man's help in here!"

"Gettin' dressed first," said Frosty. "What time is it?"

"Time to get your skinny ass up!"

Frosty reached for his phone. The time blinked next to a variety of unanswered texts and a voicemail from a burner phone number he recognized as Julius Colón's. He pressed the phone to his ear. The recorded voice came across tinny:

"My ice-cold nigga. Got us some catchin' up 'n' shit, know what I'm sayin'? Come by later 'n' we sit down. An' don' you leave nothin' out. Need me the whole play-by-play."

Frosty dressed, choosing a pair of Nikes in a color scheme called Deceptive Red. It was an obvious Blood color and, as a rule, verboten for any self-respecting Crip. If anyone were to pipe up about the shade of his footwear, his answer would be vintage Frosty.

Who? Me? I ain't all that. These is just shoes and don't they look the shit?

With meticulous relish, Frosty sat at the kitchen nook and replaced the stock white laces with a fresh set of blue satins. The afternoon light filtered in through a street-facing dining room with the occasional shadow being cast by his perpetually busy mother, Des'ree.

"Red shoes," she said, returning from his room with a basket of laundry.

"Goin' nowhere I ain't known," replied Frosty, "An' things don't go like that no more. Check it. My laces are blue, anyways. See?"

"Lord don't recognize no blues 'n' reds." Des'ree had disappeared into the kitchen cubby with the recently installed stackable washer and dryer—brand-new Whirlpool courtesy of her one and only baby boy.

"Where's Gran'nana?" switched Frosty.

"Where she's always at," said Des'ree. "It's a weekday and she old and somebody she knows gettin' planted in the ground . . . Pickin' her up after and we goin' to Bible study. Wanna come?"

Frosty gave his mother a smirk. In return he received a wink and a row of crooked yet brilliant white teeth. Frosty once offered to pay for braces. But his momma wouldn't have it, replying that God made her perfect just like he'd made her young Lamar perfect. Her smile was infectious and framed by an incredible roundness that reached from her ankles to ears. When she unleashed that beaming grin on her boy, he felt the only true warmth he'd ever known. The rest of the world had left him pretty cold. And he had treated it in kind.

"You was out late," said Des'ree, trailing off into another of the house's tiny rooms.

"Workin', workin'," returned Frosty.

"Didn't know all them trees you growin' grew at night."

"Trees never stop workin'," said Frosty. "Just like my momma never stop workin'."

"But unlike me, their bark ain't worse than their bite."

Frosty released a gentle chuckle. "Ladies and gentlemen. She here all week."

"Hungry?"

"I get somethin' when I get there."

"Get where?"

"Bossman calleth."

"Same fella you call King Julius?"

"Jus' Julius. Ain't nobody call him king."

"Because there ain't but one king and that's the one up in you-know-wheresville."

"And you be the queen."

"And don't you forget it." Des'ree reappeared, barely five feet tall but wide enough to fill the doorway. She wore a turquoise shift of lightweight polyester and what little of her hair that remained was pulled into a neat topknot.

"Be home for dinner, I think," volunteered Frosty. "I can pick up somethin' to cook."

"Coupla whole chickens. Make that brick thing again."

The flow between mother and son was comfortable and breezy. More to the tune of a contented married pair than a thirty-eight-year-old momma and her boy. Frosty tugged on the last loop of his laces, strode two lanky steps, and kissed his mother's cheek.

I love that woman.

And if things worked out in a year or so—if the plans Frosty was part of bore the promised fruit—he'd not only have the capital to start his own urban tree nursery, but some leftover Benjamins to buy his momma the house she truly deserved. Somewhere beyond Compton. Perhaps further inland to Riverside, he thought. Or the sun-kissed knolls of Chino Hills.

13

The yellowed tiles of the former Compton PD showers dated all the way back to the swinging seventies. But the fixtures, corroded down from their peeling chrome finish, still delivered a scalding spray with significant force. Nothing like the lousy water-saving shower heads required by state building codes. Lucky chuckled at the irony of a sheriff's deputy breaking water conservation statutes just by taking an office shower.

After enduring one of his thrice-weekly rehab sessions with his *physical terrorist*, Lucky had arrived at the station with time to shower, stretch again, then prep for the shift ahead. He toweled himself to a cool semi-dry and settled in front of his locker. As he dressed, a young deputy whose name Lucky had yet to memorize slid in behind him.

"Son of a bitch," remarked the young deputy.

"Got a problem?" hissed Lucky, barely a look over his shoulder.

"Sorry," said the young deputy. "I just didn't believe it. Least not till now."

Lucky twisted at the waist. He had just pulled on a T-shirt when he realized the young deputy had keyed in on the Reaper tattoo covering most of his left calf.

"Is there a number on it?" asked the deputy. He was thin enough to blow over with a kiss, with hair cut short on the sides and choppy on top. The fit of his uniform was something akin to an oversized condom.

"Yeah," said Lucky, neither volunteering the digit nor inviting the young deputy to take a closer look.

"Lennox motherfucking Reapers," grinned the young deputy, who finally introduced himself. "Gil Ramirez. Hey. I bet you got some stories, yeah?"

"Don't we all," said Lucky, pulling on the neoprene kneepads he wore under his uniform pants.

"Me, man?" said Gil. "I'm too new. Like, only two years on the map, you know?"

"Compton map?"

"Yeah. But Lennox Station was top of my list. This is as close as I could get."

Compton was, in fact, an easy map compared to some of the other sheriff's stations. The street grid was simple and nearly every inch of it ran north/south and east/west. And if a deputy ever got lost during a pursuit, a scan of the horizon would usually provide a glimpse of the thirteen-story Compton Courts building. The concrete white monolith—not so affectionately nicknamed Fort Compton—stood well above all other buildings in the zip code and was an easy visual for a cop to use for quick orientation.

"Can I ask something?" asked Gil, not so much waiting for a response. "Did you have to shoot your way in?"

Lucky lifted one eyebrow.

"To be a Reaper," Gil continued. "You had to be in a gunfight, yeah?"

"Have a good shift," was Lucky's retort, thus ending the conversation.

The evening brief was scheduled for 9:00 p.m., but it could be later depending on station watch. The five-minute warning came over the locker room's public address system.

"Evening brief at ten after," buzzed a voice with muffled articulation equal to that of a Metro driver announcing the next bus stop.

Lucky found his back already stiffening—a pronounced restriction in mobility his physical terrorist had ascribed to his taut-as-drumheads hamstrings.

Note to self. No foot pursuits tonight.

The folding chairs in the briefing room were dated and once painted a chocolate brown. The color on every seat had been worn through to a metallic sheen. Lucky sat at the back of the sparse gathering, having little trouble keeping to himself. While other deputies were trading trash talk or making plans on where to meet for their post-midnight lunch, Lucky kept to the comfort of his own skin as well as his position as the outsider. He was hardly shiny, but was still considered someone new—known mostly as "that transferred badge from Kern County" or "the ex-Lennox Reaper with the sinister tattoo."

"Okay. Got a list, so let's get to it." Torres took to a badly veneered podium still bearing the fading emblem of the defunct City of Compton Police Department.

Lucky swiveled his eyes to the doorway, still missing his trainee.

"Before you start," cleared Lucky. "Anybody seen my greenie?"

"Babysitting your ride-along," said Torres, his porno stache hardly stirring above his ChapSticked lips. "Surprise to me too. Talk to you when we're done with all this Fourth of July crap."

Lucky sat back and privately commiserated over the bad news. He wasn't a fan of ride-alongs. A police officer's job was to serve and protect the everyday Janes and Joes. Not play tour guide to some connected bureaucrat or thrill-seeking reporter. In addition, he was in training mode with a deputy who'd spent half her first night drying off from a near drowning.

"Before we get to the Fourth of July memo," said Torres, "the department is once again delayed with the issuing of body cams. Temple Street says the week after next. I will believe it when I see 'em. And for those of you who look upon this as a two-week reprieve, remember: body cams will be as much for protection of patrol deputies as they will the public. Questions? No? Good. Moving on."

Lucky would like to have lodged a complaint. He'd policed just fine for sixteen years without needing a stem-to-stern recording of his in-uniform activities. Yet he also knew he couldn't control the future nor the challenges that came with it. But had there been body cams back when he'd started with L.A. Sheriff's?

There wouldn't have been Reapers.

"So tomorrow night is you know what," repeated Torres. "Forecast is a record breaker heat-wise. So, more fun with that. And if you haven't worked a July Fourth down this way—and I'm talking Compton, Lennox, Century—it's nothin' short of Baghdad on the first night of the invasion. Any of you served, you get me."

The Mustache had fought in both Iraq and Afghanistan. Or so Lucky had heard. But the heat in the Middle East had a predictability and purpose. In L.A., when the offshore breezes shifted to the Mojave-driven Santa Anas, the population on the semi-cool flatlands between Hollywood and Long Beach would often react like insects travelling across a pancake griddle.

Bad things happened when it was hot.

The watch boss carried on with his reiterations of the dangers when dealing with the seemingly trainloads of illegal fireworks that were sure to be uncorked within his jurisdiction. July Fourth was generally a night that guaranteed law enforcement officers would be chasing their tails, hoping to bag bad boys with guns and more than likely coming up with trunks full of illicit Chinese- and Mexican-made bottle rockets, roman candles, and air-burst projectiles.

"Of course," droned Torres, "as is their usual modus operandi, LAFD has new and—these are their words—'improved procedures for disposal of confiscated incendiaries.'"

"My douchebag bro-in-law is FD, and I got an improved procedure where he can stuff illegal fireworks," announced Gil to the room's belly laughter.

If Lieutenant Torres had an explanation for saddling Lucky and his trainee with a ride-along, he had forgotten or had been urgently distracted post-briefing. No matter, decided Lucky. If the Mustache had gifted his newest TO with a slice of fertilizer pie, it would be Lucky's job to stir it into a teachable meal.

The night air had turned uniquely thick. A thin cloud ceiling hung amorphous and gray against the reflection of dim city lights. Lucky, standing on the curb overlooking the motor yard, lowered his gaze to the Crown Victoria radio car that was backed up and idling with three of its four doors open. Shia climbed out, new smile stretched across her face and appearing no worse for wear after the harsh dunking she'd suffered the night before.

"Dry and ready to ride," she grinned. "Can't say the car is quite what we had last night."

"Partial to Crown Vics," said Lucky. "No matter what I do, seems we end up back together."

He scoped the ride-along's legs as they stretched from the Crown Vic's back seat. Spindly and long inside a pair of perfectly faded denim. White Converse All Stars with no socks, shaggy beach hair in a designer cut, and a muscle T-shirt underneath a fresh-from-the-plastic-wrapper black ballistic vest.

"Hey there," introduced the ride-along. "Atom Blum. I'm your tourist."

Lucky measured the man as roughly thirty-five to forty years with a youthful exuberance underneath hard-partying skin. Entitled. The skinny SOB stunk of a zip code south of Mulholland and west of the 405. Some kind of showbiz asshole, that was for sure. Despite all instinctive reservations, Lucky greeted the boy wonder with a handshake.

"I'm Lucky. I expect you've met Deputy Saint George."

"Already familiar," said Atom. "Second night on the job, I hear."

"Gonna see if we can keep her dry tonight." Lucky nodded

toward Shia, knowing full well the undertow of sexual innuendo. Night two of hazing had already begun. Sure enough, the movie director's eyes widened with puerile delight.

"New body armor," noted Lucky, ambling around to the driver's door. "Ride-along expecting a gunfight tonight?"

"Oh, the vest," exclaimed Atom. "Yeah, that. Paul McGill suggested I wear one."

If Atom's name-drop was meant to impress, it slipped past Lucky like a haymaker missed wide. Not that Lucky didn't take stock in the name. Paul McGill was the department's number two in command. Assistant sheriff. Top brass.

"Connected guy, huh?" said Lucky.

"Good to know people," said Atom. "Anyhow, Paul thought I should maybe think about putting some L.A. Sheriff's in my next picture. You know? For PR. Make you front-line cops look good."

"You in movies?" asked Lucky, more pro forma than profoundly awed.

"Director," said Atom, trying and failing not to sound dazzled at himself.

"Mr. Blum directed the *Roadkill* movies," volunteered Shia.

"I'm Atom," the boy wonder insisted. "My step-daddy's the only mister I know."

"Rules of the back seat," segued Lucky. "You get out when I say get out. Stay when I say. And if, for any reason, I tell you to hit the floor, don't ask why. Just do and we'll all be okay."

"Hey," said Atom. "All good. You be you. I'm here to observe and nothin' else. Call me Mr. Invisible."

"Thought you weren't a 'mister,'" played Shia.

"Shoots and scores," clucked Atom. "Cuff me and do with me what you will, Ms. Deputy."

"Let's have a good shift," refocused Lucky.

"Yes, sir," agreed Shia.

14

"**P**izza *Wang*," Lil Rod sang into a crust-covered phone receiver. The kitchen of the former Pizza King was steamy and the decrepit ventilation unit installed to suck the cooking gasses out of the building contained a rattle that sounded like loose change tossed in a tumble dryer.

"It's Pizza *Wing*, dumbass," yucked Tuba as he slammed the oven door shut so hard the push of hot air licked his eyelashes.

"S'all about the sound," argued Lil Rod, scribbling down the phone order. "Throw down some *wang* on our *wing* an' our shit's got game."

"Keep it up and J's gonna have me pop this paddle upside your brains." Tuba jokingly pretended to bat with the giant metal spatula used to shovel the pies in and out of the oven.

It had been nearly three years since Julius Colón had bought out the old Pizza King on Compton's East Alondra. The deal was legal down to the lawyers and the ink despite the longtime owner's polite resistance. Once Julius had purchased the block of storefronts, he had handpicked the business from which he wanted to operate his less-than-legit ventures and began raising rent until the original proprietor had no choice but to capitulate. As Julius's first order of business, he added a deep fryer and wings to both the menu and the street sign, which soon read Pizza Wing. Adding chicken to the delivery service was an instant boon to the business.

"Pizza *WANG!*" danced sixteen-year-old Lil Rod, trying to Frisbee a handful of pepperoni slices one by one onto a pair of extra-large pies. "Say it, Tubes. The *wang* got the *swang*."

Tuba, the nineteen-year-old assistant manager, shook his head, his short dreads wagging as if made from springs.

The back office door had a squeaky hinge. High pitched. It was Tuba's only warning that Julius was on a path to the kitchen. Unconsciously, Tuba swiveled his view to gather in his bantamweight boss, who favored skintight workout wear to show off his MMA-sculpted physique.

"You better be countin' them meat slices, young'un," rang Julius, arm raised and pointing the length of the kitchen to a handwritten chart outlining exactly how much meat could be expended per each pizza size. "And what does bein' cheap earn me?"

"All da money," chimed both Tuba and Lil Rod.

"Jews ain't stupid," said Julius. "Why those tribesmen still own most of what they survey."

"Maybe you was a Jew in another life," added the hulking Big Otis, Julius's bodyguard and self-appointed right hand of God. Prostate cancer drugs administered by a Tijuana clinic had left every hair on Big O's three-hundred-plus-pound body in permanent retardation and his skin a constellation of Rorschach blotches.

"A Blaxican Jew," joked Julius. "Rich *and* badass. Now there's a super race I can use to beat ass on the world."

Hands in his pockets, Frosty appeared from behind Julius, wearing a blue skully to match those new shoelaces on his Jordans.

"Hey, Fros'," tipped Tuba from the open oven.

Frosty chinned his acknowledgment and smiled thinly, grateful that he'd long since graduated from Julius's school of thug work ethic. All the Colón Bad Boys were schooled in hard work to balance out what Julius called gang life lazy. Slingin' and stealin' and protectin' turf wasn't so hard when compared to the character-building toil of a day laborer. Julius made every homie his legal employee, empowering them with part-time, minimum-wage positions at his various businesses. Frosty's tutelage was at the Greenleaf Nursery, a quarter-mile strip of tilled earth under the DWP high-voltage towers that striped southern Compton. It was a backbreaking job, which Frosty had initially hated. That was before he'd discovered his passion for all things trees and glimpsed his way out of the streets.

"When you knock off?" asked Julius.

"S'posed to clock at midnight," said Tuba. "But that's if last shift shows up right."

"After you clock," said Julius. "Want you to go over and keep a watch on my hole."

Lil Rod failed to muzzle his giggle. The sixteen-year-old's imagination wasn't so firmly tucked in his extra-baggy American Eagle jeans.

"Shut your baby ass," barked Julius. "My hole. The big mess in the middle of Poinsettia. Power fuckers are too cheap to keep a twenty-four-seven crew on it so we gotta keep it clean. Ya feel me?"

"We gotcha, boss," said Tuba, meaning to slap his chest out of ownership. Instead he caused a mammoth ripple across his fatty middle.

"And watch you don't overcook no more wings," finished Julius, crossing through the kitchen with Big Otis, Frosty a languid step behind.

"Hey, yo," said Tuba, putting down the spatula. He chased Julius by the order counter and a yellow-tinged dining area smaller than a Starbucks bathroom.

"You leavin' Raydon alone in my kitchen?" shot Julius, referring to Lil Rod by his birth name.

"Got somethin' you might wanna know," hushed Tuba. "Somethin' my cuz heard over at the sheriff's."

"Who's your cuz?" asked Julius.

"Explorer scout kinda cuz."

"Wanna be a cop?"

"Naw. He just got ambitions. Checkin' his options."

"What he know?"

"What he heard. 'Bout a new fella with a leg tattoo."

"Tattoo? So what?"

"Lennox tattoo. You know. Reaper shit."

Frosty observed the already posture-perfect Julius stiffen. At five-foot-seven, Julius was all pectorals and bulging thighs and had the soft brown facial features of mixed races. Dominating in the ring as well as the streets had taught him the art of looking down on his lesser.

"You heard too many stories," said Julius, betraying his truest feelings. "That Lennox shit's behind me."

"Oh, right," corrected Tuba. "Jus' thought you might wanna know."

"That some fat ol' Reaper be workin' Compton?" faked Julius. He forced a business pose to mask the belly full of flame the word Reaper wrought inside—memories of an embarrassment the street would not abide. "Your heart's in the right place and I appreciate it. But we don't dust up with sheriffs. We take care of *our* business. They takes care of theirs. Now, what's your job?"

"Clock out. Watch your big hole."

Julius thumped a friendly fist on Tuba's chest.

"Good. Now, get back in there before Raydon fucks up my pizza game," gestured Julius before turning to Big Otis. "You waitin' on me to tell ya to get the car?"

Otis performed an awkward pivot and hulked off around the corner. This left Frosty to lead Julius fifteen paces west to the Escalade parked against a curb darkened by an overgrown ficus.

"Love this ol' tree," remarked Julius, "but it's kicking the ass of my sidewalk."

The businessman knew all about liability. The concrete had long ago stopped containing the tree's clamoring roots. Surrounding pieces of cement were either loose in chunks or dangerously and unevenly protruding.

"*Ficus microcarpa*," said Frosty, with the correct Latin for the Indian laurel fig tree.

"Well, whatever it called, some ol' woman gonna trip, break her hip, 'n' dial that 222-2222 motherfucker on the back of all them buses."

Frosty laughed.

"You laugh," warned Julius. "But you wait till you get your first legit biz. Insurance? Liability premiums don't know nothin' but how to ask 'pass the lube.'"

After a cautious read of the street in both directions, Frosty used his remote to pop the rear gate of the Escalade. He was lifting the top off the spare wheel well when Julius interrupted.

"Don't want your bloody underwears," touched Julius before snapping his fingers. "That's your shit to burn. Jus' need me the pop gun."

"Why? Was gonna drop it in the harbor."

"City idiots got a buyback goin'," answered Julius. "Givin' away gift cards from Walmart 'n' shit for turnin' in guns. And I'm talkin' any gat no matter if it works or not."

"Y'ain't serious."

"As a hard-on. Them city assholes dumb enough to trade dollars for any bang bang that chambers a bullet, let 'em pay me for the gun that kilt one of their own Water 'n' Power bitches."

Frosty paused, wondering if Julius had been kicked hard in the head during a sparring session.

"Nothin' for your skinny ass to worry about," explained Julius. "They go right from the buyback to the place where they melt 'em down. Use the metal to make wheelchairs or some such do-good bullshit."

"Makin' good from the bad," surmised Frosty.

"Don't care what them fools call it," said Julius. "Call it leavin' no easy dollar behind. That, and you gotta love the irony. Yeah. I said *irony*. Know that word?"

Frosty didn't think it cool to scratch his head. From the bag of bloody evidence, he lifted a gallon-sized Ziploc containing the Taurus .22 he'd used to execute the Tarzana man and his screeching ex-wife.

"Shell casings?" asked Julius.

"Jackers don't stop to pick up their trash," answered Frosty. "Left no prints on 'em, so . . ."

The rest was left unsaid, considering Julius's plan to trade the palm-sized pistol for certain destruction and a gift card.

"When they handin' over them gift cards? Any of 'em from Olive Garden, you send my way, 'kay? My Gran'nana loves her some breadsticks."

Julius accepted the Ziploc, tucking it into his armpit just as Big Otis rounded out of the alley in a metallic gray Chevy Suburban.

"Still scoutin' property?" asked Julius before slipping into the Suburban's passenger seat.

"If it's got source water and transmission towers," said Frosty, "I'm eyeballin'."

"Almost there, Frostman," grinned Julius. "We're almost there. You *will* have your garden."

15

"Hotter 'n Hades," moaned the boy wonder from the back seat of the black-and-white. "Seriously. My skin's gonna crack. Any air conditioning in this bitch?"

Lucky flicked an eye to his rearview mirror.

"Tell our guest why sheriffs roll with windows down," suggested Lucky.

"It's because L.A. sheriffs use their ears," replied Shia. "All year round it's windows down. That way we hear what's happening outside the vehicle, like whistles or shouts for assistance. Or triangulation of gunfire—"

"Right, right," complied Atom. "Must be hell on your skin and hair, though."

"My second night, sir," replied Shia, keeping her eyes forward and scanning the ghostly corners and storefronts. "Time will tell."

"Complexion like yours," said Atom. "I mean, it's fucking beautiful. Like, camera-ready—art-school beautiful. And I would know because I've directed hours of cosmetics spots."

"Spots?" asked Shia.

"TV commercials," said Atom. "When I'm not making a movie, I shoot ads for television. Easy money if you're A-list."

"Wouldn't know about that, sir," said Shia.

"Hey," said Atom. "Ever heard of an actress named Lupita Nyong'o?"

"No, sir," fibbed Shia. She didn't want to appear too interested in anything as shallow as showbiz—at least not in front of Lucky. Shia had obviously both heard of and been compared to the *Twelve Years a Slave* actress, especially after the mixed Kenyan-Mexican performer had collected an Academy Award. Their rich complexions and bone structures were striking in similarity. Once while standing in line for a nightclub, Shia had even been mistaken for the actress and escorted past the velvet rope by a bouncer. She hadn't protested.

"You are every bit as spectacular as Lupita," impressed Atom. "Especially now that I've been this close to both of you. I'd say your uniform thing gives you the edge."

"Didn't know I was in a competition," fended Shia, flat and trying to sound unflattered.

"Come on," laughed Atom. "All women are in a competition, whether they admit it or not. Ain't that right, Sergeant Lucky?"

"Sir?" asked Lucky, pretending not to have been listening. He'd already reached what he sometimes called his "douchebag threshold." If there were a switch he could have flipped to shut the visitor's mouth to the off position, Lucky would have thrown it.

"All women," confirmed Atom. "And call me sexist, but in one way or the other they're in competition with all other women. And I'm talking the planet earth."

From his left, Lucky marked a beige mid-nineties Lincoln Town Car slow-rolling through a stop sign before turning right onto East Compton Boulevard. He clicked the flashlight between his legs and, in an instant, crunched the math. Three men in the front, four deep in the back seat. Teens to early twenties. A fresh square of gauze poked out from under the driver's white wifebeater—the telling signature of a new tattoo.

But more importantly—as Lucky would calculate—not a single head inside the Lincoln so much as twitched when his black-and-white rolled past. The lack of interest informed Lucky that inside that car he'd likely find something arrest-worthy.

Like a gun.

Lucky spun the steering wheel and U-turned the radio unit into an immediate one-eighty.

"See 'em?" asked Lucky to his trainee.

"Counted six or seven," said Shia. "Rolled the stop sign."

"Kind of a chickenshit infraction, dontcha think?" suggested Lucky.

"Four in the back. There's at least one riding without a seat belt," she countered. "So that's two. I'll run tags."

The beams of the black-and-white's headlights converged as Lucky closed the gap on the Lincoln. Yet before the license plate was even readable, Lucky could see the rear of the vehicle had been custom lowered.

"It's gonna come back clean," said Lucky. "Custom car out for a cruise."

"You're right," said Shia, proving to have keen eyes and quick fingers on the Box.

Both cars slowed at the west-facing stoplight, the black-and-white slipping in a mere two feet from the Lincoln's lowered bumper.

"You gonna light these bad boys up?" asked Atom from behind the protective screen that separated the back seat from the radio car's occupied front.

Lucky ignored the director, keying his vision on the near-finished cigarette pinched between the middle and index fingers of the Lincoln driver's left hand.

One. Last. Puff.

Sure enough—and as if on telekinetic command—the outstretched arm crooked at the elbow and the trail of smoke disappeared back into the car as the driver took a final drag. When the hand returned, the cigarette had been relegated to a flick position, momentarily perched on the driver's cuticle.

Ready. For. Launch.

The light turned green. Simultaneously with the turning of the Lincoln's front wheels, the cigarette's remains were unconsciously discarded, catapulted end over sparking end into the Compton air.

"Littering," spoke Lucky in a throaty whisper. "Now there's an infraction I can get behind."

Atom pressed himself up against the right side of the screen, hoping to get close to Shia's ear.

"What do you think we got in the car?" asked the boy wonder.

"You're here to observe, sir," reminded Shia. "Sit back and we'll see what comes."

Lucky engaged the button cuing the light array, spinning up the cherry and hot blue mirrored bulbs into an unmistakable frenzy. And certainly it was zero surprise to the seven male occupants of the Lincoln. Nary a silhouette in the back seat so much as swiveled. The driver acknowledged the sheriff with an empty-handed wave and glided the custom car nearly a quarter mile before indicating he was looking for a place to pull to the curb.

Like all those traffic stops the night before, Shia observed Lucky placing the black-and-white in park, popping the front door, and unskinning his pistol.

"Stay in the car, sir," ordered Lucky without even a glance back at the director.

As for Shia, she'd already learned to set her rhythm to Lucky's. During a near-sleepless day leading up to her second night of training, she'd tuned her radio to a meditation stream and mentally practiced syncing her movements to her TO's. She'd replayed Lucky's every movement from the night before—awkward or otherwise—trying to make a memory metric of all his ticks and twitches. Still, when she found herself drifting off to sleep, her brain would scan back to that rare Lucky Dey smile. With that, she'd jerk awake, left to wonder if the warmth Lucky had reserved for the dogsledding Mush Man and his team of goofy mutts was what some call a "soul window"—a tiny indication of the man's true self.

She could only hope.

As Lucky neared the Lincoln's open driver's window, he observed the driver wisely had both his hands on the wheel. A quick strike of the eyes and he'd clocked the hands of the two young men nearest him in the back seat. Nothing concealed. Palms on knees.

These boys know the drill all too well.

"What I do, officer?" asked the driver without even a lift of the chin.

"My name's Deputy Dey. What's yours?"

The driver calmly eyed Lucky, the corner of his mouth forming an indifferent smirk.

"Guess it's okay if you call me . . . Howdy Doody," said the driver to audible giggles from his crew.

"Okay, Mr. Doody," said Lucky without a hitch.

"You can call me Howdy," joked Howdy Doody, his glibness on full drip.

"Here's what it is, Mr. Doody. I got nothin' against smokin'. But you know what happens when you drop a butt in the street?"

"Called litterin', right?" asked Howdy Doody, whom Lucky surmised was as old as twenty-five and rather vain, manicured from his fingernails to his five-day beard.

"Cigarette butt stays on the pavement till it rains. Then it's the storm drain to the river and out to the ocean with all the other trash people toss from their cars."

"Sorry, officer," said Howdy Doody. "S'pose I could be more—like, environmental, you know? That means I'm gonna get me a ticket, well, I guess I deserves one."

Lucky bent slightly at the waist, checking the hands of the skin 'n' bones fourteen-year-old squeezed between the driver and front passenger. All Lucky could see of the teen's face were acne scars and hanging dreads, yet clear as day, he noted the boy's cell phone recording the traffic stop.

Lucky finger-waved a hello at the tiny mobile camera lens.

"Hey, we knows our rights," claimed the acne-prone teen.

"Expect you do," said Lucky, returning his attention to the driver. "So let's start with you. One at a time, I want you to step out of the vehicle."

With that, the mood shifted into an altogether different gear. Some groans erupted from the car. But mostly it was the eyeballs—initially resistant to making contact with Lucky, each pair now switched from indifferent to a deadly stare.

"All cuzza my fuckin' cigarette?" bitched Howdy Doody, pushing open his door. "You harassing us now."

"Reasonable suspicion," replied Lucky. "Now, turn around, hands behind your back."

From the black-and-white's back seat, Atom Blum pressed his face against the screen in hopes of getting his least obstructed view. To him, the traffic stop routine appeared orderly. Safe. Hardly how he'd imagine filming the scene.

While Shia was poised near the sidewalk, left foot forward and clearly prepared to face down any unwarranted conflict, Lucky allowed every young black male to exhume himself from the Lincoln one at a time. Each was instructed to spread his legs shoulder width while Lucky patted him down for weapons then freely dug into his pockets, temporarily depositing all contents onto the Lincoln's hood. When he was satisfied, Lucky directed each to the curb to sit on his hands.

Wow, thought Atom. The compliance of it all. As if they were following some scripted routine.

"Borrrring," he whistled to himself.

No. Were Atom to have captured the traffic stop on precious film, he would've built up the scene's tension by having deputies sweat the suspected gangbangers while remaining seated in the black-and-white. Next, he'd set his camera low and on a forward-moving dolly track. A medium wide-angle lens would best capture Shia stepping onto the curb, hand on the grip of her pistol, and unconsciously sashaying that dynamic ass in the direction of the suspects' vehicle. So sexy, Atom thought, the way the gun belt and all the equipment hugged the top of the woman's hips, both rocking and squeaking with every purposed step.

"Don't be afraid to sex shit up a little," demanded Atom to nobody whatsoever.

Worried his senses were dulling, the boy wonder released his brain to obsess over the beautiful young deputy. He loved dressing women. And suddenly he ached to be dressing Shia. From silky, bejeweled underthings to her Kevlar vest, Atom imagined Shia waking. Showering. Buttoning herself down for the day. Only the way Atom imagined it, she'd be climbing into clothes sewn by his favorite costumer. Tighter in the thighs and buttocks. Tapered at the waist. Slight padding in the bust to offset the obvious constraints of the body armor.

Oh, and please, some red flippin' lipstick.

"Seven on the sidewalk, sir," announced Shia the moment the last of the passengers had parked on the curb. Shia eyed the last to sit, a freckled gangster in a bright red skully. He kept shifting from cheek to cheek as if inconveniently uncomfortable. "I said, sit on your goddamn hands!"

Lucky stuck his flashlight inside the Lincoln for a cursory look-see. After circling around the front end of the town car, he repeated the same routine on the passenger side. Peek. Flashlight. Sweep. And out. He eased over to Shia.

"Mr. Doody," addressed Lucky. "Got license and registration?"

"Already took my wallet," bemoaned the driver. "Registration's in the box, you know?"

Lucky gestured for Shia to retrieve both the driver's license and vehicle registration.

"So my guess is you're all of the Blood persuasion." It was hardly much of a guess considering the amount of crimson each man was wearing. Two in the middle, seated butt cheek against each other, wore twin Los Angeles Clippers home jerseys, the dominant crimson over blue. "Particular set you wanna affiliate?"

"I'm settin' on taking me a nap," pissed the retro one with the

kinky afro. He wore a whimsical SpongeBob character comb stuck
in his man bun.

"Outta the pocket trash, I got some weed and—looks like
maybe Xanax and a few hits of MDMA," Shia called out as she
organized all Lucky had removed from their pockets. "Got the DL.
You Lawrence Holmes?"

"An' I'm sober as a church mouse, Ms. Dep-u-tee," sang back
Howdy Doody. "And this is some sheriffs' ass bullshit."

Shia crouched at the Lincoln's passenger door and twisted the
latch on the glove box. It dropped open with a heavy *kuh-thunk*.
Out spilled wads of bubblegum wrappers, empty jeweler bags used
for single servings of drugs, and two unopened twelve-ounce bottles of Mexican Coca-Cola. One tumbled onto the floor mat.

At the curb, Lucky paced behind the line of young black men
who were either squirming on their hands or slump-shouldered
on meditative pause. He keenly let his eyes scour for temple or
neck sweat or perspiration stains spreading from the creases of an
armpit. The row of semi-obedient young men revealed some beady
scalps and wet necklines. Yet the wettest of the crew was the red
skully at the end with the freckled face. He kept wiping his palms
on his cargo shorts before replacing them under his butt. Of the
seven, Freckles as Lucky cast him, hadn't once made eye contact
with either police officer.

The trainee had to empty the glove box to find the registration slip. Whether it was out of a penchant for neatness, hating
to leave things undone, or her mother's voice chirping in her subconscious, Shia chose to restock the glove box with what she'd
unleashed. Searching for the missing bottles of Mexican Coke,
she reached under the front passenger seat and allowed her fingertips to explore. But instead of touching a cool, glass cylinder of
pure cane-sweetened cola, her middle finger brushed something
steely and all too familiar. Shia crouched deeper, twisted, and lowered her head until her screwed-down cornrows pushed against
the floor mat. Though underneath the seat was almost opaque
with blackness, the faint illumination coming from headlights'

reflection and the micro lamp in the driver's door left something in clear relief.

A gun muzzle.

Dipping into her belt with her left hand, Shia found her tactical flashlight, buttoned the end with her thumb, and set the passenger seat undercarriage ablaze with 120 white halogen lumens.

"Sir!" shouted Shia.

"Sheeeeeeeiiiiiiit," griped Howdy Doody.

"What she find?" asked Lucky, as if he hadn't already suspected.

"I got guns, sir!" answered Shia without being asked.

"What flavor?" asked Lucky, withdrawing three steps and unsheathing his .40-cal in case any of his detainees chose to up and rabbit on him. He keyed his shoulder-affixed mic and quietly requested backup units.

Under the blast of that small fistful of tactical light, Shia counted two weapons of the semi-auto variety, neatly attached to the underside of the seats with Velcro. A quick scoot inward and a swing of the beam under the driver's seat revealed two more automatics and a machine pistol with at least a thirty-round clip, also secured with black Velcro.

"I count five," said Shia, almost breathless. "All semi-autos!"

"A gun party," cracked Lucky.

"Hey, fuck you!" angered the afro-man with the SpongeBob comb. "We don't know shit about shit."

"Shut your holes," ordered Howdy Doody, before demanding, "Only word we gotta say is 'lawyer.'"

Howdy Doody checked his crew. Nods rippled up and down the line of Bloods like a stadium wave. Each appeared resigned. Pleased enough with himself, Howdy Doody lifted his chin to discover Lucky unsnapping the lock on a leather-bound citation book.

"What's that now?" asked Howdy Doody. "Gonna write me up for this shit?"

"Straight up? You're goin' to jail for the guns," said Lucky. "But I'm still writing the ticket for improperly discarding that smoke."

"All this *and* you're writin' me a fuckin' ticket—"

"RUNNER!" shouted Shia.

Freckles was up and digging his feet into the sidewalk, arms pumping at full throttle. Lucky showed a hand signal for Shia to hold in place while directing the remaining six bangers with his gun muzzle.

"On your stomachs!" ordered Lucky. "Fingers laced behind your heads!"

"Sir?!" asked Shia.

"Hold 'em and wait for backup!" barked Lucky, all the while his hamstrings were cursing at him for considering a foot chase.

Shia unsheathed her Beretta, arms extended and stepping a few feet to the rear to keep the remaining gangbangers in her weapon's sights.

"HE SAID STOMACH—FINGERS LACED!" demanded Shia.

As the Blood crew slowly twisted and rolled over to their stomachs, Shia expected to see Lucky charging after Freckles, who'd already turned up a driveway and disappeared into a backyard.

But the Lincoln's engine turned over in a gutty roar. Lucky had dropped behind the wheel and thrown the vehicle into drive with his foot pushing on the gas pedal. The wheels spun and smoked for eight feet before the g-forces took over, closing both open doors as the Town Car accelerated away and carved a right turn at the nearest corner.

Shia—half gobsmacked—was retraining her weapon when she noticed Atom Blum had emerged from the black-and-white for a better look.

"GET BACK IN THE UNIT!" ordered the trainee before keying her radio mic. Her voice shook, "Seven-eighty, where's our backup?"

In Lucky's hands, the low-riding Lincoln felt like a slow-galloping beast that cornered like a bowling ball. The lowered shocks felt like they were holding on for dear life while Lucky executed a second right-hand turn, powering up the block. After quickly picturing the route he imagined he would have foot-raced after the Blood, Lucky guided the Lincoln on a course to intercept the punk.

The visual reward came quickly. Freckles, shining from his sprint through two backyards, showed up in the Lincoln's headlights coming out from behind a heavy-trunked tree. At first Freckles seemed bent on keeping pace, crossing the street with plans to hop even more properties. Yet when he saw the Lincoln's headlamps the Blood stopped in the middle of the street and waved as if flagging down an old friend.

Perhaps Freckles thought his pal Howdy Doody had also up and run, making haste in his classic Lincoln.

Los Angeles Sheriff's policy would have been for Lucky to brake the vehicle, hop out, and attempt to apprehend his escaping suspect. Then again, he reasoned, borrowing the big, bad Lincoln to chase down a suspect wasn't precisely procedure.

You wanna run on sheriffs? began the rhetorical question formed under Lucky's skullcap. *I'll teach you to run.*

Lucky eased on the gas as if he were swooping in for a fast pickup. Still, he aimed the Lincoln's right headlamp on at twenty miles per hour heading for Freckles's left femur. After that, it was the larger object's momentum versus a semi-stationary Freckles that completed the chase. The elusive Blood was summarily clipped and cartwheeled head over tail to the pavement.

Standing outside the Lincoln, Lucky swept the landscape for passersby or Blood friendlies . . .

. . . or witnesses . . .

Satisfied there'd be no more than neighborhood looky-loos peering out from behind window screens and ghetto bars, Lucky rotated to the passenger side of the Lincoln to assess damage to the suspect.

"You hit me!" squealed Freckles, rocking on the ground, hands gripping his thigh.

Lucky keyed his radio's mic.

"Seven-eighty. Suspect injured. Requesting EMT." Settling down to his haunches, Lucky addressed Freckles with a sympathetic rejoinder. "Another night? Woulda seriously foot-chased your ass. But too bad for me I been on your side of a wreck one too many times. You'll mend. But do yourself a favor and don't skip the phys therapy."

16

Mush Man cherished the clatter. When his dogs and shopping sled found maximum speed, the sonic ruckus created could be heard from blocks away. Especially at night. The Food-4-Less grocery cart, held together with scavenged wire, plastic zip ties, and brick-hammered framing nails salvaged from local construction sites, was half packed with crushed cans and bottles. It added to a cacophony that Mush Man calculated was as satisfying to the ear as hand-laminated skids against Arctic ice.

"Slow left, slow left," ordered Mush Man, dropping his left foot and braking with the duct-taped toe of his K-Swiss sneaker.

The mutts and the cart used the entire street to execute the turn up Poinsettia. In his mind's eye, Mush Man expected the familiar view of a street he was partial to sledding. The asphalt crown at the center of the lane created a ridge that was a challenge to straddle.

If he could keep the dogs on an imaginary center stripe, there would be an increased sense of gliding. Mush Man's trick to stay on course without streetlights was by dead reckoning on the lone porch light where the street T'd to a stop two short blocks ahead.

There was an inky density blanketing the neighborhood. Every single bulb inside every residence was extinguished. It was a veritable blackout that carried as far as Mush Man's weakening eyes could focus. A single solar-powered hazard marker lay ahead blinking a yellow warning every other second.

"Whoa, whoa, whoa," cried Mush Man, dragging his right foot from toe to heel. He pulled back on the center leash, signaling lead mutt Oprah to ease to a slow trot and stop. The dogs panted and shook their hides. Hank whined. Mush Man kept waiting for his eyes to adjust. The dogs, he knew, could see ahead. They had the canine *eye shine*—an ability to discern light at five times the distance than that of a human.

"What I give to be one of y'all," remarked Mush Man.

A breath of wind jiggled the yellow emergency tape roping the DWP site. The slight glint read against Mush Man's straining retinas, telling the sledder he had arrived at the source of the now-dry river. He'd heard on the street that a hole had opened up in the earth and nearly swallowed a police unit.

Lucky's? he wondered.

"That's gotta be some story," he said to his pups. "Shit-piss-shit-shit."

Mush Man was abiding a simple credo: following destruction is construction. The Department of Water and Power would surely be on the case to fix that dangerous hole in the middle of Poinsettia. That guaranteed a daily influx of union work crews, regarded as refuse machines by urban salvagers. Refundable cans and bottles were likely to be surrendered wherever the clock-watching hardhats sipped their last traces of sodas and energy drinks.

"We needs us a—sucky suck—a light," said Mush Man. Easing forward he was able to make out three short concrete blockades to keep cars from venturing too close. The solar-powered hazard blinker was riveted to a metal strap on the center barrier, a standard K-Rail. Mush Man was able to twist the light free of its rusty mooring, fully planning to return it to its rightful place once he'd scoured the site for recyclables.

"You guys watch the sled, 'kay?" he instructed the team. He blocked a front wheel of the cart with a loose chunk of asphalt, unfurled a garbage bag, and ventured deeper into the site. "I be back—cock-suck-kerrrrrs."

The pups needed water. So, Mush Man made a mental note to salvage what he could with some haste. He carried no watch or phone. His concept of passing minutes was a matter of clicks in his head. He'd imagine his brain had a voice timer, singing "one Stevie Wonder, two Stevie Wonder, three Stevie Wonder" upon his silent command.

The quandary was whether to start inside the hole and work his way out? Or outside in? Realizing there could likely be water at the bottom, Mush Man quickly doubled back to the cart and unhooked the old VW hubcap he used as the dogs' drinking bowl.

"Back with sometin' to drink, mutty-mutts."

The solar-powered hazard light, a double-sided medallion the size of a butter plate, pulsed with enough yellowish pop to show Mush Man an easy ingress to the crater. A single fifteen-foot aluminum ladder had been left with express access to the bottom. Mush Man could see water lapping where the ladder's feet rested.

Mush Man left the hubcap at the edge of the hole before throwing a leg over and descending. He felt the air change from hot to cool. Moisture clung to his cheeks. As if he'd just climbed into a river cave. Mush Man thought of his dogs—how he'd love to engineer a way to get all four mutts down in the hole.

Find out who a swimmer and who not.

He imagined the animals, once they'd had their splashy fun, would climb out, shake the water from their fur, and be left with that wet-duck-dog smell of a happy animal.

At the ladder's bottom, Mush Man discovered he was ankle deep. He could feel his 140 pounds squishing bubbles out of the soles of his tired sneakers.

"Oh well, Musher," said Mush Man. "You a wet sponge now."

He swung the blinking hazard light, hoping to catch a glint of a can or bottle bobbing across the massive puddle. But all he could read were some exposed cables drooping across striations of dirt underneath a crusty asphalt cap. At the other end, he could make out a three-inch drainage hose connected to a gas-operated pump scaffolded across the top of two half-sunk saw horses.

"Lookie like nothin' down here," realized Mush Man, before he answered back to himself, "Unless your schizo-ass wanna go snorklin' for it—fuck-fuckity-fuck."

Mush still had to scour the site as well as fill that hubcap. Turning back to the ladder, he was about to slip the hazard light into his pants for the climb up when he flashed on a face staring into the hole.

"What the fuck you doin' in my man's hole?" carved out a voice.

Mush Man fumbled for the hazard light, hoping to better reveal the man. He could see little more than a black scowl on a young man near the top of the ladder before he lost his grip and the lamp careened backward into the water.

"Ain't nobody's hole," defended Mush Man to nobody he could see.

A cell phone glowed above and to the left, followed by a tiny but almost blinding blast of white light. Mush Man couldn't make out who held the device. He tried to shield his eyes.

"This hole belong to my boss man, J," said Tuba, rattling the top of the ladder. "That means you are trespassin' on his shit."

"Fuck yeah," chimed Lil Rod, revealing himself behind the phone light.

"Don't mean nobody no—cocksucker—trouble," relented a nervous Mush Man.

"What you say?" flared Lil Rod.

"I said—fuck you, fuck your mother—said I mean no harm to nobody—shit-shit-shitter."

It was rare for Mush Man to hear the result of his own

Tourette's. The affliction was painfully more pronounced when anxiety spilled over into his mental cocktail. Unfortunately, hearing his own uncontainable curses only increased his stress.

"You just tell me to fuck my momma?" angered Lil Rod. "Somebody should smoke your homeless ass."

"Step off," warned Tuba.

"Didn't he say he wanted to fuck yo momma?" argued Lil Rod.

"Don' wanna fuck nobody's—cock-cocksucker—momma."

"Nigga? Get the fuck out the hole!" shouted Tuba. "'Fore I pull this ladder and you got no ways out."

"Piss-fuck-piss-fuck-piss-fuck!" blasted Mush Man with no verbal control.

"Man, what's wrong wit you?" realized Tuba.

"Playin' us," said Lil Rod. "That shit won't go. Not from no homeless nigga."

"Climbin' up now—YOU CUNTS," stammered Mush Man. "Sorry, sorry. Didn't mean—YOU'RE ALL CUNTS!"

"Shut your shit 'n' climb," forced Tuba.

"Suck my balls," vomited Mush Man. "My dogs . . . Lemme just get water for—GUZZLE MY CUM, NAPPYHEAD MOTHERFUCKER!"

"WHAT YOU SAY?" angered Lil Rod.

"My dogs—"

"You said something—"

"SHITSTAIN, SHITSTAIN, FUCK-FUCK-COCKSUCKER!"

Tuba was feet away from Lil Rod. And despite what he sensed evolving, he could neither summon the words nor cover the few yards in time to prevent the sixteen-year-old pizza slinger from turning the moment into a mistake.

"Don't wanna fight nobody—Mister Fucknut," pleaded Mush Man, hands open and arms wide in a universal sign of surrender. "Mush Man just wanna love his puppy dogs—"

Pop. Pop. Pop.

The three shots from Lil Rod's revolver sounded like successive firecrackers. Lil Rod had lowered his phone just before squeezing off the initial .38-caliber volley. Bullets one and two had whizzed right and higher right, striking only the mud-caked wall. Somehow, with the third squeeze of the trigger, Lil Rod had unconsciously corrected his aim and, once the hammer had snapped back to the cartridge, the cheap wad-cutter had drawn a straight line downward and through the target's inner thigh.

Mush Man squealed, unleashing a cacophony of sympathetic howls from his dogs. They bellowed and pulled at their leads.

Whether or not Tuba was caught up in the moment or just feared further screams into the night, he lifted his own pistol—a 9mm Glock 19—and emptied the entire twenty-two-round magazine in the direction of Mush Man's screeches. Lil Rod limped in with his final three pops, aiming at nothing, only to quench what was left of his bloodlust.

A haze of spent gunpowder hung. Then, in the following quiet as the dogs' howls subsided, Lil Rod lifted his phone and shone the flashlight feature into the hole. If there was a body, neither he nor Tuba could put eyeballs on it.

"What we do?" asked Lil Rod.

"Get the fuck out," answered Tuba.

"An' Julius?"

"We get the fuck out," repeated Tuba. "Then we figure out what to tell J." Tuba withdrew from the edge of the hole and began the first steps of a two-block sprint. Lil Rod stayed on Tuba's heels, happy to leave behind both the hole and whatever was left of the vagrant inside it.

17

The arrest procedure involving the seven gun-toting Bloods should have been a pro forma process. Drop the three black-and-white loads of Bloods at the Compton Station, where they'd be detained until formal charges and arraignments, then return to patrol and write up all reports at the end of shift.

"If we don't fall into another sinkhole," Shia had quietly joked, succeeding in getting Lucky to reveal only the slightest up-tilt at the corners of his mouth.

The station's booking officer, Sergeant Mike Yang, had been suffering from IBS—irritable bowel syndrome—which sent the twelve-year vet on beeline trots to the men's room. Add to the mix a van full of Salvadoran juveniles selling illegal fireworks out of the back of a pickup truck and a joint task force sting of prostitutes and pimps working the by-the-hour flophouses on Long Beach

Boulevard, and the backup at the booking desk was beginning to look like the line at the DMV.

Lucky suggested they make use of their wait time with a lunch break. That would have usually resulted in a vending machine sandwich had Atom Blum not treated the station house with a surprise order of pizza. The delivery driver from Pizza Wing unexpectedly entered through the front door of the Compton station hauling three vinyl hot boxes holding a dozen extra-large assorted pies, enough for the walk-ins stuck in the lobby to each sample a slice.

Lucky rolled an empty office chair from the dispatch room onto the sidewalk that separated the back of the station house from the motor yard. He propped his boots on the bumper of a black-and-white, rested his head on a knob of concrete coping, and hoped to coax his body into a nap. His low back pain was manageable, but hardly vanquished. A fistful of Advil would probably last him through the rest of the shift, but that would require him to fill his stomach with something starchy—like the free pizza—which would surely lead to an uncomfortable shift in his ballast.

Lucky's plan to lower his eyelids was spoiled when he glimpsed Atom talking up his trainee. The boy wonder seemed to have Shia trapped in a cinder block corner near the outdoor barbecue pit and tiki bar named after a fallen deputy. The only prop that separated Shia from the towering movie director was her drooping paper plate and the pizza she carefully picked at with her fingers.

He's a hound.

So what? thought Lucky. Lots of men were. Cops especially. And surely Shia knew as much. Between time in the academy and then working the jail, she was certain to have been dubbed the hot girl—attractive to a fault and accustomed to a dog pile of male attention.

Yet there she was—his trainee—nearly cowering under the come-on moves from their Hollywood ride-along.

Politics-wise, the movie director reeked of *hands-off*. He was rich, famous, and connected to top sheriff's brass. If it weren't for the station house backdrop and Shia in uniform, Lucky would have sussed the duo's pickup bar posture as another horny guy hitting on another uncomfortable girl. Was he correctly reading the trainee's body language? Or was the moviemaker so persistent that he figured it was only a matter of time before he turned her nonverbal rejection into a consensual roll in the hay?

Then Shia flicked a glance in Lucky's direction.

Was it a check-in with her TO or a call for help? Lucky attempted a reread on the situation. Shia was a big girl. If she felt harassed, there were both official and unofficial remedies, the latter being something as simple as a knee to the groin or a reminder that she was a trained bundle of badass. Then again, maybe she'd assumed the politics were such that rebuffing come-ons by the clearly connected ride-along might come with early and unwelcome career consequences.

Again, Shia flicked her soft brownies.

Please save me from this asshole.

Lucky found his frame of view suddenly cramped with deputies—young Gil Rodriguez in his drooping uniform partnered with a top-heavy cop with a name tag that read F. Petrie. The larger of the pair, who stood no less than six-foot-five, put such a strain on his shirt that the creases had nearly been erased.

"Hey, Lucky," said Gil. "You met Franco Petrie?"

"Just now," said Lucky, offering his outstretched palm. "Deputy."

"Deputy," replied Petrie, "welcome to the Grid."

"Is that the line for booking or the free clinic?" joked Gil, gesturing inside and overstating the obvious.

Lucky forced a polite smile.

"So they got you on training?" asked Petrie, seeking conversation.

"Plus a ride-along."

Both deputies pivoted to take in the cornered Shia. Even the young deputies stiffened slightly at the obvious macking underway at the hands of the film director.

"Hey, cowboy!" barked Lucky, following with a penetrating

finger whistle. Atom perked and unconsciously obeyed, instantly twisting himself in Lucky's direction. "Meet a coupla more of the good guys."

Atom pasted on a practiced grin and strode over, open hand as ready as a politician's.

"Atom Blum," the director introduced.

"Movie dude. Directed all the *Road Rage* flicks," erred Lucky. On purpose.

"Kill," corrected Atom, *"Road. Kill."*

"Love those movies!" pimped Gil. "I even got me the PlayStation games."

"You workin' on somethin' about the sheriffs?" asked Petrie.

"Might be workin' on finding my next leading lady," puffed Atom. "Unless you can tell me that all your female sheriffs are as hot as Deputy Saint George."

"She's sure as shit a step up," replied Gil. "Know what they used to call Compton Station? The Dog Pound."

"No shit," laughed Atom, as if he'd just logged himself a moment of real cop talk before turning back to Lucky. "Seriously. You got five months ahead sittin' next to that? Hope you're not married."

"And if I am?" asked Lucky.

The trio joined in a nervous, knowing guffaw.

"I getcha," muted Atom. "Five months, shit. What I would pay for *five hours* with that."

"You've been introduced," shifted Lucky as he straightened from the chair. "Why don't you young studs share your stories with Hollywood's finest?"

Lucky stretched, adjusted his utility belt, and left the movie director with Gil and Petrie. His exit served as punctuation.

"What's your movie about?" begged Gil, eager as hell to be included.

"Dunno yet. Love story in a black-and-white?" teased Atom. The deputies laughed with the director at the sexual possibilities. "You guys ever do it? Not with each other. You know. In a police car. With a lady deputy? Or not a lady deputy?"

The deputies traded distrusting looks as if to test the other on how much off-the-record funny business they were willing to share.

"Hey. Get this," switched Gil. "Some shit hardly nobody knows. Couple nights back, Air Support is flyin' up 'round Malibu way, checking on a stolen car report when they light up this Lambo parked at some scenic turnout. They're slingin' the spot and they light up this ass-clown at the bottom of a ravine. Pants 'round his ankles. Big ol' hard-on."

Atom's face dropped into that of a slack-jawed statue. Was he really hearing what Gil was passing along?

"You're shittin' me," laughed Petrie. "Was the dude by his-self?"

"When they found him, he was," continued Gil. "Supposedly there was some swimsuit honey up there doin' him when he crack-over-tits falls into the ravine. Drunk as a monkey."

Atom felt his knees weaken. The flush of blood rising beneath the skin on his face. Good God, had Lucky been waiting to spring this? Was it some kind of joke sent along by Assistant Sheriff Paul McGill—his supposed top-brass friend who'd promised to *fix* the embarrassing episode forever?

"Really?" Atom forced after his fake chuckle. "They say who the dipshit was?"

"Man, I must know twenty deputies up at Temple Street," answered Gil. "But this guy's gotta be somebody or know some-body 'cause there ain't no written report—no names—no nothin', 'cause Christ knows I asked."

"And if you could find out?" asked Petrie.

"I'd go find the dude and ask to be his wingman," laughed Gil. "I mean, imagine a girl hot enough to be worth that kinda spill? That dude's gotta be a pussy magnet."

"Drives a Lambo," agreed Petrie.

"Wow," was all Atom could manage, nearly wheezing his sigh of relief. Not just from learning that his identity was still intact, but also over his decision to leave the Lamborghini in his Malibu garage and drive his Range Rover to the Compton station instead.

* * *

Shia splashed water on her face and, for a minute or so, appreciated the cooling quiet of the ladies' washroom. A lingering low-rent perfume left an annoying sting in her nostrils. One of the dispatchers, she figured, recalling a squat woman named Sunny with a mop of black curly hair and a pronounced curve to her back.

Spinal scoliosis.

One bugger of a deformity.

Wear as much of that stinky scent as you want.

Shia made a mental note to schmooze the mostly female civilian staff just so they'd view the new trainee as a deputy who didn't see herself as a cut above.

She dried her hands, swung the door open, and was surprised by the voice behind her.

"You all right?" asked Lucky. He was leaning on the wall, arms crossed.

"Fine," replied Shia. "Why wouldn't I be?"

"Checking in. That's all."

"You mean Mr. Impressed with Himself?" Shia asked. "Not a problem."

"No complaints? Formal or otherwise?"

"He's just one of those guys. Gets slapped a lot. But probably gets laid a lot because he's not afraid to get slapped."

"Okay then."

"Not like he's droppin' roofies in my coffee," shrugged Shia, referring to the date-rape drug Rohypnol. "Handled way worse than him . . . Asked me to model for him. By his pool. So lame."

"Maybe he's seen enough for the night. Kick him loose."

"Said I'm good. Jacked for our arrest."

"Your arrest." Lucky offered his fist. Shia softly knuckled him.

"Let's get some more," she gamely offered.

18

Lucky swung the black-and-white into a wide right turn from East Greenleaf onto Sante Fe, the steering wheel gliding underneath his fingertips as if he were the maestro of all road-weary Ford Crown Vics. He set his sights on a closing pair of oncoming headlights, readied his tactical flashlight, and snapped a quick beam at the unknown driver of a panel van. The man behind the wheel—African-American, middle-aged, and scowling from the invasiveness of Lucky's curiosity, appeared as if it was all he could do not to return a middle finger.

"Think that guy feels just a little harassed?" joked Atom from the back seat.

It was painfully obvious Atom loathed dead air. Every peaceful moment seemed shoehorned with his shallow observations, most of which Lucky ignored.

"Seriously," pressed Atom. "Is it harassment? You know? The flashlight thingy?"

"Legally?" replied Shia. "No."

"But say you live here," continued Atom. "I mean, lucky for us we don't. But say you did. You're black. Every time you drive by a cop car you get a face full of candlepower?"

"Might feel harassed," argued Shia. "But how I *feel* and the law. That's two different things."

"I'd sure as shit feel harassed," admitted Atom. "See that guy's face? He was hacked off."

"After 2:00 a.m.," infused Lucky. "You're driving a panel van in a high-crime area? Odds increase that you're up to no good."

"Maybe the guy was driving home from his job," pressed Atom.

"Just a flashlight," defended Shia. "And maybe the next car we lamp is fulla van-jacking thugs following Mr. Hacked Off to his home where his wife and babies are sleeping. See where I'm going?"

"Hear ya," said Atom. "But come on. Isn't any wonder why minorities feel oppressed by the police."

"That what your next movie is about?" asked Shia, hoping to shift the conversation.

"I'd tell ya," joked Atom before dropping a tired punch line. "But I'd have to kill ya."

"That might be considered a threat to a police officer," matched Shia.

"Flirt all you want," teased Atom. "But you won't get it out of me before I get it into you."

Eyes on the rearview mirror, Lucky caught the twisted grin on Atom's face a split second before swiveling right to catch the reaction from his trainee. He expected something akin to an eye roll as she shrugged off or just endured another overtly sexual pass. Instead, Lucky saw Shia practically wince, inhale, then release air through secretly gritted teeth. Shia didn't even chance a look in her training officer's direction. Embarrassed. As if her tolerating Atom's overt crassness were somehow her own fault.

Lucky eased back on the accelerator until the black-and-white was rolling under twenty miles per hour. Next he quietly slung his seat belt across himself until the tongue clicked in the receptacle. Shia picked up on the cue and followed suit, the retractor on her restraint unwinding in hushed ticks until the telltale metallic snap of the lock.

"Hey," said Lucky to the movie director. "Got a question for ya."

"Fire way, Sarge," replied Atom, clueless that Lucky was not a sergeant.

"In the movies, you got something called a screen test, right?"

"Yeah," said Atom. "For actors, usually. Big screen doesn't suit everybody. So, we use screen tests to see how an actor comes across."

"No shit," said Lucky. "Did you know us poh-lice? We got ourselves somethin' called a screen test."

"Really?" asked Atom, hoping for some insider L.A. Sheriff's juice. "What's that?"

"I'd tell you," mocked Lucky. "But I'd have to kill ya."

Atom wasn't quite certain whether or not Lucky was joking. Following the awkward pause, he decided to risk a laugh. Lucky and Shia relieved Atom with their own chuckles, joining in the fun.

"Naw," said Lucky. "Just kidding. Why don't I just show you?"

"Show me?"

"A screen test. Sheriffs' style."

"You're gonna *show me* a sheriffs' screen test?"

"Only if you ask me to."

"Fine. I'll bite," said Atom, getting slightly impatient. "Please show me how L.A. sheriffs do a screen test."

Lucky lifted his right hand and gave a come-closer gesture. Two fingers, beckoning Atom to lean closer to the mesh partition that separated the radio unit's front and back seats. Atom shifted and leaned forward.

"Closer," said Lucky.

"Close enough?" asked Atom, only inches from the wire.

With the sole of his boot, Lucky struck the brake. Hard. The shift in gravity sent the boy wonder's face slapping against the acrylic partition. The sound was akin to that of football players colliding.

"OW, FUCK!" howled Atom, his body recoiling into the back seat, hands cupping his face.

"Screen test," quipped Lucky.

"Not fuckin' funny!" blasted Atom.

Shia covered her mouth, trying with all her might not to sound out her pleasure.

"Now, that's harassment," said Lucky. "But only if you're a suspect. Good thing you're not a suspect. 'Cause it mighta been a lot harder."

"Fuckin' A, I'm not a suspect!"

"No. You're a ride-along. And you *asked* for a demonstration."

"You're an asshole!"

"Affirmative."

Atom glimpsed Shia's shoulders, bubbling up and down as she continued to stuff any sounds of her laughter.

"Oh, yeah?" bitched Atom. "It's funny to you?"

"Only laughing because all trainees get screen-tested," fibbed Lucky.

"She got . . ." pointed Atom. "He did this to *you?*"

"All trainees," repeated Lucky.

"Screen Test Society," recovered Shia, getting a grip on her amusement. "STS."

"Fuckin' club?"

"Consider yourself initiated," nodded Lucky.

"Think my nose is broke," Atom moaned.

"Pay attention," chirped Lucky. "You have now been instated in a secret society of sheriffs. You tell anybody else about this, we'll just state the facts. That you *requested* a screen test."

"Didn't ask for my nose to get broke!"

"Looks manly on you," teased Shia. "Like you just scrapped your way out of a cage fight."

"Screen Test Society," waned Atom.

"*Secret* society," reminded Lucky.

And there it was again. An unsettled pause. The boy wonder shifted his perspective from Lucky to Shia, then back again. Were they messing with him? Or were they truly welcoming him into a clandestine club of cops?

Atom pushed out a defensive chuckle, not wanting to give away how much his face hurt or that he wanted to cry. He could taste the old bitterness at the back of his tongue. All the childhood slights he harbored were queued to rush in—reminders of why he chose to make movies and live such an over-the-top, over compensating lifestyle. The director didn't require a paid psychologist to dissect his motives, nor was he ever one to apologize for anything to anybody. In Atom Blum's playbook, saying I'm sorry was for pussies, peons, and as soon as he had his way, Los Angeles sheriff's deputy Lucky Dey.

Wednesday

19

Eagle Rock. 4:04 a.m.

What Cat Rincon would have paid for more than two hours' sleep. As it was, two hours was as good as it would get. Unless, of course, there came some giant leaps in science. Sixteen years earlier, as a UCLA sophomore, she had been diagnosed with severe melatonin deficiency. In the years since, she'd tried everything from supplements to sleeping pills, but nothing agreed with her. The only regimen that worked was intense exercise. Sometimes up to three times a day. Cat had learned to live and thrive despite her malady.

She had awoken shortly after three. Try as she might to return to slumber, she eventually conceded defeat, snatched her iPad, and caught up on social media posts before padding into her perfectly restored bathroom to shower under a spray of eighty-two-degree water. Like a summer afternoon swim in a black-bottomed pool. Cooling, but without that freezing, shocking sting.

Instead of toweling off, she opted to air dry, crossing into the small but wide-open living space originally penciled by famed architect Pierre Koenig. The thrusting glass and steel structure, built in 1960, was designed to minimize both square feet and angles and maximize the surrounding views. Cat's recently restored house was a hilltop residence with panoramic vistas of the lower San Rafael Hills. The sprouting humps and junior-sized valleys were conveniently two short miles northeast of downtown L.A.

Cat stood fully naked at that vast floor-to-ceiling window, air-molecules working to evaporate the water beads from her chestnut skin. She stared out at those Hobbit-like mounds, none taller than 240 vertical feet, haphazardly arranged like molehills stretching from Griffith Park to Pasadena. Each mound was dotted with domiciles, old and older, with twinkling lights fueled by electricity delivered exclusively by her beloved Department of Water and Power.

And all you bastards get to sleep.

Once dry, Cat found herself jonesing for a run.

But you just showered, bitch.

Cat didn't care a lick about water consumption. After all, she pretty much *was* the DWP. She could take as many tepid showers as she desired without any concern whatsoever about any god-damn water shortage or rationing.

The drive from her hilltop house to Pasadena's Rose Bowl Stadium took a matter of minutes. She parked under a blazing vapor lamp. Against the flat expanse of the venue's southernmost parking lot, her fire-engine red Audi convertible appeared no bigger than a wingless ladybug, entirely alone against the hulking vine-crept concrete of the old coliseum.

She began her run when the sky was still black, a full hour and a half before her normal run time of 5:30, when the Arroyo Seco would turn from dark to dawning gray. The ancient watershed, long ago settled as a cozy West Pasadena enclave, boasted the famed Rose Bowl as a centerpiece. Two public golf courses surrounded the vintage stadium. And ringing the acres of manicured grass and sand bunkers was a popular loop perfect for biking, walking, and jogging.

For Cat, running early and on weekdays had a secondary purpose. If she didn't start with the early risers, she could barely finish the 5K course without some middle-aged, testosterone-ingesting warrior stalking her from behind, ogling her poppin' ass for a quarter to half mile before accelerating up next to her. The horny men would start the conversation with lame icebreakers like, "How far you runnin' today?" or "You like the way those Sauconys feel?"

The 4:00 a.m. start was something new for Cat. And not until she'd parked, lightly stretched, plugged in her earphones, and begun her trot up Rosemount Avenue did it actually dawn on her that any hint of daylight was still more than an hour in the making. Her counterclockwise habit began on a northward heading, making easy work of the initial mile of incline before button-hooking over the top of the golf course and picking up speed as she covered the long, gentle downhill grade.

A mist clogged the arroyo. No matter the time of year or the weather—or even when the Southland was suffering under a record heat—that canyon bottom was a trap for moisture. The heavy air would hang in suspended relief, leaving all streetlamps and porch lights as eerie, glowing orbs.

On a normal morning run, Cat would marvel at the sense of peacefulness the southbound stretch instilled—usually only passing a clockwise runner or two, maybe a cyclist, or a local resident walking a dog by the time she'd reach mile three. Yet twenty-five minutes into this unusually early run, she hadn't crossed paths with a soul, nor was the promise of breaking day anywhere in sight.

A shadow slipped ahead and to her right. Forty-five feet away. Tracking alongside Cat through the brush. She heard a crash of branches. Dry leaves crunching underfoot. She instinctively slowed instead of speeding ahead toward the next deco-styled torch lamp. Bursting from a flowerless oleander came the shadow and then the form of a fearless coyote. Large. Healthy fur. Well fed, thought Cat as she eased back on her pace. Probably fattened from a diet of kittens and all those pedigreed lap dogs that were the rage. She hated seeing those Westside, plastic surgery–addicted bitches lugging their miniature canines like they were designer handbags.

"Good for you," she uttered aloud. Where Cat was concerned, one less pint-sized pet made for one less asshole owner.

Instead of taking flight, the coyote oddly braked, straddling the avenue's center stripe and staring back at Cat.

"Wanna race?" she gibed at the animal.

She was about to gesture with waving arms and wiggly jazz fingers when the coyote's attention jerked ten degrees left. What followed was a slight but audible car brake squeaking. As the coyote bolted, Cat unconsciously pivoted toward the sound. All she could see was the slow curve of the road under the glow of two distant streetlamps. The space in between fell off into complete darkness—impenetrable under the pre-daylight conditions.

But I heard what I heard.

Cat strained to see though the black, cursing herself for not biting the bullet and getting Lasik surgery. She was, after all, five years from forty. Her body might've been bangin' enough to compete with women in their early twenties. But her damned eyes were her damned eyes.

Without overthinking, Cat returned to her run. Between breaths and her size-five running shoes gently spanking the asphalt, she tuned her ears for footsteps. Hoping, praying for another early runner to enter the void. She imagined she heard car tires chewing the pavement. A glance back over her shoulder revealed nothing but the same—streetlamps and the opaqueness between. Cat upped her pace and scanned for landmarks, recognizing a large green letter M hanging from a twelve-foot-tall cyclone gate defending the golf course from unwanted intruders.

M means what? Halfway, Cat? Two and a half miles to go?

Cat picked out a pair of headlights slipping from a side street before aiming in her direction. Fear gripped her chest. As if her Lycra running wear was shrinking about her. Her instinct screamed for her to flag down the oncoming vehicle. But her rational brain fought back. Why? What are you scared of, bitch? The dark?

Nobody but nobody is following me . . .

The headlights approached, the driver flashing high beams to let Cat know he was closing.

You paranoid little twat.

Cat acknowledged with a wave, but retracted her arm. Intellect had won out. And why shouldn't it? Cat Rincon was whip smart. Reason and wits had delivered her from a shit-box existence, growing up the youngest of seven kids in a two-bedroom rental house on the west side of Albuquerque. Neither her parents, brothers, sisters, teachers, nor school chums had, in Cat's razor opinion, contributed to her meteoric success from academia to Los Angeles politics.

That, and the liberal yet selective utilization of my platinum-lined vagina.

The approaching car, a tiny gray Fiat, puttered north and beyond Cat. Normally, she'd have jogged on, checking her heart rate against her pace to ensure she was in her optimal cardio zone. But doing so would have been moot. Cat could feel her heart pounding—elevated in response to autonomic fear.

Cat slowed and turned.

As the Fiat trailed away, its headlights swept the road and scraped past a navy blue Chevy Malibu parked in the shadows between the streetlamps. The Malibu was illegally parked and in a spot where Cat had seen no cars whatsoever as she'd run past.

And something else the Fiat's lights caught?

A man seated low behind the Malibu's wheel. Black. Wide-set eyes. Yellow and feral. Staring back at her.

Cat stopped and glared at the man in the Malibu. More accurately, at where she'd seen him in the Fiat's headlights. From Cat's perspective, the 150 yards between streetlamps had again fallen off into a light scale unreadable by the human eye. Or at least, her eyes. It was a blank space. A black hole. Yet stare at it she did, as if in her mind's eye she could still read the sun-eaten paint plaguing the roof and hood of the vehicle.

Stare at the motherfucker. Let him know that you see him.

Cat recalled her self-defense training—a six-week-long Impact course she'd attended with two girlfriends from the mayor's office. The instructions were to stop and stare at a potential attacker. Reduce the moment to its most primal. Let the predator know that you recognize him and are *not* afraid.

The fear wouldn't subside. If anything, her heart rate had kicked up a notch, sending vibrations up her esophagus and into her molars.

Then the Malibu's engine revved with an ugly, unmistakable belt-slip squeal. High-pitched. The headlights remained extinguished while the sound of the car pushed toward Cat.

Time to find a way out.

She moved at a firm knife-angled left toward the fence separating the running path from the golf course. Swift and fleet. Cat was, after all, in the best shape of her life, barely clearing a hundred pounds soaking wet.

But faster than a wheezing Chevy accelerating downhill? The engine squeal muted as the Malibu's engine found second gear. How close? Cat didn't turn to see. She homed in on that tall gate marked with an M. It was double-chained and padlocked. A gap, though, between the gate and gravel. Could she slip through?

I have to fit!

Cat slid headfirst—a verboten move when she was sixteen and played fast-pitch softball. Her body bounced off the gravel. She reached through with her right arm, slipped her shoulder then her head into the gap, and pulled at the rest of herself. The padlock rattled and rang, sending a panic of sound ripples down the fence line.

Headlights erupted. The Malibu's lamps switched on in a high-beam blast of white. That's when Cat twisted her view and clocked the distance. Fifty yards and gaining. She rotated her hips and nearly cursed her maximized gluteus. Her running shorts snagged and ripped without a lick of care. She continued to kick her way through until she was free of the gap, but her right running shoe caught at the laces. It stopped Cat dead until, with a desperate yank, she dropped the sneaker and left it behind.

Cat righted herself, retreating backwards into the dark and

keeping the fence between her and the street. She watched the Chevy Malibu swing back to the middle of the road. The man shadowed behind the wheel was clearly eyeballing that impossible gap under the fence through which she'd escaped.

She stood frozen until the Malibu was out of sight. If it hurt to jog, she was assisted by adrenaline. Ignoring whatever scrapes or bruising she had suffered, she kicked off her remaining running sneaker, then covered the remainder of the distance across the golf course grass using the dim lights of the old stadium for navigation.

The sky was still black. Daylight was an hour from its appointed arrival. The trek across the greens and fairways gave her time to attempt some calculation on what the hell had just happened. Failing to do so, she faced one more obstacle, which, for the ten minutes she'd paused at the edge of the parking lot, felt equally as frightening as her escape through the gate's gap. It was her Audi convertible. Parked under that vapor lamp, her prized ladybug was a hundred-yard walk across the vacant, semi-lit parking lot. Before approaching in her stocking feet, Cat scoured the landscape for the man in the Malibu. At last, she hurried, ignoring the sting of every loose gravel chip that probed the soles of her feet.

When Cat climbed behind the wheel she noticed the paper pinned underneath her front windshield wiper. It was folded and glued to the glass from the predawn mist. She reached over the top, felt the flimsy newsprint, and gingerly unfolded it while returning to her bucket seat. What she saw sent waves of icy cold down her neck and arms.

Oh. My. God.

Gripped with a need for flight, Cat punched the ignition button and sped away in no particular direction—as if putting some speed under her would prevent Hal Solomon's ghost from gripping her any harder that it already was.

20

Compton. 5:28 a.m.

Lucky knew there'd be no automatic overtime if Shia was slow in completing their written reports. He'd showered again, slipped on a T-shirt and jeans, and waited out his trainee while seated in the driver's seat of his primer gray '99. The driver's door was half open, his legs were crossed, boots propped up in the open window. The car radio was semi-quietly tuned to an alternative station that crunched rock music from the grungy nineties.

Still in her uniform, Shia approached with a handful of forms.

"That was fast," remarked Lucky.

"I'm a little hung up on this one thing," replied Shia.

"Show me."

"The gun arrest. You said check the glove box for the registra-tion."

"Yeah?"

"I opened the glove box, some cans 'n' stuff fell out. I found the registration. But it was when I got on the floor to pick up this Coke bottle I saw the first weapon."

"It wasn't in plain sight?"

"When I was on the floor it was. But not when I was going for the registration."

"That's a problem."

"Really?"

"Did you have PC for guns?" asked Lucky, referring to the probable cause required before police officers can search any property.

Shia rewound the tape in her brain and replayed the sequence of before and after the arrest. The memories included the back slaps and accolades she'd received from her fellow deputies as well as the proud watch commander.

"I don't know," she said. "I was ordered to get the registration. If I wasn't cleaning up some stuff from the floorboard . . . I wasn't looking for guns."

"If you'd just grabbed the registration and left the shit on the floor," clarified Lucky, "would you have seen the guns?"

"No," she answered flatly.

"Then all seven bad boys walk," shrugged Lucky. "On your way home, might as well stop by the jail and unhook 'em yourself."

"Shit," griped Shia, wanting to flog herself.

"I could go with you. Hold your hand."

"I don't want 'em to walk!"

"Why?"

"Are you joking?" angered Shia. "Those assholes were looking to put a kill on somebody."

"No doubt."

"And so they walk?"

"Depends on you."

"How me?"

"You said shit fell out of the glove box."

"Yeah?"

"What if—included with the shit that fell onto the floorboard—was the registration?"

"Because that would be untrue . . ."

"Untrue?" asked Lucky. "I asked you to fetch the registration. In the course of fetching the registration you discovered the guns."

"So you think that's how I should write it?"

"You want those bad boys to walk?"

Shia made a slow-to-acknowledge nod before her about-face and march back into the station house. Lucky resumed his former pose. On his phone he composed a text for Gonzo as to his expected time of arrival. It wasn't a demand that he check in. Lucky just knew she'd appreciate the simple gesture and, for appearance's sake, it might earn him points for maintaining the relationship. He was about to press send when he realized the time. The morning was just beginning to reveal itself. Gonzo would surely still be sleeping. Lucky canceled the text and sent the message as an email, finishing the note off with a pair of uncharacteristic Xs and Os. Perhaps because he was looking forward to sharing with her the tales of his obnoxious ride-along and the resulting "screen test."

Shia returned and, after handing off the completed and signed shift report, placed her hands on her hips and momentarily gazed at the renewing sky. Instead of passing the papers back for Shia to file, Lucky exhumed himself from his car and stood over her.

"What?" she asked. "Something wrong?"

"I got the rest," said Lucky. "I'll file."

"No, you won't," she insisted. "You're showered and dressed. Go home. I got this."

"No," said Lucky firmly. "I got this. Same way I got you."

Shia screwed up her face while trying to figure out just what Lucky was implying.

"I got you," he repeated, gently waving the fistful of paper. "You signed shift and arrest reports that you know to be false. That's perjury. Nice work for your second night on the job."

Lucky watched as the wind expelled from his trainee's lungs. Behind that layer of defeminizing body armor, he could see her chest sink, her eyes wide and shocked reservoirs of *what the hell just happened to me?*

"But you suggested . . ." she searched.

"And you signed."

"To keep it a good arrest."

"Perjury all the same," said Lucky, knowing that Shia knew—as would any self-respecting deputy fresh from the academy—that perjury of any shade was a silver bullet to a cop's career.

"Why?" she asked, her delicate eyebrows beginning to pinch the bridge of her nose angrily.

"Trust," answered Lucky. "Now I know you have my back. Same goes for every other deputy you partner with. They will trust that you are there *for them.*"

"Wait, wait, wait, wait," she stammered. "You sayin' every trainee—"

"Sayin' that outside those walls is a grid with no rules. *Bad guys* don't play by rules. That means the day-to-day shit which is you 'n' me in a black-and-white might demand more than following policy and procedure. You get me?"

Lucky couldn't gauge what had penetrated. Some of it would have to sink in later. He'd said his awful piece and now it was Shia's to either swallow or reject.

"Go home. Sleep on it," said Lucky. "And when you show up for shift, know that I will have your back from today to the grave."

"And if I choose to protest?"

"You can. But you won't," said Lucky. "Welcome to the circle of trust."

He left Shia looking like a complicated tumult of heart-break, random victimization, and unexpressed rage. Lucky didn't know for sure what kind of trainee he'd find once their July Fourth shift resumed at 9:00 p.m. After he made digital cop-ies of the shift reports, he filed them, returned to his '99 Crown Vic, and rolled out into the dawning day, steering out of the motor yard and pointing himself north.

* * *

Because of the holiday, Lucky anticipated minimal traffic on his commute home to Altadena. As he figured it, he had between Compton and Altadena to hogtie his feelings of guilt and stuff them into the vault where he kept all his other indiscretions—Reaper and otherwise.

Sixteen years earlier, young Deputy Lucky Dey had been inducted into the circle of trust by his own training officer, Flip Bledsoe. Lucky could argue that what he'd passed down to Shia was for her own good as much as the good of the L.A. Sheriff's. At no other time in recent history were cops under such a microscope. To do the job demanded faith in one's partner as much as faith in the department as a whole. Otherwise that thin blue line would crumble and the bad guys would use their newfound upper hand to cause even more urban chaos.

Then Lucky wondered if his own young face had looked as stung as Shia's when Bledsoe had dropped the perjury hammer on him.

The sun was cresting enough to paint the sky a sapphire blue while leaving the Los Angeles Basin in shadow. As a defense, Lucky grabbed for his Ray-Bans before hitting the Alameda on-ramp. Only his sunglasses weren't in the center console, where he normally left them. He patted his chest to see if he'd inadvertently hung them from his T-shirt collar, then the top of his buzzed scalp just in case he'd absently saddled them up high.

Damn it, Lucky.

He shook the image of Shia's hurt face in exchange for the recollection of his sunglasses parked on the top shelf of his station house locker. For a split second, he wrestled between turning around and retrieving the sunglasses or braving the blistering sun for the twenty-minute drive home.

Lucky's boot stomped on the brake pedal. The '99 Ford's wheels locked instantly and rubber bled against the asphalt.

His path was blocked by a tangle of recognizable mutts dragging a tipped-over shopping cart. All without the help of their beloved Mush Man.

"Shit," said Lucky, assessing the picture with a reservoir of worry.

He jammed the '99 into park and climbed out, scanning a quick three-sixty, half expecting to see Mush Man careening around a corner, out of breath, uncontrollably cursing for his dog team to halt. Yet there was little sound but for the scraping of the crippled cart across the pavement along with some yowls from the tangled mutts.

"Where's your boy?" asked Lucky, approaching the dog team. "Mushy take a tumble?"

The dogs perked up at Lucky's smell and wagged their tails. He righted the cart and ushered the knotted mongrels over to the sidewalk, where he crouched and gave each pup some scruffy attention. He took Oprah's muzzle and looked into her eyes.

"C'mon, sweetheart," he urged. "Where's our Mush Man?"

21

With so many embarrassing and frequent mainline blow-outs plaguing the Department of Water and Power, quick response teams had been formed, serving both practical and public relations agendas. Seeking the opportunity for a bump in both salary and overtime pay was twenty-six-year-old waterworks mechanic Mike Keough from Hesperia, a high-desert enclave more than eighty miles from Compton. Because he was the newest and youngest on the crew, Keough was bent on impressing his managers by being the first on every site and the last to leave. With that in mind, he had arrived at the Poinsettia Street repair dig at three minutes past six with a dozen Dunkin' Donuts and a hundred-ounce Box O' Joe. His thinking was, yeah, so what if I look like a red-faced ass-kisser? I'm first here and ready to work.

And work he did.

With a glance, Keough could see the leaky clamps had left the hole nearly a quarter filled with muddy water. So, he keyed the diesel generator, push-started it, and, before the engine cylinders had found a rhythm, he switched on the drainage pump. The hoses bucked and filled. Keough quickly traced the line to make sure that no one had moved the relief spouts from the nearby storm drain during the night. For the briefest moment, he feared he would find the business end of the hose whipping around like a deranged snake, soaking somebody's yard and house with mud-brown water. He was relieved to discover the four-inch collapsible discharge hose remained moored in the storm drain, precisely where he had left it ten hours earlier.

But the water wasn't flowing evenly. It was chugging in fits and starts. Keough could hear the pump straining.

"Crap salad," he said aloud to nobody but himself. He turned toward the hole, where he resigned himself to starting the day wet. He had to clear whatever had obstructed the strainer head.

As Keough's view tilted into the hole, his eyes followed the hose line as it looped across a ledge dug out by a backhoe and followed the teeth marks into an opaque pool of browned fluid.

Easy enough, he thought, charting his route from a two o'clock position. He descended the ladder, foregoing the last two rungs and landing with knees bent in an athletic *squish*. He gripped the hose with both hands and gave it a tug, thinking a simple readjustment might free the filter's face from the impediment. Instead of easing loose, the hose gagged and shook. The young mechanic gripped hard, set his feet, and threw his body weight back and away from the snag. For the briefest moment, he felt something give as suction resumed and the hose engorged itself. Then, *snap!* as if the filter head had re-engaged the obstruction with a shark's bite. The pump wheezed and the hose whipped.

The water splashed. And for a brain-second, a startled Keough imagined he'd hooked some kind of huge urban catfish.

"Eat me!" barked the waterworks mechanic. He let go of the hose and stumbled backwards, nearly tripping his backside into the goo.

There was no amphibious monster attached to the filter head. Or easily removed hunk of flotsam. It was a man. Small. Clothed. Not the least bit threatening. And very clearly dead.

22

Van Nuys. 6:31 a.m.

"So two nights in. How's it feel?"

Steve Wimminger was seated in a corner booth at Nat's Early Bite, a three-decades-old hole in the wall with a history of serving and employing recovering alcoholics and addicts. Across from him, picking at her plate of egg whites and limp asparagus, sat sheriff's trainee Shia Saint George.

"Okay," she nodded in slow motion, as if trying to convince herself. "Never a dull moment."

"No shit," said Wimmer, leaning in, always leading with his hard-to-forget forehead. "That *was* you I read about in the *Daily News*? Took a swim on your first night out?"

"That would be me," she semi-singsonged.

"Coulda screwed our whole deal from the jump."

"Nice to know you're thinking about me instead of our *thing*."

"C'mon," he nudged her. "Don't forget. I've been where you are."

"A black female trainee?" she shot back.

"Fair enough," admitted Wimmer. "But you know what I mean. I went through my five months in a black-and-white."

"In Lennox," she finished for him, having heard the story more than once. "With a Reaper."

"So I never got swallowed by a DWP blowout," he eased. "You're lucky to be alive, you know."

"He pulled me out."

"Lucas Dey?" confirmed Wimmer.

"Lucky."

"You're lucky he pulled you out? Or *Lucky* pulled you out?" he joked. In return, he received little more than a cocked head and a narrowing of Shia's eyebrows. "Okay. My bad. Just trying to keep it light."

"What's light about any of this shit?"

"It's not shit," he calmed her. "And I'll stop with the wordplay."

"Please do."

"Eye on the prize. Always," he reminded. "And I'm not the least bit distracted. You?"

Shia took a breath to regard the tenor of her next answer. "No," she said. "Just tired. I need to sleep."

"So we'll get down to *it*," said Wimmer.

Nodding, Shia agreed without having to clarify what *it* was. She knew all too well the stakes that came with conspiring with the feds. In this case, that meant Deputy United States Attorney Steve J. Wimminger, whose target of investigation was Lucas Dey of the Los Angeles County Sheriff's Department.

"Anything to speak of yet?" asked Wimmer.

"Like, has he suckered me into a perjury trap?"

"Exactly like that."

"Yeah," she admitted. "Coupla hours ago."

"Wow. That didn't take long."

"Quick work if I wanna be in his 'circle of trust,'" complained Shia.

"And you played it?"

"Didn't really have to play it at all," she said. "I sorta saw it coming."

"Because I told you it was coming," impressed Wimmer. "Unless he trusts you, he won't be keen on crossing any policy lines. At least while you're riding with him."

Wimmer was referring to the rules, regulations, and federal statutes forbidding police officers from violating the civil rights of the citizens they were sworn to protect. Such violations were catnip for government prosecutors. Headline-grabbing. Career-enhancing.

"Still caught me by surprise," she admitted.

"Didn't expect it to happen the first week?"

"No. Not that," she thought, reaching for her feelings. "I dunno. For a minute I forgot why I was there."

"You're there to take down a dirty cop."

"Dirty?"

"Corrupt. Badge-heavy," redefined Wimmer.

"Maybe."

"He's got the tattoo," pressed Wimmer. "He's a real deal Lennox Reaper."

"Yeah, yeah," she conceded. "Maybe I forgot because . . ."

"Because why?"

"Because he did something that felt pretty cool . . . Something he didn't have to."

"Yeah? Like how?"

The exhausted trainee gave Wimmer a condensed version of the previous night's events involving their annoying ride-along, Atom Blum. Despite Wimmer expressing eyebrow-raised surprise at the mention of the director—admitting to be a fan of the boy wonder's *Roadkill* and its subsequent blockbuster sequels—Shia kept her voice even as she described all the inappropriate come-ons, sexual passes, and flagrant, uncomfortable innuendos she'd been subjected to.

"Screen test?" chirped Wimmer, his voice carrying well beyond their booth. Nearby diners crooked their necks.

"Really?" griped Shia.

"Sorry," said Wimmer, lowering his voice to just above a whisper. "Like anybody thinks a screen test is something other than a screen test, you know?"

"Still," she reminded.

"I know, I know. Wow. He did that to Atom Blum? Friend to the assistant sheriff? Talk about some *huevos grande.*"

"He did that *for me,*" corrected Shia.

"Wanna flatter yourself or stay real?"

"I'm not being real?"

"How do you know he didn't screen test the douchebag to amuse himself or give a middle finger to the sheriff's brass?" pushed Wimmer, already sounding somewhat embittered and admiring at once. "Balls on his balls. Jesus. Once a Reaper, always a Reaper. Take it from me."

"Fine," relented Shia, bending to her desire to sleep.

"Ink this to the inside of your eyelids," impressed Wimmer. "L.A. Sheriff's is a career. But FBI is a launching pad to wherever someone smart, ambitious, and beautiful can imagine herself."

Shia could have done without the reference to her looks. Not that she was against men *or* women paying her unsolicited compliments. Wimmer, though, had yet to meet with her once without dropping some weak reference to her attractiveness. She wondered if the stick attached to the carrot he dangled came with hidden entanglements—such as an expectation of sexual congress once he'd fast-tracked her into a Justice Department career.

Quid pro quo.

Shia parted from the US Attorney, leaving him at the cash register to pay the check. He would wisely hang back to eliminate the chance the pair would be seen leaving together. And thank God for her oversized Michael Kors sunglasses. The orbital lenses served a dual purpose: cutting the morning glare and disguising her recognizable features. The last thing she needed was to bump into somebody she knew from either CSUN or the academy who found her taste in breakfast companions suspicious.

A powerfully built gent in a cowboy-styled, snap-front shirt with sleeves rolled up to the top of his biceps held the door for her. His tattoo-covered leathery face below a close-cropped Mohawk made an immutable impression. At a glance, one might mistake him for a Māori tribesman from New Zealand, decorated from head to toe in ancestral ink. Only Shia distinguished a different genus of clan. MS-13—a.k.a. Mara Salvatrucha—the murderous transnational gang of drug traffickers known for tattooing their allegiance across their faces. She'd run into MS-13s while working the county jail and knew to treat them with caution *in extremis*.

"Thank you," said Shia, staring a split-moment longer in search of recognition. It was the easy smile on the man that struck her cold. So familiar. Had they met at the downtown dungeon?

"No problem," beamed Mohawk, "and you have yourself a good morning."

And that was that. Or so she thought.

An inner tumult bubbled as she piloted her Kia Optima on the short drive to her NoHo condo. She wondered if the taste in her mouth was regret. Or maybe betrayal. Her ambitious side was excited at the prospect of attending Quantico, carrying an FBI badge, and wearing suits tailored to fit both her striking form and a service pistol. She also questioned if it was another case of the grass being always greener. How many changes in a career trajectory could a twenty-five-year-old have already made? Or how many broken hearts and promises could she leave in her wake before her own fickle collateral caught up with her?

Shia's next trick was surely to come at an inflated price. Lucky Dey. Wimmer's grim Reaper. Betrayed by his trainee and tossed for God knows only how long into a federal lockup.

When Shia imagined Lucky in an orange prison jumpsuit, she felt like choking on her own saliva. She next pictured that MS-13 member who had so politely held the door for her moments earlier. Her insides screamed that she'd crossed paths with the killer before. Most likely where there had been steel bars, electronic surveillance, and hundreds of thousands of poured concrete yards to keep men like him from mixing with the population at large. Yet there he'd been, a man who advertised his evil deeds through the tattoos on his face, behaving like any other gentlemen, a smile and a warm reply. Shia wondered what made her feel dirtier—passing within a hair's breadth of an unshackled murderer or selling her soul to the US Attorney in exchange for a career with the *federales*.

Get a grip, girl.

Before crossing her condominium's threshold Shia would need to box her feelings to face her annoyingly sunny roommate—also known as Rufus Saint George, her permanently disabled father. The blind former chemical engineer would be waiting for her in their cozy kitchenette, radio tuned to National Public Radio and already halfway through a pot of coffee. He'd expect a full debrief of her second night in a black-and-white. The best she could do was hope he'd be satisfied with half truths, perhaps an anecdote, and her pleas for sleep.

23

Compton. 7:14 a.m.

Lil Rod woke to a buzzing in his head. It was like television static being broadcast between his ears and so disturbing that he couldn't recollect where he was or how he had landed there. His only clear memory was that of hauling ass away from that big hole in Poinsettia.

"Yo, Lil Rod," called a singsong voice. "I knows you 'round here."

Young Raydon's eyes fluttered open and began to swirl for a point of reference. He was horizontal and weirdly comfortable. In a bed? Surely not his own. With Julius Colón looking for him, he'd never have returned home. Then again, whatever zombie weed he'd smoked had proven so disorienting he could barely remember his given name.

"Know how I know young nigga's here?" sang a rasping voice

Lil Rod instinctively recognized as Wolfgang's, a member of a Crips set called Original Swamps. The crew had connections to Julius.

Lil Rod pictured a quad-copter flyover of the neighborhood. Nearly everything and everyone in Compton had a Julius Colón connection—or so it seemed to the young gangster. One of J's front businesses was the old Adams Funeral Home on East Palmer, famous for its drive-thru casket viewing. Lil Rod's uncle Antoine had worked there part-time. One afternoon, while giving his nephew a macabre tour, he'd shown off the decrepit storage shed leaning against the property's back fence. Inside, amongst the piles of rusted junk, lay a long-forgotten coffin—a sample casket left by a bankrupt manufacturer. Uncle A had confided that there had been times when he had tied on a serious drunk and that satin-lined burial box had proven a handy place to sleep without his wife or bosses ending up the wiser.

"You 'round here 'cause I found young nigga's bike!" cackled Wolfgang.

Through the fuzz, Lil Rod could hear the familiar *tick-tick* of his bicycle's gears. The sound revolved clockwise around the shed, leaving the impression that the Crip was walking alongside the bike.

"Lil Rod want his hot roddy ride back?" teased Wolfgang.

The casket was on the floor. Lil Rod found his knees and eased out of the box. The shed's walls—redwood slats shrunk from years of an unforgiving direct sun—were striped in morning light. Dust and cobwebs hung. If Lil Rod still retained a childhood fear of spiders, it took a quick back seat to Wolfgang's shadow crossing over him.

"Lillllllllll Roddddddddddddd!" called the Crip.

Lil Rod hurled himself against the side of the shed. The vertical planks snapped like balsa. He found himself on his face in the back alleyway, but with his legs still churning in hopes of gaining traction. The moment the sixteen-year-old found his feet, instead of discovering Wolfgang quick-scaling the wall after him in full chase, he saw his hot rod neon yellow bicycle helicoptering over the shed and bouncing off the asphalt.

Twisting a one-eighty, Lil Rod hauled in the opposite direction, arms and legs pumping.

"LIL NIGGA!" yelled Wolfgang. "WHY YOU RUNNIN'?"

Lil Rod heard the thumps of scuffling sneakers behind him. One pair. Two pairs. Three. Wolfgang wasn't alone.

Lil Rod was light and fast and nearly rested. So, he pulled his elbows in, set his spine to the correct lean, and found the economy of speed and listened for the footsteps behind him to recede.

Willow Street crossed ahead. Houses to the north. Backyards. Fences to hop. Sixty seconds and Lil Rod was sure to lose anybody or anything biting his heels.

A white GMC Yukon screeched to a stop and blocked the alley. The doors burst open and out scrambled four more Crips, hitting the ground and spacing themselves in a clothesline.

"Okay, okay, okay, okay!" shouted Lil Rod, skidding to a stop, arms up in surrender.

Lil Rod might have had more to say. His lips and tongue were already forming a soliloquy of excuses he hoped would find the ears of Julius—excuses that would have to wait as a tattooed forearm swung into his periphery and struck him across his right ear. Lil Rod saw blue sky and little more before he blacked out.

24

Julius Colón didn't see himself as a Robin Hood or criminal savior to the poor and disenfranchised. He just hated waste—especially when it involved his own pocketbook. Example: After Julius purchased Pizza King, which served and delivered until 4:00 a.m., he'd discovered that between the mistakes in the kitchen and phantom phone orders, the garbage cans would be choked with uneaten food by night's end. With improved workplace rules in place plus some organizational changes, Julius was able to cut waste by 65 percent. A win for some, but not so for Julius. He obsessed on the overages. Then came an early morning in April. He and Big Otis stood in the kitchen, staring down at a leftover assembly of seven uneaten pizzas, six pounds of cooked wings, and three boxes of mojo-roasted potatoes.

"Put 'em in the truck," Julius had ordered.

Thus began an almost daily habit of what Julius labeled Dawn Patrol. By reheating the leftovers and placing them into hot boxes loaded in the back of the Suburban, Julius and Big Otis would cruise the streets handing out warm food to random vagrants. After only a month, the neighborhood's homeless population became less random and more familiar. Some even called Julius by name and would attempt to flag down his gray Suburban from distances of a block or more.

"Bes' part of my day, boss," remarked Big Otis in a rare non sequitur. He spun the steering wheel into a right turn while flipping down his visor to cut off the glare of morning sun.

"I feel ya," was all a weary Julius said.

The boss was less jovial than his normal morning self. Julius had been shoring his workouts with fresh injections of human growth hormone and hourly bumps of cocaine. Exhaustion was kept in abeyance.

"Stop the car!" barked Julius.

Otis applied the brakes, stalling the Suburban in the middle of the street.

"Back up, back up!" Julius's eyes zeroed out his passenger-seat window.

Ever the obedient bodyguard, Big Otis reversed the big SUV until it was perpendicular to the point where Julius sounded.

"Hey!" shouted Julius before his window was half rolled down. "HEY, I SAID! WHAT YOU DOIN' WITH MY NIGGA'S DOGS?"

Dogs were to Lucky what Kryptonite was to Superman. Over his entire life he'd suffered a special connection with dogs. But for the two vicious animals who'd bitten him during the course of duty, most dogs had loved Lucky right back. If only the deputy hadn't been cursed with a goddamn allergy. If he so much as touched a dog, he'd have to wash, douse his hands with cleanser, or seek out medicine or medical attention. Otherwise his throat would swell until his larynx was crushed.

Danger aside, Lucky wrangled two dogs per arm, hoping lead dog Oprah would guide him to their missing master. The mutts had turned him up an alleyway, only to be interested in a pair of garbage cans that smelled like last night's fried chicken.

Lucky checked his watch. By his count, he had less than sixty minutes before he'd need to walk into an ER and beg for a shot of epinephrine or find the nearest CVS, where he could gargle a bottle of Benadryl. It was when he was urging the dogs into a U-turn that he heard shouts in his direction.

"HEY! WHAT YOU DOIN' WITH MY NIGGA'S DOGS?"

At the opposite end of the alley was a gray Chevy Suburban. Though Lucky didn't recognize the scowling man framed by the passenger window, Oprah and Hank clearly did, the latter woofing excitedly while the older lead dog let loose an anticipatory howl. The animals tugged and it was all Lucky could do to follow without being yanked face-first to the ground.

The Suburban's driver turned the SUV's front wheels into the alley and closed the distance. Before braking to a full stop, the passenger door flung open to reveal a fireplug of a man yoked inside an undersized compression shirt with a Stars and Stripes UFC logo.

The dog team surged and ripped the harness from Lucky's grip. He relented, pleased at least to see that instead of running off, the sled crew bunched around the SUV's passenger.

Julius gave each of the pups a familiar rub while keeping his gaze on Lucky.

"Good," said Lucky. "They know you."

"Didn't answer my question," said Julius. "Where's their daddy?"

"Mush Man? We're lookin' for him."

"Where'd he get off to?"

"Found 'em on Alameda. No Mush. Draggin' that shopping cart Mush calls his sled."

"Yeah?" said Julius. "How you know him?"

"Just bein' 'round," said Lucky. "Way back before he got pushed out of Lennox. You know he's under psych care at the VA?"

"That so?"

"Thinkin' he mighta had a seizure." Then Lucky segued. "Dogs seem to know you pretty good."

"Not so much me," said Julius, thumb-gesturing to Big Otis. "It's what I give 'em."

Lucky flashed to Otis as the big man lumbered from the driver's seat to the back of the Suburban. The pieces were coming together. Pimped SUV. The ex-footballer doubling as driver and bodyguard. The easy math allowed Lucky to profile Julius as either a hip-hop-styled celebrity or Compton crime impresario. Lucky was leaning towards O.G.—original gangster. Only the criminal in question bore none of the usual visible and distinguishing tattoos that might connect him to a local set or affiliation. The man bore no features that labeled him either African-American or Hispanic. Racially neutral, thought Lucky. Not necessarily the best DNA combo for a criminal in Compton, a swath of real estate where color lines were best appreciated when they were easily recognized as black, brown, or sheriffs' khaki and green.

Big Otis reappeared with an extra-large pizza box. The mutts swarmed, jockeying for position. The big man belly-laughed like an eighth grader.

"Lemme," demanded Julius, flipping open the box and distributing the slices by name. "Oprah first. Big Hank. Whoa, whoa. Wait your turn. Thurgood. Rosa." As the dogs wolfed down the cheese pizza, Julius crouched amidst them. "Now, where's your daddy? Huh? What happened to Little Man Mush?"

Lucky scratched his forearm, recognizing the signal of an oncoming allergic siege.

"They safe with you?" Lucky asked.

"Yeah, yeah," replied Julius. "I find a place for 'em till Mush crawls outta wherever he be."

"Good," agreed Lucky, fishing into his wallet. "I'm gonna keep lookin' for our boy. But you hear from him first, maybe you could call me?"

Lucky produced one of his vellum L.A. Sheriff's business cards and offered it with two fingers.

"Back atcha," said Julius with a double snap of his fingers. Big Otis slipped his fat fingers into his shirt pocket and dug until he came up with one of his boss's cards—slick black, red, and embossed blue.

Lucky read the name two points underneath the company's moniker, Pizza Wing Enterprises.

"Julius," read Lucky. "Good to meetcha."

"Lucas Dey of L.A. Sheriff's," read back Big O before passing Lucky's card over to Julius.

Lucky squatted in front of Oprah. The black-and-white lead dog was licking her pink chops after devouring the pizza slice.

"We'll find your ol' man," assured Lucky. With his fingers he rubbed the scruff behind her floppy ears. Then unconsciously, with his left hand, he reached below his jeans' cuff and scratched at the itchy skin on his left calf.

Julius Colón, a man prideful about his knack for detail, noted the sheriff's deputy's posture as he pet the dog with one hand while relieving his itch with the other. As the pants leg lifted further, he recognized the bottom of Lucky's Reaper tattoo. The ink was only partially visible, but instantly identified.

Mother. Fucking. Reaper.

"So you call me or I call you," agreed Julius, his tone betraying his surge of venom.

"Thanks," said Lucky, returning to his feet and thrusting forward a parting hand. Julius grasped it with a strong fit.

Lucky's intuitions always kicked in when he turned his back to walk away. Where some cops trusted the hairs on the back of their necks or a gooey sense of heebie-jeebies when encountering evil, Lucky would rely on one of two tests. He'd either read the subject's pupils during a basic Q and A or, upon turning his back on the creature, he'd tap his gut as to whether or not he expected a blistering bullet expelled in his direction.

As Lucky strode from the dogs, Big Otis, the Chevy Suburban, and the enigmatic Julius Colón, he listened to the chain of muscles knotting his back. Without asking, the fibers between his shoulder blades clenched with certainty and expectation. As if the sinews themselves could read the thoughts of the man left behind. Definitive.

Julius Colón equals . . . bad guy.

When Lucky landed in his '99 Ford, his eyes were already beginning to itch and water. If he didn't attend to the allergic reaction soon, he might get to that ugly point where he'd consider using a Brillo pad to relieve the discomfort in his eyes.

Righted next to his car was Mush Man's shopping-cart-cum-urban-dogsled. Lucky considered leaving it on the sidewalk. But odds were it wouldn't last the day, let alone the time for Mush Man to resurface. So, Lucky popped his trunk, loaded what he could of the cart, then strapped the trunk lid on top of it using remnants of Mush Man's makeshift harness.

Now all I need are meds.

His natural bearings informed him that he was roughly equidistant from the nearest drugstore and emergency room. Choosing a bottle of Benadryl over the hassle of walking into a local ER, Lucky keyed the engine and dropped the '99 into gear. It was 8:02 a.m. and already eighty-five degrees. The holiday ahead was promising to be a steamer.

Lucky prepped to make a left onto East Compton when a semi-tractor rig towing a mobile investigation trailer rumbled past. The white paint with a single blue stripe indicated the familiar markings of the Los Angeles County Coroner.

Lucky's curiosity was piqued.

A twenty-four-hour CVS and a bottle of chemical relief was just a turn to the left and an easy half mile away. Despite the pull, Lucky swung the '99 right, effectively tailing the coroner's truck. Considering the time of day, he tried to convince himself that the crime-scene team was headed back to the barn. He decided to give his little chase ten blocks before peeling off to seek attention for his allergy. After all, he was off duty and feeling like shit. Yet there he was, off the clock and tailing a coroner crew without a clue other than the magnetic pit in his stomach.

At Poinsettia, the coroner's truck indicated a right turn, slowing, starting its wheels left to make a clean arc onto the tight residential track. A tingle spread across Lucky's scalp, producing a cool slick of perspiration. He negotiated his own turn onto Poinsettia—already recognizing that it was the precise block where he and his trainee had been nearly swallowed alive in that water main blowout. His mind ticked off the number of emergency units already on the scene. Two fire trucks, a ladder, and an EMT. Four sheriff's black-and-whites. As well as two more unmarked units with radio arrays. Closer to the hole was the hulking machinery of heavy DWP equipment, including an oversized backhoe. A fresh ribbon of crime-scene tape was being strung out by a pair of uniformed deputies.

Either because of Lucky's sheriff's shield fixed to his belt or his experienced swagger, nobody thought twice to check whether he had business at the scene. As he snaked through the ring of cops, firemen, and DWP workers, he saw a scattering of Big Gulp–sized yellow cones—each with a different black number—placed around the eastern rim of the hole. These, Lucky recognized, were to record where spent bullet casings were discarded. From Lucky's glance it appeared no fewer than twenty rounds had been expelled.

A fire ladder had been lowered so the crime-scene techs could scramble in and out of the hole. Lucky eased ever closer, his ears keyed on a testy exchange between a pair of sheriff's detectives and a barrel-chested DWP foreman.

"I'm sayin' I can't take responsibility for any shit that happens down there," pressed the foreman.

"It's a crime scene," replied a familiar-looking detective. He appeared thirty-ish despite having already lost half his flame-red hair. "That means we gotta do our thing no matter."

"Just don't say you weren't warned," said the foreman, hands up in surrender. "I get called in as witness to your work-comp claim, I'm testifying you guys didn't allow none of my people to secure the hole."

"So warned," said the other detective, a wan-looking sort with sallow eyes, a gin-blossomed nose, and sagging khakis beneath a generous belly. "Now, mind corralling your crew somewhere over thataway?"

Lucky arrived at the edge of the hole, heart pounding in his chest. He could feel the adrenaline beating back the allergens. Fear, thought Lucky. That was the only explanation for the thumping. As he gazed downward, it was hard to make out any specifics as the six-man crime-scene team decked out in disposable blue Pyrolon coveralls scoured and marked whatever evidence they could.

"Whatcha got?" Lucky found himself asking the red-haired detective.

In return he received a requisite who-the-hell-are-you once-over from the detective along with the expected authoritarian follow-up.

"Who are you?" the detective asked.

"Lucky Dey. Compton Station."

"Someone send you to look over my shoulder?"

"I'm the cop asshole this hole almost ate," said Lucky.

"So that was you?" gaped the detective, both admiringly and amused while accepting Lucky's hand. "Jeff Lowe. Homicide Bureau."

At the drop of the detective's job description, Lucky instantly imagined the Irish-looking pug at one of those messy desks that made up the L.A. County Sheriff's Homicide Bureau. The unit—which gamely referred to itself as the Bulldogs—was housed in a nondescript office building oddly located in the nearby City of Commerce.

"Got a relative flying whirlybirds for LAPD?" asked Lucky.

"That'd be my little brother, Mike. You know him?"

"Works with my girlfriend."

"Small-ass world," deadpanned Lowe. "And this is the big-ass hole you fell in."

"You got a theory what happened here?"

"With the crime scene? All we know is there was a lotta lead in the air and one unarmed victim."

"ID?"

"Got a uniform somewhere around here," said Lowe, glancing around. "Recognized him as a local homeless dude. Said he was last seen ridin' around in a shopping cart pulled by his dogs."

There came a plunge inside Lucky. It felt like his heart had been hooked and pulled into his spleen. His eyes were already slits, near-shuttered by his allergic reaction. Yet through them he was able to track a pair of coroner techs as they climbed into the hole and unfurled a yellow mesh body bag designed for water recoveries. The team slipped into the muck and only as they worked their rubber-gloved hands below the surface of the water was the body finally revealed.

A face bobbed to the surface—the attached dreadlocks barely floated, limp and uncoiling.

Mush Man.

There was a tightening in Lucky's throat, as if the devil himself had wrapped a claw around his neck and begun to strangulate him. The allergic reaction had gone from a tickling to full bloom. His airways were under attack. Without immediate medical attention, Lucky might choke or black out or even die.

He pivoted and turned toward where he recalled seeing the paramedics' vehicle. He made a beeline while keeping his shoulders back and chin slightly elevated to lengthen and open his trachea. A puffy, baby-faced EMT appearing no older than sixteen sat outside the one open door to the emergency cabin. Lucky unhooked his shield from his belt and was lifting it to identify himself when an enormously loud hum came from behind him. What followed was a cacophony of screams, men shouting, and involuntary curses. The baby-faced EMT switched from looking at Lucky's shield to rushing toward the developing emergency.

Lucky's ear canals were swelling.

Everything to his rear sounded as if underwater. Instinct demanded he ignore the distress behind him and continue into the vehicle's cabin. He climbed, feeling his equilibrium failing, his need for air proclaimed in a gagging cough. Recalling his brief training as a fireman before getting accepted to the Sheriff's Academy, Lucky began releasing overhead bins from right to left. He dug at each, spilling everything from packaged hypodermics to gauze to decompression supplies. A handful of plastic-wrapped cylinders the size of tampons tumbled from the fourth box. Without having to read the contents, Lucky snatched one, stripped off the wrapper, and revealed a colorful epinephrine auto-injector—also called an EpiPen. He twisted off the protective cap with the gusto of a man dying of thirst and jammed the needle through his denim jeans into his right thigh.

Lucky dropped, sat, and waited. When relief didn't come as expected, he began to fumble for a second EpiPen. He was ready to jam another dose into his leg when he tasted metal in his mouth—a side effect of the drug and proof that it had found his bloodstream. He tipped his head back and rested while listening to the blitzkrieg of his ever-elevating heart rate.

It's working. Relax. Let it happen.

Lucky's ears began to clear. Satan's hand around his throat eased into a malignant but livable touch. He could breathe again.

"What the hell are you doing in here?" barked the baby-faced EMT, swinging the second door wide. Behind him were his paramedic partner and, between them, an unconscious crime-scene tech on a collapsible ambulance stretcher. Half crouched, Lucky expertly assisted, pulling the forward end of the litter. The stretcher's legs folded, allowing it to glide into the cabin. Lucky's assessment of the female victim—a heavyweight girl of Asian extraction—was that she was dead on arrival. Her eyes were fixed. Her right arm was badly burned with an electrical crease moving diagonally across her chest, the vinyl of her disposable jumpsuit melted away as if she'd been slashed with a welder's torch.

Lucky felt the stretcher lock into position. He swiveled to the right and exited through the side door without so much as a hello or goodbye or apology for the mess he'd left behind. Better that way, he thought. They had jobs to do. As did he.

His head throbbed. Another damned side effect of the epinephrine injection, he remembered. The metallic taste was receding yet still present. And with every step, his balance returned. Snagging a petite female deputy in uniform, Lucky convinced her to brief him on what he'd missed. The deceased crime-scene techni-cian had been fishing for an expended slug, which had pierced an exposed eighty-year-old piece of clay pipe, a long-ago conduit for an electricity transmission line. The DWP backhoe operator had warned her of the hazards involved in her search, but none included the danger of electrocution. Why? The DWP no longer buried power transmission lines underground for a variety of convenience and safety reasons. In the backhoe operator's opinion, the techs would be safe to explore for a bullet, an underground spring, or even buried treasure.

The backhoe operator was wrong.

Once the crime-scene tech's aluminum probe had made contact with the assumed to be dead power cable, she would have been better served if struck by lightning. Witnesses claimed to have seen an arcing light paired with an enormous, low-frequency murmur. For a moment, the crime-scene tech had stood her ground, frozen in time until her knees buckled and she tumbled into the muddy water.

Swell, thought Lucky. In a matter of thirty hours that fucking hole had claimed two human lives and a spanking new Ford Interceptor.

Lucky nosed the site for those two homicide detectives, quickly discovering they'd excused themselves once the coroner team had officially claimed Mush Man's body. From what he could tell, the undynamic duo had knocked on zero doors and interviewed just as many witnesses. There were other cases to solve with thicker files and victims with families demanding justice—far more prominent than a schizoid, street-sledding vagrant who stood no taller than your average fifth grader.

Mush Man didn't take up enough space to matter. That, and the deceased vagrant had most likely already been demoted from solvable homicide to rarely answered ghettocide.

A goddamned no-account ghettocide.

25

Until 1960, the miles of Los Angeles County–owned property that lay beneath the endless stretches of high-voltage power lines were considered near worthless. Then an entrepreneurial tree farmer made Southern California Edison a lease offer for a few unused acres. More than fifty years later, almost every square foot of real estate below the massive So Cal Edison and DWP transmission towers was greened with trees and shrubbery. It became a perfect marriage between the utility monopolies and needy urban and suburban nurseries.

Compton's power line greenbelt ran east to west along the city's southern boundary, flanking aptly named Greenleaf Street. Over the course of the previous half decade, many of the nursery owners who had leased property below the crackling, high-voltage towers had been unceremoniously bought out by Pizza Wing Enterprises.

On July Fourth, Frosty took a few moments to stretch out his arms as he walked, his fingertips tracing the leaves of young Indian laurels, *Ficus benjaminas*, *Acacia salinas*, and African sumacs. Looking down as he traipsed through the aisle, he relished the one thing that was worth dirtying his Jordans over: rich, freshly turned earth. If Frosty hadn't been there for business, he'd have been tempted to discard his shoes and run barefoot through the man-grown jungle.

"Stop kickin' dirt!" bitched Tuba. The trio was marching single file: Lil Rod at point, Frosty bringing up the rear, Tuba in the middle. "That dust you makin' is up my nose already."

"Niggas? Both you better learn to like this dirt," said Frosty. "'Cause ain't no more Pizza Wing for you."

"Pizza *Wang*," corrected Lil Rod, trying to lighten the mood.

Due to the holiday, the nursery was abandoned. They had parked in the dusty lot and Frosty had walked the pair of idiot gangsters for a solid five minutes, ushering them a quarter-mile deep into the tree farm.

"Why all these big mothers in boxes 'stead a' the groun'?" asked Tuba, remarking that every tree had its roots individually crated by size.

"Tha's some of the shit you'll learn workin' this farm," answered Frosty.

"Shiz. I really liked makin' pizza," said Tuba.

"About the discipline," said Frosty. "Gotta ask yourselves. Are you slippin'? Or are you do or die?"

"Fuck you," forced Lil Rod. "I'm all do and all die."

The pathway emptied into a small clearing with a half dozen sawhorses, stacks of pre-cut redwood, and blocks of concrete set in the dirt, each with heavy gauge rebar protruding at expanding angles like unfinished sculptures.

And there was Julius. The boss man sat atop a sun-warped picnic table. He held a framing hammer, expertly tossing it, letting it flip double-gainers before catching it by the rubberized grip.

"Here's where we make the tree boxes," began Julius. "These concrete squares here with the rebar stickin' out? These are the molds. That's so I can hire a coupla los stupidos like you all to assemble tree boxes without any worry they gonna fuck my shit up."

"Yo, J," burst Lil Rod. "I can 'splain that shit las' night—"

"You like your guns, dontcha?" interrupted Julius. "Make ya feel you all powerful? Shit. When I was twelve, I could clear the block with pop-pop-pop. Windows close. Doors. Car alarms go off. Now I thought that was power."

"Wasn't like that, J," argued Lil Rod.

"Hold your gums and open your dumb fuckin' ears," angered Julius. "No more flippin' pizzas for you. You're gonna learn to work shit the way Frosty 'n' Big O learned. Hard-ass labor. Discipline. Now there's where the real power come from."

"Yessuh," nodded Tuba. "Sling hammers 'steada pizzas. I'm good for whatever you says."

Big Otis emerged from behind a stack of boxes, wiping his hands on his baggy jeans.

"We at hammer time yet?" asked Big Otis.

"Soon 'nuff," said Julius. "First I wanna knows what happened at my hole."

"Shit, yeah, that," blurted Lil Rod. "We was—"

"Shut up!" interrupted Tuba, revealing the bubbling menace just beneath his skin. "I'll tell it."

"See my ears, Fat T?" said Julius. "They open."

"We was at your hole," explained Tuba. "Right after we finished up at the Wing. We got us some Mountain Dews 'n' went on over like you said to."

Tuba disregarded the sideways glare Lil Rod delivered before taking an extra half step near Tuba, who hardly shrunk.

"When we got to the hole, there was this homeless dude in it. With a blinkin' light he stole. Lookin' for some kinda shit. We told 'im it wasn't his hole to be messin' in. And in a weird way he started givin' lip. Cursin' us 'n' all kinda shit. That's when Lil Rod got into it—you know—like, he started bangin'."

"Hey, motherfucker!" spat Lil Rod. "You was bangin' jus' like me!"

"Fuck yeah, I was bangin'!" defended Tuba. "I thought he was shootin' back so I shot too."

"But Lil Rooster here was first on the trigger?" confirmed Julius.

"He was," confirmed Tuba.

"An' I'm sayin' it wasn't all me!" defended Lil Rod.

"No," agreed Julius. "You both shot the shit outta that nigga. Lil nigga I really liked. You know he had sled dogs he named after his favorite homies from Black History Month?"

"Didn't know, J," said Tuba. His eyes downcast as if Mush Man's death were his fault.

"See that right there?" pointed Julius with the hammer. "Tuba feels sorry for the shit he done. He got remorse."

"Yeah? I got me remorse," insisted Lil Rod. "Got all the sorry you need, J."

"Bullshit," groaned Big Otis.

"He right," agreed Julius. "Lil Rod? You ain't got no remorse in you."

"You want me to feel bad?" asked Lil Rod. "Then I'll feel bad if you say I gotta."

"Not at all," said Julius. "You don't need to feel bad. That's 'cause Tuba there? Lookit him. He's got enough feel bad for ten Lil Rods. Ain't that right, Tuba?"

"Sorry, boss," upped Tuba. "My bad . . . My really bad."

With their focus on the boss, both Tuba and Lil Rod forgot Frosty was standing behind them. Neither saw Frosty quietly retrieve the rusty clawhammer from atop a nearby sawhorse. Nor did they witness Frosty cock it, left elbow pointed at his target like a baseball pitcher prepped to unleash a fastball. Frosty delivered the hammer from an angle of two o'clock to eight o'clock, the claw penetrating deep into Tuba's skull a half inch in front of his left ear. There was the muffled crack as the skull split. Tuba's knees gave way. As his body dropped and Frosty extracted the hammer, Tuba's ear came with it and frisbeed. The disconnected and bloodied ear slapped Lil Rod's cheek, lodging between his skin and shirt collar.

Lil Rod, his skeletal face a freeze-frame of shock and fright, defensively lifted his arms as if he expected the next blow to land somewhere on his skull. He heard Julius and Otis laughing behind him.

"Lookit that dead nigga twitch," ordered Julius. "That's what bein' a sorry-assed fuckup gets you. You hear me, Lil Dick? I got no needs for remorseful motherfuckers. Jus' niggas that own their shit. Ya feel me?"

"Yessuh, Mr. J," shook Lil Rod, his eyes unable to avert from Tuba's convulsing carcass.

"Now, before Frosty there learns you how to make tree boxes," explained Julius. "He gonna show you how dead niggas get buried in Compton."

Frosty pushed over a shovel. The wooden handle landed at Lil Rod's feet.

"He gonna tell you where to dig, how deep, and all that shit," continued Julius. "You do it right, listen hard, and you won't have to join Mr. Sorry-Ass Tuba."

Stiff to the point of cramping, Lil Rod mustered a nod.

"Now, you need to ask me why you still alive."

"Why . . . why 'm I alive?" stammered Lil Rod.

"'Cause your brain ain't finished growin' yet," said Julius. "Room left in there to learn some shit. Not jus' how to work hard. But work right."

Julius let go of the framing hammer he'd been flipping non-stop. Before the tool thumped to the dirt he was retreating with Big Otis trailing behind.

"Pick it up," ordered Frosty, referring to the shovel.

Lil Rod retrieved the four-foot garden spade, lifting it as if it were an alien tool. He trudged after Frosty. With each step, though, his nerve began to return. A brief idea flashed. With one swing of the shovel, Lil Rod could easily drop Frosty and take off running. But how far could a baby gangster get before one of Julius's unlimited gang tentacles snagged him by the ankles and dragged him under? Permanently.

Some thirty yards beyond where Tuba lay dead, Frosty used the murder weapon to mark out a rough six-by-three-foot rectangle.

From his back pocket he extracted a pair of oil-stained work gloves and tossed them at Lil Rod.

"Lesson one," said Frosty. "Gloves keeps your baby skin from getting all blisters."

Lil Rod dug, learning to use his foot and his ever-so-slight 140 pounds as leverage to sink the shovel into the dirt. After retrieving Tuba's body with a wheelbarrow, Frosty sat in silence, watching Lil Rod sweat and plow that spade into the ground until his reedy muscles shook. Once the hole was no less than four feet deep, Tuba's body was deposited and Lil Rod was assigned to fill in the hole. The final act was up to Frosty, who employed a gas-operated pneumatic forklift to move a four-year-old California walnut tree in a thirty-six-inch container. Frosty expertly lowered the tree box squarely atop the grave, returned the lift to its shed, and cut the engine. As he climbed out, he discovered Lil Rod had chased him all the way from the scene of the crime.

"How many?" asked Lil Rod, drenched, out of breath, yet piqued with excitement. "You know. Niggas buried here at the nursery?"

"Not for you to know," said Frosty. "All you need to worry over is doin' what you're told and keepin' your skinny shit aboveground."

26

Covina, California. 11:12 a.m.

Tim Gilligan's July Fourth began as a disappointment. His first divorced family—or "family number one" as his soon-to-be ex-wife number two called them—had plans to spend the holiday on a powerboat on Nevada's Lake Mead. The compromise Tim negotiated was to treat his twin fourteen-year-old boys with a holiday breakfast before they hit the highway with their mother and step-daddy. After stuffing themselves to the gills on an all-you-can-eat pancake special at the Fontana Courtyard Marriott, Tim bid his boys so long and was back on the road, pointing his DWP-owned Hyundai back toward the San Fernando Valley. Because family number two had evening plans with their Santa Clarita cousins, Tim's daddy time with his five- and three-year-old daughters had been relegated to a four-hour afternoon window at Burbank's Chucky Cheese.

In Tim's hungover opinion, he'd drawn two shitty July Fourth hands. Then, as if the stomach acid in his mouth weren't foul enough, he found himself on the receiving end of a group text from the DWP's Office of Emergency Management while re-fueling his company car.

Another flippin' blowout.

Or so Tim had incorrectly guessed. With one hand operating the pump and the other holding his smartphone, he was reading a missive about an accidental electrocution involving a sheriff's department crime-scene tech when the text dissolved to an officious DWP publicity photo of Catalina Rincon. He could choose to reject or accept her mobile phone call.

"I was just reading about it," Tim answered.

"Reading about what?" wondered Cat after a half-second pause.

"Some kind of accident," said Tim. "Compton blowout. You didn't get the emergency text?"

"I'm driving," said Cat. "Where are you?"

"Kinda halfway between Fontucky and Burbank."

"Fontucky?"

"It's what some people call Fontana—cuzza the racetrack and all the rednecks out this way."

"And why the hell you out there?"

"What do you need, Cat?" shifted Tim.

"Need to talk."

"It's a holiday. And I didn't read enough of that text to know if I'm gonna have to deal with somethin' more with the Compton hole."

"That's what I need to talk to you about."

"Thought you said you didn't read the text."

"I don't know shit about a text!" Cat's voice pierced through the tiny speaker. "Now, where can we meet? Like, right now!"

"Where are you?" asked Tim.

"Almost downtown. But the freeways are clear so I can pretty much go anywhere."

"Head east on the ten," instructed Tim. "There's a Chili's in Covina. Right off the freeway. North side."

"Twenty minutes," finished Cat before abruptly hanging up.

The Covina Chili's was spitting distance from the Interstate, set cozily amongst a cornucopia of franchise restaurants, chain retail stores, replanted palm trees and sprouting evergreen shrubbery to soften the acres of concrete, stucco, and stacked faux stone trim. Tim secured himself in a comfortable booth and returned to that emergency text.

fatal electrocution . . . crime scene tech . . .
lasd homicide detectives . . .

Tim scrubbed his fingertips over his wispy scalp, instantly feeling the cold transfer from his beer mug. He thought about whom to call. Carefully. Because of the holiday, those in the know would all be on-site. Tim guessed it would be the emergency engineer with the least seniority. Tim dialed and, sure enough, he connected with Adesh Singh.

Don't ask Tim. Just listen and don't give yourself away.

So listen he did, making certain whatever questions he asked sounded innocent or tinged with surprise. He made mental notes only, forgoing his usual scrawl on cocktail napkins. Then he waited for Cat to crawl in.

"What the hell are you wearing?" Tim asked before Cat could so much as slide into the booth.

The DWP board member, known for her crisp fashion, was in a pink T-shirt with a silk-screened Barbie logo that traveled armpit to armpit, teal foam-rubber flip-flops, and black yoga pants with the price tag still attached to a front pocket. It wasn't until Cat removed her oversized sunglasses that he noticed the bruise underneath her left eye.

"Couldn't go back to my house. It's the goddamn Fourth of July. Quickest place I could get a change of clothes was Walmart."

"Who were you with?"

"Who was I . . ." stammered Cat. "A man didn't do this . . . At least, not directly. I was out for a run."

Tim wondered if the beer had already gone to his head. Or if last night's abuse had left so much residual ethanol in his veins that half a draft of suds had left him missing beats.

"Sorry," said Tim, "you've lost me."

"I went for a run in the arroyo," said Cat, leaning in across the table. "It was early. Like, zero dark early. And I was being followed."

"By who?"

"Not sure. To get away I had to squeeze under the golf course fence. That's how this had to happen." Cat mimed a circle on her face, then splayed her fingers to show off her scratched mitts. "And don't say it was a stalker. Never seen the guy or the car before."

"Guy in a car?"

"Black guy in a car. And the way he was looking at me? Those eyes? I knew right then and there."

"I'm sorry," said Tim, even more confused. "But what does that have to do with the blowout in Compton?"

"It has to do with Hal Solomon!"

"You find out something?" leaned Tim. "You told me that it was just the way it looked. Carjacking."

Cat shifted in her seat, looked for her yoga pants pocket, discovered the hanging tag, and snapped it free. Next she retrieved a folded news clipping. Damp. Carefully, with fingernails only, she peeled the parts from itself and laid the article in front of Tim.

"It was glued to my windshield."

Noting the font and print style, Tim recognized the clipping was from the *Los Angeles Daily News*. In the upper left corner was a two-by-one-inch black-and-white photo of Hal Solomon followed by a headline and short story sketching the DWP board member's untimely murder.

"Son of a bitch . . ." mumbled Tim. "You said Hal had nothing to do with anything."

"I said 'probably' or 'most likely,' but not 'nothing.'"

"Hal was having second thoughts," worried Tim, working through the possibilities. "But you said you had it handled."

"Think this is just a warning," cautioned Cat, an accusing finger pointing at the news clipping. "Keeping us to our commitment."

"Christ's sake. I haven't stepped out or indicated . . . Have you?"

"You know I haven't," said Cat.

Tim sat back, his head on a slow-motion side-to-side swivel.

"What?" asked Cat.

"The blowout."

"So? What's that got to do with our deal?"

"Someone got killed last night." Tim cleared his throat. "On the site. Homicide. Some vagrant—or at least that's what I got from my guy."

"What's the blowout got to do with us?"

"Crime scene," said Tim. "And one of the techs came in contact with an old transmission line."

"You mean *your* transmission line?"

"*Our* transmission line," Tim reminded, nodding equally slow. "Electrocuted. Dead. An accident for sure. But she's dead all the same."

Cat's eyes were swimming. Her elbows came off the table and she let her back pop the padded rest behind her. She was at a loss for words, let alone a coherent thought on the matter.

"So far it's just an accident," reminded Tim. "Sheriffs' don't know or probably care that we don't run power underground anymore. Family of the tech, maybe the union'll make waves. But how long does a lawsuit take? Keeps it internal. Gives us time—if we're lucky—to find a workaround."

"And if *you* don't find a workaround?" she pressed, though her tone was more rhetorical.

Tim heaved with his big chest and let his eyes rest upon hers. In his view, she was scrubbed of any of her usual hotness. Cat appeared small and weak and hardly the kind of soldier with whom one would want to share a foxhole.

"Without a workaround?" Tim asked. "We're screwed."

"Then fucking find one," Cat insisted. "And fast."

27

Altadena. 1:00 p.m.

It wasn't like Gonzo to chase. When she was angry at Lucky, she preferred to disappear into an array of errands—keeping her out of the house and the offender out of her periphery. Her secondary reaction was to seek a soft spot to recline, stretch out her nearly six feet of limbs, and play endless hands of solitaire on her phone.

July Fourth was different.

While Lucky showered once again, dressed for a hot day, and gathered up pieces of a clean uniform, his lover and co-parent nipped at his heels in full protest.

"You, most of all, should get this," defended Lucky. He speed-sifted through the hallway closet, where Gonzo usually deposited the dry cleaning.

"Maybe I should," agreed Gonzo, if only halfheartedly. "And maybe I'm not the least bit out of line to expect more."

"More," repeated Lucky. If it was a question, he didn't voice it as such.

"Our first Fourth as a family," reasoned Gonzo. "I get you're on the clock tonight. But that's not until nine. Between now and then *we* had plans."

"Barbecue," agreed Lucky, keeping up his string of one-word retorts. He paired some regulation green work pants with a khaki L.A. Sheriff's shirt and hustled toward the kitchen.

"Think of the kids."

"Right now I'm thinkin' 'bout Mush Man."

"He's not your family."

"'Least I got a family." Lucky opened and browsed the refrigerator for something portable to square his hunger. The appliance buzzed loudly. "Didn't we get this fixed?"

"Just this once," pressed Gonzo. "All I'm asking."

"Mush had nobody but his dogs," said Lucky, choosing a box of leftover chicken legs from Popeye's. "I'd bring 'em home if they hadn't near killed me already."

"How come I never heard of this Mush Man till today?"

"Are you really gonna do this to me?" said Lucky, finally facing her, his arms awkwardly loaded with dry cleaning, a four-day-old box of chicken, and in addition to his service pistol, a pair of SIG Sauer 1911 .45s—one a standard Fastback model, the second a small, seven-shot Ultra Compact for his boot.

"You're doing it to *us*."

"To *us*? Or *you*?"

"Goddamnit! You're not a detective this time!" argued Gonzo. "You're just a TO. So, let the homicide crew do their job!"

"Dead homeless guy in a hole? Please. Someone used him for target practice. It's already a write-off."

"It's not your job."

"I don't do this, nobody will."

"Then leave it and do it tomorrow!"

Lucky shook his head no. He'd already explained himself. If the streets and potential sources were left unworked for forty-eight hours, chances of finding Mush Man's shooters fell to south of nothing.

"We're going without you, then," was all Gonzo could muster.

"Have fun," Lucky returned, attempting a kiss to her cheek. She held up a hand and turned. The rebuff spoke volumes.

Lucky made a move for the front door, slowing at the doorway to Travis's room. Relieved to see the boy was blissfully lost under his headphones, face stuck eighteen inches from the game on his computer screen. Lucky notched at least one child who hadn't recorded the fight.

But where was Karrie? Lucky knocked on her door, then peeked inside. The room was practically wall-to-wall purple with a bed so tidy it would have passed boot-camp inspection, impossibly neat for a teenager.

You're an asshole, Luck. Not cut out for this family hooey.

Viewing the household from his gutter-high prism, Lucky knew they deserved a better husband and father. He liked them all. Loved them, even. Would gladly bleed to death for any one of them. Despite that, he'd yet to find a comfort zone within that nuclear structure that rivaled anything he felt on the street. Lucky's bloom came on the job, in or out of uniform. Until those feelings flipped to something otherwise, he'd have to keep up the pretending.

Fake it till you make it, ass-cactus.

"Hey," greeted Karrie, in jogging shorts and a retro Nirvana T-shirt. She was leaning up against Lucky's '99 Vic, arms crossed with what appeared to be automated disappointment.

"Found you," played Lucky. "You mind?"

Karrie opened the rear door for Lucky, where he hung his dry-cleaned uniform.

"Just want you to know that I get it," said the teenager. She'd either heard the argument from outside or possessed astonishing perception.

Lucky straightened and got momentarily lost in her preciously freckled face. He saw the part of him that desired to be her father and protector. The connection was palpable. If she had asked him to stay for the day, he might not have been able to deny her.

"I get it," Karrie repeated. "You gotta do what you can for that Mushy guy. Find his killer."

"Gonna give it a go," said Lucky.

"Then what?"

"Then we'll see," said Lucky.

The teenager nodded her understanding, pushed up onto her tiptoes, and kissed Lucky on the cheek before wrapping him up in a forever grateful hug.

"Don't really like fireworks anyway," she finished.

"Yeah," said Lucky. "Me neither."

The teenager stood on the driveway and regarded Lucky as he backed into the street, reversed gears, and rumbled away. It wasn't aloud, but Karrie could hear her own sage voice as if in prayer.

Yea, though he walks through the valley of the shadow of death . . .

28

L.A. Sheriff's Station. Compton. 9:02 p.m.

The moment Lucky glimpsed him, the words of the late, great New York Yankee Yogi Berra pinged between his ears.

It's like déjà vu all over again.

Leaning against the front right fender of Lucky and Shia's assigned black-and-white was the familiar, lanky Atom Blum. The boy wonder was identically dressed as he had been the night before, replete with that form-fitting Kevlar riot vest. The only addition to his look was a bandage to his broken nose, a clear plastic shell protecting the injured appendage.

"Sir," said Shia from behind Lucky. "Lieutenant wants to talk."

"Night number three," said Lucky. "No more of your 'sir' shit."

Shia trailed Lucky to Lieutenant Torres's office, a cramped utilitarian box no larger than most public bathrooms, and poorly lit despite the waist-high window facing the busy corridor that cut between the men's locker room and the dispatcher's bay.

"Screen test?" began Torres. "Seriously?"

Lucky gave a sideways glance at his trainee. The set of her jaw gave nothing away. From whoever or however Torres had heard about the duo's mistreatment of their ride-along, it hadn't come from the trainee.

"And if he asked for a demonstration?" asked Lucky, not at all trying to sound convincing.

"Really?" The sarcasm in Torres's voice was further enhanced by his comical mustache.

"Technically, yes," answered Lucky.

"Okay," straightened Torres. "Let's say he's a big, ripe asshole. Racist, annoying beyond reason, whatever. Can't imagine what he could've done that would've deserved getting his nose broke."

"Is that a question?" asked Lucky.

"As in, do I wanna know what kind of douche-knob behavior incited the incident?" waxed Torres. "Not really. Because *that* Hollywood shit-heel is buddy-buddy with the assistant goddamn sheriff. Paul McGill? Heard of him? Yeah? Our Captain Daniels gets a call from him this morning, inquiring as to if Compton Station has an initiation policy that involves giving all new deputies a surprise 'screen test.'"

Torres punctuated his annoyance with a pair of comical air quotes.

Comfortably partnered deputies might have quietly guffawed at the lieutenant's phrasing. Even Torres might have betrayed his authority with a semi-understanding smile. Yet Lucky's de facto manner was to give little away in both words and body language. And Shia, from her training officer's perspective, showed stalwart control, nary a muscle twitch but for the occasional pulse of tension where her mandible attached to her temporal bone.

"So ask me why Mr. Blum is back for a second ride-along?" Torres knuckle-rapped his desk.

"Why?" played Lucky.

"Because the assistant sheriff didn't have an appropriate response for why you did what you did," said Torres. "So he invited Mr. Blum to return to our fine and upright station for a do-over. I suggested a change of deputies. The captain agreed, as did McGill. But it was Mr. Blum that insisted on saddling up again with you two for a second go 'round. So, go figure."

Lucky and his trainee remained seated with synchronous poker faces.

"Okay," relented Torres. "What did the asshole do that got him a screen test?"

Lucky tipped his chin toward Shia to see if she had an objection. The trainee remained stoic, squarely facing her lieutenant.

"Fine," decided Lucky, "Our ride-along was—in my opinion—engaging in improper sexual advances toward—"

"Advances?" repeated Torres. "Like, he hit on you?"

"He sent me a dick pic, sir." Shia announced, her first words in the meeting.

"Sent you what?" asked Torres.

"A dick pic," repeated Shia. "From his phone to mine. A digital photo of his manscaped genitals."

"You're shitting me," said Torres.

"No, sir," confirmed Shia. "It was when I made my training officer aware that he . . . arranged . . . for our ride-along to experience the aforementioned screen test."

"Two nights in a black-and-white," said Torres, turning his attention to Lucky, "and your trainee already knows about screen tests. I expect she understands the policy against such acts."

"I am aware, sir," said Shia. "But Mr. Blum was neither a suspect nor in custody. My opinion, sir?"

"Yes?"

"Deputy Dey's actions were . . ." Shia searched for the word, not certain she'd landed on the perfect descriptor. "Chivalrous."

"Defending the honor of his trainee," Torres tried to confirm. "Is that it, Lucky?"

"I'm good with it," said Lucky. "But if a ride-along had sent snaps of his junk to a guy trainee? Not sure I woulda done it any different."

"You know," said Torres. "Let's not go out of our way to split sex identity hairs. 'Cause between you and me and ghosts of Lee Baca, this shit gives me a migraine."

A pause followed as Torres tried to untangle the wires in his brain. Across his desk, the duo was in tandem, reading each other's body cues with little more than peripheral glimpses.

"What do we do?" shrugged Torres.

"Your call," said Lucky.

"A dick pic? Jesus."

"I'm good if Mr. Blum wants another ride-along," volunteered Shia. "I'm pretty sure he'll behave."

"And if he doesn't?" asked Torres.

"We return him to the station. And what the assistant sheriff doesn't know . . ." Lucky left the rest unsaid.

Sated, Torres released Lucky and his deputy sidekick to a third night of training and bid them "good luck and be safe" before shutting his office door behind them.

Four strides down the corridor, Lucky broached the subject. "Dick pic?" he said, suspicious as hell.

"I might've had the timing wrong," confessed Shia. "But douchebag sent more than one. Woke up around four this afternoon, my phone blowing up. Each pic in various stages of attention, if you know what I'm sayin'."

"Lucky you."

"For every dick pic he sent, I returned him a photo of a chlamydia-infected genital," she shrugged. "Seemed to do the trick for the moment, sir."

"Sir?"

"Lucky."

"And don't you forget it."

29

Compton.

Shallow blooms of fireworks sprouted from inside the walls of Compton's Woodlawn Cemetery. An extensive party had assembled inside the historic walls. Some fifty Independence Day revelers, armed with a cornucopia of illegal rockets, mortars, and malt liquor, joined the hundreds of buried dead, including the eighteen Civil War veterans interned beneath the monthly mown sod.

The historic graveyard, designated a Los Angeles Historic Landmark in 1946, had since suffered a dubious legacy. As the Crips, Bloods, and Sureños gangs ran roughshod over Compton in the seventies and eighties, Woodlawn had become even more famous as the funeral ground for countless young men, mostly black—victims of a ceaseless war over turf, drugs, and foolish pride. By the turn of the twenty-first century, the approximately ten acres had become overcrowded and so shoddily managed that graveside visitors would find randomly scattered human bones poking through the grass like skeletal fingers grasping for a mid-day scare.

All four windows of the black-and-white were rolled down and the dry Compton air was tinged with whiffs of spent sulfur and weed. The constant cacophony of crackles and pops made it nearly impossible for even the best ears to distinguish between the firecrackers and actual gunfire.

Lucky, though, wasn't listening for gunshots as much as he was for loud whistles.

Barely an hour into the shift, Atom Blum had fallen asleep in the back seat of the unit. This came as no surprise considering that upon being reunited with his ride-along hosts, he'd bragged about having caught no sleep whatsoever since the previous evening's hijinks.

Shia had a notion the time might be ripe to ask her training officer about the plastic container he'd secured just forward from the center console.

"So you gonna tell me what's in the Tupperware?" asked Shia.

Lucky fired her a sideways look. Knowing. Yet without recrimination for the knowledge he held.

"Okay, so I peeked," admitted Shia, slightly unnerved that he'd pegged her well enough to make the assumption—and that with just one look from him she could practically read his words.

"What you need to know?" asked Lucky.

A call came across the Box, directing the nearest units to Woodlawn, ostensibly to shut down the block party, confiscate whatever was illegal—be it unspent fireworks, liquor, or drugs—give warnings, and scatter the participants.

"Not worth our time," announced Lucky. "Go ahead. Ten-six us."

Shia obediently keyed the code into the computer. Next

she reached forward and popped the lid on the container. She returned her hand with a pink plastic ring around her index finger. Attached to the ring was a pink plastic whistle with a pink plastic crucifix.

"Warning. Blow it and you might wake up you know who," advised Lucky.

Shia twisted, caught a glimpse of the still-sleeping boy wonder, then twirled the ring on her finger as if to invite Lucky to explain.

"Rape whistles. Patrol confiscated 'em from some nut-job wannabe priest," explained Lucky. "He was going up and down Long Beach Boulevard, encouraging the hookers use 'em whenever a john rolled up to proposition 'em. The girls complained to the PD. Whistles ended up in storage."

"And now they're in our unit."

"What's left of 'em," winked Lucky, who went on to explain how he'd spent his afternoon and early evening instead of catching up on his sleep. Shia had already heard about Mush Man, the murder, and where the body had been recovered. She'd expressed her condolences to Lucky, assuming she'd properly read his affection for the homeless character. He'd barely muttered thanks. After, she thought that was that.

But now as Lucky told it, he'd covered Compton corner to corner, seeking out Mush Man's fellow street people. He had given one of those pink rape whistles to whoever he could, strongly encouraging them to blow it loudly at any deputy driving by if they had discovered or unearthed any information that might lead to Mush Man's killers. Lucky promised a crisp hundred-dollar bill from his own pocket as a reward.

Shia was moved. Impressed, even.

"Homeless don't have cell phones to call in tips," she admired. "So give 'em whistles. Nice."

"Probably a dry hole. But worth a shot."

"So . . ." said Shia. She was unconsciously flicking the plastic pink crucifix with her index finger. "We're listening for whistles tonight *instead* of gunshots."

"Go easy on Jesus there?" suggested Lucky. "Think maybe he suffered enough."

"Didn't take you for Catholic."

"Too late for me."

"Not the way I heard it."

As usual, Lucky chose a poker-faced reply. As if trading any more words wasted time and attention. To the northwest, he could track the sparks from rockets rising from behind Woodlawn's stone ramparts. To the thrill of those partying amongst the gravestones, there would be a burst of gold and green against the low, gray-black sky.

"Last question." Shia twirled the rape whistle on her middle finger. "Can I keep one for—"

"FUCK SOUP!" came a shout from the back seat.

Startled, Shia turned all the way around while Lucky merely shifted his eyes to the rearview mirror. Both cops discovered their ride-along guest in a cobwebbed, waking state.

"What . . . ?" asked Atom once he realized that both deputies had eyeballs zeroed in on him.

"You all right?" asked Shia.

"Huh?" said the director. "Why wouldn't I be?"

"Got a problem with soup?" quipped Lucky, sounding more like a mock-interrogator.

"Oh, man . . . Was this crazy dream about my stepmom making me eat bowl after bowl of mushroom barley." Atom suddenly remembered that he was in a sheriff's black-and-white, not on a psychotherapist's couch. "Whatever . . . Guess I don't like soup."

"No shit," said Shia.

"So here's my question. Are we gonna get into some actual shit tonight?" shifted Atom.

Lucky caught the boy wonder's expectant expression. It crinkled the white tape employed to secure that clear, nose-shaped protective cup centering his face.

"On patrol," measured Lucky. "Means we take what comes."

"As long as what comes is some serious cop shit," replied Atom. "I'm all good."

The director left little to the imagination. His obvious and rather entitled expectancy had surely been fueled by his relationship with the department's number two in command.

"Asshole," whispered Lucky under his breath.

30

Culver City. 11:50 p.m.

"Goddamnit, nigga!" angered Julius into the disposable burner phone he kept in the pocket of his spa-styled robe. "Call me back, you fat fuck."

He shut his eyes and coaxed himself to breathe slowly in the elevated air of his Culver City loft.

The new lease property came with a bounty of luxury amenities. On the gentle slope south of the Santa Monica freeway, the fifth-floor corner space boasted twenty-five hundred square feet of hardwood with sparkling floor-to-ceiling views of the old MGM studio lot and beyond, Los Angeles International Airport, and the South Bay. The basement gym rivaled most of the better-known monthly fitness clubs. There was a rooftop pool, a garden atrium, synthetic putting green, four tennis courts, and even an indoor climbing wall. But best of all for Julius, the complex was approximately halfway between Compton and West Hollywood, where, some three or four nights a week, Julius poured himself into a Lycra muscle shirt and cruised the nightclub scene in search of anonymous gay sex. His come-hither line to prospective hookups hadn't changed in years.

Ever done it with a Blaxican?

And if the propositioned young stud were to answer glibly in the affirmative?

Are you a Blaxi-can? Or a Blaxi-can't?

Julius kept his secret sex life separate from his ever-expanding Cholo Original empire. In both black and Hispanic gang cultures, no tolerance was given to alternate lifestyles, especially that of a homosexual man. To be gay was to be shamed. If even a scent of Julius's private proclivities were to trickle down to the streets, he'd be rolled up and assassinated for sport or bragging rights. Thus Julius's need for his business plan to grow exponentially beyond the ghetto and into more legitimate and progressive real estate. Only then could his virtual closet door be demolished.

The condo's lease agreement contained the basic prohibitions. No smoking. No drugs. Noise abatements. Hot tub hours. And no more than two pets, none weighing more than twenty pounds. The pet clause demanded a thousand-dollar surcharge to the security deposit.

Goddamn Otis and goddamn dogs!

It had been forty-one minutes since Julius had begun calling Big Otis in anal-retentive five-minute intervals. His fat man Friday had asked for, and been afforded, the holiday evening to spend with Inglewood cousins. The big man had delivered Julius along with all four of Mush Man's orphaned beasts to the Culver City condo. Otis then made a quick run to Kmart for provisions, including four huge dog beds, a fifty-pound bag of top-priced kibble, feed bowls, a two-gallon water dispenser, collars, and leashes.

The original plan had been for the dogs to overnight at a kennel. But with the holiday, no doggie hotel in a twenty-five-mile radius had room. Plan B should have been for Julius to dump the animals on one of his employees. Instead, a heartstring inside had been plucked. The idea of spending the holiday evening on his apartment balcony, four furry friends for company, smoking a genuine Cuban cigar and sipping twenty-five-year-old McCallan while watching the various fireworks displays had tugged at Julius in a rare romantic way.

Then came the fireworks.

With the distant but sharp *pop-pop-pop* of exploding rockets and firecrackers, Hank, the youngest of the mongrels, panicked and began tearing about the condo, scratching for an exit. His unmanicured toenails scored every surface. And when Julius tried to leash the beast, the animal cornered itself, growled, and snapped at his would-be-savior.

Julius wanted to beat the stuffing out of the mutt for his sheer ingratitude. Instead, he withdrew to the kitchen for some raw meat in hopes of salving the poor dog. As he crossed to the center island, the strip-mall king stepped in a fresh pile of hot dung. It squished under his bare left foot, warm and slippery. Julius skidded and crumpled to the floor with a gooey splat. He scrambled, found a grip on the travertine cap, and quickly righted himself.

"Muthuh-FUCKER!"

It was downhill from there. If only Julius could have thrown open his front door and released the hounds without any repercussions from the homeowners' association. But for sweet Oprah, Julius realized, he couldn't identify Rosa from Thurgood from Hank. With the passing hours and the unabated sound of fireworks, Julius discarded his clothes into a trash bin, steamed himself clean in the shower, then surrendered to his bedroom balcony with a bottle of cold Chablis in lieu of the scotch he'd earmarked to go with that Cuban reserve cigar. He shut the glass slider behind him, sat in a lounger, and speed-dialed Big Otis in five-minute increments. He was halfway through the bottle before he remembered to snip and light the cigar. He reached into his shorts pocket for a cutter, only to come up with a plastic pink rape whistle.

Oh, yeah, he replayed. In his zeal to give the big mutts a home for the night, Julius had all but forgotten the silly pink whistle with the attached crucifix, gifted him by a young Crip brother from his stable of legitimate employees. A homeless woman—unhinged by her cravings—traded the whistle and a rotted mouthful of information for a quarter gram of meth. She talked of a sheriff's deputy named Lucky who was willing to pay Benjamins for information leading to the identity of Mush Man's killer. She gleefully added how much she hated the little vagrant and his foul dogs who'd scared her witless at every encounter.

"Whistle," Lucky had said to her. "If you know anything, whistle when you see a black-and-white."

Julius placed the whistle between his lips and pushed the minimum measure of air to make it barely audible. It gave a faint, high-pitched wail. And with it the rage inside him swelled—a primordial call to his lizard brain. He blew again. Louder. The piercing noise provided no release. If anything, it was as if a fuse had been lit. For a third and last time, Julius blew—his full lungs into it. The little pink rape whistle screamed at the night.

Motherfuckin' Reaper.

It was like a dam had broken. The memories flooded in. Julius felt as if he were right back where he'd started. Fifteen years young. Crip blue and slingin' rock. Crack cocaine. As a baby banger, finding free corners to sell on had been next to impossible with so many of the competition willing to pop a nine into a young gangster's brain. On top of that, there had been the constant street exposure and never-ending running rabbit from the PD.

Julius's answer had come with the Catholic church and school, Our Lady of the Angels—aptly nicknamed Our Lady of the Ghetto. The grams the boy slinger sold through the Gault Street fence soon came with him to mass. Word spread that the mixed-race young gun in the back right pew was making dope deals between the Apostles' Creed and the reading of the Eucharistic Prayer.

And business was very good.

So good that Julius built his entire crack-dealing routine around the mass schedules of other outlying Catholic churches. One fair Easter, after a midnight vigil at Maria Regina in North Hawthorne, four sheriff's Reapers from Lennox Station met up with the young dope dealer and, instead of making a juvenile arrest, decided both the teen and community would be better served if Julius was taught a lesson about respecting local institutions dedicated to "bettering the hood."

The following dawn, as natty worshippers in blue and yellow pastels made their way to Maria Regina's sunrise mass, the reverent parishioners were aghast by the image of a crack-slinging baby banger, stripped naked but for his tightie whities, duct-taped to the tall parish cross like a living crucifix.

And so the memory burned in Julius.

Then he caught himself. *Purge the negative thoughts*, he reasoned. After all, the past was the past—or so his better self argued. Vengeance had upended the trajectory of many an entrepreneur. Unproductive thinking was antithetical to profit. Julius had listened to hours upon hours of success-themed audiobooks, each pounding the salient point home. With that, his mind swerved back to the dogs. The untrained mutts would soon find a short-term home with L.A. County's Animal Care and Control. If not adopted within a week—which Julius seriously doubted—the beastly foursome would be destroyed.

A week to live. Not bad.

Miles better, he reasoned, than the death sentence Julius and his not-so-better judgment were readying to level on the Reaper deputy. Not as an act of revenge—or so was his weak rationale. Julius was convincing himself it was smart business. The less known about that DWP hole in Poinsettia—be it details about the unfortunate death of Mush Man or the discovery of a live electrical transmission line—the better it would be for Julius Colón and his entrepreneurial trajectory.

Excuses all.

What the self-proclaimed Blaxican businessman needed now was for Big Otis to answer his phone. Soon the damned dogs and the Reaper would be purged—from both Julius's overactive psyche and the earth.

31

Compton.

The way Lucky played it, the one-night policing of illegal fireworks was a waste of precious time. Let the other units chase Compton teens with backpacks brimming with weed, lukewarm liquor, and aerial mortars. Atom Blum was demanding action. And as far as Lieutenant Torres and his cartoon mustache were concerned, the department powers up on Temple Street were in full-fledged public relations mode. Show the movie director a good time and maybe—just maybe—he'll make the L.A. Sheriff's look heroic in his upcoming movie.

Yeah, right.

It was cynical and naïve of the downtown brass. Yet, in the moment, the presence of the obnoxious bastard in the black-and-white's back seat served Lucky's agenda.

"So what's at the other end of these whistles we're listening for?" The director kept shifting his long legs, looking for a comfortable way to stretch out in the black-and-white's back seat.

Lucky ignored him, preferring to keep his ears clear and tuned out the car's open windows. The air was populated with a constant stream of firework *pop-pop-pops*, both far and near. Because Lucky had passed the pink whistles out to some of the Compton homeless population, he stayed off the residential streets in lieu of cruising the back alleys that paralleled the more traveled boulevards.

"Looking for tips on a murder," Shia eventually answered.

"Yeah?" piqued Atom. "Who got killed?"

"Sssshhhhhhhh," hushed Lucky, signaling to his right ear.

"Fine, fine. But what kind of whistle?" asked Atom.

"Just a whistle," answered Shia, twirling one on her index finger. "Like this."

"Football whistle?"

"I guess."

"So that means I heard something you didn't hear?" grinned Atom.

Lucky drove his foot into the black-and-white's brake. The surprise force sent Atom forward, though this time he caught himself with a stiff arm.

"Trying to give me another goddamn screen test?"

"You heard a whistle where?" Lucky's question was both blunt and urgent.

"'Bout a minute back," answered Atom. "Before we turned into the alley."

Column shifting into reverse, Lucky twisted in his seat, pointed his nose at the rear window, and nearly floored the black-and-white. The tires spun first, then screeched as the vehicle lurched backward. The rear backup lights made for dim navigation. All the while, Shia kept her eyes on her side-view mirror, calculating if Lucky was going to trade paint with the junkyard furniture and abandoned appliances lining their path. In her head, Shia was already writing the vehicle damage report, her second in three nights on the job.

The unit cleared the alley without incident, launching onto

a quiet residential street, twisting ninety degrees, and chirping to a stop.

"Ssshhhhhhhh," Lucky ordered.

"Just jealous that I heard it and he didn't," said Atom, unable to help himself.

"Said shut the fuck—" Lucky clammed his own lips, his head swiveling right and looking past Shia into the dark passage where the back alley continued.

Then they *all* heard it. Clear. Pitched over the continuation of fireworks—a distinct and unmistakable toy whistle.

Shia gripped the post-mounted light and beamed it into the alley. A block deep—perhaps two hundred yards into the alley— there returned a glint. Glass. The familiar motion of a bottle lifted to a person's lips and lowered again.

Lucky spun the wheel and accelerated. Despite the headlights taking over, Shia redirected the blinding spot at two figures.

"Count two males," said Shia.

"What we got? What we got?!" infused Atom, full of antic- ipation. He leaned closer to the screen and observed Lucky unsheathing his pistol and anchoring it across the top of his thigh.

"Gimme a sweep," demanded Lucky, slowing the black-and- white to a menacing creep.

Manipulating the post-mounted light, Shia covered the sur- roundings. The car was a good fifty yards from the nearest cross street. The hotspot lit up the scene. Unpainted cinder-block walls both left and right, separated by a strip of pot-holed, semi-loose asphalt. A large apricot tree hung its branches over a backyard wall, its fruit rotted and leaving a half circle of squishy stains on the pavement. Across from the tree were two young black men. Both were dressed in black, baggy denims and silk-screened T-shirts and both were sucking back forty-ounce bottles of cheap malt liquor. To their right and slightly shielding them from Shia's spot was a dented and rusty dumpster anchored with a heavy chain and padlock.

The taller teen with a slick, flattop fade haircut was sounding a pink whistle, amusingly stuck between his teeth. The other young man wore a reissued L.A. Raiders snapback.

"They don't look homeless," said Shia.

Lucky shoved the shifter into park and popped his door. The air stunk of days-old garbage and fresh-smoked marijuana. A quick flashlight scan revealed the back door of a fish and chips fry shop, bolted and closed. And clear across the pavement, up against the opposite wall was a leftover blunt, nearly smoked to the twist, smoldering.

"In the car or outta the car?" asked Atom.

"Up to you," said Lucky, stepping out while momentarily keeping the car's heavy door between himself and the teen drinkers. Shia mirrored Lucky, unsheathing her 9mm while staying behind her open door.

Atom hoped to let the moment unfold from the safety of the back seat. But feeling obstructed by the screen and front windshield, he pushed his own door open and awkwardly climbed out, the signs of fatigue revealed in his wobbly legs.

"Whatcha drinkin'?" Lucky asked the teens, his affect benign yet cautious.

"Steel Reserve," replied Flattop.

"S'pose you could do worse," said Lucky, holstering his pistol and stepping around his door.

"Fuck, yeah," said the teen in the Raiders cap. "Ever had that piss Ice Cube sells? St. Ides?"

"Old enough to drink those?" asked Lucky.

"Nawwwww," said Flattop, slurring with a smile. "But it the Fourth of Joo-Lye."

"How 'bout you put the forties down for a minute?" From Lucky it sounded less like a request and more like a polite command. "You can get back to 'em after we talk about your whistle."

"Not my whistle," said Flattop. "But I sure as shit blow it real good, knowwhatI'msayin'?"

"Nigga we got it from said if we needed us the po-po, all we gotta do is make a noise," added Raiders Cap.

"Forties down!" reminded Shia.

"Ain't no weapon," said Raiders Cap.

"Like he said," replied Shia. "After we talk, you can go back to your drinking."

"You need the police?" asked Lucky, easing two steps closer to the pair.

"Who don' need the five-oh," laughed Flattop. He bit down again on the plastic whistle and pushed out a sharpened tweet.

"Put the bottles down!" barked Shia.

The teen in the Raiders cap mock saluted the lady deputy and gently placed his malt liquor bottle against the graffitied wall. He nudged Flattop to do the same.

"Person you got the whistle from," continued Lucky. "They have something to tell me?"

"Tell a cop?" asked Flattop. "Or tell you?"

"I'm lookin' for certain information," said Lucky.

"'Bout a dead nigga in a big hole?" grinned Flattop.

"Like that," affirmed Lucky. "Got something to tell me?"

"Whadda you pay?" asked Raiders Cap.

"If you got what I need," said Lucky. "Then you already know."

"Whadda you care about that broke-assed little nigga?" asked Flattop.

"One with the dogs, right?" clarified Raiders Cap. "Woof, woof, woof."

"Why I care is for me to know," said Lucky. "You either got information or you don't."

"We're talking a Benjamin, right?" asked Raiders Cap.

"Hundred? Shit," said Flattop. "That don' even buy me new kicks."

"Who you?" noticed Raiders Cap, catching his first real glimpse of Atom Blum behind and to the left of Shia. "Some kinda back-seat cop?"

"I'm just observing," defended Atom, his words a reminder that he was keeping his distance.

"Eyes on me," focused Lucky. "Now, you fellas either got something for me or you're wasting my time."

"Wastin' your time?" said Flattop. "You work for us, don' ya? Who wastin' whose time, nigga?"

"You blew the whistle," said Lucky, patience still in check.

"Maybe I likes me the fuckin' noise," defied Flattop, giving the whistle three quick chirps.

"One last time," said Lucky. "What do you know about the dead guy in the hole?"

"Think he said, 'Dead little nigga,'" corrected Raiders Cap. "Motherfucker wasn't worth the bottom of my sneaker, man. Why you wanna give up a Benjamin for some midget homeless toe jam motherfucker?"

Checking his watch, Lucky asked himself how much of the shift he was willing to waste on the two teens and their malt-liquor mouths. They either knew something about Mush Man or they didn't. And it wasn't as if they were negotiating for more money. Their agenda seemed first and foremost to power up on the police. Make some noise at the authority figures and brag about it later.

"You don't know shit," surmised Lucky. He was a half pivot back toward the black-and-white when the teen with the flattop fade barked at him.

"Yo, Mister Money! Where you goin'? I got what you need. Pink whistle and all!"

"Last chance," said Lucky.

"You gonna pay?" pressed Flattop.

Hands resting just above his duty belt, Lucky gave away nothing more than a willingness to give the teen one more bite at the apple. Flattop's eyes flitted, briefly landing on Shia's and Atom's faces before returning to Lucky's give-nothing stare.

"'Kay. We know somethin' about your dead nigga," said Flattop.

"He the little nigga in a hole," revised Raiders Cap.

"And . . . ," said Flattop, before releasing a grin to cue his compadre. In bad harmony, both teens delivered their punch line . . . "And he dead."

"Fuck you both," relented Lucky. "Turn around, grab some wall."

"What we do?" complained Flattop. "Now you all gonna up and harass us?"

"Now," said Lucky, one hand resting on the butt of his pistol, the other guiding both smart-assed teens to face the wall. As the pair assumed the position, each placing his hands high on the wall, it was clear they knew the turn-and-frisk drill all too well.

Shia moved in for the assist. Atom was in follow mode, leaning in at her ear.

"Can he even do that?" Atom asked.

"Underage," she said. "Liquor and dope? Mouthing off? Oh, yeah. We're on the page."

Neither Lucky nor Atom, let alone the two flap-jaw teens, noticed that tucked between Shia's duty belt and her body armor was her mobile phone, camera lens peeking out between her pepper spray holster and extra magazines. While Lucky frisked, the trainee applied both her primary and secondary sets of handcuffs. Every second of spare air was taken up by the two teens running their mouths at the unfairness of their sudden detention.

Shia spun both teens forward just as Lucky spilled both bottles of malt liquor, dumping the remaining booze onto the pavement.

"Listen up," said Lucky. "Life gives you choices. So far, you are making lousy ones. How about I give you another chance?"

Neither teen stepped up. They stood in complete indifference. Silent. Doing their level best to keep their posture unimpressed, despite their obvious predicament.

"New choice," explained Lucky. "Already got the bracelets on. So, here's what it is. Los Padrinos? Or the dumpster?"

The dumpster? Both young faces screwed into question marks. They clearly understood the part of the equation that involved Los Padrinos, the nearest juvenile lockup. It was ten miles due east and, considering the holiday, it would mean a minimum forty-eight hours' detention. But what was the other option Lucky was giving them?

"Coupla nights in Los Padrinos," Lucky repeated. "Or you both take a short hop in the dumpster."

"That dumpster right there?" asked Flattop.

"Wasted enough of my time," said Lucky. "You have five seconds to decide. One. Two. Three—"

"Dumpster!" jumped Raiders Cap.

"Yeah, yeah," agreed Flattop. "Why not? Dumpster."

"Unhook 'em," said Lucky.

Shia, who was as confused as the teens, didn't hesitate at the order. While she moved in behind the teens to key and re-holster her handcuffs, Lucky swerved to the dumpster and pushed up the lid until it clanked against the cinder-block alcove.

The teens might have wondered about their choice as one looked at the other. Then again, the handcuffs were off and the night was still ripe. They both grinned with a unified *what the hell?* Flattop climbed first with Raiders Cap close behind. They pulled themselves up and dropped into the angled mouth of the dumpster.

"Heads down," Lucky reminded.

He lowered the heavy lid, the teens dropping into a crouch before it clanged shut.

"Now what happens?" Atom found himself asking.

Lucky answered by climbing on top of the dumpster and making himself comfortable, his legs dangling over the edge, thus sealing the mouthy teens inside. Lucky didn't need to look. He knew his trainee and the ride-along would be staring back at him slack-jawed with did-he-really-just-do-that? stares.

"Hey, rook," Lucky nodded at Shia. "Radio dispatch we're ten-seven. Oh, yeah. In the trunk there's a plastic bag with waters and PowerBars. Snack time?"

Lucky swiveled his gaze over to Atom.

"Can you, like, do that?" questioned the director, who then chose to double down with Shia. "Seriously. Can you guys do shit like that?"

Shia was stuck. She remained with her boots squared on the pavement, body armor flush to Lucky on top of that dumpster.

"Rook?" cued Lucky.

"Right," Shia answered, rotating to the black-and-white's trunk, where she retrieved the bag and walked it over to Atom.

"Seriously," whispered Atom with more than a hint of excitement. "Is he allowed to detain juveniles like that?"

"He's doing it, ain't he?" was all Shia could muster before slipping back into the vehicle to attend to her business on the Box.

The teens, who'd been shouting inside the big tin can, began pounding on the walls of the dumpster in vain. The muffled complaints were mostly unintelligible. But the single syllables were most likely curses. Lucky checked his watch. The duo had been interned for barely a minute.

"I'm guessing that this, you know, right here, is outside sheriff's, you know, regular procedures?" braved Atom, handing Lucky a water and a protein bar.

"Guess that depends what side of the dumpster you're on." Lucky twisted the cap off the water bottle and sucked back a gulp before starting in on the protein bar.

The banging inside the dumpster grew louder and the boy wonder involuntarily took three steps back.

"My brother and me," said Lucky between chewy mouthfuls. "Think I was fifteen, sixteen. Tony was, like, twelve. We used to get into some stupid shit—correction—*I* used to get into shit and Tony was along for whatever ride I was on. I'd started smoking and got it in my head that I could steal a carton of Camels from this neighborhood stop 'n' shop. Tony made like he accidentally knocked over a magazine rack. I snatched the carton of smokes and headed out the back. By the time my brother met me at the other end of the alley, the store security guard had collared me. Now, me 'n' Tony were given a choice that day. Wait for the cops to come take us to juvie . . . or do some attitude adjustment time in the dumpster behind the stop 'n' shop."

Lucky punctuated the short tale with a wide, made-up grin.

"And that was the day you turned your life around," finished the director.

"Why not? Hollywood ending, right?" munched Lucky. "You gonna put that in your movie?"

As if the thought just came to him, Atom whipped out his

phone, turning it horizontally to best capture the dumpster moment cinematically.

"Nuh uh," said Lucky, index finger waving like a metronome.

Inside the black-and-white, Shia keyed in the ten-seven code, indicating to the Compton dispatcher that Lucky and his trainee were temporarily out of service. Next she retrieved her smartphone from inside her duty belt. She checked the video to see if she'd captured both picture and sound of their encounter with the two alley teens. She sped forward to where Lucky had given the boys a choice between Los Padrinos and the dumpster. She made certain the recording concluded with Lucky climbing atop the dumpster, sealing the teens inside.

Her thumbs worked fast and without error, uploading the file to a pair of email accounts. After hearing the trademark *whoooooooosh* of sent correspondence, she deleted the incriminating file from her device.

Covert task complete, Shia involuntarily glanced up through the black-and-white's windshield to discover Lucky's eyes were fixed in her direction. From that thirty-two-foot stretch, she couldn't imagine Lucky catching her betrayal. Yet still, from his perch atop the dumpster, his gaze was penetrating.

Was it accusing?

The Box pinged with a message. Shia lowered her eyes, read the missive, then pushed back out of the car.

"Message from another unit," relayed Shia. "Woman with a pink whistle over at . . ." Shia stuck her head back in the black-and-white and reread the message to make certain she didn't err. "New Wilmington Gardens."

"SCHOOL'S OUT!" Lucky rapped twice on the dumpster lid, slid off, and landed boots first on the pavement. He was half-way to the black-and-white before the boy wonder gathered there was a change in the wind.

"I'm back in the car?" asked Atom.

"Up to you," said Shia. "You can come or stick around and buy those knot-heads their next round of malt liquor."

Thursday

32

The mobile phone's buzzing radiated. The vibration amplified so loudly through the nightstand that it sounded as if it were being played through a subwoofer.

So much for silent mode.

Steve Wimminger stirred, rolled to the edge of his king mattress, and snatched up his phone before it sounded again. He cleared his throat and was preparing to answer with "Wimmer here," when he realized that it wasn't a call that had woken him. It was an email from a sender he'd flagged as critical. The attorney groaned, turned on his back, and closed his eyes in hopes of summoning the remnants of his dream. He recalled a sky filled with fireworks, and a massive expanse of grassy parkland dotted with picnicking families on blankets, enjoying the climax of a day full of Fourth of July festivities.

In the dream, Wimmer was walking hand in hand with a busy-footed five-year-old boy. He could still see the child's face turned upward in wonder at the sky. The boy had curly black hair and a face the color of a mocha latte. Though Wimmer didn't recognize the beaming kid, he knew the boy was of his making. To his giddy surprise, the child's mother grasped hold of Wimmer's other hand. Fingers laced. He felt Shia's returning smile like a spreading warmth that reached all the way to his loins.

Yes, yes. I remember the dream now. And I'm back there again.

Only Wimmer wasn't. He was awake. And the just-received email wouldn't stop tickling his semi-alert psyche. He pried his eyes open, unlocked his phone, and fumbled for his reading glasses. The sender's address would inform if it was urgent enough to interrupt his holiday slumber or if he could roll his face back into the cool pillow and will himself back into the dream.

shiasaintgeorge@lldei.com

Upon recognizing the address, Wimmer's body repeated that surge of warmth he'd felt in the dream. What were the odds he'd dreamt of her only moments before she'd emailed him? Perhaps there was a psychic connection, with the dream spurred on by some telepathic receptor hidden in his cerebral cortex.

The US Attorney's thumb clicked on the email, which came with nothing written on the subject line. There was only an attachment, which he immediately clicked on. His phone screen came alive with video. With a tweak to the volume, Wimmer was just able to hear the voices of the two teens in their hapless argument with Lucky Dey. He paused the image, rummaged in a nightstand drawer for a pair of earbuds, eventually plugging them into the phone and pumping the volume until he could match the voices to whomever was speaking.

The video unfolded with the recorder starting moments before Shia slipped it into her duty belt. In doing so, the aspect frame was reduced some thirty percent by her pepper spray and ammo holsters. The audio quality was fair enough, though, and the gist of what transpired was unmistakable, from the initial encounter to the—by Wimmer's measure—seven minutes the two teenagers were detained in the dumpster.

"Gold," he said aloud.

"Whaaaa you say?" asked Wimmer's wife of eleven years. She slid into him but kept her eyes little more than sleepy slits.

"Nothing," said Wimmer. "Go back to sleep."

"Are you sneaking porn again?" she half-sparked.

"Someone sent me an email. Really. You should go back to sleep."

Wimmer felt a hand slide from his thigh to his crotch.

"You liar," she said. "You're hard."

"Look. See?" showed Wimmer, aiming the phone screen at her.

"Too bright!" she complained. Her words came out slurred and boozy. "Anyway, I don't give a shit what you watch if it gets you hard like this."

Wimmer let her push down his boxers until he could kick them away. Then, as if to conceal any reminder of his wife's Nordic sheath, he buried his phone under a pillow, plunging the bedroom back into darkness. The trick provided instant gratification. In the opaqueness of their bungalow, Wimmer was able to imagine another wife beneath him. One from a dream, complete with skin like ebony, an unkempt spray of kinky black hair, and intoxicating breath that smelled of warm pears and saliva.

Oh, Shia . . .

33

Compton.

Over his young blockbuster career, Atom Blum had experienced plenty of head rushes. There were the red-carpet premieres and the impossible-for-the-average-male-to-date actresses willing to afford every inch of themselves for a chance to be photographed with the hit movie director. Topping the list might be his adventures with the stunt crews who performed most of the miraculous action that populated the *Roadkill* franchise. On each picture, he'd taken advantage of his position in exchange for the occasional stimulus. He'd talked himself into stunt cars and trucks and helicopters and begged the expert operators to get his heart racing. Each professional driver and pilot had wisely obliged, strapping the director in and, for insurance purposes, observing every safety concern.

Yet none of Atom's movie thrills measured up to the three-minute ride when Lucky navigated the black-and-white across the southwest corner of Compton. The Ford's eight cylinders, out of tune and knocking, strained under the deputy's heavy foot. Outside the vehicle, the city flew past. The road underneath the squeaking chassis delivered none of the smoothness Atom had experienced while driven by stunt drivers on carefully chosen roadways.

Lucky buckled his seat belt as he sped, then returned his free hand to operate the siren tones—intermittently switching between auto-wails and pulses for the desired affect. All steering was performed by his left hand, low on the wheel, relaxed as a barfly piano player's.

The black-and-white's speedometer topped out at ninety miles per hour—barely half the speed Atom had clocked with NASCAR drivers around the ovals at Ontario and Las Vegas. But the push and pull of hard braking and re-acceleration, the stomach-flipping road dips, the potholes undefeated by shock absorbers, and the unbanked, ninety-degree turns on city boulevards made for an unparalleled mash-up of excitement and concern. The boy wonder worried if he might soil his designer denims.

And as fast as it had begun, the wild drive was over. The lights and sirens were extinguished and the black-and-white's roll was reduced to a crawl. Once again the air filled with the sounds of distant fireworks. As Lucky negotiated a right turn onto Laurel, the radio car's windows filled with a forbidding stretch of real estate. The federal housing project otherwise known as the New Wilmington Gardens.

Under daylight hours, the NWG, as it was sometimes called, could have been mistaken for any other apartment complex occupying ten suburban acres. Plain. Unremarkable. The five two-story buildings were faced with taupe rough stucco. Apartments sported small balconies or patios; most of the upstairs units were outfitted with small dishes for satellite TV. On first glance, the locale appeared a rather decent place to live, especially when compared to similar classes of residences in a city as economically depressed as Compton.

Then came night, when what looked palatable by day would

morph into an unwelcome specter. The landscape bore little to no lighting but for what bled from the mostly shaded apartment windows.

The buildings appeared ghostly, unwelcome, and purposefully removed from the sidewalk. The perimeter of the property was defended by a ten-foot wrought-iron fence ornamented with spiked finials—a first defense against intruders.

The cinematic nature of the moment was unmissed by Atom Blum, his eyeballs acting as a 3-D camera logging the visuals into his organic memory.

"Damn," he said aloud. "What's this place?"

"Housing project," answered Shia.

She had only heard about the New Wilmington Gardens. It was famous amongst sheriffs working South Los Angeles County and often referenced during academy classes dealing with gangs and rivalries. At the start the new century, the NWG had served as a backdrop for countless shootouts over turf and dominance in South Compton. Despite having never laid eyes on the property, Shia couldn't help but feel as if she knew it front to back. Or rather, inch by bloody inch.

"They added a guard booth?" she remarked as if in the middle of a conversation.

"Been here?" asked Lucky.

"Nope." Shia let her eyes fall on the complex's best-illuminated feature, a reinforced sliding gate with an armed guard occupying the hut. "Feel like I know it after all the stories. Academy, you know? Last thing I heard is it's just a den. Users only. Nobody grinds over it no more . . . Kinda makes you wonder what the guard booth's for."

"Lookin' for a lady with a pink whistle. All we're here for," reminded Lucky.

Lucky nosed the black-and-white into the narrow chute for entering vehicles. If there was any question to the make, model, or affiliation of the sheriff's radio unit, all mystery was vanquished under flood lamps serving as an early warning for residents with a view.

"Mystery solved," called Shia, her voice dipping a full octave lower into a mocking, ghetto mode. "The po-po be in da house."

With barely a nod from the uniformed gate guard, semi-obscured behind a tinted, inch-thick pane of bullet-resistant laminate, the gate rattled open.

"There some kinda spooky story that goes with this place?" asked Atom.

"Yeah, and it goes like this," warned Lucky. "Whatever happens, stay the hell in the car."

"Like, what's gonna happen?" Atom's face was the picture of anticipation, pressed up against the rear passenger window like that of an eight-year-old boy only steps from his first run at Disneyland.

"Nothing's gonna happen," replied Lucky. "I'm gonna talk to a lady with a whistle. Then we ease out the way we came in."

As the black-and-white crept down the single, snaking drive that divided the complex, Atom was noting cell phone lights igniting on and behind about half the balconies and windows.

"Jeeeezus," said the director. "Who they all calling?"

"Lookouts warning the dealers," answered Shia.

The first sixty yards of the driveway was an easy hook to the right around the northernmost building, sixteen units upstairs and down. Next, the blacktop path arced back left before emptying east into a generous parking lot surrounded by a trifecta of buildings. The units faced each other in a horseshoe shape.

"Behind us," eased Shia off her glance into her side mirror.

Lucky checked his rearview. A young male in a black hoodie was trailing them, performing lazy S-curves on a bright neon yellow bicycle thirty yards to the black-and-white's rear.

The parking lot came into view. What Lucky saw there didn't make him instantly tap the brakes, but he did remove his foot from the accelerator in hopes that the slowed crawl of the vehicle would sync up with the hyper calculations his brain was crunching.

"What the hell is that supposed to be?" asked Atom.

Lucky didn't answer. Not because he didn't know. He just wanted the next words that passed his lips to be direct, understood in their urgency, and followed to perfection. Otherwise, he, his still-wet trainee, and their ride-along were all about to be very dead.

34

For the record, Frosty had thought it was a bad idea. Not that he'd voiced an actual protest or assembled some kind of written or recorded document to be able to prove his official dissent later. His only option had been to make a mental deposit into his own private complaint box.

Below him, what had begun as poor judgment on Julius's part was about to turn into a train wreck—an irreconcilable error with consequences beyond normal comprehension. Yet there Frosty lay on the tar and paper rooftop of what NWG residents and frequenters called the Trip—or less confusing, Building Number 3. Frosty was prone beside a Chinese-built AK-47 rifle, peering down over the bracket of apartment buildings that flanked the parking lot.

His orders from Julius were simple enough. As that tattooed

Reaper was lured into the New Wilmington Gardens, assassinate him with a pair of clean gunshots to the head. The boss's rationale was plain. Any cop who ventured into the NWG knew the risk and that he would be making himself into a target. Nobody would question motive. As far as residents were concerned, cops were the enemy of everything—from the simple sale of narcotics to the survival of young black men from sea to shining sea. Whatever investigation followed was sure to turn cold from sheer lack of witnesses. That's because nobody inside the NWG was dumb enough to talk to the authorities, let alone have the gonads to testify in the white man's court.

But kill a cop? What biz interest would that be for?

Had Frosty asked Julius, he was sure as hell Julius wouldn't bother with an answer. So, Frosty shifted his thinking to his own plans: a plot of property below some power lines, a below-market lease from Julius's connections with the Department of Water and Power, and all the time in the world to watch his garden grow. The greenery. The trees.

Julius got his plan. An' I got mine.

Frosty's aspirations were directly linked to his following through for the boss. And if that meant whipping a mean-hot bullet through the melon of one tattooed sheriff's deputy?

So be it. And whatever calamity comes with.

Calamity was a good word. For Frosty it had biblical-like connotations. Someone with military knowhow might have called what was forming below Frosty something even more descriptive: a clusterfuck. Were the murder plot to unfold as Julius pictured it, the black-and-white bearing the former Lennox Reaper would nose up to the building opposite Frosty. The target would step out and—*pop-pop*—a pair of high-velocity hollow-points would greet the Reaper's skull and he'd drop like a bag of planting soil.

Frosty preferred to make his own murder plans. If a homie needed to get smoked, then he was good for it. As long as things went down *his* way and on *his* schedule. But for some unknown reason, Julius was prepared to force whatever issue he had with the Reaper. And Frosty was the assigned hammer for the job.

An ocean breeze kicked up from the west. The spent sulfur from all the illegal fireworks unleashed over the skies of Carson and Torrance crossed Frosty's nostrils. The sneeze the stink summoned was quietly relieved into the crook of the gunman's arm before he returned his eyes to the problem below.

Crips on fuckin' Crips.

Some kind of post-midnight summit was in full bloom. The NWG parking lot was crammed with bangin' rides and the bad boys who rode them. Hummers to refurbished Impalas and just about every model of over-waxed ghetto buggy in between. It was no car show. It was a gathering of, by Frosty's best guess, the Wilmington Blocc Crips and, from North Long Beach, some ten Ghost City Crips, rival sets engaged in some kind of illicit exchange of weapons or drugs. Centered amongst the vehicles were a spanked-up BMW and a Plymouth Road Runner, trunk lids open as the final points of the deal were brokered.

Frosty's cell phone buzzed with a text from Lil Rod.

5-0 + 2

The plus two informed Frosty that there were two additional sheriff's deputies with the five-oh—the Reaper in the black-and-white.

"Shit," breathed Frosty before inching forward on the rooftop and shouldering the AK-47. Using his left elbow like a monopod, he tilted the muzzle downward and sighted in on the scene below.

Wonder if this is how that Oswald biz-natch felt before he popped that black man's homie, JFK?

During a six-month sting in juvenile detention, Frosty had attempted to read a book on the Kennedy assassination. The politics failed to kindle much interest. He did, though, enjoy the descriptions of the killing itself. By his measure, Oswald's angle from the Texas School Book Depository's sixth-floor window wasn't much harder than the shot he was about to pull off.

In his periphery, Frosty read the headlights of the black-and-white. The car was slowing, most certainly because whoever was behind the wheel had just caught a couple of eyeballs full of gang-sta bling. Dead below, those Crip-blue skullies turned their unified faces in the intruder's direction. Frosty tensed, realizing that not only was Julius's plan about to unravel, but the Reaper in the black-and-white might never even enter Frosty's kill zone.

Click! Without thinking, Frosty's right index flicked off the safety selector and returned to the trigger guard. He shimmied twenty-five degrees right in hopes of improving his aspect. If providence had anything to do with anything, Frosty would get his shots off before all hell broke loose.

He pressed his cheek to the stock and aimed his dominant right eye down the barrel. The sight picture was plain and, in the mass of car headlights, easily illuminated. Of the three occupants in the car, the Reaper was an easy spot. Julius's description had been simple. White. Buzzed head. Crooked nose. Seated next to the target was a female deputy with black features. The figure in the rear seat was hardest to make out. The best Frosty could clock was a white man with sandy hair.

Sights on da tat-man.

Frosty's index finger caressed the trigger's flat curved edge. Then came a smooth, cleansing breath followed by an even slower release. When he felt most of the air had evacuated from his lungs, he was at his most still. All that was left was for him to gently pull on the trigger until the release surprised him. The firing pin struck the primer of the 7.62mm cartridge. The rifle bucked. And away the bullet spun.

Before he'd fully braked the black-and-white, Lucky was beginning the first move of his planned, three-point turn. He smiled and waved out the open window in an attempt to appeal to the nearest Crips, letting them know with a simple gesture that no harm was intended. Clearly, Lucky and his crew had stumbled onto some kind of transaction where a lone black-and-white was wholly unwelcome and completely vulnerable.

Shia, eyes scanning from one Crip blue identifier to the next, recognized the rules had changed.

"Just turning around," announced Lucky, loud enough for any ears within fifty feet of the radio unit to hear. Through the windshield, he clocked four Crips within stoning distance, their lower bodies blocked behind the open doors of their shiny ghetto rides, each ostensibly concealing a weapon that was surely cocked and ready to rock.

Meanwhile, as Lucky clicked the branch shifter into reverse, he coolly freed both his out-of-policy SIG .45s, placing the service pistol onto his lap and tucking the ankle piece's muzzle under his left thigh. Shia followed with her own 9mm, revealing visible shudders as she gripped it with both hands and held it between her knees.

"Hey, back there," rapped Lucky on the screen. "Need you to promise me something. No matter what happens, get on the floor and do not—AND I MEAN DO NOT—leave the vehicle. Am I understood?"

"What the hell's going on?" pressed Atom.

"Shut the fuck up and tell me you heard my instructions!" said Lucky.

"Yeah yeah, sure," responded the boy wonder, utterly clueless about the depth of danger. "But what—"

The first bullet soared through the open driver's window and punched a hole through the top of Lucky's left trapezius, two and a quarter inches above his Kevlar vest and missing his jugular by three. The projectile then spiraled downward, somewhat slowed, and splintered the plastic from the screen before punching like a heavyweight's fist into Atom Blum's store-bought body armor. The slug failed to penetrate, but it landed like a mule kick.

Lucky pressed on the accelerator, sending the black-and-white spinning onto the sunburnt patch of grass. Simultaneously, with his right hand, he raised his pistol, aimed it through the front windshield, and unleashed five quick self-defense shots in the direction of the nearest Crips. The windshield spider-webbed with each successive trigger pull.

The Crips, in unified resistance, dove for cover or brandished weapons and returned an undisciplined spray of fire. In typical gang reply, they shot in retreat and without regard for conserving ammunition. Thus, the tremendous volley of hot lead smacked everything from Building 5 to palm trees to satellite dishes and, on occasion, the sheriff's radio unit. The skin of the vehicle sounded with a loud metallic *pung* with each bullet strike.

Shia found herself shoved down onto the car seat by Lucky. Her right hand found her radio key and, without having to think about it, she began broadcasting.

"SHOTS FIRED, SHOTS FIRED!" she radioed. "UNIT 780—NEW WILMINGTON GARDENS—OFFICERS NEED ASSISTANCE!"

As her fingers continued depressing the mic, the overwhelming staccato sounds of gunfire were making it out over the radio waves to every deputy tuned to the channel.

"Shotgun!" barked Lucky.

With her face hovering over the electronic switches, she keyed the quick two-finger unlock code. Behind her, the shotgun released and fell into Lucky's hands. He wasted no time jamming the barrel through a hole in the windshield, jacking out the dummy round, and while steering forward with his left hand, pulling the trigger on the first round of buckshot. The shotgun roared at the crowd of Crips huddled around their cars.

"PUMP ME!" ordered Lucky.

Shia reached upwards, gripped the shotgun's forestock, slid it forward to jack out the spent shell, then reversed directions to re-arm the chamber. *BOOM!* The shotgun spoke once more.

"I'M HIT, I'M HIT!" Atom was screaming from the rear bench.

"Just stay down!" Lucky barked.

From Frosty's perspective, it was as if his single rifle shot had sparked a Fourth of July conflagration like none other. Below him, hell had been unleashed in the form of trading gunfire. The Reaper, whom he'd barely missed with his one and only trigger pull, had been quick to return fire at an already electrified gathering of gangbangers. In what seemed like the blink of an eye, the parking lot had erupted. Each and every paranoia-infected member of those ready-to-rumble Crips had filled his hands with a weapon and begun blasting in the direction of the retreating black-and-white. Seconds seemed like eons—the air full of sparks, exploding stucco dust and flying safety glass. Some spinning shards carried far enough to bite Frosty's cheek.

The black-and-white reversed direction. Its rear wheels spun on the soft sod before gaining traction and wheeling into a left-to-right arc across a phalanx of firing Crips. Out of the corner of his eye, Frosty caught a glimpse of Lil Rod abandoning his neon yellow bike for cover behind a children's swing set and playhouse.

Jeeeeezus.

They're all dead, decided Frosty. Julius's bad idea had just turned into something irreversibly calamitous. The Frostman was witnessing at least a dozen or more Crips assassinating a car full of deputies.

A motherfucking Fourth of July massacre.

"No, no, no," said Frosty at the noise below, his voice soft as a whisper.

One cop killed inside the New Wilmington Gardens was maybe worth two or three nights on the local news. A black-and-white full, cut up by two entire gang sets? That was full-on CNN. Or a wall-to-wall Fox News event. Frosty knew because his dear Gran'nana lived her nearly every non-churchgoing hour tuned to one of the three twenty-four-hour cable news networks. Both his mind and eyes flicked to the windows overlooking the debacle. Camera phones were sure to be turned on, recording the massacre in grainy video, only minutes from an upload to the Internet.

Time to bounce.

Frosty rolled away from the roof's edge, found his feet and a scrambling exit. He needed to be gone—and fast—and witnessed far away from the bloodbath, with the AK-47 hidden away until it could be properly destroyed.

* * *

Shia had heard stories from cops who had survived gunfights. She recalled a lecture at the academy from a beefy, charming former deputy named Robert Rangel, who, after being shot and nearly killed, had written a book, *The Red Dot Club*, on the subject. Amidst his own terrifying recollection he'd included accounts from other surviving cops—both sheriff's and LAPD. One of the common denominators that bound the tales was how each survivor's memories couldn't help but replay the scenes in the slowest of slow motions. Five seconds of flying bullets somehow morphed into hours of mental playback.

Such was Shia's horrifying experience.

From the moment that first high-velocity round tore though the black-and-white, the trainee's mind was unconsciously recording at a thousand memory frames per second. The projectile striking Atom Blum sounded like a sharply pitched belly slap. Next came Lucky's return of fire. With each trigger pull, his pistol recoiled and ejected a .45-caliber empty, the brass tumbling counterclockwise in uniformed arcs. The dusty mix of spent powder and windshield safety glass filled the air like a million tiny suspended crystals.

Then there were the whizzing bullets. The hot, spiraling missiles, twisting against the air and striking what felt like everything but her. She remembered being pushed downward with such force her shoulder nearly snapped the Box from its bolted mount. The barrel of the shotgun slung over her head had been shoved into one of the holes in the windshield. Though she didn't remember Lucky's precise instructions, she retained slo-mo snippets of her jacking shells in and out of the shotgun, one-handed, as if stroking off some giant phallus. Was it after-memory? Or in the actual moment had she somehow sexualized her assistive actions? Any and all undertones of the moment had ended abruptly when the scorching brass head of an expelled shotgun shell struck her cheek and burned her back into real time.

In those real-time seconds of recall, Shia felt the car's engine reverse directions and the g-forces from the acceleration. A hard left turn had pulled her back into an upright pose. That's when

Lucky had leaned into her, extended his right hand, and unleashed the entire clip from his ankle .45 through her window frame. The gunshots had snapped at the air in perfect time.

CRACK! CRACK! CRACK! CRACK! CRACK!

When Lucky touched her had he felt her body quiver? The fear in her loins? The damned knowing that her life was going to finish? Right there in a sheriff's black-and-white. Not even twenty-five. A full life yet to live, bleeding out in the parking lot of some godforsaken federal housing project in godforsaken Compton.

Then it was as if she were back underwater, plummeting into that blowout on Poinsettia when at last her toes touched bottom. With nowhere deeper to sink and death a practical certainty, a switch in her had been flipped. She was still alive. And while alive, she was going to fight.

I'm not dead yet!

And I'm not someone to be protected! she screamed at herself. *I'm a goddamned Los Angeles County sheriff's deputy!* In a purely instinctive millisecond when Shia recognized Lucky had emptied the magazine of his backup pistol, she forced herself upright, trained her 9mm out the window, and filled her gunsight with the first armed Crip her eyes could capture. Her target appeared less than twenty yards away, sliding out from behind the hood of a gold-flecked Lexus. The gangbanger was nearly as blue-black as she, but basketball tall with an ultra-thin waist underscored by his white skintight wifebeater.

For Shia, the moment was in such crystalline optics she could not only read the ribbed knit of the Crip's shirt, but could picture three of her bullets striking at center mass and turning the fabric a soiled crimson. Though the assailant was firing wildly in her direction, her picture was so acute she felt she could read the serial numbers on his stainless-steel .40-cal pistol. One of his bullets flew close to home, spinning an inch by her right ear before it struck and rattled the safety screen.

Shia clocked the Crip as dead before his body thumped the parking lot. Her first kill. In her mind, a notch was made into an imaginary mantle. All in real time. As she sought a second target, her sight picture turned suddenly to shrubs and taupe stucco a split second before she felt the impact.

Lucky wanted out. Out of the situation. Out of the New Wilmington Gardens. And in that bloodletting moment, out of Compton forever.

Had he been alone in the gunfight, he might have laid off the accelerator, stood his ground, and seen how many bad guys he could drop before a head shot cut his motors for good. Instead, he was encumbered with responsibilities in the form of his trainee and the numb-nuts Hollywood ride-along in the back seat. The movie director had already screamed out that he was hit. Which meant that Lucky was duty-bound to rescue his charge from the immediate peril rather than stay and fight.

His initial intent, once he'd gunned the black-and-white into forward gear, was for his rear tires to catch the asphalt and propel them away from the hail of scorching lead. But it hadn't rained in months and the pavement had a baked-on veneer of oil. Momentum shifted and sent the radio unit fishtailing across the drive and into the sod. That's when Lucky readjusted his aim, doing what he could to direct the vehicle to collide passenger side–first into the small outdoor deck of a corner apartment in Building 3. There was the crunch of colliding sheet metal, glass, and plaster. Like gas filling a vacuum, the inside of the black-and-white was so instantly choked with stucco dust Lucky had to hack out his orders between coughs.

"WINDOWS . . . OUT . . . NOW . . . OUT!"

Despite the dizzying aftereffects of the crash, Shia twisted herself and crawled out the window. Lucky impatiently assisted by grabbing a handful of her butt cheek and giving it a forceful shove. He followed, dropping out of the car and onto a half-collapsed kettle grill that appeared never to have been cleaned of charcoal and ash. Overhead, bullets struck the apartment's slider door, shattering the glass and extorting muffled screams from inside.

"ATOM!" Lucky shouted, just before reaching into the back

seat, arms outstretched with hands grasping for the movie director, only to come up empty. But for the violent microbes still floating in the air, the black-and-white's cabin was vacant.

What the hell?

A hundred feet beyond the wrecked radio unit, two shadows approached the left rear window. In near unison they lifted their pistols and emptied what ammo remained in their double-stacked magazines. On hearing the firecracker-like pops, Lucky lifted himself over the buckled half wall separating the porch from the landscaping and slid back to the deck while the bullets pocked both the car and the porch. Each slug striking the building sounded like a yardstick slapped against a desktop.

And then it was quiet.

Lucky expected the gunfight was pretty much exhausted. Most lasted only seconds before the bad boys would call out for a scatter. All those splashy ghetto rides began roaring out of the compound in hopes of beating the evil eye in the sky—a.k.a. the LASD air support helicopter—with all its night-vision, infrared, and vehicle tag–reading tech. It was the Fourth of July, though. Lucky, who currently shared his life with an LAPD pilot, knew response time on the holiday would be dodgy and slower than normal. Low-flying choppers and ground-to-sky fireworks mortars had the potential for tragedy. The air support team was surely cruising at a higher and less-accessible altitude.

As for his wounded shoulder, it stung at the point of penetration, the pain radiating fully into his thorax and down to the fingertips of his left hand. He was concerned about Shia, not to mention where in God's world had that idiot movie director vanished? When and how Atom had exited the black-and-white, Lucky could only guess as sometime between the first shot and the collision into the building. How long a window could that have been? Five seconds? Fifteen? Thirty?

Lucky kept low and swung into the dark apartment. He was reaching for his tac light when Shia's beam kicked on and swept the unfurnished living room. Cowering crackheads were tucked into the dirty corners. Lucky estimated around a dozen who were either stoned, in the process of smoking rock or meth when the conflagration began, or flat-out too scared to move. The floor was a pit of used newspapers, empty dime bags, and refuse from every conceivable fast-food franchise.

The radios on their belts squawked.

"Units responding," announced Shia, a mix of both shell shock and unspent adrenaline. She'd survived, she knew it, and was experiencing a strange, almost chemical elation. "Where's what's-his-face?"

"Abandoned ship—somewhere between out there and here," said Lucky. "You hit?"

"No," assessed Shia. "At least, I don't think so." So far, she was unaware of her TO's injury, keeping her tactical beam on the scrubby addicts in the crack den. "We need to find our ride-along."

"Thirty seconds," ordered Lucky, listening for the last hot rod to wheel past and the engine thunder to abate. "If dumb-fuck couldn't stay in the car, he can wait for the last gangster to clear out before we make our search."

Thirty seconds. Jesus.

Lucky couldn't list all the bad he could imagine that might take place in a simple half minute. Worlds could change between count one and halfway to sixty. Yet he still needed that one infinitesimal stretch of time to pass before he'd allow his trainee to face more danger. Twice in three nights, she'd nearly been killed. His charge. On his watch. Surely he'd be grilled on the issue soon enough. Was he taking that extra beat to protect his uninjured deputy because she was a trainee? Or because she was a woman? Or because he'd been shot himself and needed a breather?

None of the above, assholes.

Between the crack den and his future inquisition, Lucky would need to come up with a lie. A believable one. Thus adding to his ever-growing list of procedural indiscretions. All in the course of performing his primal duty—to actually serve and protect.

35

The movie viewed through Atom Blum's box-office lens had been unspooling since he had first laid eyes on the New Wilmington Gardens. The projects had appeared like a modern Gothic painting. Completely plain and architecturally benign, yet fenced like a mental asylum. The few tall palms swaying against the reflecting night sky only made the picture that much more surreal. Fantastic. A neo-modern horror dreamscape.

That was all before the reinforced guard gate clattered shut behind the sheriff's black-and-white. The unmistakable connection Atom heard was akin to a prison cell door slamming closed for good. As the radio unit rolled deeper into the complex, reality infected his moment of cinematic reverie. A cold had swept over him—a chill he tried to jettison as a complication from both fatigue and his prescription pain meds.

So obsessed was Atom with cinema he'd often dream he was in a movie. Sometimes one of his own making. And sometimes there would come a moment when the dream became a nightmare— when Atom realized that he was no longer part of something make-believe and instead in real danger. On nearly every occasion Atom would wake and be grateful to discover himself in his Malibu bedroom and no longer requiring rescue.

Neither Lucky nor Shia had acknowledged Atom's wailing hysterics. Atom had feared his eardrums would rupture when Lucky aimed his big pistol at the windshield and began blasting holes in the direction of the shooters. Then the car was lurching backwards. More than hearing the incoming gunfire, Atom could feel the black-and-white's skin getting punctured by bullets from what had to be every conceivable direction.

This is when Atom's amygdala grabbed control from his frontal lobe. The picture in his mind turned into a wide-screen, panoramic view from the radio unit's back seat. In the front seats was a pair of sheriff's deputies. Police officers. Cops engaged in a surprise and overwhelming battle with society's underclass. After all, hadn't it been plastered all over the nightly news? *The Man* was under fire. Authority deserved a righteous comeuppance at the hands of the abused.

In that microsecond of panic, Atom convinced himself that he wasn't a target. He was only a tourist there to observe and learn, caught in the wrong place at the wrong time. Just because it was Lucky and Shia's turn to die didn't mean his destiny was to become a collateral casualty in a civil war between the oppressed and their uniformed oppressors.

The left rear passenger door popped open in practical silence, smothered by the discordance splitting the air. Despite feeling wounded from the rifle round that struck his body armor, Atom was reasonably quick to his feet and bolted in a direction his gut instinct informed was the shortest distance from peril. To his immediate left was a building corner around which he might conceal himself. Then dead ahead was something altogether more inviting: a neon yellow mountain bike that appeared abandoned at the edge of the asphalt drive.

Atom's plan formed quickly. The neon yellow bike would be his means of escape. Hell, he figured. The way the bike had been left, the front wheel was already pointed in the direction of the front gate. All that was left for him to do was swoop in, right the two-wheeler, and pedal to safety.

Before he had even lifted the bike and climbed on, Atom was so far ahead of himself he was imagining how far west he'd need to travel before he'd be within range of an Uber pickup.

Then home, a hot shower, four capsules of Tylenol PM washed back by half a bottle of Jack Daniels. Then some dreamless goddamn sleep.

Tunnel vision had set in for the boy wonder. So much so that he was too impaired to notice the bike's owner. A skinny black teen nearly a foot shorter than Atom was angling sharply from his right.

"Hey!" shouted the skinny teen.

Atom was so focused on the bicycle his response was delayed. Only after he'd snatched it from the ground and set it on two wheels did he unthinkingly swivel his head in the direction of the voice.

"Fuck the police!" hissed the skinny teen.

Atom's eyes narrowed across the bridge of his bandaged nose, instantly freezing on a very obvious gun muzzle. The weapon was in the outstretched hand of the skinny teen, whose face was, if anything, determined.

"Oh, fuck," whispered the boy wonder. And that utterance was his very last.

Lil Rod's revolver, the very same snub-nosed .38 he'd unleashed on Mush Man, let out a high-pitched *pop!* To the gangbanger's ears, the noise blended nicely with the other gunshots. Only while most of the other expended bullets in the gun battle were missing wildly, Lil Rod's single pull of the trigger hit its upward mark with close-range accuracy. Without even a thought, he'd adjusted his aim at that bright white X of a bandage in the middle of the bike thief's face and let fly. The tall suspected cop stood for a surprised half second before his knees finally gave way. The body buckled to the pavement, pulling the bicycle down with it.

"Tha's my bike, nigga!" pissed Lil Rod, who retrieved it from the dead man's grasp, hopped aboard the vinyl seat, and was peddling home just as the last of the gunshots subsided into silence.

36

Downtown. 6:28 a.m.

The Xanax had worn off minutes shy of 5:00 a.m. It had been a banner night of sleep for Cat Rincon, even if she had cheated with a fair dose of prescription meds. She lolled for some time on the feather-top bed, curling herself around the pillows as if they were lovers spooning. For the hour and a half she lay there, only half hoping for sleep to return, she tried to distract her overwrought brain with pleasant thoughts. She thought of all the liaisons she'd had at the Downtown Crown—a.k.a. the Crown International Hotel, the discreet eight-story kissing cousin to the more prestigious Biltmore that stood across the street.

Jeez, Cat. Before last night had you only ever stayed here for sex?

In her hazy state, the string of lovers she'd met at the Crown seemed impossible to calculate. In contrast, she could count on two fingers the number of men and women with whom she had shared her home bed. One she called Mr. Regrettable. The other, a mercy encounter with a mayor's office missus in a bad marriage and a story too tragic to fathom.

Try as Cat did, her eyes wouldn't stay shut, peeling themselves open into slits and facing the pair of French doors that led to the balcony. Cat unconsciously recalled a year-old news tale. If the faint memory served, it was about some software success story who had murdered a prostitute then swan-dived off one of the Crown's balconies.

Is that where I am? In the suicide suite?

The haunted hotel stories about the Downtown Crown poisoned any chance Cat had of carving out an extra hour of bonus slumber. After a minute searching the sheets, she found the TV's remote near the foot of the bed and flipped on one of the five local morning shows where all the anchors, sports readers, and booty-popping weather girls looked as if they'd been spit from the same 3-D printer.

She found her tablet, intending to check her calendar to the cheerful morning chatter. Instead, there were texts. Reminders from the night before. Mayor Ramon Avila had arranged for a pair of luxury boxes at the Dodgers game to entertain the usual array of public employee honchos, key brokers from the utility and city service vendors, Democrat Party campaign bundlers, and a few handpicked council members and county supervisors. It was a veritable who's who of Los Angeles power players—minus, of course, the millionaire and billionaire classes. Mayor Ramon—or just Ram to his friends—was never one to upstage his hosts, the L.A. Dodgers management group, especially when those luxury boxes came for free.

Cat stared at the swirled patterns on the hand-plastered ceiling, trying to make figures out of them. She couldn't even recall whom the home team had played against. She'd started drinking blue tequila Dodger-ritas from the moment she'd arrived mid-fourth inning. Meanwhile, she'd convinced a trusted DWP intern to swing by her house, pack a small bag with the clothes she'd listed, and drop it by the stadium. Her excuse was that she was vacating for three days of termite tenting.

Oh, the bed you've made, Catty-Cat.

The confident, politically savvy princess of the DWP board was troubled to her ligaments. The terror she'd felt the day before at the arroyo had escalated into a problem demanding a quick solve.

Dipshit twat. This is a problem you can't fuck your way out of.

The morning news show was mostly noise to her—weather, traffic, celebrity gossip, a thumbnail of last night's news, along with more suffocating weather and butt-numbing traffic. If Cat hadn't heard the name Compton uttered, she most likely would've continued padding barefoot and naked from the running bathtub to her compact suitcase. She slowed a step, tilted her head toward the television screen, and caught some typical local news B-roll. It was edited like every other news crime story with images of swirling lights against a nightscape, police tape, and distant telephoto shots of bodies lying under tarps.

"Stupid Compton," she groused back to the TV as if the micro-city was a cold sore no one could cure.

The TV reporter's voice track mentioned a semi-familiar name—Atom Blum—identified as the blockbuster Hollywood movie director of the *Roadkill* trilogy. With her attention only slightly piqued, Cat looked up from digging for fresh underwear and took in the news story's pro forma footage of the boy wonder working one of his movie sets, setting a camera shot, instructing actors, dressed in a suit on a red carpet, waving at paparazzi while exiting a restaurant, and answering publicity questions with a rehearsed smile.

Think I know this guy.

Or Cat wondered as much. She'd seen none of his movies— the snob in her wouldn't deign to pay money for some lowbrow action flick. Perhaps she'd met Atom at a dinner party or one of those charity fundraisers designed to pluck money feathers off the entertainment pigeons. No matter. The young studio gun was dead, found shot in the head in the middle of some federal housing project. No doubt, she reasoned, the byproduct of some underground addiction.

Yet why am I still staring at the TV?

It was like an itch she couldn't scratch—a bothersome, unrelenting nag at her paranoid subconscious. Then the puzzle pieces clicked. A famous Hollywood movie director had been murdered in Compton. Whether it was a drug deal gone sideways or a pimp robbing a white john seeking some chocolate kink, it was sure to draw a very public spotlight. Atom Blum's death could very well be a white-hot klieg lamp aimed at a slice of Southland that was otherwise ignored but for the ubiquitous gang shootings that played liked wallpaper on the local news feeds. That was, in part, the beauty of doing business in Compton with Julius Colón. Nobody that mattered gave a goddamn.

But they would now.

"Shit," Cat audibled back to the TV. "Shit, shit, and SHIT!"

37

The pain in Lucky's shoulder had elevated from a searing sting to a flaming ache that referred from the wound both down his left arm and up through his neck until it dammed at the back of his skull. Tempting as it was, Lucky refused the ER doctor's recommendation that he dull the discomfort with a narcotic-based fentanyl patch, opting instead for a cocktail of over-the-counter anti-inflammatories. The primary downside was that once Gonzo had driven him home from Martin Luther King Hospital and prepared a comfortable cradle of goose-down pillows for him, sleep had remained as elusive as answers to Mush Man's murder. Thus Lucky righted himself, found the spare keys to Karrie's Prius, and navigated fifteen minutes east to Arcadia and the converted boxing gym where his sixteen-year-old emancipated girl was testing for her green tassel in Muay Thai.

Left arm immobilized in a baby-blue sling, Lucky rested on a bench near Travis. The boy barely acknowledged him with a glance before returning his attention to the game on his phone. The gym, normally a bustling crunch of fighters and mitts slapping flesh and vinyl, was empty but for the few students testing as well as a half dozen onlooking parents. The converted transmission shop was painted glossy gray from the floor to the ducting with punching bags of all weights and sizes hung like sentries waiting for war.

Karrie was on the checkerboard mat, her strawberry mane cinched in a bun. She wore black compression shorts and a T-shirt screaming the silk-screened name of the home gym—Dynamite Muay Thai. Having danced since age two, Karrie had turned in her tights and tutus for a four-day-a-week regimen of fight training. She'd landed on Muay Thai after an Internet search for "the most deadly martial art for self-defense."

Lucky approved.

"You're supposed to be in bed," reminded Gonzo after returning from the bathroom, ice-cold Dr Pepper in hand. The can sweat bullets in the gym's eighty-degree temperature.

"Didn't work out," said Lucky.

"Hurts like hell, huh?" she asked.

Lucky nodded, but only slightly, because engagement of his neck muscles resulted in even more pain. The sound of Karrie striking her instructor's hand pads made a popping noise not unlike the fireworks stuck in his skull from the night before. Sharp, like air split by bullets.

"She's somethin', huh?" remarked Gonzo. "Traded jazz hands for boxing gloves."

Lucky keyed on Karrie's hands, moving swiftly through her rehearsed routine. Her padded fire-engine-red leather grappling gloves had been a Christmas gift from her newly adopted daddy.

Whap! Whap-whap! Whap-whap-whap!

"Before long you'll *both* be able to kick my ass," muttered Lucky.

"You don't have a prayer," smiled Gonzo, before offering him a sip of her soda. "Hear anything from your trainee?"

"Like what?" asked Lucky. "A fuck-you-very-much for the worst start of a patrol deputy's career?"

"Or something like, 'How you feeling?'" corrected Gonzo. "You're her TO for God's sake."

"By the time the shoot inquest is done, my guess is she'll be cured of wanting to be a cop."

"Well, if it were me," encouraged Gonzo, "I'd wanna get right back in the car with you."

"No chance for that," said Lucky. "I'm good as done. Zero chance of survival."

"You had no control over what happened. And for Christ's sake, you kept your trainee alive."

"That I did," he acknowledged. "But I got my ride-along killed."

"That's not on you."

"Don't matter. He's news. Downtown's gonna need a head on a stake."

"The union will fight for you."

"Third day back in a black 'n' white? If there ever was an easy sacrifice . . ." Lucky let the sentence hang. But he was resigned only to losing the job, not the battle. "My head hurts. But all I keep thinkin' about is Mush Man."

"Your ghettocide?"

"Bad enough some CSI gets zapped to take the spotlight off," groused Lucky. "Now, with Atom dumb-fuck getting himself dead, it's callin' all cars to cement cap the hornet's nest. And when the crime clears?"

"I know. Nobody cares about a nobody."

Karrie's instructor hoisted up a body-sized punching pad and braced for a series of kicks from his student. The teenager's grace was mesmerizing and so fluid her sparring could have been confused for a dance. Only this routine was punctuated by bone-breaking power, with blow after blow echoing across the space. The instructor continued backing away to absorb the strikes. All while Karrie's freckled face, a usual picture of concentrated cool, had turned fetal pink with rage.

"*Hyud!*" barked the instructor, Thai for *Stop!*

Karrie heard the demand, but couldn't resist a final core-jacked *thwack* to the body pad. The last strike echoed like a broken two-by-four.

"You've created a little killer there," remarked Gonzo.

Lucky would have liked to shake his head in disagreement, but he didn't care to invite any more pain. As for any concern over creating a weapon out of Karrie? But for the example he set, Lucky deserved no credit for Karrie's martial arts transformation. The kid had clearly been marching to her own aggressive drum since she had transformed from the only child of an ugly divorce into a homeless runaway surviving in some of the darkest corners of Los Angeles some eighteen months earlier.

"Wonder what's with his dogs?" segued Lucky.

"Whose dogs?"

"Mush's."

"No. No. And no. You can't bring 'em home. You're way too allergic and I'm—"

"Not home. Just wondering who's got 'em."

"Thought you knew who got 'em. Some O.G. with the—"

"Pizza," finished Lucky. "Yeah. He was feedin' 'em pizza."

Julius, Lucky remembered. Julius Colón. Just thinking the name raised gooseflesh on Lucky's legs. Why? Wasn't Julius Colón just another criminal? Or was there more to the unfinished picture? And why in the name of Jesus was Lucky imagining Julius Colón when his mental picture was still choked with last night's Fourth of July conflagration at the New Wilmington Gardens?

38

Downtown.

Three uninvited union reps had descended upon Tim Gilligan in his most unwelcoming bunker. And it wasn't even ten in the morning yet.

"Job's stalled," shrugged burly Vernon DeMacher of I.B.E. Local 18. "Nobody steps on-site until that phantom line is shut off."

"In process," defended Tim, failing to appear relaxed even though his chair was titled fully back, his feet propped across the corner of his desk.

"Clock's on my guys," said Vernon. "And because that's your emergency hole down there, they're making double time for doing dick."

"On top of that, if we can't get in that hole," complained Ken

Chang, the municipal employees' union spokesman, "we can't do our investigating diligence for the family of the dead CSI."

"Don't think I know that?" Tim contended.

"Have to say it or we're not on record," argued Kenny.

"And I already got your email," defended Tim.

"And now I'm here," smiled Kenny.

"Who had a good Fourth?" Tim asked, lamely trying to ease the tension in the space. "Me? I had two families to—"

"C'mon, Timmy. Holiday's over," moaned Jeanette Reyes, seated in the one visitor's chair opposite Tim's über-utilitarian tank desk.

"'Timmy'?" complained Tim. Five minutes earlier, he'd never met the mannish, tattooed Ms. Reyes. He wondered if the city had paid for her sex reassignment.

"What's the holdup on shutting down that old transmission line?" she asked.

"Holiday yesterday," defended Tim. "I just got in. Right now you're all taking up my time, keeping me from my job."

"Our job to be here," insisted Kenny.

"You didn't even gimme a chance to answer your email!" barked Tim. "And since all of you had to coordinate to find me, what happened to the service employees' union or someone from Coalition? Why aren't *they* here to bust my balls?"

"Take any longer than the morning," chilled Vernon, "and my guess is they'll be right along."

"Re-routing the line today," shrugged Tim.

"When?" asked Reyes.

"As soon as you beat your clumsy-ass feet outta my office," pushed Tim.

"That's a mouthful," stood Reyes. "Especially comin' out of a management fat ass."

"And why's your office so cold?" asked Vernon, the only hand Tim was willing to shake.

"So I can see everyone's nipples," joked Tim, quickly gulping after the last syllable crossed his lips. "That was a joke. Nobody write me up, okay?"

Tim watched the trio file out, then proceeded to stare at the open door for a good thirty seconds. He fully expected a second wave of desk jockeys purporting to represent union employees using the phantom underground transmission line as a reason to shirk work.

My underground line.

If there was pride in Tim's self-admission, it was because he had done all the heavy lifting to rediscover the eons-old transmission line. His hungover eyes had trudged through volumes of ancient Compton City schematics in search of forgotten underground electrical pathways. He'd eventually landed upon a prewar designated trunk-line with branches that travelled from south to north, from Long Beach to Lynwood as it cut through the east side of Compton. The DWP manager had let out an excited whoop. As if X had marked the exact spot where bags of forgotten gold had been buried.

To be an engineer in those old days? What must it have been like to be on the burgeoning start of a great cityscape instead of on the tired decrepit end?

Back at the turn of the century, when Los Angeles and thereabouts were developing into an industrial juggernaut, engineers were at odds over the best ways to transmit power. Aboveground or below? Transmission of electricity through overland power lines was cost effective by clear multiples. Routing cables underground, though, was considered safer for the obvious reasons of weatherproofing the lines from downed trees, storms, and other potential catastrophes.

By the second half of the century, faster and cheaper had won the day and most of Southern California's power had been relegated to aboveground delivery. The landscape from the Valley to the Basin was cluttered with telephone poles and drooping power lines. In more recent decades, a significant number of residents, especially those living in higher-income neighborhoods, had judged the exposed lines unsightly, spoiling their views of sunsets, mountain desert scapes, and the gentle swaying palm trees. The demand to bury power lines was, once again, on the rise.

Shutting down his private transmission line would be the easy part. A simple text to the tech he'd paid off at the Central Avenue receiving station and the power would be reverted back into the DWP's mainstream.

But rerouting juice back to the all-important destination?

That's what scorched Tim's insides. It might take weeks. Months, even. There'd been no backup plan. And why should there have been? Along the hundreds of miles of DWP-managed water mains, who on earth could have predicted a blowout along his surreptitious underground transmission line? Only to be followed a day later by a murder and fatal accident? What were the odds?

Nobody can blame you, Timbo. Shit just happens.

Tim handled his prepaid flip phone, purchased for cash at a gas-station convenience store just outside Disneyland. He had spent all day and half an evening at the famed amusement park with his two youngest kids. As his DWP-owned car chugged gasoline from a self-serve pump and the incessant melody of "It's a Small World" pinged in his head, he'd dropped $24.99 on the untraceable number. From that point on, every time he'd handled the flip phone, that awful song cycled in his ears.

It's a world of laughter, a world of tears . . .

Inside Tim's head, counterpoint pictures played along with the song. There were the moving images from all that he'd watched on TV about the West Valley murder of Hal Solomon; the newspaper clipping slipped across the Chili's tabletop by tiny, frightened Cat Rincon in her Walmart pink; the yellow crime-scene tape, like a scarlet letter announcing his dirty secret. The more Tim reflected, the more the insufferable song fit his idea of what would happen the moment he grew the gonads to shut off the power.

It's a world of hope and a world of fears . . .

39

Frosty never tired of it.

Whether the moment was imagined or real, he'd stretch out his gangly arms and, while slowly strolling, let his fingertips graze the leaves of the plants aligned in neat, man-made rows. It was a spiritual connection he couldn't quite describe. Not even to his deeply religious mother or Gran'nana. The connectivity of it was—if he were ever coerced to admit as much—the nearest thing to heaven the twenty-two-year-old Crip could envision.

This from a man who'd not once set foot in anything wilder than the urban gardens of south Los Angeles County. A true forest or jungle might scare the wits out of him with its unevenness and chaos. Nurseries were clean and ordered and quantifiable by genus, age, size, and price.

In the nursery world, man *was* God.

Above him, rows upon rows of grow lights were arranged like upside-down church pews. As they devoured electricity, each unit hummed in harmonic unison, casting the five-acre former aircraft tire plant in an ominous yet loving magenta hue. Fore and aft, six-foot-diameter industrial fans created a controlled breeze to provide a constant tickle of agitation to the grove of hydroponically accelerated cannabis.

The plants, each raised from the Oracle seed strain, were rooted freely in buckets of clay pellets and wired like vineyard grapes, allowing them to stand at their tallest—some as high as ten feet.

Julius estimated the first crop alone would clear five million dollars.

Money, thought Frosty. Those distinctive marijuana leaves might as well have been twenty-dollar bills ripening for the harvest. Illegal? For now, sure. And not as sexy as his dream, the under-the-transmission-towers tree and shrub farm he planned to own one day. By Frosty's measure, he was more than halfway there. The high-tech, oxygen-rich marijuana factory was a poster card of modern horticulture. Each plant had been raised from handpicked seed, grown free of soil from sprout to adulthood, then potted in a deep bed of clay pellets and fed with a mix of reverse-osmosis water, pH-balanced organic grow product, and a pinch of Epsom salts.

Frosty's Magic Maryjane Mix was his alone to brew in the five-hundred-gallon stainless-steel feeder tank that was suspended on a platform to drip-line height at the north end of the warehouse.

He named the steel tank feeder the Big Tit.

Frosty acknowledged a marijuana shrub was not a tree. It was a flowering plant. So, despite the grove's rows of ten-foot perpendicular growth, the entire crop was trunkless. Yet every damned stalk demanded his utmost care.

He scrutinized each plant, making sure the leaves were healthy and green to the twig. No sign of malnutrition, root rot, or insects. At the southern end he looped around, skipped a row, and continued the inspection. Seventeen plants deep, Frosty happened upon a duo of stalks with a coating of mold on the top clusters of buds. The fuzzy gray growth was like poor Christmas tree flocking surrounding a gray-green pine cone. Mold meant unwelcome moisture had gathered on the bud.

Turning in place, Frosty checked the airflow, holding up his open palm to feel if the massive fans were positioned and moving the air molecules at the proper humidity-killing speed. Satisfied with the flow, he turned his attention to the ceiling to see if condensation was somehow pooling into a gravity-defying dark splotch, only to have it drip onto the infected plants.

His eyes were scouring the reaches beyond the magenta cast when he was overcome by a blanket of blackness. The darkness was so complete and immediate that it fooled his brain into thinking he'd been cracked on the head with a heavy object. Yet Frosty felt his feet underneath him. Balance. And then he heard the *tick-tick-ticking* as the grow lamps began to cool down.

Power failure.

Frosty stood his ground, fully expecting the juice to reignite, feeding the banks of lamps and the all-important agitating fans. East and west, the battery-operated exit lights kicked on, spraying a weak flood of incandescence into the expanse.

The minutes passed as a usually collected Frosty quickly tested the limits of his anxiety. A smart farmer would have been prepared for such a disaster. Once power to the grow lamps was lost, it would only be a matter of minutes before the farmer initiated a diesel-powered backup generator. A push of an ignition button and presto—all power would be restored as long as there was fuel to burn. After his extensive research on raising indoor crops, Frosty had strongly suggested to Julius that a proper diesel generator be added to the purchase list.

But Julius had balked.

The boss's argument had been that generators made noise and the diesel units belched readable exhaust. Any uninvited attention to his hydroponic pot farm would be nothing less than disastrous. No. The pot crop would be dependent on the single source of electricity provided by Julius's partners at the DWP. Because the giant public utility was delivering the juice via underground conduit, uninterrupted service was virtually guaranteed.

"Only guarantee in life is that God is great, and he loves you like the true child we all are."

His mother's words echoed in Frosty's ears and soul. Such was what he remembered every time anybody uttered or insinuated a guarantee of any flavor. From Julius to street hustlers to ads on the TV.

Guarantee? Sheeeiiiiiiiiit.

40

Downtown.

B lah de blah blah de blah blah blah . . .

Cat Rincon felt stiff. Her run and scuffle with that Rose Bowl gate had caught up to her in the form of an ache that encompassed her entire body. No matter how she tried to situate herself at her Indian teak conference table—upright or tilted back, resting her shoulders in the red leather chair—relief only came in ten-second intervals before her body demanded she redistribute her 102 pounds yet again.

She sat across from a quartet of private equity investors, the chattiest and most alpha of them a bulldog-looking Chinese-American with ties to Hong Kong and Beijing. He was coiffed and reeked of offshore deals. She'd heard the pitch so many times before: a consulting deal with stock options in exchange for guiding the money men through strategic commercial property buys across the Southland.

Blah de blah blah de blah blah blah . . .

Cat would surely say yes to the deal. But with the usual caveat that she'd be allowed to pluck them and their über-rich backers for some political cash to funnel wherever it might best benefit Cat Rincon. The rest would be up to the lawyers.

The business pitch droned on. Her eyes drifted out her fourth-floor corner suite's windows. The forty-two-story skyscraper stood atop Bunker Hill and sported views of the other sparkling high-rises that sprouted from the downtown zip code. Above the rooftops and swaying palms stood the low rolling hills of Echo Park and Silver Lake, replete with the world-famous Hollywood sign etched against the most distant peak.

"Besides channels for the money from the mainland," claimed the chatty investment manager, "there's already a lot of money here, brought over by all the expats who bought residences in Arcadia and San Gabriel and Sierra Madre. Those people got bank and no place they trust to put it."

"Would you excuse me to go to the ladies' room for a moment?" asked Cat. Not waiting for an answer, she painfully pushed herself up and trod toward the frosted-glass door.

Still teacup-sized in her five-inch pumps, she drove her heels like a race car driver, angling around the sunny corners of her office suite. She exited through a side door into the public corridor and performed a reverse S-turn into the women's bathroom. Once there she waited for the door to shut, then checked to make certain she was alone before shouting:

"SHUT THE FUCK UP!"

Cat wasn't screaming at the investors she'd left behind in her suite, but at the competing demands in her head.

It's not them, Cat. It's everything else.

Hands on her hips, she released a windy sigh. A chill darted up her spine. She tried to shake it off with a couple of vertical hops while swinging her arms back and forth. Then as if her bladder recognized the opportunity, she shut herself inside one of the three available stalls, pushed her panties to her knees, and sat for a prolonged pee. She stared at the latched swinging door two feet in front of her. It had recently been replaced with a panel she surmised must have been from a men's room somewhere else in the building. Though painted over in coats of semi-gloss, the scratched graffiti was still readable.

The hollowness of the bathroom only added to Cat's overarching concerns. She needed to calm her brain and problem solve. Somehow get ahead of the situation. After all, business—Cat's business—was a game of chess. Moves and countermoves. She'd been threatened. Cornered. How she maneuvered next might mean the difference between living and dying. With the situation so obviously dire, Cat weirdly wondered why the hell her eyes were fixated on a remnant of scored graffiti.

life is hard. it's even harder if you're stupid.

Cat felt the corners of her mouth twitch into a smile. The tension in her eased, if only a fraction. Then while snapping off a few squares of toilet paper, she felt the pressure change as the ladies room door opened and shut—a prompt of sorts to reaffix her business mask and get on with her day. Only through forward motion would a solution come for what chilled her.

She unlatched the door and . . .

"Isn't this how we met?" echoed a familiar voice.

Cat was so startled, the elevated heel of her right pump nearly twisted underneath her. She caught herself against the stall's jamb and regained her equilibrium.

"You asshole!"

Julius Colón glistened as if he'd just finished a workout. His clinging shorts and undersized T-shirt were smudged in sweat. At the sink, he cupped and wet his hands before using the moisture to cool his curly scalp.

"Bathroom, remember?" reminded Julius. "That's how you and me got started in this."

"So?"

"Tell me you remember."

"I got people in my office," shifted Cat. "And they're waiting on me."

"You should try answering your phone."

"Been a little distracted, as you might imagine."

"How'd we meet?" returned Julius before blocking the door. He leaned against it, arms crossed. Waiting.

"Julius—"

"Gotta ask you again?"

"I remember, okay?" she finally replied. "I remember."

Oil Can Harry's. That much Cat could clearly recall. She and Julius had first met at the gay nightclub in Studio City. Miles north of his usual West Hollywood trolling grounds, Julius had made a rare trip beyond the Hollywood Hills and Mulholland Drive to the sleepy San Fernando Valley. There on Ventura Boulevard was a warehouse-styled bar that advertised theme nights. One such evening, Cat had trailed a pair of downtown girlfriends from a city councilman's office on the promise of country line dancing. The craze, in deep decline since its eighties heyday, had been resurrected at Harry's. Gay men along with professional women seeking to swing and two-step with handsome hunks would gather, guzzle beer from long-neck bottles, and dance themselves silly to ear-thumping country beats.

Julius had arrived on a whim. He'd read that the cruising scene in the Valley was more akin to finding hookups in white-bread Laguna Beach. Julius had a taste for blond men. A penchant he cribbed Caucasian Persuasion. When he imagined a club full of men engaged in line dancing, he pictured straw-colored hair spilling out from beneath sweaty Stetsons.

As it worked out, his only Oil Can Harry's connection was with a teacup-sized "hot tamale" in the unisex bathroom. After a chance meeting on the dance floor, Cat and Julius were reintroduced at the noisy bar. Julius's sexual appetite was momentarily overwhelmed by opportunity. Unwilling to let the real estate mistress go, he'd chased her into the bathroom and pleaded for five minutes of her undivided attention.

Their impromptu meeting moved to the quiet of a darkened parking lot. Julius impressed her with his very specific interest in acquiring strip malls. With strategic locations, he argued, an entrepreneur with the right connections could open a chain of medical marijuana dispensaries—or collectives. But state and city regulations didn't permit franchising. Yet.

"I wanna be the Starbucks of pot shops," he'd pitched. "Everybody knows that full legalizing is gonna happen. Legalizing means the man with the locations and the money to back his weed game is gonna be the man with all the leverage. Ya feel me?"

And feel him she did.

Cat Rincon was more than impressed. Not that she hadn't met a fair measure of ambitious men. The city was thick with swinging dicks with big plans. And she'd been more than willing to use her body to stroke as many egos as required to meet her own designs on power. Yet in Julius, she'd been exposed to a different flavor of man—queer and completely disinterested in her sex—who possessed a unique vision. Not to build his empire by accessing entrée to the Los Angeles power elite. But on his own moxie, from the gutters to the curbs to the street and up.

"But you're an obvious criminal," she'd argued, if only as a tease.

"Know anyone in City Hall who's not a gangsta?" he'd fired back.

"No. But the criminals in City Hall are pretty much protected."

"Why you think I'm talking to you?"

It had been five years since the meeting at Oil Can Harry's. How far they had come . . . or devolved. In that half decade Cat had introduced the Compton gangster to attorneys who best understood the ever-evolving legal ins and outs of owning and operating marijuana dispensaries. And with help from Cat's real estate connections, Julius had expanded his strip mall holdings from as far east as Glendora all the way to Redondo Beach. By using age-old fronting schemes as platforms for starting up seventeen different collectives—each with its own clever shingle like the Kush Kollective, Cannabis King, and Mary Jane's Joint—Julius had laid the footprints for the franchise he hoped to brand as Bud-Stop eventually.

That would have been enough for Julius.

Then came a Sunday at Compton's new Blue Line Farmers Market—one of the many grower-friendly street fairs that cropped up on Southland weekends. An idea hit Julius. Rather than buying his pot from collectives—supposed nonprofits—his earnings would be even more robust in a farm-to-table model. He could dispense with the profit-sucking middle man.

The rest would be logistics.

"You cut my power," angered Julius, not ceding his blockade of the ladies' room door.

"Cut what?" replied Cat. "I didn't cut anything."

"You Water and Power or what?"

"You killed Hal Solomon?" she pressed.

"We didn't need him."

"Are you kidding—" Cat stomped her heels. "He was our backstop!"

"He was *your* protection. Now we back to a mo' better power balance. You 'n' me. We protect each other."

"Is that why you threatened me?"

"Was nothin' much," defended Julius. "Just in case you was wondering where you 'n' me stood."

"We're in a fuckin' bathroom. Again."

"Why you cut the power?"

"I didn't cut shit!"

"Then why our farm lose its juice?" Julius was leaning in. "Goin' on three hours with nothin'."

"I wasn't informed. I've been in meetings. I'll look into it."

"Water and Power. That's your end of shit."

"It's a hiccup. Lemme talk to my guy."

"I'll wait," said Julius, once again leaning back against the door, arms folded over his pronounced pectorals.

Cat thought of staring him down. Putting up a pose of equal inflexibility. Perhaps Julius would step off. Give her room to maneuver. Before she could decide, her subconscious was already acquiescing as she pinched her cell phone between her right thumb and forefinger and slipped it out from the waistband of her skirt. She auto-dialed Tim Gilligan's burner phone.

"What's your guy's name?" queried Julius.

"Nuh uh." Cat shook her head. "That's my side of the fence."

"That dead Jew was on your side of the fence," he warned.

"It's me," Cat said, holding up a shut-up index finger to Julius. "What's going on with the power?"

Julius regarded her every twitch as she listened to the unknown man at the other end of her phone call. He studied her, patiently waiting for a tell—some giveaway in her body language or a betrayed bit of dialogue that informed she was playing him.

Cat clicked off.

"It's temporary," she said.

"Tell that to my crop."

"Thought it was *our* crop," she not-so-playfully replied. "My guy has a workaround."

"How long?" pressed Julius. "'Cause hydroponics don't do so good without no grow lights."

"Soon," said Cat, easing toward the bathroom door. "Now can I get back to my meeting?"

Julius cocked his head to the side. As if he wanted to view a slightly different but carefully procured angle of his business partner. He was still seeking a tell. And Cat had given him none. Julius menaced closer to her. What he lacked in vertical imposition, he more than made up for in muscle mass, especially when closing in on a woman as tiny as Cat. Even in those five-inch heels, she was virtually dwarfed.

Not since they had line danced at Oil Can Harry's had one been so close to the other. As he neared, Cat reflexively froze all but her face, from which she projected a scowl of lip-pressed fury.

Undeterred, and while keeping his eyes zeroed on her semi-dilated pupils, Julius bent his knees slightly before slowly hooking a hand underneath her skirt. He felt her breathing cease. In his ear, he detected hardly an exhaled air molecule. When his fingertips felt her inner thigh, he itsy-bitsy-spider-walked three of his digits upward until he was touching the lace mesh of her panties. Though his probe was gentle, his words were the true assault.

"I may be a fag," he hissed. "But if I have to, I will surely fuck you. Ya feel me?"

"Yes . . ." she quavered, the tremble of her voice providing tell enough for Julius to walk away.

"Have a nice day," he said, removing his hand and allowing her to slip past him to the door. He barked behind her, "And don't forget to turn on my 'lectricity!"

41

North Hollywood.

"Night damn three, Little Miss Trainee gets herself in a shootout at the O.K. housing projects."

"I didn't get myself into anything," defended Shia. "Trainees ride the passenger seat. Or have you forgotten?"

After Shia was relieved of her service sidearm in lieu of the mandatory and certain-to-be-laborious post-shooting investigation, she'd been separated from Lucky as per sheriff's policy and delivered by ambulance to Martin Luther King Hospital, where she was cleared and sent home. During the Thursday morning drive back to her condo she'd called Steve Wimminger. Her verbal debrief to the US Attorney had lasted nearly the entire commute from 120th Street to her North Hollywood address. Instead of risking losing the mobile signal, Shia parked on the street in front of her corner Starbucks. It was there, while she subconsciously counted the hipster to non-hipster passersby, that she received an unwanted lip-lashing from the federal prosecutor.

"You think that dumpster video gets me a grand jury? Gets my Reaper?" spat Wimmer.

"I'm *suspended*," Shia repeated, both her body and voice box exhausted from answering questions. "Did you expect me to get everything you needed in three nights?"

"You want what I got to give?" Wimmer flatly stated. "You get me what I need."

"We got our ride-along killed!"

"Is that something I can use?"

"I don't know."

"Then?"

"I'm on *suspension* pending *investigation*!" Shia repeated again. "My career might be over and out. I'll be lucky to get shuffled back into jail rotation."

"I don't care what you have to do and who you have to do it to," demanded Wimmer. "I'm your lone ticket to Federal Employment Land."

Shia didn't squeeze in a shower or change her clothes. She didn't even elevator upstairs to attend to her old man. She U-turned and pointed her Optima back in the direction of Compton. All while Wimmer's tin voice pinged behind the membranes of her eardrums.

"You're a smart girl," Wimmer seethed. "Figure it out. Solve the problem. Get me what you promised."

Shia didn't precisely recall promising Steve Wimminger anything other than to give her utmost effort. Had she done as much? Obviously, not in his DOJ opinion. With downtown Los Angeles prominently engorging her windshield before she transitioned to the 110 South, she was speed-dialing the watch desk at the Compton Station.

"Watch desk," answered the female voice. "Sergeant Menendez."

"Hello, sergeant," said Shia. "This is Deputy Saint George. I was following up—"

"Deputy!" interrupted the excited desk sergeant, her honey-smoked voice so welcoming. "Helluva night you had. You holdin' it together?"

"I'm fine," said Shia. "Wouldn't have made it without my TO."

"Lucky you had Lucky," grinned Menendez over the phone. "See what I did there?"

"Speaking of Deputy Dey," continued Shia, "were there any messages left on our call box? Just following up before I clear the shift log."

"Unit 780," Menendez repeated from memory. "Your black-and-white is still in the back lot. On the tow truck. Nobody's punching in without first giving it their own once-over, you know? There go we all but for the grace of God."

"Don't I know it."

"Okay. Pulling it up now," said the desk sarge. "Y'all got two pings. One from Deputy Kenya in 820. It says, 'No luck with finding out about status of dogs.' Another from Deputy Rodriguez in 750. Says, 'Got one of your whistles.' He added his mobile number. You want that?"

Whistles, thought Shia. Pink and full of promise. If there was one thing she'd gleaned from her three nights with Lucky, it was that he was like a dog with a bone. There was no way, suspension or otherwise, he'd let go of his ghettocide. If Shia could gift Lucky with a lead, he'd probably bring her along for the ride.

"Yes, please," said Shia. "Give me Deputy Rodriguez's number."

42

Altadena. 2:48 p.m.

In news parlance, the murder of Atom Blum was a fast-evolving narrative. While it was initially reported that the blockbuster film director was killed in a drug deal gone awry, the story quickly morphed from a tragedy brought on by the victim's own personal frailties to the rumored malpractice by the L.A. County Sheriff's Department. The leaks were everywhere and mostly without foundation. Some online sources wildly claimed the boy wonder had been killed by a deputy's stray bullet; others that he had accidentally administered the deadly shot himself.

Yet it was the gossip website TMZ that was first to get the story straight.

After paying off a qualified source inside the LASD, TMZ was able to reveal that Atom Blum had been in the black-and-white's back seat as a guest ride-along. A simple cash transaction had produced crime-scene reports that also included the names of the tour-guide deputies tasked with the director's safety. There was no mention whatsoever that prior to the ride-along, Atom Blum had soberly scribbled his famous signature on a standard LASD liability waiver.

"Mooooooooommmmmmm?" called Travis from the living room of the Altadena rental house. The young teen, his face temporarily removed from behind his electronic device, had the ears of a fruit bat. Upon hearing the distinct rumble of a diesel engine idling, he'd trundled into the living room to get a better look-see out the street-facing picture window. A mobile satellite truck, courtesy of a local television news station, was framed by the room's lacy curtains. Moments later, a news van with a microwave antenna and a competing station's call letters emblazoned across the side panels pulled up to the curb.

"MOOOOOOOOMMMMMM!" repeated Travis.

"I'm right here, so stop yelling," began Gonzo, wiping her hands on a dish towel. Then she saw the gathering of news crews. "Jesus H. Christ."

"Does anyone around here respect the nap?" complained Karrie, her hair a static mop on the side where she'd been sleeping.

"Where's Lucky?" asked Gonzo.

Instead of answering, Karrie caught sight of the TV news throng assembling outside the house.

"Ohhhh," said Karrie.

"Oh, what?" asked Gonzo.

"Why I just saw Lucky going over the backyard fence," answered Karrie. "I heard Travis and thought it was about Lucky, so . . ."

"So, yeah. It *is* about Lucky," chimed Gonzo, releasing the curtains from their hooks and struggling to slide them shut. Karrie joined the cause, assisting in blocking all uninvited eyes, not to mention camera lenses, from prying.

Lucky had been sorting through boxes in their detached, cobweb-infested one-car garage at the end of the rental's driveway. Unsatisfied with the mobility the hospital sling offered, he'd been rummaging for his rope-ring of duct and electrical tape. With an unconscious glance down the driveway, he had glimpsed the satellite truck angling for a parking space. That was all he required to connect the media dots. A famous movie director had turned up murdered. The sergeant in charge of the victim's safety had been Lucky. In the unholy search for ratings, local news directors would be demanding some kind of televised reckoning.

The door at the dark rear of the garage led into an overgrown vegetable garden Gonzo had planned to bring back to life. Lucky pushed past the stacked bags of soil conditioner, peeled off the sling, and ignored the soaring pain as he pulled himself up and over the ivy-covered fence. Before he landed on his feet, he could feel the wound-sealing staples pop and tear. Damn, he thought. Bleeding would likely follow. It wouldn't be long before the bandages were soaked through.

In his speedy dash, he hadn't considered the Rottweiler mix that normally patrolled the yard of his neighbor's property. Lucky was grateful to mark the beast as boisterous, yet restrained, behind the house's back porch slider.

At least one thing is going my way.

Despite the tempered glass barrier, the dog's bark was still piercing. Lucky quickly hurried up along the west side of the lot, churning up the gravel as he ran along the side panels of the house, then emerging through a wooden gate and into a front yard and a street empty of news trucks.

The phone in his jeans pocket buzzed. Certain it was Gonzo, Lucky answered without checking the incoming number.

"Hey, sorry," said Lucky into the phone. "Best I'm not around to feed the circus."

"Circus?" asked the voice. "Um. This is Shia Saint George."

"Not the best time right now," said Lucky, slowly jogging east down the sidewalk. "And you're not supposed to be talking to me, or me you."

"Got something on your pink whistles," she braved. "I know we're on suspension pending—"

"Who and where?" asked Lucky, slowing only slightly to better his hearing.

"Deputy Rodriguez," continued Shia. "Last night. He pinged our box. I couldn't sleep so I thought I'd come back this way and check it out."

Lucky's trainee was officially out of bounds.

Along with her training officer, Shia was on suspension pending a shoot investigation, during which period neither were allowed to so much as communicate a human or digital syllable. It was also departmental protocol to examine every discharge of both deputies' weapons. The chaotic shoot-out at the New Wilmington Gardens promised to be so complex that Shia's paid leave could last from months to as long as a year. Add to the bloody stew a dead movie director who just so happened to be pals with LASD's assistant sheriff and Vegas might have taken bets on how the internal investigation would eventually spin to a conclusion.

It was Lucky's sworn duty to show Shia the ropes—both inside and outside the confines of the black-and-white. His better judgment tapped on his shoulder, begging him to demand she step off and go home. But then there was Lucky's gutter side. The part of him that often trolled the waters of his darker impulses. If his young trainee had shown the initiative to follow up on his ghettocide, who was he to deny her the co-satisfaction of solving Mush Man's murder?

"Where are you?" Lucky asked.

"Northeast side of the grid," she said, referring to their patrol beat of Compton.

"Get up to Altadena. Need you to be my ride."

"You sure? We're both—"

"You're gonna break suspension all by your trainee self? C'mon. Flip a one-eighty and come get me."

"On my way," promised the deputy.

43

Downtown.

R*ape.*
Cat couldn't stop repeating the word, if only inside her skull. Upon her retreat from the fourth-floor ladies' room in One California Plaza, she'd bypassed the frosted double doors to her business suite and quick-stepped her way to the elevator bank. Fully ignoring the Chinese investor group she'd left mid-business pitch in her conference room, she climbed in the first lift to open its doors, pressed the button for the thirty-first floor, and took a twenty-seven-floor ride.

Rape.

She thought of all the men who'd touched her. Those who'd made her tingle with excitement. Those who'd left her cold and indifferent. The common thread among them all was that each—

even those in her occasional forays into group sex—had been invited.

Cat was a woman. As such, she'd supported every gender-related cause with her time, political connections, and money. She calculated that she had identified with practically every women's issue from discrimination to assault.

I had no idea.

That unwanted touch. That unsolicited finger-walk Julius had taken up her inner thigh to the lips of her vulva. Though hardly the worst of violations, combined with the threat, Cat felt as if the full, penetrative sexual assault had taken place. The shock wave the act had express-delivered to her soul was without mistake.

Ding.

Cat drove those killer heels into the thirty-first-floor carpeting, travelling a route she knew well until she pushed through an oak door stenciled with:

3144
Halberstram and Jenks
A Law Corporation

"Need to talk with Willie," snipped Cat to the sweater-wearing twenty-something perched behind an impossibly high reception desk. Not waiting for permission, Cat was dead reckoning for the partner's office.

"He's on a conference call," called out the receptionist.

Ignoring the warning, Cat turned the sharp corner into the roomy office of William Jenks. The lighting was exactly as he preferred—shades drawn, an amber glow from incandescent lamps of different antique designs. The lawyer himself—tiny enough to be Cat's fraternal twin—was appropriately suited, wearing a telephone headset, seated with his feet up behind an original J. G. Stickley desk.

William Jenks held up a stalling palm indicating for Cat to give him just a moment.

"Enrique," said Jenks. "Can I call you back in a few minutes? Promise, okay?" He hung up on the call and adjusted the headset so it dangled from his ear.

"I need a lawyer," announced Cat.

"And if anyone has her pick," quipped Jenks, "it would be you."

"I want you to rep me," she insisted.

"I'm flattered," he returned.

"What do I need to officially engage you—the firm?" she asked. "Whatever you need. Just say."

"It starts with you sitting down, taking a deep breath, and telling me what's going on."

"So you're my lawyer now?"

"With a promise to pay my fee you are entitled to all rights and covenants."

"Done," said Cat, allowing her machine-carved derriere to squish into a leather chair ample enough for a man four times her size. She crossed her legs for punctuation. "You're my lawyer now."

"And why is that?"

"Because I'm a criminal," said Cat, plain as wallpaper. "I've engaged in a criminal conspiracy which, I guess you could say, has gotten out of hand. My partner in crime has threatened me and I'm now in fear of my life."

"Okay," said Jenks. He sat up, taking a more significant and curious account of his friend-turned-client. "Is that all?"

"Is that *all?*" she asked with a sharp dose of unmeasured incredulity. "How long have we known each other?"

"Eight years? Ten?"

"Have I ever confessed to being a criminal?"

"Not a priest, Cat. No confessions necessary."

"You know what I mean."

"Maybe I should ask you to start at the beginning."

"Fine," said Cat. "You need to call Enrique back?"

"Enrique is an understanding client," assured Jenks. "Now, tell me how Cat Rincon turns into a wanton lawbreaker."

"Admitting it only to you," she reminded.

"Of course," said Jenks, assembling a fresh legal pad.

44

Compton.

Lil Rod. The name was all Shia had acquired when she'd run down a vagrant woman who'd taken up residence at the Jordan's Disciples Transitional Living Shelter near the Compton recycling center. The lady, mentally challenged and naturally frail, was too afraid to give her name. She did present Shia with the correct pink whistle, the name Lil Rod, and what she'd heard on the street to be the motive.

"He kilt da Mush Man cuzza he was protectin' da man's hole in da groun'."

The hole. By late morning, with the mystery electrical transmission line shut down, union and insurance investigators had been allowed to enter the blowout to photograph, measure, and document enough of the accident scene to satisfy their professional curiosities. Never mind that twenty-four hours prior it had been tagged a crime scene with the murder of a homeless man. It was as if the killing of Mush Man had been wiped away and replaced by the tragic workplace investigation of a valued county employee's death.

The DWP construction crew arrived to continue the repairs. Their overall mood bordered on giddy at the guarantee of overtime pay. At five in the afternoon, three diesel-operated light trailers were delivered. Each trailer was self-contained with a mast affixed with four metal halide lamps, promising a worksite blast of light so blinding the nearest neighbors would hang blankets over their windows to temper the glare.

Standing conspicuously still at the southeast edge of the hole was Lucky. With each second staring into the chasm, he hoped for an answer to the question why. The burning in his shoulder had been replaced by a deep and unstoppable ache. He had been able to fortify his bandages by yoking a Kotex pad over his injured shoulder with breathable cloth tape. He'd replaced his bloody T-shirt with a FIFA-approved *Viva Mexico* jersey. All items purchased at one of the five Compton Circle K gas stations. The Sudanese-born cashier who rang up the transaction didn't bat an eye. In fact, when handing Lucky his change, he'd grinned with a "Thumbs up Mexico, yeah?"

"Crew foreman says they had a delayed start today because of the insurance investigators," said Shia, easing up on Lucky's left. "That, and the transmission line was still live until late morning, I guess."

Lucky acknowledged her. His eyes, scouring the hole, lifted slightly to survey the exposed clay conduit that carried the old power cable.

"So it's just like you said," continued Shia. "One CSI gets zapped and it's like, 'What murder?'"

"How old does a transmission cable gotta be to be cased in clay pipe?" mused Lucky. His view lifted to the nearby rooftops and the aboveground power lines that fed electricity to each home. "Houses. They get their power from where? The external lines, right?"

Lucky was pointing, his index finger tracing the air as he

followed the drooping phone and electrical lines from pole to pole. A squat, hard-hatted man in DWP overalls and rubber boots was climbing one of the ladders leading out of the hole. Lucky stepped over and offered a helping hand.

"Ask you a question?" began Lucky to the hard hat. "That clay pipe with the hot cable in it?"

"Not hot no more," said the hard hat.

"How ancient it gotta be for you guys to use clay pipe for insulation?" asked Lucky.

"Not a pipe," said the hard hat. "Conduit. And how old beats the hell outta me. Before this blowout, hell, nobody I know has ever hit a live wire."

"I didn't even know Water and Power ran underground electrical," said Lucky.

"Hey, man," said the hard hat. "I'm on the water side of this shit. But from what my boss told us, we haven't run power under city streets since before World War Deuce."

"That so?" asked Lucky. It was rhetorical as if to confirm a notion he was already considering.

"What's that mean to you?" asked Shia.

"Visit to the Bunker," said Lucky, already ambling in the direction of Shia's parked car.

"What's the Bunker?"

"Gramercy Depot. Looks like a German pillbox bunker. Near Lennox."

"What's in there?"

"Water 'n' Power switching station. Ways back, guys workin' night shift were slingin' crack through the fence between the utility property and Jesse Owens Park. Lotta foot chases in that park."

"Ergo the name," joked Shia. Her punch line missed wide. Thus the sideways squint Lucky passed her way. She tried to save it with, "Jesse Owens? Gold medals? Famous American track and field athlete?"

"Oh," said Lucky. "Like, maybe I didn't run down 'em all."

"Did you?"

"Real world, kiddo," said Lucky. "Not everyone gets caught."

45

Downtown.

Hard as you work, Timbo, you'll always be fat.

He'd stayed late into the day, holed up inside his DWP cave, catching up on paperwork. All the while, worrying how—if at all—he'd be able to cover his tracks.

"Last to go makes all the dough!" called out Front Office Peggy as she slipped by his door.

"I'm a civil flippin' servant!" replied Tim from behind his computer.

"Yeah, but you're management!" she said, her voice trailing as she exited.

Tim checked his watch. It read almost half past six. With nowhere to go but his depressing week-to-week apartment, he locked his office door, elevator'd down to the garage, and drove the five short blocks to the Athletic Solutions Fitness Center, where he'd been a member since January. By the time he climbed onto one in an endless row of west-facing treadmills, the sun was dipping behind the Ritz-Carlton Hotel. The geometric-tipped high-rise, overlooking L.A. Live—the posh downtown destination that included the Microsoft Theater and Staples Center—appeared magically backlit in glittering gold. A fitting sight, thought Tim, considering the hefty price he paid for the gymnasium membership.

Paying to get fit.

That was going to be Tim's bonus for the cash he'd accepted from Cat Rincon and Hal Solomon. He'd drop a fistful of Benjamins and lose the weight, transforming himself into a more attractive photo to post on dating sites. Live bait for his future wife—the yet-to-be-discovered Missus Tim Gilligan Number Three.

In the six months since Tim joined the gym, he had scanned in a total of five times. And a scant fifteen minutes into his Thursday-night workout, he'd practically sweat through his 4XL T-shirt, turning the light gray into a shade closer to black.

"Dude, you're wheezing," said a trainer, stepping up next to the machine and reducing both the treadmill's speed and angle.

"Know what I'm doing," coughed Tim.

"Bad for business if you yack and I gotta call the paramedics," smiled the trainer. "I got nothin' right now. How about a free half-hour session? I'll hook you up with a circuit you can maintain."

Tim wiped his face on his forearm, took one look at the muscle-head with the bullshit tan, shaved, chest and bulging pecs, and wanted to spit.

"Did I ask for a trainer?" panted Tim. As he stepped off the moving track, he nearly lost his balance. The trainer's arm shot out and pinched Tim's greasy forearm, righting the heavyweight from a near spill.

"Dude. Just doin' my job—"

"Outta my way," spat Tim, shoving past the trainer and making a beeline for a column of perfectly stacked towels, which he knocked over with an embarrassingly awkward soccer-style kick.

Tim wouldn't look back. He didn't stay for a shower. And the rage he felt bubbling up within was a horrible surprise. It was as if months of resentment—from the divorce to his rejections by women to the stress of the crimes he was committing to the muscle-turd trainer in his red wifebeater—had teamed up to bust down whatever door he'd locked himself behind.

Screw me.

With his shouldered gym bag making his silhouette even wider, Tim rode the escalators down three flights into the underground parking. With every shortened breath, he waited for the heart attack to mule-kick him dead. Fell him like some sickened hardwood tree.

Would serve me right.

As his knees began to weaken, Tim instinctively began drawing air in through his nose, holding it a second, and then exhaling through his mouth. In through the nose, out through the mouth. All while the escalators delivered him lower and lower. His heart rate eventually slowed. The sweat on his face turned chilly under the force from a basement air-conditioning vent.

"Backtrack, Timmy," he breathed to himself.

He mentally retraced his steps. From sending the text message to shut down the uninhibited transmission line 439C to ordering the temporary tap of power from two local middle schools. It would be days—or maybe even weeks—before the schools discovered their meters spinning from the stolen electricity. But it would serve as a quick fix until he configured another workaround, collected the $55,000 in cash he'd hidden from his ex-wives, and made a run for God knows where. It was either that or engage an attorney to seek protection from prosecution preemptively.

No way 'round it, fatso. You're toast.

"Hey, Tim!" called the voice to his rear and left.

Tim started and twisted. He didn't recognize the fit-looking specimen in loose jeans. He briefly wondered if it was the asshole salesman who'd sold him the gym membership. The man was flanked by a spectacular woman—onyx black and in her twenties—in a V-neck T-shirt and black jeans.

"I'm fine with my membership," excused Tim. "Now, leave me the fuck alone."

"Slow your roll, fat man," expressed Lucky, displaying the six-point star of the L.A. Sheriff's Department. "I need you to come this way, please."

At first, Tim looked as if he'd been cracked with a wet washcloth. Then his spine seemed to straighten as a defensive question formed.

"What's this about?" asked Tim, wondering if they'd be able to read through his lie.

"Need to talk for a moment," said Lucky.

"Do you know me?"

"You Tim Gilligan of the DWP?"

"Yeah, but—"

"You wanna walk over here with me?" asked Lucky, dripping with mock politeness. "Or you wanna be flat on your fat face with your hands cuffed behind you?"

It was a total authority play. All cops pretty much knew it. And Lucky had performed it a thousand times. Without a warrant, simply make a request to a suspect. If the request is denied, offer a negative choice. It wasn't precisely a threat. Yet it worked just the same. In Tim Gilligan's case, he slightly lowered his head in automated guilt and allowed Shia to lead him to her Kia Optima. Lucky opened the door to the front passenger seat and assisted Tim until he was comfortably situated. He shut the door then lowered himself into the back seat. He landed with a painful *crump*.

"This doesn't look like a police car," suspected Tim.

"It's my car," said Shia. "So do your best not to drip your goo all over it."

"Mr. Gilligan. I'm Deputy Dey," started Lucky. "In the driver's seat is Deputy Saint George."

"Okay," said Tim.

"I would like you to tell me about underground transmission lines," said Lucky.

"What about 'em?"

"Just one," said Lucky. "Runs through Compton. You paid off a couple of homies at Gramercy to power it up."

"Lawyer," shot Tim.

"Say again?" asked Lucky.

"I want a lawyer."

"You aren't under arrest," said Lucky. "We're just havin' a talk."

"Still want one."

"All I want to know is why."

"Why what?"

"Why you powered up that old line. And for who?"

"Lawyer."

"You said that already."

"I have my rights, okay?" strengthened Tim. "I have wives and kids to think about."

"Wives?" chuckled Shia.

"Know what?" said Lucky. "I can understand you not wanting to speak in front of a female officer."

"Nothin' do with it," insisted Tim.

Meanwhile, Lucky caught Shia eyeballing him through the rearview.

"Understood," said Lucky. "Deputy Saint George? Would you mind stepping out?"

Obediently, Shia popped her door open. Only she stalled, keeping her eyes in the rearview mirror. She pulled the door back shut with an atmospheric *whump*.

"Deputy?" pressed Lucky.

"I'm good," replied Shia.

"I said you can step outside," repeated Lucky.

"And I said I'm good," insisted Shia.

There was an immovable force in her. If she'd been a man, Lucky would've regarded it as the moment her testicles had dropped. Only the trainee was all woman. Five full inches shorter than his beloved Gonzo, but fully female with bricks of her very own.

Lucky slid forward on the back seat, reaching both his arms

around big Tim Gilligan. He fed the seat belt from his right to left, engaging the tongue in the receptacle with a confirming snap.

"Why . . . why you buckling me?" asked Tim.

"For safety," breathed Lucky.

"You can't do this!"

"But I just did."

"I want the fuck out!"

"The hot wire in Compton. Why and who for?"

"I asked for a lawyer!"

"You did."

"So you have to get me a lawyer."

"People watch too much TV," sided Lucky to Shia.

With the little slack left in Tim's seat belt, Lucky quickly looped it around the engineer's neck.

"Hey, HEY!" shouted Tim.

Forced to favor his left arm, Lucky swiveled at the waist, reached over Tim's right shoulder and underneath the seat belt's sash guide, and gathered a handful of belt into his left grip. Instantly, Tim felt an increase in tension beneath his chin.

"I wanna know who gets the juice," insisted Lucky.

"Don't know who! Don't know why!" fended Tim.

"But you know where, right?"

"I know where it goes," confirmed Tim.

"Swell," said Lucky, easing back on the belt. "Now you get to show me."

"In my office. Everything's on my desktop."

"Nope," said Lucky. "You're gonna take us to where that transmission line ends."

"I don't think—"

"You're all buckled up," said Lucky. "Strongly suggest you take us for a ride."

Taking her cue, Shia strapped herself in and keyed the ignition. Only not before switching her smartphone off the video function and pocketing it in her jeans. The trainee's ground-standing play had been a mask to record covertly the entire ugly and way-out-of-LASD-policy episode of fat and afraid Tim Gilligan being threatened with torture at the hands of Lucky Dey. Shia was uncertain what kind of video she'd secured. The audio, though, would all be there, certain to give US Attorney Steve Wimminger a federal ear-gasm.

"Where we going?" asked Shia, dropping the Optima into gear.

"Compton, of course," said Tim. "Do I really have to go with you?"

As was his habit, Lucky left the dubious question unanswered. He gave his trainee the simplest of nods and leaned back, allowing his head to tilt backwards and his eyes to shut. Sleep might not follow. Yet even thirty minutes of short rest might allow his batteries a quick charge.

He didn't know it yet, but Lucky was going to need everything in his tank if he was to survive the night.

Friday

46

"Maybe you didn't hear me ask you nicely," complained Des'ree.

"I heard you fine, Momma," returned Frosty, the warmth of his mother's low-octave voice piped into his ear canals via a pair of form-fitting earbuds.

"But you didn't say nothin'," she said.

"'Cause I'm a good listener," jested the son. "You taught me real good."

"Don't play me like that. I made a request."

"Church, Momma? Really?"

Frosty shifted in the threadbare bucket seat of the '92 Olds Cutlass he'd borrowed from a livery driver. The car was worse than a beater with an engine so far out of sync it had already rumbled to a dead stall at two stoplights. He cursed himself for not testing the shit-mobile before deploying it on his stalk. At least it had a valid registration and the damned brakes didn't squeak as Frosty kept a safe distance on the snaking uphill and downhill road.

"How long it been since you took me?" asked Des'ree.

"Since you couldn't get there on your owns," miffed Frosty. "Your ankle was broke."

"Had a nap today and I dreamt that you was with me at church. And Jesus was smilin' down on us."

"Was just a dream, Momma."

"Woke up I was cryin'. My heart was in pieces."

"Aw, Momma."

"You too busy bangin' not to give me that one thing?"

"Not bangin'," defended Frosty. "I'm workin' the nursery."

"This time of night?"

Frosty was tired as hell. Tired of lying to his mother. Tired of making excuses. He was tempted to lay out his present position for her.

I'm drivin' this dark-ass shitty street in some part of the city called Mount Washington. Followin' some thirty-five-year-old cholita in her red Audi.

The preamble was the same as Frosty's smoke-job in Tarzana, when he'd popped that old Jewish man and his fake-tittied ex-wife. Only the stalk on Cat Rincon left Frosty with constant stirrings of unease. The woman in his sights had no predictable routine. Since he'd delivered the scare message at the Rose Bowl, Cat hadn't once returned home or repeated an action. He'd followed her for miles, covering real estate as diverse as Huntington Beach and Covina to what felt like everywhere in between. She attended meetings between all her mealtime meet-ups and made pit stops at cocktail functions and charity fundraisers with the swiftness of hitting corner 7-Elevens for coffee refills. And now he found himself on the snaking roads of Mount Washington, two miles northeast of downtown. He kept a safe distance while mentally clocking every on and off flaring of her taillights. Cat also appeared unfamiliar with the terrain, uncertain where each curve led. Making matters more frustrating, Frosty hadn't yet received the actual green light to slay the *ese chiquita*.

Such was the game.

The uneven roads were rarely wide enough for two cars and only guard-railed for half of the most precarious turns. Between what appeared to be newish, post-modern homes and hippie chalets were dark, unlit sections of dangerous blacktop. If Frosty were a careless or impatient killer, it would have taken little more than an angled fender from the heavy Oldsmobile to bumper-thump the Audi A4 convertible over a cliff and into a fatal four-hundred-foot tumble. It could take weeks for a dead body to be discovered in the uninhabited canyons below.

As Frosty came upon a rise in the road and a meandering, left-sweeping turn around the edge of the mountain, he caught a dazzling view of downtown. The Mojave-heated Santa Ana winds had all but pushed every visible particulate out toward the ocean, leaving the night air unobstructed all the way to the twinkling shore.

"Well?" asked his momma.

"Church?" returned Frosty. "Or what I'm really doin' right now?"

"I'll take church."

"Whatever," relented Frosty. "I'll go with ya, okay? But I ain't doin' no singin'."

"Only if God inspires you to," Des'ree smiled over the phone, pleased as Sunday punch.

"God already knows, Momma, Frosty-dog don't sing for shit."

"What if God don't call out to Frosty? He may still call you Lamar."

"Jesus can call me a no-good nigga and I'm still not singin' no Bible hymns."

"Love my Lamar," she sang.

"Love my Momma," said Frosty, clicking off the call and carrying on with the stalk.

Less than a quarter mile after he'd hung up with Des'ree, the

Audi braked opposite a gated stilt home guarded by a neat flagstone wall. Frosty eased off the gas pedal. In the hundred or so yards between his borrowed Olds and the idling Audi, he could make out the silhouetted figure in the driver's seat kissing her passenger goodnight. The passenger stepped from the car, revealing herself to be bone white, thin, raven-haired, and poured into a black cocktail dress. It was nothing more than an end of the night drop-off. Cat appeared to be waiting politely for the woman to enter the gated property before she released the brake and motored on. For the next five minutes both cars wound down Mount Washington to the Pasadena freeway for a short, near traffic-free route to the Crown International Hotel.

And that was where Frosty left Cat. The remainder of the overnight stalking was subbed out to a pair of Crip babysitters on Julius's payroll.

Yet Frosty's apprehension remained.

If the order to kill Cat Rincon were to come that day or the next or even a week hence, Frosty wasn't near ready. To him it was all about *his* careful execution of the execution and not Julius Colón's recent and odd impulses. And without a consistent routine or pattern to plot by, Frosty would be unable to predict an outcome resulting in Cat Rincon's certain demise and—of comparable importance—his certain escape. Anything short of perfect was plain dumb and might result in catastrophes like that reckless bullshit at the New Wilmington Gardens.

On the ride back to Compton, Frosty began cementing his own three-point plan.

Get paid by Julius.

Sever ties with Julius.

Start a nursery business and get on with the gettin' on.

47

Compton.

Tim Gilligan hadn't needed to access his office computer. He *knew* the address to which he'd directed untold watts of unregulated power via that long-forgotten underground transmission line. This, despite having never once laid eyes on the location, let alone completely understanding the scheme behind it.

"All I know is that it was an old aviation tire plant," admitted the DWP manager. Still buckled into the front seat of Shia's white Optima, he was gazing upon the shadowy address for the first time.

"What's it used for now?" asked Shia.

Lucky was 99 percent sure of what ongoing crime was concealed therein, but didn't feel the need to answer. It was no secret that both federal and state police agencies trolled public utilities to uncover illegal marijuana grow sites. The juice required per square foot to operate an indoor pot farm, be it in a converted one-car garage or a long-abandoned airplane tire factory, was far beyond normal consumption. The simple algorithm, once applied, was akin to unmasking a bank robber.

But not these bad boys.

By arranging unmetered and unregulated electricity, clever marijuana farmers could produce crop after crop with minimal worry they'd be discovered because of some power anomaly.

From Lucky's vantage, the decrepit factory appeared to occupy half a city block. Rimmed in rusty cyclone fence, topped with triple strands of sagging razor wire, the defunct plant looked the part of a landlocked oil tanker. Lucky instructed Shia to circle the property, allowing him to count off four sentries. One at each corner. Crips all, each occupied as much by his phone screen as his mind-numbing job.

"Both of you stay here," ordered Lucky once they'd parked. "I'm not back in ten minutes, call in a double-oh and make sure you get lost." Lucky opened the back door. "Got any spare Kevlar in your trunk?"

"All I got is a furniture blanket I use for my daddy's wheel-chair," answered Shia.

"That'll work," said Lucky. As he shut the car door and rotated to the rear, Shia triggered the trunk switch.

"Can I ask somethin'?" asked Tim, his words audibly timid. "What's a 'double-oh'?"

"Ten-double-zero," said Shia. "It's a call sign. Means officer down and needs assistance."

Lucky ambled into the dark, the folded blue furniture blanket tucked under his right arm. He was feeling unusually stiff in the joints, every step a reminder of the night before. An onshore breeze had cooled the air, adding to his discomfort. He wondered if this is what old age felt like. Then just as quickly he thanked Jesus that, considering his headstrong history, he probably would never reach the age of sixty.

The chain-link was eight feet high. The razor wire added another foot. Lucky unfurled the furniture blanket, gripped it wide, and spun it upward and across the top strand. It was a one-shot try with the half-inch blades snagging it dead.

Sweat gathered on Lucky's brow as well as the creases of his palms.

This shit's gonna hurt.

Up until the blanket toss, Lucky hadn't once deigned to lift his left arm over his shoulder. The dull ache had been replaced by a pain so acute and burning he imagined the staples used to seal his wound had completely lost their grasp. He found himself with an opioid craving. What he wouldn't do for a handful of Percocet. He could almost taste the tablet on his tongue.

"Piss on it," Lucky hissed.

He reached up and gathered handfuls of chain-link. The rest was absolute will. Because the tread of his sneakers couldn't find a toehold, it all depended on upper-body effort. Grip over rusty grip. And so fast, time wouldn't allow for an adrenaline release. Lucky hooked his right arm over the top strand of blanket-defended razor wire. It sagged under his weight with a single barb busting through to puncture his bicep.

"Shit!" he bitched to the night.

He pushed over the top, making sure to hang tight to the top bar. He let go to keep his good shoulder from separating. His feet touched concrete on the other side and his natural balance took over. His legs, though, were shuddering as if he'd just sprinted a mile without warming up.

Lucky tracked westward, easing closer to the ancient concrete and metal behemoth in search of a way in. He thought he detected a faint electrical hum coming from inside the building, but nary a leaked lumen. If it was a grow house, the owner had sealed it so not a lick of light escaped. And whoever the illegal proprietor might be, he surely wouldn't allow it to be guarded only at the corners, thus Lucky gripped his SIG .45 and held it tucked against his ribs.

A five-step metal staircase—no more than a half flight in elevation—hung from the side of the building. Lucky found the bottom step, climbed by mostly feel, and tried the corroded fire door. It sang a sour note as it scraped against the concrete floor, yet revealed nothing but a blackness so opaque it betrayed reason. In the darkest of dark, Lucky's eyeballs still searched but could land on nothing at all. It was as if a sack had been pulled down over his head.

Reaching out into the void, his fingertips touched something smooth, dry, and so familiar. Plastic. It gave in like a two-ply garbage bag. Stretching. He could feel it vibrating like a sheet in a breeze.

The droning thrum, Lucky figured. They had to be agitating fans, a must for any indoor pot farm. With the muzzle of his .45, he probed deeper until the light-impervious sheet of plastic tore at the edge and released the magenta rays from the banks of grow lamps.

It was as Lucky had expected—only far more ambitious in scale: a wall-to-wall weed farm. The factory floor was a veritable plantation—thousands of green cannabis plants in various stages of growth. Tiered by age. Perfectly fed. A horticulturist's wet dream.

Damn, mused Lucky, begrudgingly impressed.

This was what required an unfettered electrical feed worth protecting.

This was why that hole in the ground mattered.

This was why Mush Man had been murdered.

A mirror duplicate of the exterior stairwell led Lucky to the farm floor. The unconscious ten-minute clock in his head had long stopped ticking, replaced by awe-struck astonishment at just who could have built such a ballsy operation.

Lucky realized he was very exposed.

He must have been detected. An investment so appreciable would not be without defenses. Cameras. Armed guards. An encounter was not only expected but damn sure imminent. Lucky's heart pulsed all the way to his knuckles. He kept his .45 in play, muzzle just south of horizontal, hoping to wound only the first comer. He would need to apply pain to extract the information his DNA demanded.

Lucky's thoughts were overtaken by the sound of barking dogs. Angry. A hard-charging racket. He coolly swiveled toward the sound, but was shaken by the sight. The marijuana plants' perfect vertical stalks were shaking, agitated by fast-approaching beasts. In the seconds it took Lucky to assess the danger, the guard dogs had covered more than half the distance across the pot field. The quivering stalks betrayed their ever-widening swath as they charged their target.

One attacking dog, he could put down. Maybe two. But three or more teeth-gnashing beasts? Not a chance. Lucky's only escape was the way he had come in. So, he reversed his path. The pivot he made was, he thought, five strides from the foot of the steps he'd only just descended.

His mental math was wrong.

Three swift paces and he was at the rusted stairs. His timing was poor. His toe caught the underside of the first step and, before he could catch himself, his oft-busted face only partially broke his fall. He would have growled a worldly curse if his jaw hadn't been clamped from the immediate shock of it. His ears rang with blood. Or was it just the reverb from his body slam into the timeworn stairs?

But where were the attacking dogs?

The barking had stalled. The beasts should have been upon him and ripping into his legs. That's when he heard steps. Light. Dog paws on his left, panting, and wet noses fighting for sniffs at his ears and neck. Lucky forced himself to roll to his left and open an eye. Through semi-blurred vision he saw fur and mutt-ish, slobbering dog mugs radiating a familiar hounds' stink.

"Oprah," muttered Lucky.

All four of Mush Man's sled team were upon him, lapping up Lucky's familiar smells. He righted himself, re-gripped his pistol, and searched the perimeter for human approach. He sighted no one. Not a solitary biped. But then came a not-so-distant voice.

"STUPID GODDAMN DOGS!" shouted a barrel-voiced man. "GET YOUR FURRY TAILS BACK OVER HERE!"

A piercing two-fingered-whistle followed. The dogs' ears briefly perked, yet they remained expectant and stuck at Lucky's side.

"Here we go, gang," whispered Lucky, pressing back up to his feet. "C'mon, yup."

Lucky climbed the half-flight with all four dogs at his heels until they were outside and well beyond the cannabis farm's magenta pall.

As Lucky escaped, Big Otis balanced upon one of the industrial stepladders used for pruning and harvesting. His eyes, hampered by a mix of color-blindness and astigmatism, strained for movement. The best he could catch was the last two dogs scampering up a stairwell and out through one of the fire exits.

"Bomb them dogs," pissed Otis, already scraping at his fat brain stem to come up with an excuse as to how and why he'd just lost Julius's smelly mutts. The boss had not just burdened Big Otis with the chore, but had also made him clean up the mess the dogs had made of his condominium, including a kitchen floor smeared wall to wall with their excrement.

Still parked outside the defunct tire factory, Shia remained alert behind the wheel of her Optima, Tim Gilligan strapped in at her side. Both were keenly aware that they were two full sweeps of the second hand beyond Lucky's order on when to bug out and place the officer-needs-assistance call.

"Twelve and a half minutes," jiggled a nervous Tim.

"Shut your mouth," was all Shia cared to reply, keeping her gaze fixed on the silhouetted monolith framed through her windshield. There'd been reason aplenty for her to follow orders. Leaving Lucky behind while dumping Fat Tim at a convenient corner to thumb his phone for a ride would have left her alone and in possession of her ticket to Washington. The kidnapping and threatened torture of the DWP civilian had been duly captured on her camera phone—all procedure and due process ignored by Lucky Dey. Shia's mission was accomplished. So, why the hell stick around beyond Lucky's arbitrary countdown?

You should've left after two minutes! her inner voice shouted.

"We wait him out," hushed Shia.

She was half ready to switch on her headlamps and shock the desolate scene with her high beams when—

KER-WHUMP!

The Optima's atmosphere felt like the air was being sucked

out as one of the rear doors was yanked open. Violently so. Only instead of Lucky folding himself into the back seat, four large and dirty mutts vaulted inside, one after the next, instantly spoiling the last possible whiff of the vehicle's new-car smell.

Lucky joined the back seat fray and pulled the door shut.

"What are you waiting for?" Lucky demanded. "Let's get outta here!"

"Right," said Shia, turning over the engine and jetting the car into a stealthy U-turn. "Where to?"

"Nearest twenty-four-hour drugs," moaned Lucky. "Need Benadryl."

Big Otis looped the old factory three times, once clockwise and twice counterclockwise, all the while cursing the stupid beasts as well as Julius for not turning the four mongrels over to Animal Control for destruction. None of the four sentries reported hide nor hair of the dog pack. On his last rotation, Big Otis decided to flashlight every oxidized foot of the chain-link at dog height. Though his low gaze entirely missed the blue furniture blanket hooked and hanging over a three-foot section of razor wire, he did discover a corroded section of fence pushed through to the sidewalk.

Mystery solved, thought the big man. *See ya later, mutts. An' good goddamn riddance.*

Big Otis pulled the fire door shut, repaired the blackout plastic with duct tape, and ambled back to the observation platform that had once been the factory foreman's post. Set up with a folding buffet table, stackable outdoor chairs, and a humming mini-fridge, Big Otis planned to put up his size-fourteen feet, get nostalgic with some Tupac on his headphones, and take his sweet time working up a plausible excuse as to how he lost the dogs.

"You back from fixin' your fuckup?" asked Frosty, seated at the buffet table, the operation's lone laptop open to a mosaic of security camera images.

"What you 'bout up in my shit?" angered Big Otis.

"Checkin' my pot stalks."

"Then go check on 'em," urged Otis. "Or you gonna take over my squat?"

"You gonna tell Julius 'bout the bust-in?"

"Wasn't no bust-in. Was them stupid-ass dogs."

"You sure?"

"Damn sure. Saw where they pushed themselves through the door and then the fence. You like dogs?"

"Got no problems with 'em," said Frosty. "And yeah. I'll take yer squat."

"Bam!" said Big Otis with a touchdown dance. "I. Am. Gone!"

Frosty didn't need to look up from the computer screen to know when Big Otis had checked out. His ears tracked the man's thumping exit all the way to the squeaking door underneath the foreman's tower. With his eyes fixed on the mosaic, and the digital dexterity of a fifteen-year-old, Frosty enlarged each individual camera frame and rolled back video for a full hour. Next, he fast-forwarded through each camera's view until he spotted the intruder. White male. Six feet, Frosty guessed. And no doubt 100-percent cop. By keying up various camera angles, Frosty tracked the dogs' path through his cannabis forest to the intruder, who had stopped near the bottom of the fire stairs. Frosty chuckled when the white man face-planted on the stairs. But the questions were adding up.

If he was a cop, where was his radio?

Why did he run like he was scared by dogs, only to rescue 'em as like he knew 'em?

Who the hell is that white nigga?

48

"This'll do," said Lucky, pushing open the Optima's rear door with his sneaker. The four mongrels had already been deposited at a local shelter with Lucky's promise to return and collect them the following day. What was left of the bottle of Benadryl lay on the back seat, cradled by a messy cushion of recently shed dog hair.

"Instructions?" tested Lucky.

"Return Mr. Gilligan to where we found him," answered Shia. "Go home and wait for the phone to ring. Maybe somewhere between I get my car cleaned?"

"Call could be tomorrow. Could be weeks," said Lucky. "Listen to your deputy reps. Do as you're told. And whenever shit gets hard to answer, it's all on me. I was your TO. You were following orders."

"So what about me?" whined Tim Gilligan.

Lucky hesitated as if deciding whether there was an answer better than none at all.

"Get a lawyer," croaked Lucky before shoving the door shut and double-rapping his fist on the trunk.

He watched the Optima's taillights until Shia made a left turn and disappeared from sight. The boulevard was empty. Were it not for the occasional streetlamp, the locale might have been mistaken as some post-apocalyptic dystopia—with horizons in both directions appearing endless and uncomfortably unpopulated.

Lucky rotated his view across the four-lane track to the mostly dark strip mall and its lone light-burning business. The establishment's sign, once a white bubble-styled fixture backlit by fluorescents, had yellowed over the years. A red plastic W had been pasted where a K appeared to have been peeled away with a dull paint scraper, changing the sign from Pizza *King* to Pizza *Wing*. Light from the restaurant bled from a storefront window partially concealed behind a folding security screen. A closer look revealed the green, white, and red panels of the Italian flag painted in liquid chalk.

Using his fingertips, Lucky checked to see if his wound was bleeding through. The fact that it hadn't leaked since his gas station fix was a testament to the technology of feminine hygiene. He checked his pistol, hooked and holstered against the small of his back along with the two spare magazines clipped to his belt.

He wet his chapped lips, tasting the bitter remnant of cherry-flavored Benadryl. He hoped whatever adrenaline he could summon would act as a bulwark against the doze-inducing diphenhydramine. He smirked to himself, imagining that whatever he encountered inside Pizza Wing there'd also be a parallel chemical cage match raging inside his brain—sedative versus adrenal hormones.

And may the better drug win.

He crossed the threshold of the pizza shop and was hit by a blast of oven heat spilling through the propped-open door. It slapped everyone who entered with a face full of hot, dry air. Lucky noted how claustrophobic the one-table dining area was and wondered how he would manage to maneuver through the cramped space in a scuffle.

To the left was a display fridge with a variety of cold drinks in cans, plastic bottles, and sixty-four-ounce jugs. The aging unit thrummed loudly and practically drowned the voices coming from the kitchen. Lucky approached the lift-and-hinge counter and stood waiting for one of the two aproned cooks to take notice. Both young men were black, in their late teens, and, by Lucky's read, gang-affiliated based on the tattoos creeping out from underneath their respective sweat-marked T-shirts.

"Counter," chirped the pizza cook who, between sliding pies around the oven, twirled the paddle like Bruce Lee wielding a Kendo stick.

The younger of the pair wore a red IHOP T-shirt smudged with flour and pizza dough. He wiped his hands on his apron and approached the customer, his gait ever wary with each step closer.

"Help you?" asked IHOP.

"Lookin' for your boss," said Lucky. "Gave me his card."

"Who dat?" asked IHOP.

"Julius," said Lucky.

"Yeah, man. Julius, like, owns us. But he owns lotsa places and not like he comes in here much."

"This is the card he gave me," said Lucky, sliding it across the counter. "Tell him I wanna talk about the dogs."

"Dogs?" laughed the pizza cook.

"I'll eat while I wait," assured Lucky. "How's that?"

"Order up whatever," said IHOP. "But can't say if the boss'll come 'round none."

"Sausage and cheese?" requested Lucky. "Small oughta do me."

"Somethin' to drink wid dat?" asked IHOP, writing down the order on a self-carbonating pad.

"Can of Pepsi," said Lucky. He peeled off a twenty, left it on the counter, and relaxed into the corner seat of that lone table for two. Lucky was glad to feel his belly rumble from hunger. A good sign that despite the adrenaline, Benadryl, and pain, his body demanded fuel. In that pinprick of a moment, Lucky imagined a mouthful of hot pizza would feel nothing short of sublime.

He popped the soda can with his left hand and, with his right, pulled slightly on the butt of his pistol to test the ease of a quick reach.

Just in case.

"Never thought I'd say puh-leeeaaaasse put my nigga ass *back* on the farm!" bitched the hard-breathing voice outside the door.

A shadow crossed the window separating the storefront from the sidewalk. Lucky heard the *tick-tick-tick* of smooth rolling bike gears. Through cracks in the chalk paint, he made out what he could of the figure. The cyclist sported a multi-colored cycling jersey and was diminutive despite the volume of his voice.

"Used to *like* workin' at da *WAAAANNNGGGG!*" bellowed the cyclist.

Lucky felt sucked into a vacuum. His skin tingled and the hairs on his arms stood as if electrically charged.

The front wheel of a neon yellow bicycle rolled in, stalling halfway through the pizza shop door. The rider, incongruously sporting black cargo shorts with that skintight jersey, propped the bike against the doorjamb and swung a tattered vinyl hot box onto the counter.

"You gotta tell customers we don't deliver nothin' east of Central 'n' west of Avalon—"

"Wa-wait!" interrupted IHOP with a laugh and fumbling for his phone. "Wanna get me some video of Lil Rod's complain face."

Lil Rod?

Lucky's nerve endings, already tweaked, were fully prepared to leap connections and act with deadly purpose.

Lil Rod.

The move—as pictured in Lucky's mind—was in a filmic series of skip-frames. As if there were a time-cut between Lucky raising his pistol and Lil Rod's skull being split by a 230-grain slug. Yet Lucky remained seated. Still. Externally calm. Reminding himself that the ultimate prize was Julius Colón—Pizza proprietor, cannabis entrepreneur, and supposed dog lover.

El ultimo hombre.

At least that's what Lucky presumed. He didn't know to an absolute certainty if Julius was truly the responsible party. Nor whether the skinny young pizza deliverer had been, in actual fact, on the trigger for Mush Man's murder. The ghettocide. It was conjecture and conjecture alone that had led Lucky to this singular moment. At Compton's Pizza Wing. Seated. Sipping cold Pepsi and waiting for a sausage and cheese pie. All the while, his subprimal sense informed him that he was indeed in the right place at the right time for the right primitive reasons.

Lil Rod was only half joking about his preference for pulling shifts at Julius's south side nursery over the stifling kitchen at the Pizza Wing. The long day he'd spent assembling tree boxes had left him with a sore back, splinters and blisters, and craving a long line of tall, ice-cold forties. When the text from Big Otis had landed on his phone, informing him that he was needed to fill in at Pizza Wing, he'd been chuffed, thinking his brief time toiling in plantation hell had come to a close. He hadn't given a second thought to the end of the text, instructing him to make sure to bring his bike rack. If the trigger-happy gangbanger had put it together that he'd be peddling bicycle deliveries all night, Lil Rod might have summoned a fake injury.

"What's with bleach boy?" Lil Rod didn't care a whit that lily white Lucky was seated a mere ten feet from him.

"He's sausage and cheese," barked the pizza cook as he pulled open the seven-hundred-degree oven to see if the pie was ready.

"That you?" mocked Lil Rod to Lucky. "You a sausage and cheese?"

"Asked for a vanilla milkshake and saltines," shrugged Lucky, "but your man behind the counter said they was all out."

Lucky's comeback secured a belly laugh from somewhere deep in the kitchen. From whom he couldn't see. Lil Rod, though, didn't find it funny. In fact, the teenager stiffened and dead-eye-stared at Lucky.

"Think unless you Johnny Law, you in the wrong side of the 405," challenged Lil Rod.

"Maybe I heard this is top pizza," said Lucky. "Best dough south of Lennox."

Lil Rod's murder glare remained fixed on Lucky until IHOP slid a stack of three pizza boxes into the vinyl hot box.

"West 163rd," said IHOP.

"You shittin' me," moaned Lil Rod.

"Bitch your lips at Julius," slammed the pizza cook without looking away from his job. "Now git before shit gets cold."

Lil Rod picked up the hot box, but wouldn't leave before one more unwelcome glower at Lucky. He bungeed the hot box to the bike rack, flipped on a battery-powered headlamp, and backed out. The front wheel barely cleared the threshold when Lucky's pizza landed on the counter with a metallic crack.

"Gonna eat that here, right?" confirmed IHOP. "Red peppers, Sriracha?"

"I'm good," said Lucky, retrieving his meal and returning to the seat. He unconsciously spun the pizza like a wheel of fortune, letting the slice choose him instead of the other way around. The crust was hot enough to sting his fingertips, a pain he welcomed. Anything to encourage his adrenal glands to produce more hormones. Strangely, Lucky's olfactory sense was suppressed and he couldn't smell the ingredients. He ate anyway, working to maintain his patience with every bite. All the while he flogged himself for not separating Lil Rod's head from his body when he'd had the chance.

With half the pizza consumed, Lucky slid the chair and let it tilt against the plaster-coated wall. Without a plan or thought, his eyes closed shut for a reprieve. In the darkness, he hoped to clarify his purpose—ease his angst over the missed opportunity. Instead, his mind involuntarily slipped into a non-REM dream sleep—a.k.a. the nearly awake hallucinatory stage. In the dream he found himself seated in his home dining room. Not the table shared with Gonzo in their Altadena rental, but the blue-collar Mar Vista home of his youth. The walls bore the same faux wood panels. Dark. Faded finish. The cobalt blue shag carpet was worn and stained. Yet neither his deceased mother nor brother was seated for the meal of sausage and cheese pizza.

Gonzo sat opposite Lucky in her blue-black LAPD pilot's jumpsuit. Flanking him left and right were Karrie and Travis, both as if dressed and ready for a regular school day. The trio's faces were as cold as metal. A voice from the kitchen was calling out for instructions on how to operate the oven, a mid-century gas dinosaur with too many dials to decipher. After some ear strain, Lucky recognized the distant words as belonging to Shia. The trainee was struggling to reheat her slice of pizza. While Lucky yelled back that the oven was off by as much as fifty degrees and she needed to adjust, Karrie was dividing the congealed pie and serving slices on paper plates.

In that five minutes of alpha sleep Lucky had no appetite whatsoever. He craved only pills to kill the pain. A fistful of Percocet would have sated him. With a Vicodin milkshake chaser and a day or two of coma-like napping.

"Finished with that or ya waitin' for it to get colder?"

Lucky's eyes snapped wide, the dream sleep interrupted. Seated in the other chair was Julius Colón—between them the half-eaten sausage and cheese pizza.

"I can have my kitchen reheat it for ya," offered Julius.

Lucky tried to clear his corneas with a couple of complete blinks. It was very obvious to him that the struggle between the adrenaline and the Benadryl had been won by the over-the-counter juice. How long had he been sleeping? Two minutes? Ten?

"No matter," said Lucky, answering his own mental question.

"Was it good?" asked Julius. "My pizza?"

"Did the trick," replied Lucky, summoning his wits. He felt fuzzy from his hair follicles to toenails.

"Got a text message," Julius leaned in, gesturing toward the nearby entrance. The entire doorframe appeared to be occupied by Big Otis. "Said you wanted to check on the Mush Man's dogs?"

"Yeah," said Lucky, straightening the slouch in his spine. "They okay?"

"Doggies are good. Get yourself good Samaritan points for checkin' on 'em." Julius turned his wristwatch—a platinum-cased Breitling—to face Lucky. "But at after three in the mornin'. That's some weird checkin' on shit hours."

"I'm sheriff's," said Lucky. "I'm used to an upside-down clock."

Julius leaned back in his chair, drummed his fingers twice before snapping them at Big Otis.

"Got my phone, O?" asked Julius.

Big Otis lumbered the four steps to his boss. A smartphone was produced. Julius checked the screen, manipulated the image until it suited him, then turned it around for Lucky's benefit. On the screen was a still-frame from one of the weed farm's security cameras. The image was zoomed and grainy, but doubtless in identifying the subject: Lucky Dey as he ushered Mush Man's four mutts out of the abandoned tire factory.

"Here's what I don't get," complained Julius. "You all about them stupid dogs? Or law enforcement got some play I don't see? And I mean that like this way. I know you sheriffs. But you just a patrol motherfucker. That, and you on suspension for that Fourth of July shit show over at the NWG."

"You know almost about as much as me," throated Lucky.

"Almos'. But what do you know that I don't?"

Lucky considered an answer. He weighed the satisfaction of assisting Julius by explaining how the DWP blowout hole in Poinsettia had led him to Tim Gilligan and then the abandoned airplane tire factory. Yet the connections were far clearer than the conclusion. Had Lil Rod gunned down Mush Man on Julius's direct order? Or just as a matter of consequence? Lucky's gut wouldn't offer a concrete answer.

Both Lucky's hands rested on the table, fingertips rotating the cold pizza in more counterclockwise turns.

"You gamin' me?" pressed Julius in a gangster pose. Eyeballs fixed on Lucky's. "Or this about you and that little Mush motherfucker? Like, personal, you know?"

Personal, indeed.

"About a ghettocide," said Lucky.

"Ghetto what?"

"Both of us know nobody's gonna answer for Mush Man," continued Lucky. "At least, not officially."

A slow-motion smile spread across Julius's face.

"You a badass?" said Julius. "You and that Reaper shit. Lennox badasses all. Like that tat still give you permission to fuck shit up."

"Just some old ink," said Lucky. "This right here? Is about what happened to the Mush Man."

"You here to justify me? That what this is?"

That's exactly what this is.

Lucky left Julius's question unquenched. It thickened the air so that Big Otis, who was back to filling the front door, nervously shifted from side to side. A poorly concealed .40-cal was gripped and hanging in his left hand. He was waiting for a sign. A move. A reason to perform for his boss. Julius's pupils were packed with movement and squirreling over Lucky for twitches or tells.

Lucky remained the picture of calm. Stoic. Pokerfaced. Prepared to die, but not until he'd kicked over the two-man table and blown hollow-point punctures in both Julius and his supersized bouncer. This was because nothing in the world spoke more to actual guilt than Julius's playing offense. And, in a moment, it would be worth it. The fog would lift and clarity would win the day despite the mortal consequences.

"Got family?" asked Julius.

"Got nothin' to do with nothin'," replied Lucky.

"No? Well, let's see," said Julius, returning to his mobile phone and tapping out an unknown text. "'Scuse me a sec while I talk at my number-one ninja. Hey. Here's a question. You got any ninjas?" Julius paused his texting before continuing to thumb his message. "Swear to Jesus, everyone should have one or two. But this particular ninja, see? I'm tellin' him to take care of business if I don't make it back to my crib or my farm or any of my other responsibilities. That means if you, Deputy Lucky, gots people? My ninja's gonna smoke 'em dead and gone. And that's as sure as I'm sittin' here with you and your half-eat sausage 'n' cheese."

Lucky recalled the recent dream sleep—the one with his

made-up family seated around his mother's dining table. The image was still etched in Lucky's eyelids. If he closed his eyes again he'd see them—their expectant faces—each begging Lucky to be both father and husband. The feeling warmed his veins and pulsed to his limbs. He felt a cool sweat bust out on his forehead.

Jesus Christ, thought Lucky.

Why do I put myself in these positions?

"Sure. I got people," said Lucky with purpose. "But Mush Man? All he had was his dogs. And all his dogs had was him."

"Not so. You forgettin' they got you? Otherwise, why you here?"

"Maybe I just came lookin' for something to kill this pain I got." Achingly, Lucky slow-shrugged his bullet-torn shoulder. "I could use some Vikes."

"I look like a drug dealer?" defended Julius.

"Say you're just a weed farmer with a big fat bodyguard?"

"Deputy fuckin' Pill Junkie," dismissed Julius. "Bullshit."

"Recovering," admitted Lucky. "But after the last forty-eight, I'm reconsidering my options."

The conversation reached its rhetorical maxim. Neither man was eager to engage or share another thought or existential observation. All that was left between the pair were the silence and the question of who would make the first move. The second hand of Julius's oversized Breitling continued to sweep in perfect, Swiss-engineered ticks.

As Lucky would later recall, it was the minor weep of a panel van's brake pads putting the squeeze to a disc that drew his eyes sharply to the left, sneaking a peek through that same crack in the window paint where he'd first spied Lil Rod and his neon yellow bike. A sky blue panel van slowed to a stop. Rusty. Precisely the style of vehicle he would have profiled for a traffic stop. Broken tail lamp. De-illuminated license plate. The passenger-side window obstructed with cardboard and duct tape. The vehicle screamed as either a stolen handyman's van . . .

. . . or an assassin's coach.

In equal motions, as the panel van's door was shoved wide,

Lucky palmed the edge of the two-top table and thrust it away from himself and into Julius. The strip mall king was caught by surprise and was struck by the table with such force it sent his chair into a backward tilt. Before Julius could catch himself, gravity took charge, tipping his chair toward the floor.

Big Otis, more concerned with Lucky's assault than the panel van, swung his left arm upward with the fully efficient intent of unleashing a half clip of .40-caliber slugs into the deputy. Perhaps it was his massive size that made him the initial target. In the eyeblink before Lucky witnessed the Pizza Wing's window implode, he saw the first bullets cut through the bodyguard. They spun with such velocity, the projectiles tore through Big Otis before puncturing the soda fridge in a carbonated explosion. Big Otis's knees gave in and he dropped.

Lucky chased Julius to the floor. He hurled himself downward in hopes of surviving the spray of glass and sizzling copper. Behind the crashing window was the sound of a machine gun. The high-speed sputter sounded more like chainsaws on full throttle than gunfire. And as fast as the onslaught had been unleashed, it ceased.

Whoever they are, they're reloading.

Lucky crawled ahead on nothing more than adrenaline and instinct. He fully expected to find Julius either dead or injured and panicked. Lucky found neither. Amidst the shattered glass and splinters, where Julius should have been after the initial tumble, remained nothing but the tipped chair.

Julius Colón had vanished.

49

The man with the Mohawk had his thoughts on ice. Not that he was distracted from his extant task. If anything, he was *pinche experto* at eliminating the competition. Mohawk's proficiency was such that while in the midst of accomplishing his chore, the early morning ice time at the Artesia Skate Palace was at the forefront of his thoughts.

Goddamn ice hockey.

Mohawk had grown up on Cesar Chavez Avenue as Oribe Diego Alves. Some twenty years earlier, to celebrate his fifteenth birthday, the East Los Angeles teen had borrowed his sister's electric Lady Groomer to shear off his unruly mane save for an inch-and-a-half racing stripe of black curls. From that day forward, he was happy to go by the nickname Mohawk or, more simply, Mo. But that was only if the dude was *carnal*.

In those adolescent years, Mo cared for two things: baseball and gang life. And being a cholo came with too many vacations in state incarceration. Preston. Pine Grove. Solano. San Quentin. Each institution a career-killer for a baseball player. His final hardball hope was to father a son or two someday. He would teach them to play the game he so revered, never skipping a precious practice or missing a single inning.

Then came marriage and Mo's discovery that he could only father daughters. His wife insisted on tubal ligation after their fourth screaming baby girl. Despite that, he signed up every daughter for park leagues, praying that softball might salve his desire to play baseball dad. But not even those *pinche* optic yellow softballs would stick. None of his daughters showed the aptitude for sports until his last girl, Alma Juanita. As her story unfolded, Alma Jane accompanied a figure skater friend to an after-school workout at a local rink, witnessed a sloppy junior hockey scrimmage, and summarily announced her sport would be that of pucks, pads, and ceaseless early morning ice times.

Jesus.

While Mohawk found it weirdly incongruous to bundle himself in a winter parka to attend his daughter's summer hockey practice when it was a hundred degrees outside, there was nothing unordinary for him to receive a kill order. He'd long passed on a managerial role in MS-13 organized crime in lieu of ice time. The transaction required an O.G.—or original gangster—like Mo to act as an on-call assassin. The order to take out Julius Colón had come from the cartel via a criminal attorney on a yearly retainer. Mo's instructions were to the point and required immediate action.

The early model Chevy panel van was easily stolen from a driveway where it wouldn't be missed. Mo had a crew of five, three fifty-five-gallon drums of diesel fuel, and a belt-fed M249 Squad Automatic Weapon, known amongst Marines as a SAW, partially named for its ability to cut down whatever was in its sights. While a tattooed minion tracked Julius, the sky blue van circled the tire-factory-cum-weed-farm. One by one, Mo quickly assassinated the corner sentries. After, the drums were rolled out the back and left in the care of the two Mara Salvatruchas assigned to put flame to the entire cannabis crop.

Unbeknownst to Julius Colón, he'd been tailed since his midnight weight-lifting workout at the Gold's Gym in El Segundo. But it was during the meet-up at Pizza Wing when Mo felt it opportune to strike. The driver obediently eased the Chevy van parallel to the storefront. Before it had fully braked, the panel door slid open. Behind the SAW machine gun was Mo, prone on a grease-stained carpet remnant, the weapon's barrel propped level on a folding bi-pod. With the SAW's mechanism primed, Mo pulled the trigger. His plan was to fire smooth and level from left to right, beginning with the bodyguard propped in the doorway. He'd glide the barrel until the primary target was cut down, then finish on the stranger shadowed behind the chalk-painted window. The SAW erupted in flame and bullets. The recoil surprised Mo in such a way that a level spray was impossible. The barrel bucked upward and, after the bodyguard was felled, getting the weapon to behave along a horizontal plane was more of a chore than anticipated.

Mo watched the sheet of window glass fall like a curtain. The old gypsum rock wall separating the kitchen from the one-table dining area disintegrated into a dense plaster fog, making any movement hard to distinguish.

Then the lights went out.

One of the SAW's high-velocity rounds had met with so little resistance it had travelled through the first Sheetrock wall, carried the length of kitchen, and bull's-eyed the fuse box adjacent to the rear door. In an array of sparks, all lights in the Pizza Wing went out.

Where are the goddamn bodies?

Experience had taught Mo to lower his sights in search of fallen men. But in the dark, the best he could do was tilt the muzzle downward and spew lead where he imagined Julius Colón had fallen. He saw only muzzle flashes and the dust-up of hot concrete as bullets skipped off the sidewalk.

"Let's go!" Mo barked to the driver.

With military efficiency, the van's door closed and its gears engaged. For the next half block the van drove without front or rear lights. At the first side street, it made an effortless right turn and vanished into the night. Inside a linear mile, at a preordained spot, the Chevy van was parked, emptied of all weaponry, and set ablaze with the leftover diesel, to be discovered later as just another burned-out automotive carcass that littered so many ghetto land-scapes.

Lucky couldn't put a clock on how long the gunfire had lasted. Or the weapon used. Or if he'd even been struck, considering the level of pain to which he'd already become accustomed. In his violent career he'd never experienced such a shocking volley. And the usual slow-motion gunfight recall was utterly nonexistent. It was more like a bomb had been uncorked rather than a machine gun unleashed on the pizza joint. Big Otis and the sheet glass window had appeared to cave in unison. Whatever had sent Lucky to the floor—be it alarm or reflex—hadn't mattered beyond the self-preserving result. Through the splinters and dust and microscopic glass, he'd barely glimpsed Julius's snap reaction.

And then the damned scene had gone dark.

Absolutely and temporarily opaque. Somewhere, somehow, the machine-gun assault had ceased and the vehicle that delivered the assailants had hurried off into the night. This left Lucky crawling. Not into the street, where the air might have been more breathable. Instead, he shuffled on the route he imagined Julius had escaped. How far? Lucky hadn't a trace of an idea. At any moment, he fully expected to clamor over the strip mall king's bloody bullet-pocked corpse.

Lucky snaked into the kitchen, maneuvering underneath the hinged countertop. A battery-operated emergency light sputtered over the rear exit. Through the staccato light, Lucky spied the two pizza makers, motionless and bleeding out from a multitude of life-ending punctures. The pizza oven was open and spilling its seven hundred degrees, the pies inside burnt and smoking.

Lucky stood, crossed to the phone on the wall, listened for a tone, and dialed 911. He left the phone to dangle knowing full well the operator would scramble both fire and police to the traced location. Then he stumbled for the already opened rear door.

The alley behind Pizza Wing was worse than dim. Before choosing a direction, Lucky was forced to wait for his eyes to adjust. He heard a distant bottle skitter, kicked off a human foot. He snapped his head left and began his run before he could even read the ground beneath him.

You're alive, okay? Now get after it.

The *it* was a man. Julius Colón. No doubt he'd been in foot chases with cops before. What self-respecting thug hadn't begun his criminal career hot-footing from some Johnny Law bastard?

Only Lucky wasn't on the job. He was on suspension, warrantless and with zero authority. What good was phoning for backup when the off-book deputy was moonlighting as a one-man death squad?

You're on your own, idiot. Try not to wind up dead.

The alley ended at East Myrrh Street. Residential. A customary Compton landscape of tiny stucco hovels fenced in by corroding, three-foot chain-link fringed a roadway so clogged by parked cars it was reduced to a single lane. Nearly one hundred yards away there was a lone streetlamp casting a dull, yellow apron of shine. Through the pale light Lucky saw a running man—Julius—favoring his left leg. Whatever injury he'd sustained appeared not to slow him. He ran like a running back with an extra-moving part. A double-hitch. And Lucky, his lungs already aching for oxygen, was barely keeping pace.

Experience had taught Lucky to conserve. Arms tight to the body, shoulders switched on relax. Keep the target in sight. Let the suspect bust something pulmonary. Blow a shoelace. That's when a bad guy would choose shelter over speed. Corner. Try to fight his way out against a cop armed with experience and a gun . . .

. . . and usually an entire PD to back him up.

Julius kept to his line. Due east. He ran without deviation or, from Lucky's still far-off perspective, even a look behind to see who or what was pursuing him. His pumping arms worked overtime to make up for whatever ailed.

"SLOW DOWN!" Lucky found himself shouting.

The waste of precious air lost out to his own frustration. Like Julius should retard his pace? If Lucky could, he would have laughed at himself. The pair had just survived a machine-gun attack by who the hell knows. As if that shared experience was something they could halt the chase and build on?

Lucky found himself wishing for air support—a helicopter—loudly hacking at the thickening atmosphere with its elevating rotors. He thought of Gonzo and pictured her point of view from behind the chopper's stick. Apart from barking at Lucky to call off his illegal pursuit, she would have mapped the scene and pro-jected a route. As darkness loomed ahead of Lucky, a grid formed in his head. It was the plot of Compton he'd required his trainee to memorize. He himself hadn't studied it, but had learned it by testing her—Shia, his overeducated trainee.

East Myrrh blunted into the Long Beach Freeway. Beyond the freeway was one of the broader tributaries of the concrete-hulled L.A. River. Wherever Julius was headed, this was his backyard. For Lucky to keep pressing was at his own increased peril.

Screw it, decided Lucky.

I'll cut 'im down when he's on the fence.

The street concluded at a sixty-foot slant of scrub and sand. An eight-foot chain-link safety fence cheaply screened with green vinyl slats was all that defended the freeway from intruders. To Lucky, scaling yet another fence with his screaming shoulder felt like a game-breaker. If he were going to finish off Julius, he was better off doing it with a grain-heavy slug to the man's spine.

Lucky eased off his run and dropped to one knee. With no chance to recover his breath, he'd need a steady hand and a trig-ger finger with more squeeze than spasm. His ears filled with the sound of speeding cars as they pushed the freeway air. He could see Julius cleanly ahead. The chugging silhouette didn't stop to size up the fence. He leapt and expertly hooked an arm over the top. His climb was going to be fast, and his fall onto the other side would be hidden from Lucky's view. It was now or not at all.

Reaching back into his waistband, Lucky felt for his .45. With eight loads in the mag and one in the pipe, he'd have nine squeezes to stop the runner.

But that supposed he had a pistol to aim.

Lucky's hand, so practiced at unsheathing his weapon, releasing the safety, and dropping sights on a target, came up empty. There was no gun in his waistline holster. Somewhere between the Pizza Wing and the patch of asphalt where he knelt, the pistol had loosened and fallen away without him having the slightest inkling. There followed an instinctive three-sixty-degree search in place, as Lucky prayed to find the .45 within quick reach.

No gun was anywhere in sight.

The scream of a southbound motorcycle split the night air. Some kind of Japanese bike. Rice rockets, the Chippies called them. It turned Lucky's attention back toward the freeway and that fence he'd have to overcome if he was going to keep with the chase. Julius, for sure, had expanded the space between himself and Lucky. His advantage was becoming more obvious with every one of his pursuer's heaving breaths.

Last chance, dumbass.

If Lucky didn't continue, he reckoned his chances of meeting up with Julius without a phalanx of Crip bodyguards or an entire law firm present would be cut to nil.

So move your feet.

Lucky leaned and pushed off against the pavement, charging into another run, leaving any remnant of his being a sheriff's deputy behind. His will was vengeance. And what lay ahead was no more and no less than a street fight leading to loss or ultimate resolution.

To the death.

It was like being a teenager again. Flipping over fences. The churning of dirt and loose asphalt underfoot. Beating his feet as fast as he could to grind out a clean escape sucked Julius right back. He was lighter back then, minus thirty pounds of muscle. And without a hitch in one of his motors. A running back, his Pop Warner football coach had lectured, had nine engines: two legs, his glutes, a muscled core, a pair of arms, the heart, and most importantly, his brain. But one of Julius's motors had been scored by one of Mo's high-velocity bullets. Back right thigh. Millimeters from severing his hamstring.

Evading capture by cop wasn't an exact science. Not in the hood. The proliferation of PD helicopters had made it all the more difficult. Yet there were some timeworn exits the cagey Blaxican could employ. One was what some bangers called the "Freeway Run." Taking a dead reckoning for the Long Beach Freeway—or the 710, as the westside locals called it—a fast footer could flip over the fence, climb the bank, and dodge speeding cars across eight lanes of north- and southbound traffic. No cop, from L.A. Sheriff's to LAPD, would risk causing a multi-car accident resulting in injury, death, and most relevantly, countless lawsuits. But for a fearless gutter punk, playing chicken with a bunch of commuters was worth the risk.

Part two of the Freeway Run—as an evasion tactic—would involve circumventing the eye in the sky—a.k.a. the helicopters. Beyond the Long Beach Freeway stretched one of the L.A. River's original arteries. After a second fence hop, an escapee only needed to find a way into the channel and look for the nearest spillway connecting back to the Compton storm drains. Most evacuation spouts had long lost their protective grilles to corrosion or vandalism. Fetid and forbidding as the environs might be, the shafts made for a near-certain escape.

Injury notwithstanding, Julius felt confident he could shake Lucky. It was the deputy's posse that caused him worry. With every stride, his ears were tuned for sirens. Perhaps the CHP had been alerted and, once he attempted to cross freeway traffic, they'd overrun him in their super-charged Ford Explorers. Julius crested the slope shy of the road's shoulder. With hard looks both north and south, he spotted not a single spinning red light.

His worry shifted to the helicopters. Julius chided himself for having to stop for even a breath. He forced an efficient turn, using the freeway's elevation to scan the horizon for any oncoming chopper. He sighted one bird, but it was beating out a tight circle around a city block roughly two miles to the west. Centered underneath the helicopter's sweep, the O.G. spied a city block–sized structure fire with flames reaching three or four stories. Julius could practically count the fire engines. Four alarms. He was even able to make out the arcs of pressurized water streaming into the pyre.

That's my fucking farm.

The realization sucked the wind from his chest. The blaze was at the old aviation tire factory. By the abundance of smoke, Julius reckoned his cannabis plantation was a total loss. All the planning. All the investment. Gone. Never to be recovered.

Julius's fixation was shaken by the sound of rattling chain-link. His pursuer was below. That Reaper. Alone and with no visible backup. Still pressing the chase.

Goddamn him.

Julius stepped backward onto the road's shoulder. He spun and returned to running mode, fueled as much by anger as the pain of survival. The crease behind his thigh, bleeding down his calf and into his right trainer, was less a sting than an oncoming Charlie horse. Would his leg cramp and fail before he could clear all eight lanes? If so, the chase would end with him a red smear inside parallel rails of tire marks. Turning around wasn't an option. Julius made himself a snap promise: should he survive the scramble across the freeway, there would be one hell of a reckoning.

Traffic screamed past. The average speeds near seventy-five miles per hour. But due to the hour, the wide spaces between cars beckoned.

It's Friday, Julius remembered halfway across the southbound stripes. Fubar and Mickys—his favorite nightclubs—would be slamming with man flesh. Something to live for?

Absofuckinglutely.

A box truck in the far left lane flashed its high beams to warn Julius, who only surged ahead. The miss was so close that Julius heard the truck's brakes lock before a howl of skidding rubber. There followed a rush of turbulence, the prevailing wind reversed by the drifting truck. Julius didn't see the sidewalls collapsing under the box truck's weight. He was already advancing over the concrete meridian when the truck landed on its aluminum side. Had the opportunist in him not seen a massive gap in northbound traffic, Julius might have glanced back. All cramping aside, he pushed himself over the last four lanes and butt-slid himself down the opposite dirt slope.

Behind, he heard the squealing tires of cars, all growing ever distant the further he lowered himself toward the flood channel. Whatever mayhem he had left in his wake, he hoped it would slow the deputy. Crush him, even. Perhaps the cop was already dead on impact. Julius could only pray as much to the god of his own criminal imagination.

And for a lick of good fortune.

Bad as the future looked, Julius painted it with a silver lining in the hair's breadth of digression he'd allowed. Ahead was the climb down to the dry bed of the L.A. River and a chance to find a dirty spillway. Then he could disappear for a time. Reconstitute and recalculate. Live to kill Lucky on another day.

50

Lucky caught not a glimpse of Julius nor his gimpy sprint across the 710's eight lanes. While cresting the slope to the freeway's shoulder, he'd slowed at the high-pitched shock of shrieking tires. A box truck wiped past, tipping like it had been jiujitsu'd to the pavement. Rooster tails of sparks arced as the hobbled truck scraped to a stop. Cars swerved. Three more locked up their wheels, drifting or spinning like metallic pinwheels. Fenders met bumpers met car doors, but impacts were well less than severe as the four out-of-control passenger vehicles careened off each other like carnival bumper cars.

The box truck was Lucky's shifting concern. His reflexive worry was that the driver could have been ejected and crushed by his own rig. No sooner had he switched angles than he spied the truck driver sprightly clearing himself from the horizontal cab and grabbing his cell phone.

The multi-car accident stalled traffic in both directions—the northbound lanes because of man's predisposition to rubberneck at carnage. Lucky seized the opportunity and ran full tilt without obstruction or incident.

His shoulder wound burned from the salt in his sweat. His left side was sticky and leaking with blood dripping to his fingertips. He stained the asphalt with a DNA map of his own one-cop crime wave.

Lucky slipped off the freeway and plunged himself back into the darkness. He slid down to another stinking chain-link fence— his third that night—toed and grasped his way over, landing on the top edge of the concrete channel. His eyes were already adjusted. Up and down the riverbed he scanned, locating neither sign nor sound of Julius.

A rusty access ladder was bolted to the wall of the channel forty yards south. Lucky eased himself onto the first rung to see if it would take his weight. He then descended, the last five feet a straight drop to a chalky floor. When his sneakers landed, the slap echoed along the squared culvert, announcing he'd touched down.

Lucky knew suspects would sometimes infiltrate themselves up and into the spillways, temporarily hiding out inside the storm drains. The ambient night light reflected off the sun-bleached concrete. Lucky swerved his view from north back to south, barely regarding the lone ribbon of water working down the center. It was like a slow-moving brook, no more than two feet wide and four inches deep. Wasted water, meandering its way to the Port of Long Beach. It made a slightly perceptible babbling sound. Peaceful, even. Any moment, it would be drowned out by the sounds of sirens—emergency services bearing down on the accident scene on the freeway above.

The stripe of water was blackish muck. Grossly contaminated with all matter of street residue. Yet in the dark gray of those early morning hours, something in Lucky wanted to lie in the stream, cool himself, and allow it to soothe all his aches.

Then Lucky heard it.

A scrape. A shoe, perhaps? South of him. Perhaps from under the Alondra Street bridge, which carried cars back and forth from Compton to the incorporated City of Paramount.

Lucky jogged closer. His eyes scoured the landscape, seeking any manner of weapon. A stick. A shorn length of rusty rebar. A concrete chunk. Yet nothing availed. The shadow cast by the span was nearly impenetrable to the eye. Lucky thought his pupils must have been dilated to the size of opioid saucers in their demand to gather the threadbare available light. He slowed, easing into the black overcast from the overpass, begging his eyes to adjust.

The massive, paved culverts snaked throughout the county. And once inside, the constructs all looked the same save for the angles. The city boulevards and bridges crossing the channels served as natural cover and shade. During dry times, entire tent and cardboard communities of homeless would spring up practically overnight.

Lucky noted the sound of dribbling water. High and right. He guessed there must be a storm drain outflow. He could barely make out the circle carved into the slab wall. Like a darker hole cut inside an even darker hole—black inside of blacker. If Julius were crouched inside and could make out Lucky's form, he could quickly land upon the deputy, laying Lucky out in a single airborne tackle. Knocked to the concrete, maybe unconscious, Lucky would be defenseless.

Lucky eased his progress, straining an ear for echoes of Julius working himself deeper into the drain. With the overpass buffeting nearly all freeway sounds, that singular trickle of water was all that registered.

A chill worked its way through Lucky. There was a veritable absence of sound. Lucky heard his own inhalation followed by the emptying of air from his spent lungs. And little more.

Then landed the rope—and an unexpected cinching around Lucky's unprotected neck.

* * *

Julius had heard the ringing as Lucky descended the rusty ladder as well as the slap of the deputy's shoes landing on the channel floor. If he could have continued his run, he might have been able to create more distance. His right leg, though, had cramped and practically quit. The swelling from the bullet wound had gripped his hamstring. The limb was seizing, close even to paralysis if Julius didn't stop pushing for more yards. He found cover under the darkness provided by the overhead span, then heard that trickle of water coming from the spillway. Julius ran his fingers along the concrete wall, hoping to find both moisture and the bottom of the outlet. What his fingers found instead was a rope. Dangling. Nylon. With plastic filaments wound into the kind of strand utilized to fly red, white, and blue flags above used car lots. It was shredded from age.

Julius clamped his fingers around it and, without assistance from his right leg, pulled himself up and into the four-foot-diameter spout.

The spillway's floor was slimy. Julius's mind briefly narrowed to his wound and what matter of infectious swill was gathering in his torn flesh. He spun and tried to crawl deeper, only to find that particular mouth had an intact protective grille.

Of course it has a grille!

To what else would the rope have been attached? The shaved hairs on Julius's neck made themselves known, setting off a hot flash tracing all the way to his pelvis.

Julius was cornered.

In the slight ambient light, he could see into part of the channel when he peered left from the spillway's mouth. That asshole deputy was hustling toward the underpass. In a matter of seconds, he was sure to be struck by the blackness just as Julius had been.

Julius had made a career out of recognizing even the tightest advantage. And there, while crouched in the spillway, he embraced his moment of opportunity. His eyes had adapted. He couldn't see much, but it was surely better than what Lucky might in those initial moments of plunging darkness. Julius thought he might be able to leap upon Lucky, knocking him hard to the pavement before finishing him off in a flurry of hammer fists. But the cramping in his leg was so complete he couldn't imagine putting together more than a controlled fall.

Then Julius remembered the rope, still in his hands. He first gathered all of it as a defense to keep Lucky from making the same discovery. Only when he reached the last length of the ratty nylon did he picture how he would end Lucky's life. By little more than feel, Julius fashioned a noose. Simple. The plastic braiding, though worn, provided a stiffness that allowed a loop to form—one that remained wiry and oval. Like a cowboy's lasso.

Easing to his stomach, Julius stretched himself, hung the noose, and held his breath—a feat he imagined he could do to a count of fifty.

One . . . two . . . three . . . four . . . five . . . six . . .

Julius needed only to still his breathing until twenty-seven. As the deputy eased deeper into the underpass, stalking the same trickle of water just as Julius had, he stalled for a moment.

Twenty-one . . . twenty-two . . . twenty-three . . .

Then Lucky edged ahead just one more step. With that, Julius dropped the noose and coiled his body, pulling on the rope with everything he could muster.

As Lucky felt the rope cinched around his neck, his instinct was to fire his hands straight to his throat, slipping a finger or two inside the snare before it tightened. But before he could even manage one digit, the lasso constricted and throttled his windpipe.

Julius was going to choke him to death.

Lucky thought to spin away with his legs. Instead, he was like an untrained dog on a leash, yanked backward into compliance by his master. He found himself turned around, off balance, and backpedaling in hopes of finding an inch of slack.

Only there was no lack in tension as Julius reeled Lucky in. All the core work from all the mixed martial arts workouts had tooled Julius for this one act. Inside the hole, he was able to brace his one good leg against the sidewall and continue looping the nylon length around and around his forearm until he heard the foot scrapes stop. That's when he knew he had him. The sheriff's deputy—dangling at the end of his noose—hung by the neck, moments away from unconsciousness due to blood starvation to the brain, and then, death.

"Got you, motherFUCKIN' REAPER!" growled Julius, a grin behind his grinding teeth.

Lucky stretched with his toes, hoping they'd reach the floor of the channel and give just the slightest relief from the asphyxiation. How far was he off the pavement below? Two inches? An inch? Was that going to be enough to snuff him?

I'm a dying fish on a hook.

Taking a subconscious cue, Lucky began to flop, at first hoping to jar an inch or two of rope from Julius's titan grip. Helpless to do anything with his arms, he convulsed yet again, turning himself ninety degrees and realizing his last hope. One more spasm and Lucky had reversed himself to face the concrete wall. He released his futile grasp of the burning braid around his neck and gripped the length just above him. He pulled, getting just enough relief to plant his feet against the wall. The deputy prayed he'd found purchase enough to shift the deathly paradigm.

Lucky arched his back and ran his feet further up the wall until he found leverage enough to push off. The give he felt was human. Yet Lucky was at a precipice. His head was spinning for oxygen. Blackout and whatever followed was a second or two away. With his last measure of thrust, Lucky fired his legs. Something had to snap. Would it be his neck, the rope, or the man at the other end?

Whatever leverage Julius had earned within the diameter of the spillway was lost in an instant. One moment he could feel the life slipping from the man at the end of the rope, the next he was hurtling from the storm drain. The feet of nylon weave around his arm held tight as his body flipped around it. There was an audible popping sound as his arm dislocated, followed by a crush of hard pavement against his skull as gravity had its way. There were no stars for Julius. Just ear ringing and a visual whiteout that looked like television static had been plugged into his optic nerve.

Lucky didn't register his return to terra firma. With the noose still working against him, he randomly worked his feet until he was righted, his body slumped against the wall while his finger-nails dug to get beneath the nylon and free his half-crushed larynx. The rope came loose as he unleashed a gagging cough. With each inhale came a spasm of putrid convulsions. The adrenaline gave away and his head spun.

Lucky's vision returned with a moment of strange clarity—as if the blood rushing to his skull had opened his pupils like an evening primrose collecting moonlight. Everything was grainy. But definitive. Julius was ten feet away and struggling to stand up. Without forethought, Lucky beset upon the man. He tilted and thrust himself forward until he was astride Julius with conviction and a flurry of fists.

Julius, down to only one working pair of limbs, forgot his training. While Lucky was straddling and dropping unshielded knuckles onto his face, the strip mall king twisted and gave Lucky his back. But not in surrender. Julius tried to crawl, rocking his hips and pushing off with his one good leg. He had no leverage to throw an elbow and defend himself. With all his weight, Lucky placed both hands on Julius's skull and ground it into the pavement with debilitating force.

"Quit!" sucked Lucky through his teeth.

If anything, the word had a reverse effect. Julius found a knee and twisted again, this time tossing Lucky sideways. The deputy hung on, locking his own body to Julius's. The force of the spin worked against Julius, turning him a full rotation and into the same precarious position.

Only with a very different result.

Lucky heard the splash and gurgling before he recognized that he was also wet. Any pleasure to be gained from the sensation of coolness would have to wait until Julius stopped struggling. It was the stream. The runoff from lawn sprinklers and leaking pipes, and possibly even the fire hoses at the airplane tire factory fire, ran like a charcoal ribbon down the center of the flood chan-nel. Just two feet wide and mossy bottomed to a deep green slick.

And though only four inches deep, it offered water enough to drown a man.

Lucky applied every meter of his own might, his arms locked at the elbows and hands palming the back and sides of Julius's squirming head—all without a lick of remorse. For Lucky, all mercy had been wrung from him, leaving nothing but the will to accomplish what God wouldn't.

Justice.

How long Lucky was astride Julius would remain unknown. He would only remember it as a fog of combat. Eventually, when Lucky was certain Julius had inhaled enough putrid liquid to drown to death three times over, he climbed away and slid himself only yards from his victim. There Lucky sat, arms resting on his knees, returning air back to his lungs, waiting to be arrested.

Some forty feet above and a football field and a half to the north was the accident scene on the Long Beach Freeway. Lucky was able to identify the CHP units by the sound of the sirens. Five by his count. Followed by fire and EMT vehicles. In moments, Lucky reckoned, accident witnesses would recount to the Highway Patrol the foot pursuit that had spurred the road mess. He fully expected to see flashlights and patrolmen investigating the claims. Hastening his discovery was the appearance of the L.A. Sheriff's helicopter. The aircraft practically fell out of the sky, held at an altitude of five hundred feet, and began a tight counterclockwise circle. The blinding spotlight ignited the freeway below.

Any moment now . . .

If the patrolmen didn't come, his capture would surely be expedited when the helicopter beam crossed over. How hard would it be for the pilot or observer to miss the body laying at the edge of the overpass's shadow and the depleted male seated a can's kick to the side?

Minutes ticked on. Eventually forty-five of them passed. Patrolmen never moved on to scour the riverbed. Stranger still, the chopper's white-hot beam never touched the channel bottom before it was called away to another emergency. Nobody, it would appear, was at all curious about how or why the freeway accident had occurred. Perhaps because there were no serious injuries, the initiative was to get the asphalt cleared and returned to an unchecked flow of traffic.

Or perhaps, because it was Compton, nobody gave a rat's ass.

Lucky sat without moving until all authorities had withdrawn. He could hear the heavy tow vehicle arrive, position, and scrape the tipped box truck off the roadway above. Only when the diesel engine roared and throttled ahead was Lucky certain he was going to be left alone to give a final regard to Julius Colón's puddle-soaked corpse.

"Way it goes, Julius," remarked Lucky. "You're just another ghettocide. That's how your shit ends."

51

The Standard Hotel. Downtown. 7:48 a.m.

Out of an abundance of concern, Cat had switched hotels. This after already paying for a second night at the downtown Crown. She'd only just crossed her suite's threshold when the chill had rushed her. It was followed by a paranoid whisper in her head.

He knows you're here.

That had been enough. Cat had gathered her belongings and called for a car to deliver her to the Standard. She barely slept. After a treadmill run in the hotel gym followed by a bracing shower, she was in a hurry to make the eight-thirty Mayor's breakfast at the Westin Bonaventure.

She raided the hotel room's mini-bar, stocking her Marni handbag with two Red Bulls and a Diet Coke. She double-checked to make sure the ring volume on her phone was loud enough that she wouldn't miss either call or text from William Jenks, informing her that "the problem" had been managed. She didn't want to calculate the political cost of such a favor. Most likely, the shady lawyer would be skinning her for years to come.

Just as long as Julius the Prick is dead.

The cab line was five riders deep, so Cat chose to walk the few city blocks. Her pace was brisk and her joints felt lubricated from her jog. The sleeveless dress, thank God, was vented and cool. The five-inch heels were her big mistake. The thought of spending the entire day in the killer pumps nagged her with every new step. When a city bus swerved to a corner stop a mere quarter block ahead of her, she shouted piercingly, waved an arm, and jogged the final yards down the sidewalk.

The bus driver, a spreading fat man with a jolly grin, was more than happy to keep the door open just to watch the pint-sized *chiquita* shimmy up his steps and jangle her purse for change.

"Thanks for waiting," she breathed.

"Thanks for being you," winked the driver.

Before Cat could come up with the fare, her phone sounded. She held up one finger to the driver while the other hand pounced once she saw it was William Jenks.

"And?" she asked without a hello.

"This isn't a full confirmation," he monotoned. "But my initial report is to expect a positive result. Talk to you later."

The lawyer hung up, propelling Cat to thumb for Tim Gilligan in her contacts. She had to send the text she'd already composed in her head. All was going to be well. Put a cork in your panic, fat boy. Crisis averted.

"Got a route to run," prompted the bus driver. "You got fare for me?"

"Shit. Sorry," replied Cat, shoving both her hand and phone back into the $600-handbag in a frenzied search for her wallet. The Diet Coke, agitated from her sixty-yard run, breached. The snap top on the can unsealed just enough to release the carbon dioxide–pressured goo upward in a misty spray. The caramel plume hit Cat directly in the face while succeeding in spritzing the driver and even a portion of his windshield.

"Oh, crap!" screeched Cat once she realized that what hadn't soaked her face had detonated inside her bag, leaving all contents fizzy, sticky, and ruined. She tried to save her smartphone, wiping off the moisture. The phone was done, though, already infiltrated, the electronics ruined.

"Two seconds ago you was Holly Hot Body," laughed the bus driver. "Now you just a hot mess with no fare."

"Fuck you!" spat Cat, turning and nearly tripping her way back to the sidewalk. The doors shut behind her and the bus roared ahead. She spun and pissed aloud, "Shit, fuck, shit, fuck, shit, fuck!"

Along with Warner Brothers Studios, the distributor for all three *Roadkill* movies, Atom Blum's agents at William Morris Endeavor had been quick to step up to organize a memorial service for the tragically murdered boy wonder. The service was set for Sunday at Warner Brothers' storied Burbank lot, an empty soundstage reserved to stand in for a church. Atom's favorite production designer, German-born Hans Heiger, was tasked to oversee the studio's art department appropriately dressing the set and erecting seating for at least one thousand slick-suited mourners. The event would be invitation only, each envelope hand-delivered via studio messenger. Press would have access, but only to cover celebrity comings and goings. A marketing honcho floated the idea of hurrying up the release of a *Roadkill* DVD boxed set to take full advantage of all the overwhelming goodwill aimed at the deceased movie director, not to mention the mountains of free publicity.

L.A. County Assistant Sheriff Paul McGill received his personal invitation at the department's Temple Street office. The gold-embossed envelope was waylaid on his secretary's desk, only feet from the utilitarian armchair where Shia Saint George awaited alongside Steve Wimminger for an audience with the department's second-highest domo.

For Shia it had all felt horribly rushed. Only hours earlier she'd been well outside her orders and comfort zone playing sidekick to Lucky Dey while he'd nearly tortured Tim Gilligan into giving up information. They had no warrant. There had been no arrest or scintilla of due process. Her only defense for her part was the recording she'd made for the US Attorney on whose authority she'd been spying.

"You look great," offered Wimmer, his tailored suit bellowing power lawyer with every pinstripe. "And that's considering you probably haven't slept much, yeah?"

"Yeah," was all Shia could muster. She wiped her sweaty palms on a pair of navy slacks while keeping her eyes focused on the four-inch crack in the assistant sheriff's door. She could hear the man's murmur from the other side as he paced and carried on with a conference call. Since hearing from Wimmer that they'd scored a noon meeting with Paul McGill, she'd been shredding her brain for any memory of having met the man. The best she could summon was that she'd shaken his hand at her academy graduation ceremony. Would he remember her? Did he have preconceived opinions regarding female deputies? Black women in general?

After a twenty-five-minute wait, Wimmer rose—that familiar hitch to his gait—and insisted on meeting with the department's number two prior to inviting Shia to join the discussion.

"Just foaming the runway," Wimmer calmed her. "I know this feels fast, but opportunity is everything in politics."

"Feeling over my head," was the best Shia could reply.

"No worries," Wimmer finished. "You've got the power of the federal government covering your adorable ass."

The assistant sheriff's door must have been defective, she reasoned. For after Wimmer had been ushered into the inner sanctum, gravity had delivered the wooden door back to its precise four-inch deficit. Shia shifted in her seat and attempted to listen. The assistant sheriff's murmur and Wimmer's higher-pitched whine were impossible to decipher, making for a torturous swath of time. Twenty minutes became thirty. Thirty became forty-five.

Foaming the runway? Or buttering the goose?

The secretary's desk unit buzzed. Without answering the handset, the fat-fingered deputy with an unfortunate chin spoke.

"They're ready for you," said the deputy.

Shia rose and pressed her fingers to the door panel. The door opened to reveal a modest office that was all sheriffs to the khaki and green marrow. Utilitarian and dull, with walls and a window buffet table adorned in service accolades—the clear and present collection of a man who'd dedicated a lifetime to law enforcement.

Standing behind his desk was Assistant Sheriff Paul McGill, a tall and triathlete-thin sixty-five-year-old. His uniform was creased and freshly pressed. A pair of romantic blue eyes was unable to refrain from giving Shia a heterosexual once-over.

"Don't worry about the door," said McGill with an outstretched hand. "It's got a mind of its own."

"Deputy Shia Saint George, sir," greeted the trainee.

Seated in a wooden chair turned to the assistant sheriff's desk, Wimmer patted the open seat next to him.

"Sit yourself, deputy," said McGill. "Sounds to me like you've had a Mr. Toad's Wild Ride of a first week."

"Mr. Toad, sir?"

"Old-school Disneyland attraction," clarified McGill. "You've been to Disneyland, haven't you?"

"Not my favorite place," replied Shia. "Long story, sir."

"For another time," smiled McGill, seating himself in a high-backed power chair.

"We've been discussing," said Wimmer. "I believe the assistant sheriff is going to be a fan."

"The barrel can never tolerate a bad apple," said McGill. "Spoils the whole stew. So, I want you to know that you are safe and have Temple Street support."

"Guarantees," added Wimmer.

"Assuming," held up McGill's bony hand, "you can corroborate the recordings your federal friend here has just played me."

Shia felt as if under a million-kilowatt glare. Her hands hadn't ceased perspiring. When shaking the assistant sheriff's hand, he'd surely felt the sweat slick transfer from her pinkish palm to his.

"It's okay," nodded Wimmer. "We're right where we wanna be."

We wanna be? Or where you *wanna be?*

"What'd you show him?" asked Shia.

"Lockin' boys in the dumpster," grinned Wimmer in such a fashion Shia wasn't certain if it was in glee or amusement from the phone video. "And last night's big hit. Stuff in the car with that fat DWP guy . . . what was his name again?"

Shia didn't reply. She slipped her fingers into her front pocket and withdrew the same phone she'd used to record her betrayals.

"I actually have some more video," she conceded.

"Sorry?" joked Wimmer. "Say you've been holding out on me?"

"I'm both a deputy *and* a woman," Shia teased. "Think the assistant sheriff will admit even lady cops are allowed some mystery."

The aging bureaucrat let trip a toothy smile. He was charmed, for sure. Shia, in turn, tapped the phone screen until her video files appeared. She paused, opened a video, and made sure the volume was fully audible.

"Hey, beauty queen," sounded a voice. "Thought I'd give you a tour of my private dojo."

The eyebrows below Wimmer's considerable forehead shifted with unknowing concern. McGill, on the other hand, let his long face droop in sudden recognition.

"Yes, sir," said Shia. "That's Atom Blum's voice. He was your friend, is that right, sir?"

"He was," replied McGill.

"My condolences, sir." With the gentle push of her finger, Shia eased the phone closer to the assistant sheriff.

Wimmer stood to get a better angle.

"'Kay, so that was a Tiffany glass door we just walked through," continued Atom on his camera-phone tour. "Foyer here. Living room that way, office and kitchen down there. Classic Paul Williams design. You know, Paul Williams, the architect?"

"Why are you doing this?" Shia was heard asking on the other end of the video phone call.

"'Cause you gave me your number," said Atom, his face appearing on the recording. "Need I say more?"

"I'm hanging up now."

"Not before the money shot!" pleaded the boy wonder, shifting the camera angle back to tour mode. "Here we go up the creaky fun stairs."

While the video played, Shia never let her gaze leave the assistant sheriff's ever-lengthening face.

"Correct me if I'm wrong, sir," said Shia to McGill. "But the reason Mr. Blum was afforded two ride-alongs with myself and Deputy Dey was because your office had insisted. At least, that's what our watch commander passed on to us."

"Wait. Is that the dead movie director?" quizzed Wimmer.

"Shut up," said McGill, drawing the phone even closer. "Deputy? Is there a purpose to you showing me this?"

"Keep watching, sir," assured Shia. "I think Mr. Blum advertised a money shot."

"Guest bedrooms there and there and down there," showed Atom on the video. "Bathrooms are all-new granite with sub-floor-heating for your sweet feet."

"I am never coming over," replied Shia to the movie director. "And you are making me seriously uncomfortable."

"Heeeeeeeeere's the master bedroom. Classic. Nothing for swingers. King-sized bed for a King Kong. And that's me, if you haven't guessed."

"Nice knowin' ya."

"Don't hang up!"

"Did you not hear me early tonight when I told you your shit was way outta line?" angered Shia's voice on the video.

"What if I told you you're the most beautiful creature I had ever seen? And I'm talkin' EVERRRRR."

"I said I was flattered, but not interested. Nothing's changed. Goodnight."

"But I've changed! Or you've changed me. Look here!"

McGill's seen-everything glower revealed not a molecular tick. As if the man knew exactly how the offending video would end.

"Is he showing his junk?" twisted Wimmer.

"At full salute," deadpanned Shia. "Sorry as I am for the tragic loss of your 'friend,' sir, it seemed, while he was alive, he was as proud of his erection as he was his stupid movies."

"Manners wasn't Atom's strong suit," heaved McGill. He shoved the phone back in Shia's direction.

"Shia?" said Wimmer. "For the life of me, I don't see how this helps our cause."

"Mr. Wimminger," said McGill with understanding. "Would you excuse us?"

"Sorry?" asked Wimmer.

"I need a moment with my deputy," forced McGill. "And on your way out, make sure you shut the door all the way. Please?"

"And what we discussed?" Wimmer pled.

That's right, thought Shia. *Exactly what did you discuss?*

For the forty-five-plus minutes Shia had been left alone while Wimminger and McGill had conferred, the trainee had been seized by her own sizeable imagination. There'd been time enough for her to replay every particular of her relationship with the fed. Boiled down, his plan had been simple enough: build a federal civil rights case against former Lennox Reaper Lucky Dey. In exchange for Shia's assistance, he had promised her a fast track into the FBI Academy at Quantico and a Washington career.

But what about building a federal case against a sheriff's deputy involves informing higher-ups in the department?

Shia wasn't certain about the Department of Justice protocols, but she was educated enough to concoct a reasonable scenario. Wimmer had used the word "opportunity" with relish. Having secured the strings as her personal and professional puppeteer, the lawyer had dreamt up a bigger canvas on which to splash his paint. Where there's one civil rights–bending cop, there sure as shit would be more. And what's better than an informant trainee? How about an assistant sheriff to open the gates to a department-wide federal shakedown?

In a crystallized moment, Shia puzzled out that she was more than likely a pawn in a much larger game. And any chance of her receiving a reward was minimal to none. Or miles upon miles away.

"Right," said McGill once it was only Shia and himself in the inner sanctum. "Clearly, you're a smart trainee. Maybe too smart for your own good. But we'll see."

"Sir?" she said, polite and unforgiving. Though the unspoken leverage in play was obvious. Shia was a triple-harassment threat. Trainee. Female. Black. Atom Blum had been placed in her and Lucky's radio unit because of his relationship with McGill. Not once. But twice. If it could be proven the dead wunderkind was a known pig when it came to women, McGill could be found culpable—but not before the media burned him at its holy First Amendment stake.

"US Attorney plays you," said McGill. "Now you're playing both him *and* me. You are the fulcrum and I am about to get tossed off the seesaw. Yeah? So, what's your expected outcome?"

"Finish my training, sir," said Shia.

"Finish your training?"

"Exactly that, sir."

"Dunno what the hell slick willy out there promised you," tapped McGill with his index finger. "But it had to be better than bottom-rung deputy. Now, what do you *really* want?"

"Finish my training, sir. With Deputy Dey as my training officer and you as my administrative . . . Dutch Uncle?"

"Like lawyer-boy out there thought I didn't know about the Lennox Reapers. You know how far back I go in this department?"

"Sir. The video I showed is embarrassing," reminded Shia. "But I don't believe we should be personally judged by our embarrassing friends."

"The videos of your TO are embarrassing. Disgraceful, even."

"I don't think they tell a complete story, sir."

"I expect they don't," groused McGill. "And now they want every deputy to wear a camera. Body cams. How's that gonna work for you and your training officer?"

"Can't say, sir. Only time will tell."

"You're suspended, yes? Pending the shoot investigation?"

"Yes, sir."

"Assuming you and your TO come up clear . . ."

"Sir."

"You choose to resume patrol with the very same training officer," he warned, "he might bring you more trouble than you deserve. Or than I'm willing to cover."

"What's deserves got to do with it, sir?" smiled Shia.

"I assume I'm not going to get a copy of young Atom's video?"

"What video, sir?"

The assistant sheriff revealed a confident smirk before he reached for the handset link to his desk deputy.

"Please thank the US Attorney for his time and efforts," instructed McGill. "Then have deputies escort him out of the building."

Shia rode the elevator to the parking lot alone. She was slightly numb inside, not entirely certain what she'd done or how she'd done it. The landscape had shifted so fast. She questioned whether she had behaved out of pure, feral survival—or because once she'd reached the precipice of betraying Lucky, she'd acted de facto out of loyalty and duty. Shia wanted to believe the latter about herself. Still, something that feared otherwise tickled her insides.

No matter, Miss Shitheel. You're sheriff's, now and forever. Live or die with the decision.

One thing for sure, Shia wished she could phone up Lucky and reveal all. Confess. A voice inside cautioned her to think again. Lucky, she reflected, was so much more about *do* than *tell*. Soon, she thought. Lucky and Shia would be back in the black-and-white. With time and miles of Compton blacktop to cover, the truth would find the right place and time.

Until then, bad guys beware.

52

Downtown.

It was the same café on cobblestoned Saint Vincent's Court. Tim Gilligan—showered and dipped in antiperspirant for fear of sweating out all his fluids—arrived early. He'd chosen the same table he'd shared with Cat on Tuesday and wedged himself into the very same uncomfortable chair. He had two ice waters poured as he waited, checking his watch in less than thirty-second intervals.

"So glad you got my message," said Cat, breezing in wearing running shorts and a vintage T-shirt. "Wasn't sure you'd realize it was me texting from a borrowed phone."

"Casual Friday?" Tim quipped.

"Hardly," moaned Cat. "After this morning—or, Jesus—this week? Think I deserve an early start to the weekend. You order drinks yet?"

"Not drinking today," said Tim. "Thinkin' I might be done with all that."

"Well, start tomorrow. We have to celebrate our . . . whatever. Lemme tell you about what I did to my phone."

"Order wine if you want," said Tim. "I'm good with water."

"You have to hear this. So, I'm running to this breakfast with the mayor. Heels. Such a mistake. So, I'm hauling tail for a bus, but I forget that in my bag—my six-hundred-dollar handbag, might I add—I had two Red Bulls and a defective can of Diet Coke—"

"Cat," interrupted Tim. "I went to the LAPD this morning."

"I'm sure you've got a good story. But lemme finish mine—"

"I talked to a detective in the homicide division. I told him about Hal."

"Told who about Hal?"

"Homicide. LAPD. I laid it all out."

"Laid what all out?" she stiffened.

"What I know. Which, I admit, isn't everything. But what I know. I called a lawyer friend. He went with me."

"Tim?" reflexed Cat. "What have you done?"

"You need to get a lawyer too."

"I already have a goddamn lawyer!" Cat slapped the stainless-steel outdoor tabletop with an open palm. "That's why we should be toasting . . ."

"You got a lawyer? When did that happen?"

"I got a lawyer and fixed this shit."

"I don't understand."

"I had it fixed, you fat fuckin' moron," she hissed. "Taken care of. No ties to you or me."

"Wait. I'm lost. How can a lawyer—"

"We're done. I don't want to know you. I don't wanna talk to you." Cat pushed back her chair and began her walk back to the hustle and bustle of South Hill Street.

"Cat!" stood Tim, the chair lifting with him before it clattered away. "WHAT DO YOU MEAN YOU FIXED IT?"

53

Altadena.

The sun was setting across the San Gabriels. It was a time of day when Frosty would usually pause to look to the sky. Twilight was coming when the trees turned black against the darkening heavens. Yet on that evening—that one particular extinguishing of a day—Frosty was not interested in pausing for anything. Not even the voice of reason under his skullcap.

You're doing it all wrong.

Frosty acknowledged as much to himself. He wasn't on his usual game or sticking to his normal killing routine. He was mad as hell—angry to such a degree he hardly felt able to organize his thoughts. His trees. His beloved trees and plans to start his own nursery may as well have gone up in flames along with the hydroponic cannabis crop. Julius was missing or more than likely dead, considering the damage at the Pizza Wing.

His customary precautions—using public transit to do the job—or even a stolen car—had been ignored in the heat of his rage against Lucky Dey.

If only I hadn't missed.

The failed shot from the rooftop of the New Wilmington Gardens haunted Frosty. He'd excused his own guilt with reminders that the whole New Wilmington mess was Julius's idiotic play. But that had been two full days ago when Frosty was still chock-full of hope for his future.

With a tip from Tuba's cousin who worked inside the Compton sheriff's station, Frosty had scribbled the address on a yellow Post-it and driven his own Cadillac Escalade to Altadena. After a pair of afternoon drive-bys past Lucky's house, Frosty returned to Lake Avenue, stopped at the nearest Circle K for a fifty-four-ounce Mountain Dew, then parked his SUV pointed north toward the impressive San Gabriel Mountains, where he'd waited for dark to begin its nightly assault on day.

The plan kept changing. At first, he was simply going to camouflage himself from head to toe, storm into the house via a back door, and kill whoever was there, leaving no witnesses. It was his comic, red-faced version of a murder—the angriest of acts scaled by the sequence of faces on the anger scale.

My anger scale.

Frosty's personal metric was based upon a pain assessment scale he'd once memorized while waiting in a Compton medical clinic. There, on a paint-chipped wall, was tacked a row of happy to sad cartoon faces. Each face registered degrees of discomfort with an ascending number scale from one through ten. Only Frosty hadn't seen physical pain in the cartoon mugs. He'd imagined the scale as something to do with feelings. Ever since seeing the graph he'd graded his own temper based on those happy to angry faces. Number One was content and happy. Number Ten was red-faced livid and barely under self-control.

Seated in his Escalade, Frosty calculated his present number at a 9.8. Too brain-fried to operate. He couldn't imagine even handling the easily leveled, bull barrel Ruger .22 without shaking. He tried the basic breathing exercise of inhaling in through the nostrils then exhaling out the mouth. Rhythmic. Over and over. Despite what felt like a disciplined effort, the shudder in his fingers continued unabated.

Frosty's phone rang. Before he could reach for it, the Escalade revealed the caller on the console screen: *momma*.

"I din't forget," Frosty moaned.

"We're not meetin' there," said Des'ree, his mother's oh-so-familiar voice sharp and conditional. "You're drivin' me an' your Gran'nana like a proper gentleman."

"Jus' church, Momma."

"No such thing. God wants a man to bring his best. Meetin' us a' the church your best?"

"S'pose not," answered Frosty, rolling his eyes to nobody but the rearview mirror.

"Open your ears and you can hear him say so."

"Yes, Momma."

"Gonna dress nice?"

"C'mon, Momma. Lemme back to it."

Get back to puttin' smoke to the man who fucked up my future.

"See you in an hour," said Des'ree.

Frosty needn't have seen her face. He could hear it in her voice. Wry. Looking right through him. Or thinking she could look into his soul. Thank Jesus, she couldn't. What would his dear Momma think if she knew the truth—that her sweet Lamar was a nerve-settling minute from putting two bullets through a white man's cranium?

When the call ended, Frosty noted a shift in his own demeanor. His jitters had diminished some. And the cartoon face he ascribed to his anger was closer to a six or seven. Manageable. Clarified.

No time like now, nigga.

He'd parked under a hundred-year-old oak tree offering shade from the streetlights. Acorns crunched underfoot when he stepped from the SUV and drew an easy arc to the sidewalk. He assumed the walk of a local. Direct but in no hurry. A point-A-to-B-styled gait, shoulders back and without a care. Blue and red snapback L.A. Clippers cap pulled low. A half block north, a ninety-degree right turn on Dolores, a three-minute cruise, and Frosty would be in front of Lucky Dey's rental. The rest, he imagined, would come naturally. A measure of patience seemed to have returned. Small but workable. And based on the tingling in Frosty's nerve endings, his external calm wouldn't last long.

While ambling, Frosty's phone rang, reminding him to switch the device to silent mode. On the screen was the same name from earlier: *momma*.

Jeesuz. What now?

Did his mother already suspect Frosty's lie? Had she read through the spaces in his voice that he'd had no intention whatsoever of driving her and his Gran'nana to church and would return home later with a lame "work" excuse? Frosty assuaged himself. He slipped the phone back into the front pocket of his lightweight hoodie and walked on, pretending a greater sense of purpose with each continued stride.

A man was about to die.

A deserving man.

Who knows? Given time—especially considering all Frosty had unwittingly forfeited—including his plans to move his family far away from Compton—sweet momma Des'ree might even forgive him, if not approve of the Godless act.

It was 8:11 p.m. when Frosty eased opposite Lucky's house, staying semi-distant from the sidewalk across the street. Passing cars were few and random. The light was the gray, dim netherworld between day and night. Murky. Perfect. Unless a witness was face-to-face with Frosty, he'd be impossible to identify in a photo lineup of random black males of similar age.

Frosty crossed at the street corner, then reversed west with his sights set on the Craftsman bungalow with the queen palm tree and its spray of fronds in front of a large picture window. In the ungated driveway were parked a Honda Accord and a primer gray '99 Crown Victoria. Frosty utilized the space between the six-foot hedge separating properties and the parked cars to shield his creep up the sloped drive.

Quick feet, Frostman.

Swiftly, he padded between the unkempt hedge and the pair of parked vehicles. Ahead was a side window with winged panels, both cranked half open to take advantage of the cooling air. TV light projected from the inside—as well as the sounds of video gaming. As he closed, Frosty thought he recognized the manufactured cracks and booms playing over what sounded like a pretty decent speaker system.

C.O.D.: Black Ops: Declassified.

As Frosty edged nearer, he could make out the back of two silhouetted heads seated low on a couch. A single incandescent lamp spilled into a small converted bedroom, partially shelved with books, walls collaged with framed family photos in no discernible design.

Family den. Gaming. Go, Frostman, go!

The silhouetted heads—one shaved and the other curled into an unruly hairball—made for easy division. Lucky was on the left, a teenage boy on the right. Lucky's boy? Who cares? Every young scrub had a sperm donor. So what if another pimple-faced tit-squeezer had to grow up hard?

Frosty inched closer and more of the room came into view. A woman sat in an armchair next to the floor lamp. A tall Latina with a wild mane trained back into a ponytail. Despite the ear-splitting video game she appeared lost in a book.

Or deaf as my Gran'nana.

The gun felt snug in Frosty's grip, the weight balanced from breach to barrel. The high-pitched *snap* of the .22's gunshots, once unleashed, would mesh neatly with the sounds of the game.

Two in the back of that shaved skull.

Ignore the shattering glass.

Crouch and run back down the driveway.

Brisk walk back to the Escalade.

Frosty curled around the nose of the Accord, knees bent,

cleanly below the window frame. Barrel first, he slowly rose, pivoting the muzzle against the glass. There was no more than a foot separating the business end of the pistol and the back of Lucky's head. The millisecond pause that followed offered little more than a moment of personal recognition. Frosty had indeed been correct about the video game. *Call of Duty: Black Ops: Declassified.* On the fifty-inch TV was a two-player split screen. PlayStation controllers in both Lucky's and the teenager's grips.

Two shots. Bang bang. And all would be good.

For the first few hours, the antibiotics administered at the Altadena urgent care had made Lucky want to puke. After he'd told the desk nurse he was a sheriff's deputy recovering from an on-the-job gunshot, he was hurried in to treatment. The wound was flushed, sewn shut again with a drain, and then redressed before he was excused to go home and rest. A seven-hour nap later, Lucky reconnected with his made-up family, scarfed down some cold leftover meatloaf, and retired for a few hours of gaming with Travis. The suspended cop felt all thumbs with the controller and could barely get four steps in the game without losing life, only to be re-spawned with a full magazine of ammo.

"If only the real world was like this," he quipped to the teen boy, who may or may not have registered his words. Travis's face was a picture of practiced concentration, his fingers and thumbs eradicating computer-generated insurgents with expert grace.

"Loud enough for you boys?" deadpanned Gonzo, her rhetorical finesse matching her concentration on the novel she'd rather read in the company of her men than elsewhere and alone.

For Gonzo's sake, Lucky contemplated turning down the volume. On the other hand, he was happy to have his headspace dominated by the constant wall of images and sound built expressly to feed a floor-shaking subwoofer. Any reduction of the barrage might easily lead to a flood of thoughts and images from the prior week. The last pictures Lucky wanted in his brain were the memories of for-real dead bodies.

Mush Man.

Atom Blum.

Julius Colón.

Realistic as the action on-screen appeared to a civilian, to Lucky it was both innocently counterfeit and oh-so-welcome. With even more effort, the distraction might have dulled the constant ache along the left side of his body.

Then came the *tick*.

Was it an actual sound? Or merely a feeling posing as the slightest noise at the base of Lucky's sensitive neck? After all, he'd been shot there before. A survivable .25-caliber hunk of lead had remained lodged behind his soft palate for years. Ever since, he'd experienced a strange sensitivity—not unlike a driver who'd been rear-ended once too often.

So Lucky engaged his neck. Slowly. Clockwise, following his uninjured right shoulder. He registered danger, death, and another slo-mo mortal moment.

The looming darkness married with the mostly blue spectrum rays from the TV made for a harsh reflection. Nonetheless, Lucky was able to discern two faint shapes. First, a gun muzzle, the fat piston of metal with a straw-sized hole bored through it, only a half inch from the glass, aimed between his eyes. Beyond the barrel he could make out no more than a dark shape in a hoodie. Utterly featureless but for the most dim impression of two widely set yellow eyes. Moistened. Lost in space.

Before Lucky could flinch or reflect on the imminent moment his motors would be cut and his life extinguished, the shape withdrew as if sucked back into the gray. Not realizing he'd been holding his breath, Lucky exhaled in a lung-dumping whoosh.

"You okay?" asked Gonzo from pure impulse.

Next came a shout—or scream—completely unmistakably—

"Karrie!" popped off Lucky.

He was off the couch and slashing through the open door into the corridor. He bounced off the opposing wall, sent a framed kindergarten painting crashing to the floor, but kept enough balance to turn the kitchen corner and shoot for the side door leading into the driveway. Only when Lucky pulled the door open did he realize he was without a weapon. As he swung the door open, he may as well have been miles from the bedroom where Gonzo and he kept their pistols locked in electronic quick safes.

His mind flashed forward. Any second he'd be sure to hear gunfire. He expected to fall out the side door and find Karrie slumped between the cars, sucking for her last breath.

Only there was a different kind of ruckus.

Both Karrie and the stranger were flat on the concrete. The girl had already felled the would-be assassin. The young man in the hoodie was on his side, arm pinned while Karrie used the power of her left leg to unleash kick-stomps to the side of his skull.

"MOTHERFUCKER!" she kept screaming with each strike of her heel against Frosty's face.

Frosty flailed with his free arm, begging as he was losing consciousness.

"Stop, please . . ." he croaked.

Lucky swooped in, kicked the .22 Ruger under the car, and dragged Karrie away.

"He's got a gun!" Karrie wailed.

Frosty, freed for barely a second, quickly found himself flipped over and his head pushed to the pavement, a sharp knee fitting into the thin space between his shoulders.

"She said gun!" yelled Gonzo, leaving no ounce of her considerable skill wasted in pinching the assailant between herself and the driveway.

"Under the Honda," said Lucky, moving in to frisk what parts of Frosty Gonzo hadn't secured.

"What's going on?" asked innocent Travis from the doorway.

"Not another foot, Trav!" demanded Gonzo. "Stay right there."

"He was pointing the gun at the window," cried Karrie.

"I know," breathed Lucky.

"You *know*?" questioned Gonzo. "Or you know him?"

During the frisk, Lucky came up with Frosty's vibrating smartphone.

"Was gonna shoot," pleaded Frosty. "But I din't!"

"Was gonna what?" pressed Gonzo.

"Shoot me in the back of the head," finished Lucky before reading the name on the phone. "Who's 'momma'?"

"But din't!" repeated Frosty.

"Why didn't you?" asked Lucky.

"I dunno . . ." wheezed Frosty, still pinned. "Cuzza church, I think."

"Who is he?" asked Karrie, confused and in semi-shock. "Why's he at our home?"

"Your momma calling you?" Lucky squatted and aimed the screen at Frosty's face.

"She ain't got nothin'," said Frosty. "Was all me."

"You came here to kill me."

"But I din't!"

"Why didn't you?"

"Said so . . . I think."

"You fucked up on shit?" asked Lucky.

"Don't do no drugs. Not nothin'. I'm straight up—"

"You were gonna straight up put a cap in me."

"Yeah, but I din't! You saw me walk away."

"You wanna explain this bullshit?" glared Gonzo at Lucky.

"What's your name, kid?" asked Lucky.

"Frosty."

"Like the snowman?"

"Frosty," he repeated.

Once again, the mobile phone buzzed with Frosty's mother retrying her luck.

"Jus' wanna take my momma to church, 'kay?" cried Frosty.

"He is *so* high!" insisted Karrie.

"You didn't put one in me," said Lucky, "'cause you wanted to take your momma to church? That it?"

"All it is," insisted Frosty.

"Okay." Lucky stood, put the phone to his ear, and clicked the green icon. "Hello?"

"You ain't—" began the voice of Des'ree. "I don' know who you are, but you put Lamar on the phone right now!"

"Who's Lamar?" asked Lucky.

"Lamar's my—he knows his name's Lamar," said Des'ree. "But you probably call his skinny butt Frosty or somethin', ain't that right? Now, may I please talk to my son?"

"Lamar's kinda busy right now," answered Lucky.

"He ain't got no kinda busy that forgives him for what he supposed to be doin'."

"And what's that?"

"Drivin' me 'n' his Gran'nana to church," Des'ree braved. "And I don't care what fun his friends make of him for it. He'd a man doin' what a man's supposed to do."

Lucky paused as if capturing the moment as a still picture. Gonzo wearing a T-shirt and Star Wars pajama bottoms, her sharp knee pinning the thin, young black man to the driveway like a fly under a rolled newspaper. Karrie, flushed from her five-mile run and the unexpected scuffle, staring down at the assailant, prepared to pounce and carry on with her Muay Thai beatdown.

"Hello?" came the voice over the phone.

"Where's the church?" asked Lucky.

"Lamar knows where it is," she said. "And it's too late now for him to drive us. He just better meet us or go home and move himself outta my house."

"No worries. Lamar'll be there," assured Lucky. He clicked off and pocketed the phone. "Travis. You know where your mom keeps her handcuffs?"

Travis twisted in the doorway and was off on the errand.

"Lucky," warned Gonzo. "Call the Altadena station."

"S'okay," said Lucky. "I got this."

"Lucky. He brought a gun to our home," added Gonzo. "Our home!"

"I know." Lucky put his arms briefly around Karrie, squeezed her tight, and kissed the top of her head. With that, the formerly broken runaway melted into a stream of sobs and tears. "You did so good, sweetie. So proud."

"He was gonna kill you," she huffed.

"Like he said," assured Lucky. "He didn't."

Travis returned with a set of matte-black handcuffs dangling from one hand.

"Give 'em," said Gonzo before hooking Frosty up and ratcheting each bracelet tighter than regulations permitted.

Lucky stood Frosty up and walked the Crip around to the front passenger seat of his '99 Ford. Frosty didn't resist a muscle, resigned to whatever might come. Lucky looped the retention seat belt through Frosty's joined wrists and essentially lashed him to the seat.

Gonzo approached from behind.

"Last thing you should be doing is something off-book," Gonzo cautioned.

"I'm good," promised Lucky. "Travis? I'll be back soon to finish our game. Okay?"

"'Kay, Luck," said the teen boy.

"Lucky!" insisted Gonzo.

"I promised," shrugged Lucky. "So there it is."

"We'll see," she said without any certainty whatsoever. "We'll all see, and you know what that means."

Lucky nodded, but didn't dare try to kiss her goodbye. Gonzo wasn't wired for token affection. Actions were all the meaning she required. And with a would-be assassin at her home she was angry beyond consolation.

"Cocked and locked," said Lucky, reminding Gonzo to keep the doors and windows shut and her weapon close. "Pretty sure this is all over. But just in case . . ."

54

Lucky drove, windows down and in a general state of silence, save for asking Frosty for the names of cross streets and his mother's house of worship.

"Greater Zion Baptist."

As was his preferred habit, Lucky kept their travel to surface streets. If asked, he would have said it was because stoplights and streetlamps and cross traffic added to his gravitational pull. It brought constant context to the expansive horizontal plane that was Los Angeles, where good neighborhoods bled into bad and vice versa.

"You like church?" asked Lucky.

"Like trees." Frosty had propped his head between the headrest and the doorpost, his eyes fixed on the constant streak of lights playing off the front windshield.

"Trees," repeated Lucky.

"Yeah . . . trees is good."

"Okay, I'll bite. What's good about trees?"

Lucky kept glancing over to his prisoner, who, by his calculation, had barely shifted a muscle in the thirty-plus minutes they'd been on the road.

"Trees," began Frosty. "They like all of us . . . Start as babies. Need lookin' after till they strong enough to be on they own, you know? Better they root, harder they are to knock around. An' once they put down the roots, see, they don't really go no place else. That home. Tha's they life."

"Sounds like you know more than somethin' about trees."

"I know bucket about trees. You can ask. Ain't nothin' 'bout trees I don' know or can't find out."

Lucky could've tested the young Crip, calling out the first tree that caught his eye. Would it have mattered? Not in the least. Lucky believed him. And that was enough.

"You came for Julius?" asked Lucky.

"Julius dead. I came for me."

"Yeah? What I do to you?"

"Trees, man. Fucked up my trees."

"The weed farm?"

"Weed farm, shit. Cannabis jus' a shrub. Lotta trouble, weed . . . Mean, liked learnin' the hydro. Liked that . . . You know pot roots is white? Least when they hydro'd. No light down there so they roots is like ghost fingers. Spiderwebby ghosty fingers."

"So how—"

"No matter now," said Frosty. "Feel me? S'all over. Weed. Future."

Frosty hadn't yet realized they'd parked. The '99, engine still humming, was in a passenger loading green zone in front of Compton's Greater Zion Baptist Church. It was a low-slung three-building complex, better resembling a small primary school. All appeared dark but for a subtle glow leaking from the sanctuary door.

"Little late for church service," remarked Lucky.

"Not for Momma. She go anytime somebody slingin' the Word. No matter, no how."

"She gonna be happy to see you?"

"Might slap my face. But she kiss it after."

Lucky gestured for Frosty to twist a bit. He unwrapped the seat belt and keyed the cuffs until Frosty's wrists were freed.

"'Kay," said Frosty. "You did that. Now what your game?"

"No game. Your momma wanted you to take her to church."

"Yeah, but I don't deserve no church."

"Maybe not. But maybe it's what you need more than a trip to County."

Frosty looked hard at his captor. Not certain at all if he could trust the man or the moment.

"You just lettin' me off?" asked Frosty. "Like that?"

"I know who you are. You know where I live. Maybe that makes us straight. Maybe inside church there you can find a new plan."

The young hood continued with the stare-down. As if still waiting for a trap door to open and send him to hell.

"You know, little Lady Justice did me tight," said Frosty, rubbing the bruises. "That blondie girl. She yours?"

"Kind of adopted each other. Long story."

"She was gonna bust on my head till I was smoked."

"Probably."

"Woulda served me right too."

Lucky agreed, then reached across and pushed the door open.

"Not lyin'," said Frosty. "Was my mom callin' why I didn't do it."

"And here you are. So, go get it done."

"Hey," said Frosty, his expression finally shifting from permanent distrust to a semi-brightened, near smile. "Why don't you, ya know? Come in. Meet Momma. My Gran'nana."

"Me? Church?" Lucky shook his head. "That ship sailed for me a while ago."

"Not too late for me. Not too late for you."

"Git on," impressed Lucky. "Or we can start this all over again."

Frosty's chin dipped. He understood. He climbed out, shut the car door without looking back, and tried to keep a straight back while limping to the front door. When he swung it open, singing voices and music poured out into the night, reaching Lucky's open window as he pulled away from the curb. The upbeat tune, lost in the rush of air circulating through the '99, stuck in Lucky's ears for the four-minute drive to the canine shelter where he'd boarded Mush Man's team of mutts.

The elderly couple who ran the shelter were only too glad to return the animals, hoping Lucky would find the street beasts a happy home. Each of the dogs had been washed and brushed out. The four-legged crew smelled of detergent and baby powder as they happily piled into the back seat, tongues out, panting and drooling. Oprah, who felt deserving of the front passenger side, settled in for the best angle to lick at Lucky's right ear.

"Enough of that," said Lucky. He reached into the console, came up with a fresh bottle of Benadryl capsules, and dry-swallowed a pair with the same verve with which he'd once sucked back pain killers.

Hello. My name's Lucky and I'm a Benadryl addict.

"Look at you," Lucky said to the mutts in his rearview mirror. "Now what the hell am I gonna do with you?"

Thinking the animals might want to bark a final goodbye to where they last saw their beloved Mush Man, Lucky wheeled the '99 into a U-turn and pointed it toward Poinsettia and the DWP reconstruction. Despite being a Friday night, Compton appeared quiet, darker, and more subdued than normal—as if the city were still hungover from the Fourth of July celebrations.

Turning from Rose Street to East Peck, Lucky cruised slowly as if on patrol. Perhaps a force of habit. Or even as a way of slow-rolling himself back home. Gonzo would be awake and expecting an exhaustive debrief.

Wait until she sees the mutts.

A bicycle appeared from his right, the rider hopping the curb and busting into the street with little regard for driver or car. Lucky tapped the brakes, less to avoid a collision than to give the rider more room.

The hairs on his forearms prickled as the air around him took on a static charge. The teacup-sized cyclist, weaving his neon yellow mountain bike in and out of Lucky's headlights, glanced backward with an almost snide purse of his lips. Had Lil Rod recognized Lucky from the sidewalk before he had dashed in front in such a taunting gesture? Or was it just because Lucky was a white dude in a '99 Crown Vic? An obvious police officer, off-duty or not, and surely worth a second or two of cheap ghetto provocation. Whatever reason, the player on the bike was neither packing heat nor holding drugs. Otherwise, no respecting gangbanger would deign to play chicken with an obvious cop.

For half a block, Lil Rod continued his serpentine tack, swinging the bike from curb to curb, keeping within the wash from the headlamps.

What would it take? thought Lucky.

To finish off the little killer would mean little more than switching off the headlights and a quick and clean acceleration of Detroit horsepower. The '99's front grille would swallow whatever was in its path. Fatal hit-and-runs were epidemic in the Southland, especially in the sectors where better than a third of the drivers were uninsured and nearly impossible to track down.

What's one more bloodstain on Compton blacktop?

The urge was there. Present. With a touch more gas he could right the ugly wrong that was Lil Rod.

"If only I didn't have other plans," breathed Lucky, barely audible enough for even the dogs to register. "Soon enough, little banger. You 'n' me'll dance. Soon. Enough."

Saturday

55

Pasadena.

It was a crusher of a headache. Advil, Anacin, Tylenol. None had eased the aftereffects of Wimmer's bender to end all benders. With the clock on his dash another minute beyond the 10:00 a.m. start time of the Pasadena First Presbyterian AA meeting, he'd hoped that the cobwebs might clear enough so he could accept the help he so desperately needed.

Prior to that Saturday, Wimmer had never classified himself as an addict or an alcoholic. It had been a ruse, he'd explained to his wife, to get near the subject of his investigation, Sheriff's Deputy Lucky Dey. After a few initial meetings, he'd been secretly displeased—hurt, even—that the former Lennox Reaper hadn't so much as recognized him, especially considering their ugly history. Once Wimmer moved beyond the disappointment, he had been surprised to find he'd actually begun to enjoy the meetings. The sharing. The camaraderie of wounded men and women, all trying to bootstrap themselves back into the land of the healthy mind and body. It was uplifting. Spiritual. Even if Wimmer considered himself no more than a tourist.

Then came the bender. After the crushing and embarrassing defeat he'd suffered at the hands of the L.A. County Sheriff's Department—escorted out of the Temple Street building by armed deputies—he'd bypassed his parking space at the Federal Building for the valet stand at Westwood's W Hotel. He'd handed his credit card to the bartender and begun a drinking binge that had lasted until closing. Too drunk to drive home, he'd ponied up for a room and continued the bender by guzzling down the alcoholic contents of the minibar before passing out next to the toilet.

When Wimmer woke, he couldn't imagine driving anywhere but to an AA meeting. Was he truly addicted? He didn't know anything beyond the compulsion he felt to sit and be motivated by his broken brethren.

At fourteen minutes past the hour, Wimmer hobbled from his car, fought off the urge to dry heave into the gutter, and followed the brick footpath leading to the church's basement. The meeting, in full progress, was stuffed to the gills—sixty, seventy-five strong. He found a folding chair in the rear right and lowered his head into his hands in hopes the throbbing would subside. His ears, despite the thumping of his heart in his head, were able to tune in to the words from the audio-assisted portable lectern propped front and center.

". . . pleased for all the shares," growled the speaker, a shaggy man in a flannel shirt rolled up to the elbows. "And we're gonna pick up on 'em after we get our speaker through. But he's got somewhere to be so I'm happy to turn the mic over. Lend your ears to my man, Luck."

Wimmer thought he'd heard the man incorrectly. At least initially. After all, what were the odds? Yet despite how much it hurt to sit up, straighten his spine, and twist his neck ten degrees, Wimmer could see the figure easing up to the front of the room was none other than Lucky Dey.

Lucky's left arm was in a sling strapped over a faded T-shirt. At first, he appeared wholly uncomfortable to be addressing his fellow alcoholics. He had to bend down to the microphone to say:

"Hey. My name is Lucky and I'm an addict."

"Hello, Lucky," chimed most of the others assembled, hardly in practiced unison. It sounded more like a group grumble than an actual call to answer.

Wimmer's first inclination was to rise and skulk to the exit. He had no curiosity whatsoever as to what Lucky might want to impart to the gathering of so many lost and like-minded. But the idea of even standing made Wimmer's stomach flip so violently he feared he might vomit on the spot. So, Wimmer remained from fear of embarrassment, butt glued to the chair, hands cradling his immense forehead.

"Wait," began Lucky. "First there's this."

He stepped away from the lectern and lifted his left leg onto an empty chair. With his one good arm, he rolled up his denim pants until his left calf tattoo was fully exposed.

"I know," said Lucky. "Just ink. S'pose there's enough of that in here. And this one's no more special than any other, except that it's mine . . . If you can't see it too good, it's a grim reaper tat. The reaper there, if you can make it out, he's holding his scythe in one hand and, in the other there, he's got a pistol. Also there's a number. Seventy-three. That's me. I'm number seventy-three."

With his cuff returned to normal, Lucky resumed his pose behind the microphone. To Wimmer's view, the deputy looked unrehearsed and to be searching for his next sentence.

"Why the reaper? I guess is the next question. I guess the best way to explain it is that if you were a sheriff's deputy in a certain division, it had a certain kind of meaning. A club . . . or a brotherhood. To get a Reaper tat you had to be invited. And a deputy didn't get invited unless he'd been in a good shoot. That's a justified gunfight, for any of you who don't know. Mine was my second year. Barely smart enough to keep the shit off my shoes. Anyway, we answered a call to a domestic dispute, had to kick down a door. That's when the bullets started. I got off a good coupla pulls and knocked down this big Mexican dude who'd been kickin' the snot out of his baby mama. He lived. So did I. Month later, I got asked to be a Reaper."

Lucky tried not to peruse the attendees. He worried that catching a face or two of his fellow addicts might throw him—cause him to lose his already less than sanguine place. So instead, he focused on the back wall of the basement room and tried not to ramble.

"So it's not just about a tat. There's a meaning to it. And an oath. And if you were on the outside lookin' in, it might've looked like Reapers were some gang inside the Sheriff's Department. And who knows? Maybe we were. And maybe, in the course of our duty, we looked after each other just a little bit harder than the other deputies. Can't say it didn't feel good to belong, because there was trust. Real trust. Reapers, man, we had each other covered. And because we had each other, we were able to do some serious policing. We saved lives and we cracked heads. Who knows? Maybe we cracked one of yours."

The room erupted in laughter, some of it a nervous truth. It buoyed Lucky. His shoulders relaxed and he stopped shifting his weight from side to side.

"Yeah. And we did some stuff that I'm not proud of. Now that I look back on it. But what's moving ahead without hindsight, you know? Some of us were liked. Some of our fellow sheriffs hated the ground we walked on. Cursed our existence. Some wanted to be like us. You know. In the club. Part of the gang. Which is understandable. Who doesn't want to be wanted? I got that then and I still get it now.

"That said, there was this one guy. Two-year deputy. I'd been in maybe five years at that point. But this guy, word around was that he wanted to be a Reaper in the worst way. Always trying to catch rides with one of us. Hang after shift. Serious case of the wannabes. Right? You know the kinda guy. But this one guy, see, he knows that to be a Reaper—to be inside the circle of trust—it first starts with that good shoot. Righteous use of deadly force. In defense of your life, one of your fellow sheriffs, or the public. And them's be the rules, as they say."

Lucky's eyes swirled, picturing the time and place while hoping to keep hold of his train of thought. His story was winding to a close. And he didn't want to blow the punch line. Otherwise the point would have turned moot with the final syllable.

"Was New Year's Eve. It's your basic ghetto countdown to midnight. So, this wannabe . . . the guy who so desperately wants to be part of the club, he stations himself outside this party house just shy of the clock striking twelve. Place is hopping. Music. Party bangers spilling out into the street. Then comes the five, four, three, two . . . You know. Wannabe guy, he knows some dumb drunk son of a bitch is gonna pull out his *pistola* and shoot it into the air when the clock hits midnight. You see where I'm goin', right? Twelve o'clock. Cholo pulls his gun and unloads his magazine into the sky. Full clip. Wannabe Reaper, he's there and ready—and a good shot, I might add. Lets loose a single round that snaps the cholo right in the butt cheek. Right there."

Lucky turned sideways and used an index finger to indicate a spot on his left buttocks. Amused titters rolled across the top of the gathering, as did a few sympathetic groans.

"Well, wannabe guy writes it up as self-defense. And with nobody but a bunch of drunk party bangers, who but the cholo with the gun is gonna argue? Shooting passes muster with the brass. And wannabe guy is up in all our grills expecting to be made a Reaper, tattoo and all . . . Course, none of us bought it. We had our snitches. Wasn't long before we knew what really went down. And we told him as much. That's when he threatened to expose our little brotherhood. As if he had anything on us he could prove. Somethin', though, we figured, had to be done. We drew straws. I got the short one . . . Few shifts later, it was arranged that me and wannabe guy shared a black-and-white. Maybe an hour, two, we're in a foot pursuit after some nothin' necklace snatch. I let wannabe take the lead. I hang back. Unskin my service weapon . . ."

At last, Lucky allowed his eyes to survey the other faces of those gathered, pleased to see every man and woman in the room on the edge of his or her respective seat.

"So I popped wannabe guy in the ass," Lucky finished. "Left butt cheek. Almost clean. Creased the top of his hammy. Asshole washed out on a medical."

Shifting his weight again, Lucky tried to sum up.

"There a moral here? Yeah. Somewhere. That's for you to figure out, same way it's for me to figure out. Is who we are what we've done? Or what we're gonna do about it? And that's what I got to say. Thanks."

Lucky stepped away from the lectern to polite applause. Some amused. Others shocked yet full of thought. Lucky shook the lead speaker's hand, then cut down the side of the gathering with what appeared a dead reckoning for the exit. Only once he approached the last row, he retarded his gait until he was standing alongside Wimmer. Lucky waited a few counts for the US Attorney to meet his gaze.

"Bet you thought I didn't remember you," said Lucky, plain and without recrimination. "But, yeah. I recognized my work when I saw that giddyup of yours."

"Go fuck yourself," was Wimmer's only reply.

"One day at a time," winked Lucky. "One day at a time."

And that was that.

Lucky crashed through the basement door, and though he'd have liked to go at the stairs two at a time, he climbed in pained single steps until he was on level land. There he fished his Ray-Bans out of the sling, let the L.A. sun spank his broken face, and walked on.

About the Author

Doug cut his teeth writing movies like *Die Hard 2, Bad Boys,* and *Hostage* until sharp enough to pen the Lucky Dey crime thriller series. He lives in Southern California with his wife, two children, and three mutts.

You can learn more about Doug at www.dougrichardson.com and drop him a line at bydougrich@dougrichardson.com. You can also follow him at www.facebook.com/bydougrichardson, on Twitter @byDougRich, and on Instagram @bydougrich.

AMERICAN BANG

1

Woodland Hills, California. 6:30 p.m.

Johnny B. was frustrated.

All he wanted was a Philly steak sandwich with no cheese and a Diet Coke with a slice of lemon to go. As orders went, he thought it was a no brainer. Even in his stubborn mind, he couldn't imagine how the simple request had turned into a hang-up.

"Thirteen-inch Philly steak," Johnny B. repeated to the Asian woman behind the counter. *Korean Nazi*, the teen complained to himself. For him it was like hitting the reset button on one of his video games. He tried to sound polite, but understood that what felt polite coming out of his mouth sometimes didn't come off that way. "No cheese 'cause I don't like cheese. A large Diet Coke with a slice of lemon. And that's to go, puh-lease."

"I got all that," annoyed the sub shop's co-owner and manager. She was half Johnny Boy's size—barely a hundred pounds under her white shirt and apron. Her face was as wrinkled as a dried fruit. "But I say to you, 'No lemon for Diet Coke.'"

"But the man before—he got a lemon with his iced tea," argued Johnny B. without a tinker's clue concerning the line of diners queuing up behind him. The line was out the door of the tiny takeout shop that was little more than a counter and an old, yellowed back-lit menu board hanging over a one-man kitchen.

"I say no lemon for Diet Coke," repeated the old woman.

"If I order iced tea do I get a lemon slice?" clarified Johnny B.

"You want ice tea now? You just say you want Diet Coke."

"I want Diet Coke. Just need a lemon to go with my Diet Coke."

"No lemon for Diet Coke." The old woman punched up the order on the cash register. "Twelve dollar, twenty-six."

"How about I order a small iced tea with a lemon slice? Plus the Diet Coke. Plus the Philly steak."

"You change your order now?"

"If it gets me a lemon slice."

The old woman stiffened, arms akimbo, her sagging skin jiggling where her biceps should've been. Her face was screwed into a churlish question mark.

"Why you like lemon with Diet Coke?" she persisted.

"I dunno," said Johnny B., too tense to shrug. "'Cause it tastes good?"

"Well that's your mouth!" she accused.

"Philly steak," began Johnny B. again.

"There's a line, you know?" sounded a heavy-set voice, two customers behind Johnny B.

The eighteen-year-old heard the man, gauged the voice as someone much older, with some authority, and probably unafraid to get physical. Violent, even. Johnny B. hated being touched. Without his special cocktail of psych meds, he might scream out loud if anybody pressed into him for anything longer than a brushed back or an "excuse me" while in line at an amusement park like Six Flags Magic Mountain. But Johnny B. wouldn't— or couldn't even half-turn to acknowledge the impatient people behind him. If he did he might lose his place, or his patience, or his sketchy temper.

"Philly steak," repeated Johnny B., peeling off a twenty-dollar bill from his rubber-banded roll of bills. "Thirteen-inch. No cheese. Small iced tea with a lemon slice. Large Diet Coke."

"I no care no more," mumbled the old woman. She cleared the order, re-added the total and handed the change to her blockish customer. "Takeout order wait over there, okay?"

"It's 'cause I'm Armenian," stated Johnny Boy. "I'm not stupid. Nobody likes the *Armos*."

"Next customer please," ignored the old woman.

Johnny B.—a.k.a. Johnny Boy—or John Bartholomew

Kasabian as it read on his driver's license—sidestepped from the counter and stood uncomfortably against a round metal pillar, holding his receipt in both hands, and focusing on his calm place. His face felt hot and flushed. Though that could've been from spending the day at Zuma Beach. He thought perhaps he'd stood out like a sore toe, not having thought to bring beachwear. In his black Wranglers and black T-shirt, Johnny B. was always comfortable. His redundancy in clothing was both his trademark and his armor. His mother called it his daily superhero outfit. On his feet were always a pair of Converse Chuck Taylors and his hair was a monthly Supercuts dark brown spaz of ethnic pride. With that, his stocky build and walk, and the freshly inked Armenian Power cross on his right forearm, anybody who knew Johnny B. could see him coming from a mile.

People know 'n' respect me 'cause I'm known and I'm certified Armo badass.

From behind the cooktop swerved a Korean man, equally slight as his co-owner wife, only inches taller with a drawn face under a disposable paper chef's cap. He spoke in a foggy whisper while handing Johnny B. the to-go sack.

"Wife not happy since hysterectomy," croaked the old man. "Sorry about lemon slice. I give you extra inside bag."

Nodding an expression-free thanks, Johnny B. accepted the bag and both drink cups before dumping the iced tea into the garbage bin next to the side exit. He was hungry, his stomach had been grumbling since it had long ago digested his usual morning meal of a Starbucks frap and two apple fritters. Passing three more storefronts until he reached the street corner, Johnny B. stood at the stoplight and repeatedly rabbit-punched the crosswalk button. With every strike it beeped for non-existent blind pedestrians. The Ventura Boulevard traffic washed past, the flow of cars and trucks hustling east and west in an ear-throbbing crush of Los Angeles white noise. For the moment, the ubiquitous sound drowned out his gastric bombast.

The sun had just dropped below the horizon, leaving the boulevard in shadow and the October sky with streaks of pink and vanilla. Opposite Johnny B. was the Walk/Don't-Walk display. It appeared permanently stuck on its red-letter denial. On the side street across from the Chevron station waited Johnny B.'s ride, a black Ford Shelby Mustang so damned new it still bore the dealer's stickers.

And this badass can't wait to stink up the new leather with a hot Philly steak.

Johnny B. could smell the sub through both the foil wrap and the bag. His eating instincts—sometimes described by his two siblings as those of a starved coyote—invited him to chew right through the paper sack and sink his incisors into the hot sandwich. He was eighteen though. A legal adult. With that he'd nearly learned to delay his gratification. While traffic hauled past and the *Don't Walk* sign continued its electronic indifference, Johnny B. chose to give himself a tease. Unrolling the top of the bag, he lowered his nose into the cavity and inhaled fully.

His nose curled in autonomic disgust.

Cheese!

"Korean bitch!" he screeched.

Without a thought or intent beyond his momentary expression, Johnny B. balled the sack between his meaty hands and sidearm chucked his dinner. In that instant, he saw little more than red, yet seemed to feel the million slights he'd suffered since he could first remember. The sandwich was an afterthought. No more. And his mind would have instantly switched to some other flavor of fast food satisfaction if it hadn't been for the piercing pitch of squealing tires and gnashing metal annoying his hyper-sensitive ears.

The Philly steak sandwich, balled into a projectile, then blindly hurled, had sailed across three lanes of traffic before exploding in a red meat and mayo smear across the windshield of an eastbound Hyundai Accent. The startled driver, a cosmetician and part-time coed at nearby Pierce Community College, recoiled in shock. When she reflexively stomped on her brakes, her skidding car drifted left and into an oncoming Mercedes S-Class coupe. The heavier German car practically swallowed the Korean compact.

Despite the imparting G-forces, the deployed airbags should have saved both drivers. Only the Hyundai's roof sheered and released like a horizontal guillotine. The sheet metal and carbon fiber Frisbee cut through the Mercedes' windshield and neatly decapitated the Malibu Barbie mom behind the wheel in an eye-blink.

Johnny B. had witnessed every slow-motion frame of it. And the shock of sound to his ears was closer to that of a grand piano dropped from ten stories than of two cars colliding in an ugly spray of metal and shattered safety glass. The smell though—that puke-worthy cheese and meat mélange was replaced by burnt rubber and gasoline. It fouled his senses and nearly blinded the bulky teen.

With traffic stalled and both drivers and passengers in shock or counting their lucky stars or hopping from their cars to rubberneck or call 911, a scared Johnny B. took the opportunity to run across the street. His stride lacked the coordinated grace of most eighteen-year-olds. He edged between stalled cars and past the smoking rear of the wrecked Mercedes until he had a clear path to his hot black Mustang. There, he shut himself inside with a distinctive Detroit *thunk* and waited for the change in air pressure to equalize his nerves. The silence of the interior calmed him. The new car perfume soon replaced the odor of the street horror he would leave behind. Johnny B. push-buttoned the ignition, geared the Ford into drive and slung the vehicle east and onto Ventura Boulevard. Miles ahead was Glendale and his bedroom in his parents' 1920's Spanish hacienda. The safety of home beckoned along with his PlayStation and turntable. But first, a fast food drive-thru to temporarily distract his guilt as well as satisfy his gastronomic pangs. Perhaps an In-n-Out burger—double meat, animal style and please-oh-please, no Goddamn cheese.

2

Pasadena. 7:32 p.m.

From Lucky Dey's perspective, Los Angeles and thereabouts were suffering from an overpopulation of headshrinkers. He couldn't recall the last time he'd visited any form of an office tower of three stories or higher that didn't sport at least a dozen psychotherapists on the legend. The Los Angeles sheriff's deputy had turned it into a bad habit bordering on superstition or OCD. He'd enter the lobby of a random building and, even if he knew exactly which floor of whom he was visiting, check the resident list and search for initialisms following a name. PhD, LCSW, CCMHC, MEd-LPC-CDVD. Most of the titles left him without a glimmer of whatever psychology degree they represented. A simple detective's deduction might conclude that there were too many post-graduate programs punching out too many degrees for too many couch-friendly analysts.

"You were saying?" cued Dr. Anna Sandalwood from her soft perch.

"Not sure I was saying anything," replied Lucky, wondering if he'd lost his place while staring out the eighth-floor window. The picture frame pane revealed the final streaks of what had been a bluebird day. The late October Santa Ana winds had blown hotter than usual—from across the desert—leaving cotton-ball clouds bearing little moisture hanging low, their fading shadows still dotting the San Gabriel mountains in ever-moving spots.

"Think it was my turn," said Gonzo, sharing the corduroy couch with her live-in lover, common-law husband, and emotional co-dependent, Lucky Dey. The space between the pair wasn't nearly as wide as the gaping divide in their relationship.

"Okay," shifted Sandalwood, moving one of her leggy limbs underneath herself. It left one of her favorite heels empty on the floor.

The redheaded psychoanalyst, a former volleyball spiker from Cal State Fullerton, was every bit as tall as Gonzo. It made Lucky wonder why women tipping six feet felt the need to add even more stilt to their already towering frames. Had they been so used to intimidating boys that the fashionable four inches added by their designer footwear gave them an exponential advantage?

"I feel like we're static," revealed Gonzo. "Not moving forward or backward."

"Like you're stuck?" asked Sandalwood.

"I like progress," said Gonzo. "Something quantifiable beyond days or months."

"Commitment," clarified the doc.

"Not like he needs to put a ring on it," said Gonzo. "We're supposed to be a family. But it feels like we're all just really good roommates."

Family.

Lucky had a love/hate conflict with the word. He had no trouble using the word as a reference. He shared their Altadena bungalow—the former rental which they'd finally bit the bullet and purchased—with Gonzo, her fifteen-year-old son Travis, and

Lucky's emancipated charge, seventeen-year-old Karrie Kaarlsen. But in his stubborn mind, Lucky still saw the family as something ad hoc. Made up. Did that make the family only something between temporary and for real? Or was it just Lucky holding Lucky back?

Lucky didn't dare offer that terrible tidbit in that, their third couple's therapy session. He was still sussing out the therapist's office trappings as if he were investigating something. To Dr. Sandalwood's right was a small, built-in desk on top of which was a large computer running a screen-saver slideshow of pastoral photographs. To her left was a bookshelf unit stacked with books on far-ranging subjects—from criminal sociology to climbing Mount Everest. Haphazardly strung in and around the bookcase, was an electric garland of friendly ghosts and jack-o'-lanterns. It was a reminder that Halloween was fast approaching, and also that Dr. Sandalwood's practice wasn't for couples or adults only. Children had played in that room, on that same couch. Traumatized. Troubled. And like Lucky, itching to bolt for the door.

"Bought the house," deadpanned Lucky. "That's a commitment."

"And it was practically a deal-breaker," shot Gonzo. "Like you and rehab. You did it only because I threatened to leave."

"Is that true?" asked Dr. Sandalwood.

"Probably," said Lucky.

"Lucky," pressed the therapist. "Do you need to be pushed in order for you to feel something?"

"Excuse me?"

"Threatened," clarified Sandalwood. "Pressured. Do you require ultimatums for you to reach down and find your emotional self?"

"I don't really know," said Lucky. "Not on the street or the job."

"You know," said Sandalwood. "You're not the first police officer who's been on that couch."

"She's a cop, too," deflected Lucky. "We're a cop couple. You've seen many of those?"

"No," Sandalwood replied. "You're my first. But where I was going had to do with something I've seen in other police officers. They're guarded. What's that stuff you wear to protect you from bullets? Bulletproof Teflon—"

"Kevlar," corrected Lucky.

"Kevlar," she repeated. "That's right. Cops are often covered in Kevlar. Not just on the job. But once they step across the threshold of their homes. Their families find it hard to get through to them."

Lucky gave a half-exhale and faced Gonzo.

"Do you have trouble getting through to me?" asked Lucky.

"I want to go on a vacation," said Gonzo. "And two nights in Vegas isn't what I'm talking about."

"You said that was fun," reminded Lucky. "I remember you saying—"

"You. Me. Travis. Karrie," Gonzo counted off on her fingers. "The four of us. Far away. Anyplace we can't drive to in a day. A cabin. Anything. With no TV and cell phones. I want quiet and board games."

"*Bored* games," Lucky joked. "And Travis hates 'em."

"So do you," argued Gonzo. "And don't use Travis as your excuse. That's not cool at all."

"Travis thinks I'm plenty cool," segued Lucky.

Gonzo twisted away, arms crossed and shaking her head as if to punctuate her point.

"I believe what Lydia is saying—"

"She's Gonzo," corrected Lucky. "We all call her Gonzo."

Gonzo agreed with an annoyed nod. Having been called Gonzo by nearly everybody but the Department of Motor Vehicles since grade five, Lydia Maria Gonzalez, her birth name, might as well have been someone else's official moniker.

"What she's saying," continued Dr. Sandalwood, "is that she needs a connection. Your family needs to connect. All of you to each other. Board games. Hikes. Anything analog you all could do together—as family—might lend itself to repairing those bonds."

"And if the bonds are already okay-fine?" asked Lucky.

"They can always be made stronger," suggested the therapist.

"My daughter," Lucky switched before turning to Gonzo as if to prove something. "You see. I said *daughter*. Karrie. She's got a lawyer because she wants to legally take my last name. Does that count as a *bond?*"

If there were answers from the therapist or Gonzo they would have to wait until the following week. The leggy shrink had already slipped back into her empty pump and stood for the session-ending cross to her desk. Though it was only the third appointment, Lucky had already clocked some of the therapist's physical cues, the most obvious being her way of lowering a curtain on the appointment. Instead of the *de rigueur "That's all the time we have for today"* employed by so many psychologists, the ex-volleyballer would simply rise and pivot to her desktop where she summoned an electronic calendar.

"Next week?" confirmed Sandalwood.

The cop couple walked in silence to the eighth-floor elevators, both with their emotional skin rubbed slightly raw.

"Where we going with this?" ventured Lucky.

"It's not supposed to be easy," shouldered Gonzo. "Just show up, okay? Go with it."

"Go where?"

"Wherever!" annoyed Gonzo. "It's a process."

"Feels more like a train headed over a cliff," deadpanned Lucky. He triple-tapped the down elevator button again.

"You wanna keep this going?" reminded Gonzo, "You and me? This is what it's gonna take."

"Forgive me if I don't get how peeling off each other's skin helps anybody but Dr. Ka-ching back there." The reference was to the shrink's hourly fee.

"Know what?" stalled Gonzo. "I'm not up for this shit. You keep the car. I'm gonna Uber back to the house."

"Suit yourself," shrugged Lucky, both trying and succeeding to appear as if he didn't give a rip—defensively indifferent to a fault.

No sooner had Gonzo turned her back and swerved toward the stairwell than the lift mechanism *dinged* a familiar signal.

"Elevator's here!" Lucky called out.

Gonzo's response was no more than the sound of the stairwell fire door automatically sealing shut with a secure *kuh-shunk*.

Join Doug's mailing list
for sneak previews, exclusive content, and
news on the release of the latest Lucky Dey Thriller.

visit www.eepurl.com/cRe5-v